The Spirit of Redd Mountain

❖

Larry Auerbach

iUniverse, Inc.
Bloomington

iUniverse books may be ordered through booksellers or by contacting:

iUniverse
1663 Liberty Drive
Bloomington, IN 47403
www.iuniverse.com
1-800-Authors (1-800-288-4677)

ISBN: 978-1-4620-3336-2 (sc)
ISBN: 978-1-4620-3337-9 (hc)
ISBN: 978-1-4620-3338-6 (e)

Library of Congress Control Number: 2011911029

Printed in the United States of America

iUniverse rev. date: 7/27/2011

$\mathcal{P}$ROLOGUE

❖

In the winter of 1963, a tragedy occurred in the Bitterroot Mountains of Montana. It was midseason, and while the skiing was very good, the hunting was even better. The guides and packers were having one of their best years in a long time, and many had been forced, although happy to do so, to take on extra help or turn the business away.

The snow was continuing to fall, which was making everyone happy—everyone but the ski patrol, that is. Their work was increased by the new snowfall, because it was all powder snow, which increased the danger by drawing more skiers to the slopes. This meant they had to be on guard for accidents, broken legs, lost poles, skiers who froze at the top of a slope, and the occasional drunk skier.

They also had to deal with the really hard part of the job: the lost skiers who went off the specially marked trails, thinking they were better than they really were—until they came face to face with the challenges of the harder slopes. The ski patrol was responsible for insuring the safety of those on the slopes, and that often meant protecting them from the weather and from themselves.

One of the major difficulties the Redd Mountain Ski Patrol faced was an issue of numbers. There were only twenty-five people in the patrol, and they estimated there were about twenty-five hundred people on the mountains this weekend. That number didn't include the hunters who were supposed to be on the other side of the mountain, far away from the skiers, to prevent anyone getting shot by accident.

This year the snow was coming down hard, and circling around the mountaintops today were storm clouds that looked heavy with even more snow.

Arthur Kent was watching the clouds. He knew there were supposed to be hunters up there today; Gregg had told him he had seen Amos leading a string up to Little Trout Pass earlier in the day. Now it was almost four thirty, and those clouds looked angry and ready to open up.

"Mr. Kent, you look worried, sir," his intern said behind him.

Arthur didn't turn around, but continued to look out the window at the mountain in front of him while answering her implied question. "Peggy, you got that right. I am worried. We've got a bunch of wildcat hunters up there, moving into the upper levels of the sky areas, and a group of novice skiers lost on the same mountain and maybe going into the hunting area. That spells disaster in any language. I've been scanning the tops of the mountains with my field glasses, looking for the hunters, but I've seen no sign of them all day," Arthur warned her.

"On top of that, I can hear the shooting, and it seems to be coming from all around the mountain, more so on the skiers' side, which really presents a problem. The snow on the upper slopes, beyond where the skiers are allowed to go, is looking very layered and heavy on the slopes. I can see what looks like several shelves sticking out, as well as several large towers that are very dangerous," Arthur fretted. "The risk is that one of those hunters might set off an avalanche with the shockwaves of gunfire in the wrong area—or, worse, a stray shot into one of those towers or shelves.

"From that height, the resulting tidal wave of snow would crush everything in its path, uprooting trees and smashing them down the mountain to collect at the bottom in a tangled mat of destruction," he explained to her. "Any skier caught in that wave would certainly be killed and may not be found until next summer. I'm angry because I tried to talk Amos into waiting until I could send a man up there to start a controlled breakup of the towers and that ominous shelf, but Amos wasn't willing to wait. He said he had a winter camp set up and ten hunters waiting for a chance at an elk or a deer, or even a rare moose. Now I've got to worry about them *and* those skiers working their way back down the slope. I just hope they would hurry, as it's getting progressively uglier up there," he said, turning back to the window. Peggy was forgotten as he raised his binoculars and began to scan the mountain once again.

"Come on, Warner, it's getting dark up here. We should be heading back to camp. We can get the damn elk tomorrow. Besides, I'm freezing my ass off here!" Gerry complained.

"What are you talking about, Gerry? Didn't you bring your thermals like I told you to do? I saw that damn animal just a few minutes ago; he was heading in that direction," Warner said as he pointed the barrel of his rifle up the slope to the left.

Gerry slapped the barrel down with his gloved hand, yelling at Warner as he did, "Damn it, you know better than to do that, Warner! There could be people up there! You don't ever point the rifle unless you have a clear and clean shot! If that thing went off, you could kill someone with a wild shot like that. Have you been drinking?" Gerry leaned forward to smell Warner's breath and straightened up, angrier than before. "Goddamn it, Warner, you've been drinking! You know what the rules are in this camp! No alcohol while on the slopes, and only when everyone is back at camp. You trying to get all of us thrown off this damn cold mountain or what? Give me that rifle, and let's go back," Gerry demanded.

Warner pulled back out of his reach and snarled at his companion, "No one takes my gun, Gerry. Look, I only had a sip to keep warm, anyway. Just ten more minutes, please. Then I'll come in, honest." Before Gerry could respond, Warner put his hand out and pointed. "Look! Over there, by that ridge. You see him? He's huge! And look at that rack, will you? Come on, we've got time for one or two shots!" Without waiting for an answer, Warner rushed off, high-stepping his way through the snow in pursuit of the animal he saw on the ridge. He chased the animal through the snowbank while it fled for its life, ever upward. At one point, Warner thought he had a good shot and stopped to fire two rounds. He heard the echo of his shots and saw the big animal stumble.

Gotcha! he thought to himself. He saw a slight dusting of snow tumble down in front of him, but he paid it no mind as he chased the big animal up higher, gaining on it as he climbed for the ridgetop.

At the same time, on the other side of the mountain, the ski patrol was looking for a party of six that had wandered off the marked trails. This was a three-man patrol, as the party hadn't been reported injured, just heading into the wrong area. As the men moved easily and quickly across the snowfield, they heard the shots.

"Damn it, Max, some fool hunter is still out there! With night coming in and those clouds overhead, this is no time to be shooting," Evan complained.

"Particularly with some fool skiers in the wrong place, someone is sure to get hurt—maybe even killed," Parker added anxiously as he looked around him.

"All of that is true, guys, but we still have a job to do. We have to get those skiers down before any of that happens," Max reminded them. "We all have our radios, right? Then perhaps we need to split up to get this done sooner. Evan, you're the biggest of us three—you go find the hunter and get him to stop shooting and take him back to his camp. Parker, you take the right side, and I'll take the left fork ahead. Whoever spots the skiers calls the other, so if you find them first, I'll come to you, or vice versa. Remember, guys, these people are going to be scared and may not have proper clothing on, so we will need to get them all down as quickly as possible," Max said. As the senior member of the group, it was his call.

Parker and Evan looked at each other, knowing they were all disobeying the first rule of safety, which was never to go out alone. Max didn't give them a chance to argue, as he turned and headed for the fork in the trail. The other two men gave a sigh and headed out in their respective directions.

Parker went in the direction of the last shots he'd heard, climbing up toward the towering banks of snow, hoping he wasn't heading into a problem. Evan moved easily into a gliding pace, headed for the last place the skiers were seen, hoping to pick up their trail before it got any darker. Evan was the best skier of the three men, and he had the best chance of finding them before they ran into trouble.

Max was the most determined and the most resourceful of the three. He could make something out of nothing, and the men knew if they were ever in a fix, he would be the one they all depended upon. Max never lost his head, never panicked, and never made a rash move—until today. As the three men searched for their respective targets, Max was the first to cross the trail of the missing skiers.

He saw their tracks on a hill up ahead and hurried up to them to get a bearing on their direction. He was concerned because they were already in the barrier zone, the two-hundred-foot separation zone between the skiers' side of the mountain and the hunters' territory. He had been pushing for years to make this mountain off limits to hunters, but the packers and guides provided more revenue than the skiers did, and they had the most pull with the Bureau of Land Management—or the BLM, as they called it.

What he saw made him blanch: they were headed for the woods where the hunters were operating. They were on the wrong side of the mountain, and he had to find them and get them out of there before it was too late. He saw the direction they were headed and doubled his pace, desperately trying to overtake them before they ran into the danger he knew was ahead of them—and, for all he knew, headed directly for them.

High above him, Parker was on the trail of the hunter. He had found a couple of shells that had been ejected from a rifle, and the smell of cordite was still present. That meant he was closing in, and he might be able to prevent a real tragedy. He stopped to adjust his bright red ski parka to make sure the emblems of the ski patrol emblazoned on the back and on both shoulders were easily visible to the eye. Parker then crossed himself and headed out after the elusive hunter who was up ahead.

He heard another shot and saw snow start to dribble down the hill. This sight scared him more than the hunter did, because he knew the fields up above were starting to lose their grip as a result of the shockwaves caused by the shooting. He hurried after the hunter and, as he looked to his left, saw a figure crossing the ridge above.

Warner spotted the blood because the bright red spots stood out in relief on the pristine whiteness of the snow.

"Won't be long now, boy. You're mine now," he said to the elk, who was struggling to reach a stand of trees just ahead of him.

Max found the skiers and yelled to them to come to him. Because of the bright red ski-patrol parka, they knew he was their safety line, and they turned and headed right for him.

"Hello, folks. You all are in a very dangerous position. Stay right there for a minute while I check in," he said calmly. Max picked his radio off his belt and keyed the call button.

"Parker, Evan; Max here. I've got them. We are at the edge of …" He looked around to get his bearings. "… the edge of Hunter's Run and Mosquito Run, below Moosejaw Ridge, above Otter Creek, I believe. I'm going to lead them out of here, going straight down and over into the lodge area. Evan, you join me when you can. Everyone is fine, and we should be safe at the lodge within forty-five minutes. Parker, have you seen anything of the hunter yet?" he asked.

He waited, but there was no response from either man. Max clicked the call button again, but there was still no response. He looked at the case and saw the red power-indicator light was on. He shook the case and hit it with the palm of his hand. The light flickered and went out.

"Great," he muttered to himself. "Well, people, time to get you home," Max said cheerfully, as if nothing was wrong. He headed them in the right direction and took up a position in the rear, where he could see if anyone was falling behind and help keep up the pace. They moved as fast as he could get them to go, almost straight down the mountain. His unspoken sense of urgency was felt by all of them for reasons they couldn't really explain.

Evan heard Max's message and felt a sense of relief, but he received no acknowledgement of his response. He tried again to contact Max, but there was no return. He turned down the mountain and headed for an intercept of Max's destination, which, he figured, would put him in visual contact within thirty minutes. He was concerned when Max didn't respond to his call, because that could mean anything from a faulty radio to a serious situation. While he had faith in Max's survival skills, none of those skills would mean anything if he was unconscious somewhere. He felt a chill that had little to do with the falling temperature and increased his speed and angle of attack on the snow.

Parker saw the hunter just as he fired again. This time, he clearly heard the roar of the gun. *What the hell is that idiot using, a damn elephant gun?* Parker thought. He was more concerned about the impact of that shot on the walls of snow higher up the mountain. He called out to the hunter—who didn't turn around, but rather fired again. This time Parker thought he saw some movement high up the mountain, but he dismissed it as the air and snow falling. He closed on the hunter, who was kneeling for a third shot at his unseen target. Parker reached the man just as he fired at a large elk in the tree line. He grabbed the man by the shoulder and threw him to the ground, causing him to lose his grip on the powerful rifle. Unfortunately, as it flew from the man's hand, it discharged a fourth shot. This one went wild, up in the air and in the direction of the snow field high above them. The sound that followed struck terror into Parker's heart as he recognized the opening sounds of a full avalanche building up.

He grabbed for his radio and keyed a warning to Evan and Max, who were somewhere below him. He heard the hunter yelling about his rifle and his kill and saw him rush toward the body of the elk lying in the snow a hundred feet in front of him. Parker didn't care about the elk, the hunter, or his damned rifle. Parker was only worried about his friends below him.

"Evan! Come in Evan, Max!"

"What's that sound, Parker?" Evan asked fearfully.

"You know what it is, Evan!" Parker yelled into the radio. "A damn fool hunter has triggered a massive avalanche down into the valley. It's headed for Otter Creek and coming down in the vicinity of Mosquito Run! I can't reach Max! Do you see him? I can't warn him! Oh God, I can't warn him!" Feeling helpless, Parker fell to his knees in the snow and dropped his radio.

The hunter came up behind him and hit Parker in the back of the head with his rifle butt—and, as Parker fell face down into the snow, the hunter thoughtfully turned him over so he could breathe, and then went to claim his prize. Parker never responded to Evan's frantic radio calls.

Evan watched in horror as the massive wave of snow gathered force and bulk as it raced down the mountain, collecting trees and more snow as it gathered speed. He saw a group of skiers, with a figure in a red parka in the rear, caught in the path of the massive tonnage of snow bearing down on them. He saw the figures begin to scatter, and the one in red trying to make it back to the trees the group had just broken from. Evan could do nothing to help them from where he was; he could only watch as his best friend was swept away by the roaring anger of the mountain's shedding of its winter coat.

He'd heard Parker's warning in time and had pulled up from his run downward to meet Max. If Parker had called him one minute later, he would have been in the path as well, just higher up. He hadn't heard anymore from Parker, so he was worried about his friend up high as well. He couldn't go to aid either man, because he didn't know where Parker was. It was getting late, and it would be dark very soon. He wouldn't be able to look for either man until tomorrow anyway. He knew that by then it might well be too late for them, but he also knew it wouldn't have stopped Max from looking for him or Parker if they had been caught in that white tidal wave.

As he watched the white tide sweep everything from its path in its mad rush down to the bottom, Evan somehow knew his friend was gone. He had been caught in the open with no chance to make the trees, which offered only scant protection. Suddenly something Parker had said registered in his thinking: a hunter had triggered it by shooting in the protected area. He turned to head up to the hunting camp and then stopped. It was too late in the day to do that, but, first thing in the morning, he would go and find that damn hunter. Right now he had to do his job, which was to do search and rescue.

He carefully followed the snow down the mountain to where his friend had been, but the scene was wiped clean of all trace of the group that had been there just a few minutes before. He heard a shout and looked uphill to see a red parka.

Parker was bleeding from the head when he reached Evan. "Max?" he asked hopefully.

Evan pointed to the clean white field below and just shook his head. They worked their way down to the lodge, where Parker was treated for his injury. The hunter was never identified, as no one had gotten a good look at him, and Max's body was never found. Both Parker and Evan quit their jobs and never came back. A week later, a legend was born.

CHAPTER 1

The head of the ski patrol, Oliver Barry, was excited about the new season. Nothing ever bothered or worried Oliver; no matter what the problem, he was always confident there was a solution to it. He was fifty-four, single, and starting to show a salt-and-pepper look in his moustache and goatee, though there was more salt than pepper. His hair was tied back into a long ponytail, and he had a very boyish grin—his usual expression, no matter what was going on or going wrong.

Oliver was very fit, as he played racquetball when he wasn't on the slopes or working in his office at the top of the mountain. He was known as the "old man" of the mountain, because he'd been working the ski patrol since he was eighteen, when he applied for a job on the patrol as a rookie rescuer. Well over twenty-five years later, he had outlasted every other man on the patrol, and had risen to become the head of the patrol last year. This was his first season as the new commander.

Oliver had a lot of new ideas he was anxious to implement to improve the safety and enjoyment of the guests on his mountain. He'd heard about the tragedy back in '63 and had seen what it had done to the head of the patrol—he had been forced into an early retirement and two good men had quit. He was determined not to allow anything like that to mar his administration of the department.

The first improvement he made had been the purchase of new, state-of-the-art radios with GPS transponders built into them for every man and woman on the patrol, plus a number of backup radios to ensure that no one ever went out without one. The second improvement had been to hire thirty new patrollers to reduce the load on everyone. The third improvement had been to hire a team to mark the entire mountain with GPS locators hidden in unobtrusive spots so that anyone could find their way to or from a specific location to another specific location with ease. He wanted to make it required that all hunters and skiers carried GPS locators with them, but knew this wasn't likely to happen. He had also implemented a series of training exercises once a month, with a special "lost skier" that different patrols would have to find and bring back to the lodge within a specified time.

Oliver believed in rewarding excellence and effectiveness. He also believed in promoting the best workers, and he maintained an open-door policy that was unique—he'd actually taken his door off the hinges and removed it. He was accessible to everyone, which meant that no one had to try to catch him when they could, and he actually was able to get more of his work done in the same amount of time. It didn't hurt that he had a very able and competent assistant.

Eileen Gayle was a very pretty, long-haired brunette with a very warm personality and a very curvaceous figure. She had worked with Oliver at other resorts, and so, when he started his climb to the top, he wanted her to go with him. They had been together now for over twenty-five years, and she was able to speak for him and know that she was saying what he would. She was the cautious counterbalance to his tendency to be enthusiastically impulsive. She was also very good at recognizing when Oliver was reaching his breaking point with someone, and she could divert his attention or improve his mood without anyone realizing how close he'd come to saying something imprudent. And, of course, she was easy on the eyes. This made her an excellent distraction for those Oliver didn't want to waste his time on. And she was the only one who could get away with yelling back at Oliver. In short, they worked together like a well-oiled machine.

Even if Oliver wasn't aware of it, they were an item. Oliver tended to be very oblivious to that sort of thing, and, more than once, Eileen had to rescue him from some predatory female who saw him as a good catch.

But neither of them were thinking about anything playful this morning. There had been another report of both the Red Elk and the Red Skier yesterday afternoon. This was the third one this week, and it was only Wednesday. Both of these sightings seemed to happen more on the weekends, and that was coming up. Oliver had already fielded two calls from the newspapers and one from a local TV station, which wanted him to arrange a sighting for them to film. He'd hung up on that call, as he had little patience for idiocy. Eileen scolded him for that one, to which he appeared properly contrite. He avoided calling them back to make nice, however, because he wasn't really sorry and would likely do it again.

Oliver had been hearing stories about both figures for years; they had been elevated by repeated tellings into almost mythical status here on the mountain. He tried to remember the first time he heard about either one—it must have been about a year after that ski patrolman, Max Phillips, had died in the avalanche that some had said was caused by a hunter shooting into the mountain.

Oliver turned in his chair and dug into his filing cabinet for the folder he was keeping on the two "folktales," as he called them. He had been considering a way to make them work for him, and he thought he had finally figured out the answer.

"Eileen, can you come in here for a minute?" he called.

"Be right there, boss!" she replied.

He put the folder on his desk and leaned back in his chair. He started to spin around, putting out one hand to steady himself on the desk as he turned. He stopped suddenly when he saw Eileen watching him with an amused look on her face. Sheepishly, he settled down.

"I always liked a rolling swivel chair," Oliver said with an embarrassed grin.

"Men—just big dogs that talk," she said. This was one of her favorite sayings.

Changing to a serious subject, Oliver opened up the folder and spread out the clippings, some of them going back over thirty years.

"Eileen, I have over sixty-five clippings and stories—not counting TV stories—that have been done on these two phantoms. Now we have these two new ones."

She looked down and said, "Make that five, Oliver. I had three more people this morning tell me they saw them up on the mountain last night."

"Great, just what I need. Okay, here's what we are going to do. We're not going to downplay this story any longer. We're going to embrace our legends and make them part of our history and our lore. I want you to go through all these clippings and find the place they appear more than any other, and we're going to make a public announcement that we are renaming the runs in those areas after these two phantoms. We will call them the Ghosts of Redd Mountain. No, that sounds scary—they aren't haunting us, they're helping, so we can't call them ghosts," he mused.

After a moment, Eileen suggested, "How about we call them the spirits of the mountain?"

"I like that," Oliver responded after a moment's consideration. "Set up an interview with the media for … say, what's today? Tuesday? Make it for Thursday, so we can cash in on the weekend visitors. That will give us time to put together a media package for everyone."

"What do you want in the package, Oliver?"

"I want a page giving the background of this mysterious skier—the facts, as we have them, about the event this legend is based on. Dress it up a little, make it a sympathetic phantom, you know, trying to protect the skiers, that sort of thing. Then I want some current information about the ski lodge and the patrol. Make him look like our ally in protecting our guests. You know what to do, Eileen. You know, this ghost or whatever it is people are seeing, we can make this work for us if we're careful," he said with a gleeful exuberance.

"What about the big elk the hunters are talking about?" she asked.

"What about it? It's got nothing to do with this," Oliver said dismissing the sighting. "Get on that media package and set up the meeting as soon as it's ready, okay?"

"Yes, Oliver. But I don't think I can get everything done by this Thursday. It's going to take me a couple of days to get all the information into a readable form like you want, and then to get it to the printers and back in a nice package … Well, I'll need more time."

"What about next Thursday? Can we have it to go for then?" he asked impatiently.

Eileen thought a moment and decided to cancel her weekend plans. "Yes, Oliver, I can have it ready to go for next Thursday. I'll just have to cancel my plans for the weekend and put in some overtime …"

"Hang the overtime, Eileen. Do whatever you need; I'll sign the overtime vouchers for anyone you need to help you. I just want this ready to go for next weekend. I hate to waste the time ... Tell you what: leak a teaser to the news media. Have them attribute it to the usual 'unnamed sources' they blame for everything. That will get the news sharks swimming in our direction, I'll bet." He snickered.

Eileen thought a moment, and then an idea hit her. "I can have Teddy call from a back line. That way they can trace it here, and we can deny it came from any authorized representative. They will know we are hiding something, and that will keep their interest up for the week until we are ready to announce. In the meantime, I will get some signs made up out of town, so no one will know they are for us," she said.

"Eileen, you are a real treasure. I don't know how I'd get along without you," Oliver said with admiration in his voice. "Okay, you get on that, and I will get started on the presentation speech. I want this to be just perfect for the media," he said, already moving on to that task mentally while he was talking to her.

Eileen recognized that he was dismissing her without saying so, so she gathered up the clippings and walked back to her desk to get started on her research.

Out on the slopes, the novice and intermediate skiers were starting to clog the runs in the late-morning sunshine. They were slowly traversing downhill, stopping to correct their course or reclaim their lost poles or dignity from the falls and tumbles. But for all the problems they were experiencing, they were all having fun. The sounds of their laughter filled the air, along with the soft whoosh and hiss of the skis on the snow. They were enjoying the sunny but cool weather, the crispness in the air, and the smell of the pines all around them.

When they grew too cold or too wet, they would collect their skis and poles and retreat to the lodge to get warm and have a drink. They would sit around the fireplaces, enjoying the warmth and the camaraderie of the other skiers, and they would tell tall tales of their runs. They would embellish their successes and their failures. There was a certain amount of glory in getting up again after a spectacular fall, so they would joke about them because that was part of the kinship of learning to ski. They would listen to the other skiers talk about their adventures, and they would talk about the Red Elk and the ghost in the red parka.

Stories told about the recent sightings of the two legends always started out with someone having heard about them from someone who saw the Red Elk, or with someone who knew someone who had been saved by the mysterious red-coated skier.

Only a few had actually seen either, and they had little to say about them. When pressed to talk about the skier, the storyteller would only say he appeared out of nowhere to herd them out of an area, and, when they looked for him afterward, he was no longer there. None of the people who had seen the skier talked about the fact he had often faded away from their sight or melted into the clouds of snow that always seemed to come up before he appeared or disappeared. They didn't talk about this because they didn't want to be written off as kooks or just plain crazy. They were talking about ghosts, to be sure, but they were only repeating and embellishing stories they heard in the lodge or the local pubs, because none of the novice or intermediate skiers had ever actually seen the Red Elk or the red parka-clad phantom of the slopes. They attributed it to just not being in the right place at the right time. The truth was, they were just not in the right place at *any* time, and they might never be.

This was because the Red Elk was only seen in the mountains where the hunters roamed, and the red-parka skier was only seen in the higher slopes or on the more advanced runs. No one knew why, although everyone had their theories. No one saw any connection between the two legends, although they were aware they'd started to hear about them around the same time. No one person had ever seen both apparitions or had ever seen them together.

This wasn't considered significant, as the elk wouldn't be safe around humans. Many hunters had commented they had never seen an elk with such a reddish cast to its coat anywhere before, but they attributed the color to its diet—although no one could say what it might have been eating that would produce his distinct, remarkable reddish cast. Many naturalists, wildlife experts, and even environmentalists have been consulted on this issue over the years, but there was no consensus of opinion to explain the color of the elk to anyone's satisfaction.

The editor of the scandal sheet that one celebrity once sneered he wouldn't use to "wrap up his garbage" hung up the telephone. He turned in his chair and looked out the window at the traffic outside that clogged the highway in the city beneath him. He hated the city, but always said he couldn't live anywhere else. Anywhere else would be too boring, and he craved the excitement of the big city. It was this addiction to excitement that led to his being here in this mountain metropolis.

For him, it was more of a mountain hideout—at least until the heat died down back in Memphis. His contact back east, the man he had just hung up with, said he needed to give it even more time for tempers to cool off. Wait until another scandal pushed his name to the back page, his friend had advised. But Morey Palin was here now, he said to himself, and he had to make the best of it.

He turned away from the window and looked down at his desk to see a note from one of the social-column writers who was asking for permission to do a story on one of the local legends, a fabled red deer or something. It looked like a lame, two-column item at best, but, as he read it over a second time, something about it appealed to him. The germ of an idea that could possibly get him back on top started to grow. He picked up his phone and dialed an extension.

"April, come in here. Bring your notepad and talk to me about this big red deer of yours."

Gerry Bruce was a fourth-generation rancher, hunter, and packer, who'd grown up in these very mountains, accompanying his grandfather Amos on his trips. His father, also Gerry Bruce, had stopped hunting a long time ago, shortly after Gerry was born. Gerry Junior once asked his father why he stopped hunting, but his father never gave him a clear answer—he always said he just lost his taste for it after a party had gone bad. Gerry Junior knew there was something behind this, but he respected his father's privacy and didn't dig for an answer if his father wasn't ready to talk about it.

A few years ago, Gerry had received a letter addressed to Gerry Bruce. The envelope had come from someone in Vermont, but there was no return address. When he opened it, he discovered that it was actually meant for his father. Later, he mentioned it to Gerry Senior, who became agitated and demanded it. After Gerry handed it over, it was never discussed again.

Although his father didn't take out hunting trips any more, he always asked about any hunting trip Gerry was taking out. He would ask the names of the people Gerry was taking out but then dropped the subject once he knew their names. His father had never showed any interest in where they were going or in what they were going out to hunt.

One night, while Gerry was sleeping, he decided that he needed a special theme to draw more customers to his hunts. Times were hard and money was tight, so he needed to build up his business. The stories being told about the Red Elk had given him an idea: he would limit the party to a smaller number of hunters, all with ten or more years of experience, and he would cut the time of the trip. This way, he could get perhaps two or three trips out of it before they bagged their game.

His wife, Penny, had come up with the best gimmick of all. To make it more selective and exclusive, each applicant had to send a nonrefundable entry fee of two hundred dollars, along with a letter saying why they should be given a place on this hunt. This was an old marketing ploy she'd read about—make it more desirable and exclusive by making it harder to get in the group. He placed the ads in all the major papers and hunting magazines and waited for his replies.

Within a few weeks, hunters all across the country were sitting down at their desk and looking at their checking accounts to see if they had enough set aside to sign up for a place on this once-in-a-lifetime hunt. They were also trying hard to write the most compelling letter they could to get themselves a seat in the trip. For all of them, the check was the easy part; trying to sell their right to go was hard. Most of the letters contained a brief summary of their hunting experiences, but some spoke of their desire to chase down a legend and a ghost. There were those who spoke of their passion for the hunt, some of the desire to be in the wilds of the mountains, and a few spoke of it being their destiny.

Some sent in just the initial filing fee of two hundred dollars, and a few sent in the full amount, hoping this would assure them of a place in the first grouping. A few more sent in twice his fee, in the hope this would move them to the front of the line.

Gerry was overwhelmed by the response to his ad, despite the cost and preconditions of this trip. He'd doubled his usual fee, basing this on the notoriety of the target animal. Gerry had anticipated about forty replies which he would narrow down to ten hunters, but this was turning out to be a much bigger idea than he could have ever imagined.

So far, he had received over a hundred replies, all of them containing checks for the required, nonrefundable entry fee. Gerry decided to make up a series of parties of ten, with the best in the first group. Each succeeding group would, of course, have the chance to find the elusive Red Elk if the group before them failed. There were no guarantees anyone would get a shot, but this was understood by every hunter every time they went out.

Gerry only planned to return the checks for the hunters he did not take along at any time. He spent a full day weeding out the thrill-seekers and wannabes from the hunters with real experience. He put those names at the bottom of the list, and started with the best of the best replies for his first group of ten.

He had been surprised by his father's expression of interest in reading the letters he received.

"Why do you want to read these, Dad? You haven't been involved in the hunting side of this business for a long time. What's the deal here?" Gerry asked suspiciously.

"I might be interested in perhaps going out one more time, this time with you, just to see how you do it," his father said casually.

Gerry was so excited about his father coming with him that he didn't stop to ask himself why he was doing it now. He began to think about it, but just then, the mailman came in with another handful of letters and requests for a position on the hunt, and the puzzling thought was allowed to slip from his consciousness.

"Look at all these letters, Dad! This is a gold mine! I hope they never find that wonderful animal! I could do this several times every season as long as he stays alive," Gerry said gleefully. "Take a look at some of these letters, Dad! Help me pick the winners for the first hunt, will you?"

They spent several days going through the volume of mail, dividing it into three separate piles. The first pile, and the smallest, consisted of the mail that included a check for cost of the full hunt or more, in an effort to gain a spot in the first group. The second pile, the largest, consisted of those with the two-hundred-dollar entry fee and the letter of intent promoting their cause and right to be in the first group.

The third pile, and the next smallest, consisted of those letters that had no money or were attacking Gerry for organizing the hunt. There were letters from PETA and other such anti-gun and anti-hunting groups, as well as what Gerry considered to be bleeding hearts who didn't understand the benefits of hunting.

One man sent a letter that caused Gerry to blink and get a strange feeling. The writer saw it as his right to be there, and he was quite clear in saying so. He looked at the name on the envelope and wondered why it seemed to be familiar, but couldn't recall why.

Dear Mr. Bruce,

I read about your hunt in Big Game Adventures, and I want to be in the first group. I have hunted big game all over the world, and even took a record buck elk on your mountain a number of years ago. I want to be on this hunt, and you want to have me on your hunt. I am the best hunter in these parts, and I am a good tracker as well. I do not give up on a trail just because it is hard or too dark to see. I bring technology with me that will allow me to find a trail in any environment.

I have been chasing down the biggest, the strongest, the wiliest of animals for years. I have never lost a trail or an animal I was after. I carry the latest in rifles, scopes, and ammunition, and I always get the trophy quality animals others can only dream about. I deserve not just a place on this hunt, but the first shot should be mine. This trophy buck belongs to me, and only to me.

I don't mind paying for the right to claim it, so I will be seeing you in two weeks for the big hunt.

Respectfully,
Warner Barney

Gerry picked up the slip of paper that fell out of the envelope, and when he looked at it, his eyes widened as he counted the zeroes in the amount. He had found his number-one hunter. He put it in the growing pile of checks and slid the letter back into the envelope.

He set this letter aside because he wanted to show it to his father and get his opinion on adding this man's name to the list. He turned his attention back to the pile of letters on his desk, but although he read many interesting letters, none held his attention as intently as did the letter from Warner Barney.

"The legend of the Red Elk is going to be very good for my business," he said to himself.

On the slopes at that very moment, four people were about to contribute their fifteen minutes of fame to this legend.

"Pete! Watch out!" the skier called as he zipped down the slope, headed for the man who stood in his path.

Pete looked up and called out a warning in an effort to avoid a collision. "Snowplow! Snowplow, Ed!" Just in case, Pete moved to the side about twenty feet. He watched with amusement as Ed pointed his ski tips inward. "Head up, Ed! Keep your head up and your knees bent! No! Don't—" he started to say, but stopped as he saw him fall and start rolling down the hill. Pete quickly slipped his goggles back on and headed after his friend.

Pete leaned forward and raced past him, stopping and turning uphill as he reached a safe spot. Ed's voice was muffled by the snow as he landed face down in the snow bank just to Pete's left. Pete sidestepped over to him and leaned over to extend a hand.

As Ed sat up, his goggles were twisted on his head, the lens over his ears instead of his eyes. "And this is what you call fun?" he said sourly before breaking out into a hearty laugh.

"Come on, you old faker. Let's try again," Pete encouraged him.

"I must be crazy to listen to you, Pete. Why in the world do I risk breaking my leg, my arm, or my neck?"

"Because you're a risk-taker, just like I am, and you live for the excitement of the danger. Now come on, we're gonna go up top and ride the wind on down." Pete turned and headed for the lift, with Ed right behind him.

As they went down the hill, side by side, neither looked back up the slope, so they didn't see the large shadow crossing into the woods high up on the ridge.

At the top of the lift, two college students were preparing for their first run of the day.

"Gene, I've never skied before. I don't think I should be up here; I should be on one of the bunny runs," the man said.

"Oh, don't pay that old guy any mind, Freddy. You're with me, and I've skied for years. I'll keep an eye on you and help you through it. It isn't very hard, really." Gene downplayed Freddy's worries, in part because he didn't want to be held back from the good runs. He was having second thoughts about asking Freddy to come along, because he was turning out to be a real anchor on Gene's fun.

Gene had only invited Freddy because he had the pilot's license and had been willing to fly them to the resort in return for Gene's teaching him to ski. He had thought this would be a simple thing to do, but it turned out he had grossly overestimated Freddy's level of coordination and balance. They had been here for three days, and Freddy was only minimally better than the day they'd arrived. And now, too late to do anything about it, Gene had realized the danger he was in, because if Freddy broke his leg, he would be unable to fly them home. So he did the only thing he could do—he tried to talk Freddy into going up the hill with him so that he could get at least one good run in before he chickened out and said he wanted to just go home.

"Come on, Freddy, you'll be fine. We'll take it slow—no racing down the mountain, I promise. Hey, I'll tell you what we'll do. We'll go over to the side of the runs where no one is skiing, and we can take our time without anyone rushing you. How about that?" Gene asked with concern in his voice.

"You sure you don't mind, Gene?" Freddy asked, worried he was holding his friend back.

"Naw, Freddy. I don't mind. I asked you to come with me, didn't I? I did it because I *wanted* you to come with me. Now, come on, let's get on the lift and to the top of this snow cone so we can fly down," Gene said with a hearty, but forced, laugh.

Coincidence is a funny thing. The word itself has several similar meanings: accident, chance, luck, fluke, twist of fate, quirk, happenstance. But all of these words essentially mean the same thing—an event or situation that is unplanned and unexpected. You just can't predict coincidence.

For example, Pete, Ed, Freddy, and Gene ending up on the same chair on the ski lift to the top of the mountain; in both pairs of men, one was an experienced skier, and the other was the beginner. While riding up the lift, the four men began to talk and introduced themselves to each other. They very quickly sized each other up as to their respective skiing skills and realized that Freddy and Ed were just as inexperienced as Gene and Pete were experienced, and so they all agreed to repartner up. When they got off the lift at the top of the mountain, Pete motioned to Gene to take a step back so they could exchange a few words while Freddy and Ed were looking down the slope and blanching.

"Look, Gene, I know we don't really know each other, and you can tell me no if you want to, but I was kinda wondering if you would like to take a run at the Killer with me."

"The Killer? What's that, Pete?" he whispered.

"It's the slope over there." Pete pointed to the left, beyond the barrier line.

"That run is off limits, according to the sign I see, Pete," Gene warned him.

"Yeah, it's closed off because of all the stories about some ghost skier showing up now and then. There's no reason to close the run over a ghost that doesn't exist. Anyway, I've got a camera with me, just in case there is a ghost and I can get proof of it. Regardless of that, this is the fastest run and the most challenging one, and I got the impression you like a challenge—and I thought I'd give you a chance to make the run with me. We're only going to get one shot at it, because they'll be waiting for us at the bottom. Just tell them that you got turned around when you fell higher up and didn't realize you got so off course, and you're very sorry. They'll yell at us and tell us not to do it again, and I expect they'll keep a close eye on us for the rest of our stay. But it will be a run you'll never forget!" Pete said.

Gene thought about it for a minute and looked over at Ed and Freddy.

"What about them? We can't take them on this run; they'd never survive it," Gene said.

"No, you're right about that. We'll go up with them, get ahead of them—no, get behind them and tell them we are going to keep an eye on them better that way, and when they get a bit ahead of us, we'll cut over to the run and take off. Okay?"

Gene hesitated, and then he nodded. Pete smiled and put out his hand and gripped Gene's in a strong, firm clasp. He put an arm around Gene's shoulder and steered him to the top of the run, where Ed and Freddy were waiting.

"So what's your angle, April?" the editor asked.

"I want to go into the archives and dig into the story of this mysterious skier and where he came from. It goes back about thirty years, boss," April said. April Martens was a top athlete and a fierce competitor. She was a slender brunette with short hair and a tanned, well-toned figure. April was a graduate student, three credits short of her master's degree in journalism, hoping for a real job in the sports department on a newspaper. She knew that all it would take to jumpstart her career was to get her name on a big story—and this could be it. "I think there's something to this, boss. This story's been around since the late 1960s and hasn't changed substantially in all that time. It's always the same thing, every time: someone's in trouble or about to be in trouble, and he shows up in a red parka. He either crowds them into going in a safer direction or leads them to safety—and he never utters a word. No one sees his face, and several have said he either fades away or just disappears into the snow. And that's another thing, boss—there is always a brief snow flurry whenever he appears or disappears, even if there is no wind anywhere else on the mountain. There are even a few people who have claimed they could see right through him," April said with emphasis and sat back in her chair.

There was a silence for several minutes, until he leaned back in his chair and spoke just one word. "Horseshit."

"I beg your pardon?" April said in confusion.

"You heard me, April. I said—"

"I know what you said, I just don't understand why you said it," she responded icily.

"I said it because I don't believe it, April," he said gently, leaning forward to go eye to eye with her. Holding up a finger to forestall her objections, he continued, "But I think it makes a hell of a story. Run with it; show me what you can do with it. If you do a good job, you get the byline and the front page." He leaned back in his chair.

"I want to go out to the mountain with a film crew and a producer and take a couple of weeks interviewing people on the mountain. Can I have Adam?" April asked. "He's the best man we have on the paper. Then I'll need to look up some of the witnesses from these past stories—" April started to say before she saw the look on her boss's face.

"What?"

"No producer, no film crew. You can take one cameraman with you, and you can talk to any witnesses within a one-hundred-mile circle, because that's as far as I can authorize you to drive. No plane fares, no cruises; just you and a cameraman in a car. You do it this way or you don't do it," he said firmly.

"How long do I have to get this story?" April wasn't about to give up without a fight.

"How long do you need?"

"Give me two months, and I'll have the Nobel Prize for literature," she promised him extravagantly. He looked at her for a moment and down at the papers on his desk.

"You have a month and I'll settle for the Pulitzer Prize. Now get out of here; you're wasting your limited time," he growled at her. "And take Adam with you," he called out to her quickly retreating back. "He's no use to me anyway!"

"Oliver, there's something about this story that bothers me," Eileen said.

"What are you talking about? It's not real, it's just a story. What in the world can be bothering you about it?" Oliver said, not looking up from his video game.

"Would you please pay attention, Oliver? This is serious."

With a sigh, he pressed the pause button and put the controller on the desk. Looking up at her, he put on his most serious expression and asked her to explain. "Okay, Eileen, what's the problem? Not enough information to work with? Too many contradictions and inconsistencies over the years?" he joked with her.

"No, the problem is there aren't any."

"What, no information at all? That's impossible. I have several folders—"

"No; no inconsistencies," she said.

He sat back with his hand on the folder he was about to pick up. "Say again?"

"What I am telling you, Oliver, is that there are *no* inconsistencies or contradictions in *any* of the stories, and I've gone back over the entire file. I went back to the first report in late '65 and charted all three hundred fifty-six reports of the mysterious red-coated skier and where he was seen and what time of day he was seen. Do you want to see my chartings?" she asked hopefully.

"No, just give me the salient points," he said.

"Okay, in all three hundred fifty-six reports, he was only seen on two runs and—"

"Are you serious? Thirty-five years and three hundred and, what did you say, fifty-two?"

"Fifty-six."

"Right. Three hundred fifty-six reports, and he's only been seen on two runs?"

"That's correct, Oliver, just two runs. One was the old Mosquito Run, and after that was closed, he has been seen on the Otter Creek Run ever since. Do you know what those two have in common, Oliver?"

"Not off the top of my head, but I am very certain you are going to enlighten me."

"Yes, I am. The Otter Creek Run overlapped the Mosquito Run for most of the way down, changing direction only at the last quarter. And he has *never* been seen in the last quarter. What do you think of that, Oliver?"

"Come on, Eileen. That's just a coincidence. It's got to be."

"Okay, Oliver. Here's another coincidence for you: In all three hundred fifty-six reports, he has never said a word to anyone, and no one has ever seen his face very clearly. His goggles—which, I might add, are of a style not used in over thirty years—cover his face. And one more coincidence, sir. In every reported appearance, he comes out of a snow flurry, even when there is no wind blowing anywhere else on the mountain. Those same isolated snow flurries are also present every time he disappears. And they only appear whenever he arrives or leaves—no other time. No one has ever seen any ski tracks in the snow from anyone but the people reporting the incident," Eileen said seriously.

Oliver's smile had long since faded away, and this additional fact didn't lighten his mood.

"Perhaps the falling snow covered them up before anyone came to check the trail," he suggested.

"I suppose that could have happened—if it had snowed before the patrol went out to verify the story, or if it had snowed and covered up the witnesses' tracks as well, which it didn't," she said triumphantly. "There were never any tracks except from the people who reported him, and many of the people who saw him later reported never seeing him making any tracks as he came down the run after them," Eileen added.

"What you are describing, my dear, is a ghost. I don't believe in ghosts," Oliver retorted.

"Well, I never did either—until now. And here is the strange part, Oliver."

"You are saying that none of that other stuff was strange?" he asked.

She ignored him. "He is only seen when someone is in great danger. He comes out of the snow to steer them to safety and then fades away when they are safe. Some of the witnesses have claimed, while they couldn't see his face, they could see through him. And before you say they were probably drinking, none of them were drinking until after they came in contact with him," Eileen said solemnly.

"Is there more to this, or is this it?" Oliver asked.

"Oliver, I don't think we should run this story or this promotion," Eileen said softly.

"Of course we are going to run this, it is great publicity. Our skiers are protected by a ghost of the mountain who watches over them. The press will eat it up. By the way, Eileen, what did you find out about that big red deer?"

"That's another strange thing, Oliver. The elk—it's an elk, not a deer, by the way—the elk was first seen about the same time as the skier was. And no skier has ever seen the elk; only the hunters. Even more curiously, none of the hunters have ever seen the skier. And no one has ever reported seeing the skier and the elk at the same time, and no one's ever seen both of them. It is like one apparition is serving one population and no other.

"The elk has a rather curious history, as well. He appears to the hunters, and he leads them on a merry chase until dark, when they lose him. He allows them to close on him, but when they fire, they never hit him, and the other animals run for cover. It is almost as if he's serving as a decoy to protect the others of the forest and the mountain. I've never heard anything like it in my life," she said in amazement.

"Come on, Eileen, everyone knows that certain animals protect their young against harm. You know, like cats, bears, and other momma animals," Oliver argued.

"Yes, Oliver, I know that. But you show me one other animal that protects the other animals, regardless of their similarities or differences. I know that certain animals will protect their own herd, but this animal seems to be protecting everyone in the forest. I don't know any other animal that does that, Oliver, do you?" she asked.

His silence was her response. He stood up and walked to the window and stood there, looking out over the mountain. "What in the hell do we have going on here, Eileen?" he asked in a mystified voice.

"I don't know, Oliver. But I think it's much more than we ever thought it was. And that makes me wonder about the wisdom of this promotion. I wonder what it will bring us. If it will bring good or bad for us. And that reminds me, Oliver. How did this great idea come to you?" she asked curiously.

He turned to look at her, and slowly he answered, "It came to me in a dream the other night."

As Freddy and Ed slowly stumbled their way down the slope, Pete and Gene stifled their laughter and waited for them to get ahead. When they had enough distance between them, Pete tapped Gene on the shoulder and pointed to the distant tree line.

"That is where we want to go. The run follows that tree line down to the bottom of that flat, and then it turns to the left a little more. There is a small natural ledge that serves as a small jump, and it is the rush of the run to go over the top of that jump. It gives you a burst of speed when you come down, and it will carry you to the bottom of the mountain. Now, when we get to the bottom, if anyone says anything to you, you took a fall near the top and when you came up, you lost your bearings and hadn't seen the warning signs. Here, drop down into the snow and roll a bit, make it look good for the act at the bottom of the hill," Pete suggested.

Both men jumped up in the air and rolled on the ground to coat themselves with a dusting of fresh snow to bolster their story. They then pulled their goggles into place and headed to the trees to begin their run.

A little way below them, Freddy and Ed had stopped after snowplowing into a fall that left both of them tangled up with the other. They sat up, laughing and throwing snowballs at the other. Suddenly Ed put out his hand and pointed back up the hill.

"Hey, look there. Is that Pete and your friend, Gene? They're going off into the restricted area by the trees. That run was closed off—they're gonna get into trouble there for sure."

"It doesn't surprise me, Ed. I don't know about your friend, Pete, but Gene is always looking for a new way to get his tail in a sling. And mine too, come to think of it,"

"Well, that sounds just like Pete too. The hell with them, Fred. Let's just have fun ourselves. Hey! You feel like doing something a little dangerous and fun too?"

"Like what, Ed?"

"Something I've always wanted to do: we link up, side by side, each of us using our outer ski and lifting the inner ski, and we ski over to those trees. When we get to one of them, we go around it and link up again on the other side and go down for a ways. Can you picture the faces of the people who see that as they come down?" Ed said, as he fell down laughing at the image in his mind.

It took Fred but a moment longer to get the image of the tracks coming to a tree and going around them on both sides in his mind, and he fell down laughing and joined Ed rolling in the snow.

The fact that neither of them were good enough skiers to pull off this stunt was overlooked in the enthusiasm of the effect. It was only a small decision, but it would lead to momentous consequences. Neither of them paid any attention to the cloud that was forming about one hundred yards up the mountain or gave any thought to the fact that it seemed to be following them as they made their way across the slope.

Gerry took all the letters he had received by his deadline to his father to show him the volume of response he had to his idea. One of the letters was the demand from Warner Barney, but when Gerry Senior read it, he wasn't as enthusiastic about giving the man a spot as he had expected. In fact, he was somewhat negative about it.

"This man seems like a hot dog, son. I think you should be wary of him. Hell, I think you should send him his money back and skip him altogether. I've had people like that on a trip before, and they're bad news. They complain about everything you do and hog all the shots. They won't take turns, and they create a lot of dissension and hostility. They're not team players, and they won't follow your rules. Don't take him along, son. He's just not worth the money or the stress he brings. I know his type, and I guarantee you'll be real sorry if you get involved with this man," Gerry Senior said vehemently.

"But, Dad, he sent in the fee for the entire hunt, plus his filing fee, plus a lot more. I can make all my expenses for this entire season on just this one trip! Hell, I can make them all just on this one hunter! I have to take him—he's the good luck charm for this hunt," Gerry Junior said.

"Do what you want, son, but remember this: luck comes in two flavors, and it doesn't always come knocking. Sometimes it sneaks in the back door and you can't always chase it back out later," his father prophesied ominously before he abruptly changed the subject. A short time later, he left the house, saying he had some chores he needed to attend to on the ranch.

Gerry was very puzzled by his father's reaction and his dire words of gloom, but didn't focus on them as he was writing out his acceptance letters to the lucky few—and Warner Barney was the first on his list to be written.

Gerry Bruce Sr. wasn't a very religious man, not like his father had been, and he remembered only a few of the Bible's parables and lessons. The one that came into his mind at this time, however, was vividly imprinted: "The sins of the father are visited upon the sons," is how he remembered it—although he wasn't sure he had it *exactly* the way his father always said it. When he took that letter from his son a few years ago, he had read it in private and burned it. He never answered it, hoping that no response would send the message that he didn't want to have anything to do with him anymore.

Now, here that man was again, trying to involve his son in his criminal ways. Gerry was torn between staying as far away from that man as he could and wanting to protect his son from that man's influence. He knew what he had to do—he just didn't know if he could go through with it. He had to find the courage this time—not falter like he had done the last time. Because he knew what was at stake here, he decided to get his affairs in order, just in case he didn't make it out of the mountains alive.

He didn't have a wife any longer; Casey Bruce had left him years ago, when he went into his alcoholic freefall after that last hunting trip. They went through the motions for a time, but he continually withdrew from her and could never get himself to tell her what was wrong. Between them was the secret he couldn't forgive himself for. He hadn't wanted to burden her with that guilt, so the only way he could see to protect her was to push her away.

Their son was only a year old at that time, and he allowed her to take him. Gerry had only limited contact with Gerry Junior until he sobered up five years later. He hadn't told his counselor the real reason he was drinking, only that he had been depressed because of the accident on the mountain. He never told him about his part in that tragedy, because no one could prove it had happened the way he knew it had.

The sights of that last hunting trip never left his memory, and he could still hear the sounds when the wind blew; he could hear the screams in his sleep—when he could sleep.

He was finally getting over it when that damn letter came and brought it all to the surface again. *Well,* Gerry told himself, *it's time to end it once and for all and to pay for my sins so my son won't have to.* He had heard all the stories and was sure he knew who the ghost was

21

and what it wanted. He had been responsible for creating it, and it was his responsibility to give both of them peace at last. Maybe it was a good thing Warner was coming back—maybe it was meant to be some cosmic reckoning.

Whatever it was, it was going to happen, and he needed to be there so it could go the way it should have the first time. Maybe he was finally going to get a chance to make amends after all these years. Maybe he could finally be the father that he had always wanted to be, but never had the courage.

Two days later, he went to his son and said he wanted to go with him on this trip.

"You want to go with me? On a hunting trip? Why now? I've been after you to come with me for many years. You wouldn't even go out with me and Grandpa when he asked you to go. Why suddenly now?" Gerry Junior asked suspiciously.

"Just for the hell of it, son. To see the mountains in the winter again," his father replied lightly.

"No dice, Dad. You never do anything 'just for the hell of it.' You are one of the most meticulous and planning-oriented individuals I know—and you taught me to be that way too. You never left anything to chance or failed to have some plan for the unexpected event you had not anticipated, so this line isn't going to work on me. I want to know what is going on, Dad," Gerry Junior said stubbornly.

His father looked out the window of their home at the lightly falling snow and back at his son. He took a deep breath and decided to tell him about the worst day of his life. It was the very last time he had ever been out hunting on the mountain.

April and Adam were driving to the mountain resort and singing together, out of tune, to the songs on the radio. Between songs, Adam worked on the video camera he held in his lap.

"So tell me again, April, what it is we are doing?"

"We are going to do a story on a ghost skier. But what we are *really* going to do is get into who that skier is—or who he *was*—and why he is doing this," she responded.

"I hope you're not saying that we're going to interview a ghost," Adam said with mock seriousness.

"No—not unless he wants to be interviewed, that is," she said with equal seriousness. "No, Adam, we're going to interview everyone who has seen the skier, and we're going to look into his origins and see just what his relationship with the mountain is. We're going to dig as deeply as we can into where he came from and why he is here. I want to emphasize the human interest as much as I can," she said with intensity. "This could be my chance to make the big time, Adam, and if you help me, I'll take you with me."

"So this could be my big opportunity too?" Adam asked, suddenly motivated to get the best story he could.

"Yes, Adam, this could be your ticket as well."

"What kinds of pictures do you want, beside the standard interview photos?"

"Well, I think we definitely need to make the mountain come alive, so some good pictures of the mountain from all angles, particularly the slopes where he is reported to be seen the most. So you will need to get some shots while we are skiing," April said.

"Whoa! I don't ski, April. I'm not getting in any open chair as it goes up the mountain. What if I fall out?"

"Well then, the skier will probably come to your rescue," she responded with a carefree air.

"Probably? *Probably* isn't good enough for this boy, April. Sorry, but I am *not* getting up on snow skis. *Oof!*" He stopped talking when April hit him in the chest with the back of her fist. "What the hell did you do that for?" he asked in anger.

"Listen, you: this is my big break, and you're not going to sabotage me! You will get up on skis if I have to tie you to them, or I will find another photographer who wants this job, and I'll send you back to that little jerkwater paper we just left, where you'll never get beyond taking animal pictures and photographing car wrecks," she said with a hiss.

A moment of silence followed her threat, and then Adam responded meekly, "I suppose I could learn to ski there—if they give any lessons, I mean."

"Of course they do, silly," April responded sweetly, seemingly relaxed now that she was firmly back in control. "I'll sign you up for lessons as soon as we get there, before we take any of the mountain photos. You can start off by getting pictures of the lodge and the locals—for background color. I'll go to the newspaper office and dig up all the history I can find on this place and the ghost. When I have the lay of the land, we'll go to the top of the mountain and talk to the head of the ski patrol and see what he has to say about his phantom," she advised him.

"What about the other phantom, the deer or whatever it was?" Adam asked.

"What deer are you talking about, Adam? We are going to do a story on a ghost skier, not on a deer. Stay with me here, please," April said impatiently.

"Well, when we were getting our things together, I did a quick web search on ghosts on Redd Mountain, and I came up with two hits. One you know about—the skier. But there is another story—of a phantom elk that is leading hunters all over the mountain, and no one gets a clear shot at him. When they do get a shot, they all seem to miss, because no one has seen him get hit or seen any blood in the snow to suggest he might have been even nicked," Adam patiently explained.

"As I said, Adam, what's that got to do with our story of the ghostly skier? A resourceful deer—"

"Elk."

"Fine, a resourceful *elk*, then; I still don't see what it has to do with our story or why I should even give a crap about a big, dumb animal like that," she responded nastily.

"Well, I'm not saying they are connected; I'm just saying it's interesting that this one showed up about the same time the skier did, that's all. I only mentioned it because he's reported to have a reddish color to its coat, and no elk I ever heard of is red. They're all tan and brown in color," Adam retorted.

"Well, if we have any time left over we'll look into it, but our primary goal is the skier. Understand me?" she asked him in a voice that left little room for discussion.

"Okay, April, you're in charge of this expedition. I'm just here to take the film you want of what we're looking at," Adam said in submission.

"Good, I'm glad that we're on the same page now, Adam, because I like working with you. You are easily the best cameraman at the paper." Now that she had won the fight for control, she was willing to be generous and complimentary again. "You get the shots that others dream about, and you always put more emotion into your pictures than any of the other photographers, and that's the reason I wanted you to come with me. This is going to be my shot at the big time, and I need the best you can do," she said, flattering him. "I want you to put all the feeling and pathos in the pictures that you can give me, Adam.

"I will tell you what I am looking for, but I'm not going to tell you how to take your pictures, because that is what you do best. If we can make this work out like I think it can, we both will be on our way up, Adam. Can I count on you to make this happen for us? I'll really be grateful to you," April asked him seductively.

"I'll do my very best for you, April, I promise," he said with sincerity—and was rewarded with a big smile that showed off April's white teeth. Adam smiled back, but he wasn't deceived by her sweet words and warm tone. He had seen her work before, and he knew just how much loyalty April had to anyone whose first name wasn't April and last name wasn't Martens. But Adam was a very practical man, and he knew that, even without April's "help," he could make his name known on this photo shoot if he got the right photo. He was willing to help April get her story, and she would help him get his career on track, even if it wasn't her primary goal or her intention to do so.

As they continued the drive in silence, they looked at the landscape through two different sets of eyes.

April saw a land of opportunity, adventure, and career advancement, while Adam saw the natural beauty of the land, as well as its cold and danger. Adam devoted his attention for the rest of the ride to getting his cameras ready for the difficult job ahead, because he could do this without thinking about it—and he had a lot to think about now. Adam had a feeling this just wasn't going to end well. He owed it to her to do the best job he could for her, despite his misgivings. And, although he knew this was his opportunity to get recognized by his peers and future employers, he also was well aware he wasn't as driven to achieve the level of success as April was, because he had never had to prove himself over and over again or be better than everyone else. Adam thought about how his parents had raised him; he'd always found them to be supportive of his interests and activities.

His father had been a football hero in high school and college, yet, while Adam always heard about his father's gridiron accomplishments, he was never pushed to get into sports. His father had always recognized that Adam wasn't the same person he was, and so, when he had decided he wanted to be a photographer, his father hadn't said a word against it. After Adam won his first award for his black-and-white pictures at the county fair when he was sixteen, his father had given him a week's vacation at a photography camp as a reward.

When Adam had come home from that, both of his parents' cars were out in the driveway. He went inside and asked why they weren't in the garage. His mother buried her face in her magazine, and his father just scowled and said they couldn't fit them in with all of his stuff that was in there.

Smiling to himself, Adam remembered the confusion he had felt at his father's words and angry look. He'd run to the garage and opened the door. He hadn't understood why he was seeing another door with a red light bulb over it—but suddenly, the significance of it registered, and he threw the inner door open to find out that his father had converted the garage to a fully equipped photography studio. He looked around the garage and it was instantly clear—all his father's trophies, mounted clippings, ribbons, and photographs were gone.

Instead, he saw several brand new shelves containing rows of the chemicals he would need to develop and print his own pictures, as well as all the equipment needed to operate a first-class photography studio. Behind him, he'd heard his father's voice, no longer angry or upset, and he realized it was just an act. He turned around to see both of his parents standing there, smiling and crying. He ran to them, hugging them both at once and crying with them.

He would never forget his father's words that day, for his father had told him how proud he was of his son. He had told Adam that his own football achievements were nice, but Adam had a skill that far surpassed his own talents. He wanted to give Adam the chance to reach his dreams, and he was looking forward to telling all his friends about his son's accomplishments and showing off his photographs. His father then told him to open the cabinet behind him and look inside. When he had done that, he found a professional portfolio with all of his photographs expertly mounted and indexed. His father had put this together for him to help him in his career choice. Adam had always known how his parents felt, and this only showed him how lucky he was to have them.

From the things April had told him about her childhood, he knew that he came from a much different world than she did.

April didn't mind Adam not talking, although she didn't understand why he was being so negative about this golden opportunity. She could see the enormous potential in this assignment, why couldn't he? This was her chance to hit the big time, to get her own byline, and to start on the fast track to success. Success was very important to April; it always had been.

Growing up, she had always been told that she would never amount to anything. Her mother had left the family in the middle of the night without any warning when April was six. She never heard from her mother again after she left. While no one ever told her why she left, it wasn't hard to figure it out why she left—particularly when her father kept throwing it in her face every time he was drinking. She never understood why she didn't take April with her, though. Whenever he started drinking, her father would always compare her to her mother, listing all of her mother's failures as proof that April was destined to be one as well. He never helped April with her schoolwork, never attended any of her school functions, and he never gave her any praise or encouragement for anything she did.

When she earned a B, he said it should have been an A. When she earned an A, he would say it was what she was supposed to get. When she would dress up for a dance, he would look at her funny and comment on what she was wearing, speculating on what she was doing or going to do. He would call her names and say she was just like her mother and was sure to end up the same way. He would never say she looked nice, but would instead make suggestive and insulting jokes about her physical development. At first she didn't understand, but later on, when they made sense, they hurt her.

When she was eighteen, just before she graduated, his insinuations turned into action, and that was when she moved out of the home to stay with a boyfriend. She had never told the police, because she didn't want to be put on the public display a trial would be sure to create. She didn't go back to her house, and she never talked to him again.

April was determined to be a success; no one was ever going to be able to take advantage of her again. She was willing to use whatever skills or edge she could find to help herself up the ladder.

In college, she learned to use her looks, her easy charm, and the occasional sleepover to get her borderlines grades bumped up to the next level and get the better assignments in her journalism classes. While the other girls in class talked about her ethics and behavior, April ignored them, taking their snide comments and criticisms as just jealousy. She was focused on climbing the ladder, and there was no hesitation or turning back. Her professors wanted something from her, and she wanted something from them, so it was a fair trade. She didn't see her behavior as taking advantage of anyone, because she figured she gave as much as she got. Her father had always told her it was a dog-eat-dog world, and he had been chewed on many times. She learned to chew first.

She had considered this the only good advice he had ever taught her.

Coming out of college, she had used her charm and willingness to do what it took to get her first job. She'd seen the position being offered in an ad on her roommate's desk and called the paper herself from her roommate's cell phone. She went in for the interview wearing something low-cut to show off her best assets, as well as her portfolio of stories and letters of recommendation.

One of the letters was from a professor she had become involved with during her last semester, and this recommendation was the most glowing of them all. It was this letter that got her the job. She was at that paper for a year before she moved up to her current paper in a bigger market. She'd left behind many rumors—some having to do with how she managed to get the best assignments, and some about her ability to get the stories no one else seemed to be able to get. Once again, April considered these tales to be fueled by professional jealousy of her superior talents.

Now she had her chance to move into the big time, and no one, not even Adam, was going to ruin it for her. She didn't know what she was going to find, but she didn't believe there was anything to this story she couldn't spin into a prize-winner and her ticket to superstar status.

CHAPTER 2

Pete and Gene just reached the edge of the woods after a mad dash across the lanes of other skiers. They had cut off two people coming down, and Gene had actually run across the back of the skis of one skier. There had been no collisions, however, just a few threats, shaken fists, and the occasional upraised middle finger directed at them. They laughed it off and turned their attention to the rest of the course. They were just a little way down the mountain at this point, with the major portion of the run yet to come.

Gene looked ahead, and he could see the line of trees, dark and forbidding, just a few feet inside the edge of the run. As he lifted his goggles to get a better view, he thought he saw something moving down the hill at the edge of that dark stand of forest. He blinked to clear his eyes, but didn't see anything when he opened them again.

"So where is that jump you were talking about, Pete?" he asked, annoyance evident in his tone. "I don't see anything that looks like a jump."

Pete turned to look downhill, but he couldn't recognize the ledge he'd heard about. He didn't want to admit to Gene he'd not yet seen it for himself, only heard about it, but he didn't see anything he could point to.

"It's a little farther down the hill," he lied. "It's on the left side near where the trees come up to the edge of the run, and it points back into the middle of the run. It will give you a lift and a lot of speed going down the rest of the run, so you want to be in the middle of the course as you go down," he said with a bravado he didn't really feel. "You want to go first? I'll follow you?" Pete suggested, but Gene wasn't really as big a daredevil as he had painted himself.

"Well, Pete, actually, I think you should go first, since you know where it is, and I'll follow your track to make sure I don't go off the course."

Having talked himself into a corner, Pete had no choice but to play the part and hope for the best. "No problem, Gene. Just follow me down and get ready for the ride of your life—one I bet you'll never forget." He laughed and turned his skis downward.

Pete had no idea just how true his words would soon prove to be for both of them. Both men secured their goggles and gripped their poles to push off with. Pete lifted off to start his downward run, his heart in his throat as he realized he didn't know what was ahead of him or what he was skiing into—but he didn't want to admit that to his new friend. And he didn't want Ed to hear that he had chickened out of a run he had proposed; he would never be able to live that embarrassment down. As he picked up speed, he looked back over his shoulder to see Gene coming up behind him, far enough back he could follow him however he turned his skis.

Gene could feel the wind and snow stinging his face as he flew down the run, and thought to himself Pete had called it pretty accurately. It was fast, and he could see the trees flying by in a blur. Suddenly, he thought he saw something out of the corner of his eye, but when he turned his head slightly, there was nothing to see except a low-hanging cloud and a small snow swirl caused by wind blowing through the trees. He quickly put his eyes back on Pete to make sure he stayed behind him in the safe channel of the downhill run. It slowly came to his awareness there were no other skiers around, except for Pete. This caused him to feel a slight anxiety, but it was quickly replaced by exhilaration from the speed of his descent.

Pete was right, he thought to himself. *I am flying! If I hit the jump just right …*

Then that thought changed to, *If I hit the jump wrong . . .* And then things began to go terribly awry from that point on.

To be good at a sport requires concentration and the ability to block out distractions from one's thinking and awareness. Gene had just violated that rule, and, as a result, he broke his concentration and lost his confidence. He started to sway, and his knees began to lose their angle, causing his skis to start separating from the tight parallel he had been maintaining to keep his speed and balance. This led to him starting to slip sideways in his track, which in turn led to him heading right into Pete—who couldn't see what was happening behind him, as he was having his own problems.

Pete was starting to be worried about the ledge he couldn't see. He didn't know when to expect it, he didn't know where it was going to be, and he didn't know how high it was. But the biggest worry was whether or not he would be able to negotiate that jump when he came to it. Virtually everything about it worried Pete, because he didn't know where he would come down—but mostly he was worried because he had never taken any jumps before. Oh, he had talked about it a lot, and he watched a lot of videos of it, and he had even done it on a small rise before; but he had never been on real skis on real snow on a real jump before, and now he had to do it right the first time. Pete was concerned, to be sure.

Suddenly he saw the ledge in the distance. It didn't look too bad to him, so he started to relax a little. He stuck his pole in the snow to make his adjustment turn and shifted his weight to aim toward the ledge that was coming up fast. Too fast. As he tried to get lined up with it, he saw, out of the corner of his eye, a blurry figure coming at him out of the woods. Before he could get a good look at the figure, he was hit from behind and knocked off his feet. He felt himself fall backward onto something soft. He turned his head toward the blurry figure, and his eyes bulged as he stared at what he saw coming at him. The soft object underneath him slipped, and suddenly both of them were sliding faster toward the ledge—which suddenly wasn't a ledge, but a rock outcrop with the rough side facing them.

Pete heard Gene calling out, and he realized they were tangled up and both headed right for that rock face and very serious injuries—possibly fatal injuries if they hit it head-on. Three feet before impact, the figure Pete had seen in disbelief came racing between them and the rock, and Pete felt something cold and hard push him. It was not so much as a push as it was a nudge, but it was enough of a nudge that they missed the outcrop by inches and slowly slid to a stop two feet past it.

They looked at each other briefly, and then both of them threw up.

Freddy and Ed picked themselves up from their laughing fit and practiced standing up together on one leg. It took them several tries for them to maintain their balance for more than just a few seconds before one of them fell over, pulling the other down on top of them.

"Okay, Fred, now let's see if we can move together in unison. We have to be able to ski downhill together without falling down if we're going to make this look good. I don't want to get partway down and fall down and look silly, so we need to be real good at doing this three-legged race, okay?"

"Sure, Ed. I'm looking forward to seeing the stunned expressions on these people's faces when they see our tracks!" Freddy laughed.

After another ten minutes of skiing back and forth on the snow, both men at last felt they were finally ready to make their run.

"Okay, Fred, let's take it slow for a bit, until we get a clear space between us and the next man down. We don't want anyone seeing us set up this trick."

"Sure thing, Ed."

For the next ten minutes, they alternated between slowly moving downhill and stopping to pretend they were just resting. Finally, they saw a break in the number of skiers coming down the hill, and Ed pointed this out to Fred.

"Okay, Fred, here's our chance. Give me your arm, and let's aim for that tree down there on the edge. See the one I mean? The one with the branch sticking out in the front?"

"Yeah, but maybe we should find a safer-looking tree? That big branch could be dangerous if we don't do it right, and I sure would hate to be stuck on it like a bug on a pin," Freddy said nervously.

"Don't worry, Fred, we'll be fine. Tell you what, I'll take the side with the branch and you take the open side of the tree. When we get on the other side, we'll reach out to each other and link up again, and head for the opening about a hundred yards down—do you see it?"

"Yeah, I see it. It's—what was that?" Freddy asked curiously.

"What was what? I didn't see anything," Ed said, looking around in the direction Freddy was staring.

"I guess it was just snow blowing in the wind or something. Well, I'm ready to do this. After you, friend." They shook hands, laughed, and stood up, side by side.

"Put your arm around my waist, and I'll hold on to yours, and that way we can stay balanced and not fall over. I'll count to four, and then we push off and go together," Ed said as Fred nodded his understanding.

Freddy was still looking downhill, at a spot at the edge of the woods just a short distance ahead of their target. He was also looking at the tree, which suddenly seemed to be warning him to keep his distance. Fred felt cold—not just from the snow, but for some reason he didn't fully understand. He almost told Ed he'd changed his mind, but then Ed began his count and it was too late for him to back out.

"One." They held on to each other, and each man raised his inside leg, hanging onto his pole for balance.

"Two." Both men planted their ski poles in the snow.

"Three." Both men leaned forward in unison.

"Four!" Both men pushed off and started down the hill toward the tree. They didn't go down the mountain fast because they didn't have their skis aligned as well as they could have. They were making a fairly believable set of tracks as they traveled downward. Fred noticed with concern that the snow was flying in their wake, and the wind was picking up in front of them.

The tree was fast approaching them when Ed called out, "Break!" He dropped his arm from Fred's shoulder, while, at the same time, Fred pulled his from Ed's waist. Somehow their wrists crossed at the same time, and Fred's watch got tangled in Ed's sweater, with the result that they couldn't separate from each other.

"Break, I said!" Ed called out again, this time in a very scared voice.

"I'm trying!" Fred yelled back. "But I can't get my arm free of your sweater!"

"Then drop down, and we'll just roll in the snow!" Ed yelled out, truly scared now.

But before either Ed or Fred could drop in the snow, they were bumped off their feet. As they went down, Fred caught a glimpse of the person who had hit them. It was a glimpse he would remember for the rest of his life, because he had never seen anyone like that before. The man who knocked them off their feet and out of danger of hitting that tree was wearing a bright red parka. But that wasn't what made Fred's blood run cold—it was the fact he could see the rest of the forest right through him.

Not behind him, but through him.

Fred and Ed picked themselves up from the snow, and Ed shook his head to clear the snow from his face.

"Damn, that was close! It's a good thing you … What is it? Are you hurt? What's the matter, Fred?" he asked with real concern.

"I … I … I saw him," Freddy stammered.

"Saw who, the guy who knocked us down? Where'd he go? I wanted to thank him," Ed said as he looked around. There was no one, only another snow flurry farther down the hill, swirling around two other skiers. As the powder settled, they recognized his friend Pete's blue and green sweater on the back side of the now-thinning snow cloud.

"Hey! There are Pete and Gene—down there, see? Come on, let's catch up to them," Ed urged as he awkwardly rose to his feet.

"Ed. Stop. Listen to me. You know all the stories we heard about that ghost who is supposed to be haunting the slopes?"

"Yeah, it's just a story, Fred. Don't go spooky on me, now."

"No. I saw him, Ed. That's who bumped us. It wasn't me, Ed. He came out of the snow and he bumped us. And, Ed … I saw right through him. He was there, and he wasn't there. I could see the forest ahead right through him; do you know what I am saying?" Fred rasped out.

"Yeah, I know what you're saying. Do you mind allowing the blood to flow in my arm again?" Ed said sarcastically as he tried to loosen Fred's grip.

"Huh? Oh, sorry. Ed, I saw him. He's real—well, as real as any ghost can be. But he was here. He saved us from hitting that tree! He was suddenly there, and he bumped us, and then he was gone. I didn't see where he came from, but I saw him go into that cloud of snow, and I saw right through him as he faded away! You go ahead. I have to collect myself, Ed. You didn't see what I did. I'm going to take my time going down."

"Are you saying you really saw the ghost?" Ed asked incredulously. They helped each other back to their feet, and gathered up their poles.

As they did, Fred looked around. "Ed, look around us. What do you see?"

Ed, clearly not understanding what he was being asked to do looked around him. "I see our tracks; there they are." He pointed.

"Yes, there are our tracks. Where are the tracks for the man who hit us, Ed?"

Ed took a second look around and saw no other tracks. "Maybe the blowing snow covered them up?"

"The blowing snow covered up his tracks but not ours?" Fred asked witheringly. "Yes, Ed. That's what I am saying. Didn't you see him?"

"Well, no, not really. I saw something in a blur come up from the backside; I felt myself being knocked down away from the tree, and I saw a flash of something ..." His voice trailed off. "I saw a flash of something red, and then it was gone. *Oh ... my ... God!* It *was* him!" Ed said in shock. He sat down hard in the snow, Fred dropping down beside him.

"What do you think we should do, Ed? Should we tell someone? Should we tell Gene and Pete what happened? Should we ..."

"You should just shut up right now, while I get my head together—please!" Ed said shortly. "I need to sort this out. I've never been a believer in ghosts or spirits, and this is a shock to me. I think our best bet is to keep quiet, because we don't want everyone to think we're crazy. Do you agree with me?"

"Okay, Ed, if you think that's best," Fred said reluctantly. They got to their feet again, somewhat unsteadily, and made their way down to their friends, who were also just standing by themselves while other skiers zipped past them in a steady stream.

"Hey, guys," Ed called out. "How was the run down? Hey, what's wrong? Pete, you look like you've ... seen ... a ... ghost ..." His voice trailed off.

Pete and Gene looked at each other with strange expressions on their faces.

"What makes you say that, Ed?" Pete responded with a very harsh tone.

Ed looked over at Fred, who just nodded and looked away. "Because we did. We saw him, Pete! We saw the red-coated skier! He saved our lives. We were tangled up and headed right for a tree with a low, jagged branch, and he bumped us out of the way just in time. Fred said he could see right through the spirit, didn't you, Fred?"

"It was very spooky, Gene. He came out of nowhere and went back into nowhere after he pushed us out of danger. It's like he knew we were in danger and came to our rescue just in time. And he was wearing red, just like the story says he does. He came out of a blowing snow, and he went back into it. Gene, I could see right through him. It was a very surreal moment—and, frankly, it scared me. I'm going back to the lodge to have a drink and think about what this means. You can come or not come, Gene," Fred said in a low voice.

"I saw him too," Pete said softly. "He saved our lives too, Fred. We were taking a run at a jump, and he got between us and disaster. I didn't see through him—I didn't even really get a good look at him, but I did see a flash of red as he went by me, and I felt something hard and cold brush my shoulder. I've heard all the stories, but I never believed any of them ... until today ... until now. And I'm going to join you for that drink. Come on, guys, the first one is on me," Pete offered.

Gerry Bruce Sr. was sitting at the bar in the lounge, nursing his third Jack Daniels and rum, and trying to sort out his thoughts and his feelings. He couldn't shake this feeling of impending danger, and he wasn't sure why he felt this way. He knew it had something to do with the ghost of the mountain and the sudden reappearance of his former client, but he wasn't sure how they were connected—although he had his suspicions. He also had his suspicions about how the stories of the elusive elk were related to the ghostly skier, but those suspicions didn't make any sense and defied common rational thought.

Gerry had been hearing about the elk for years, ever since that terrible night up on the mountain. He'd never seen the animal himself, as he had avoided going back up ever since then, but he had occasionally talked with other packers and guides, and they all had told him the same thing, with the only change being where it was seen. The essential details had been identical every time.

It seemed to come out of a cloud or blowing snow, and while it allowed hunters to get close, they never had a really clear shot at him. The wind would kick up, or a tree would be in the way, or some obstacle would interfere. Even when they took the shot, they never seemed to hit it.

Old Charley Weeks had sworn on a Bible that he'd seen the limb of a tree fly off behind the critter when he fired at it and was steadfast in maintaining he hadn't shot over the animal, that the limb had been behind it. Of course, everyone knew old Charley was known to pull a cork on his hunts, so no one ever paid any attention to his claims; but Weldon Trakler was known to never imbibe, and he had made the same claim a year later.

Gerry was an expert tracker, and that meant being able to see signs no one else could—and he was seeing some now. These two apparitions were connected to each other in some way and were equally connected to him. He felt drawn to the spirits, as if he had something he had to do or get done—some mistake he had to correct. He had a strong idea what mistake was involved here, but he did not know how to fix it.

As he sat at the bar, he heard four young men talking about their encounter with the ghost of the red skier that afternoon, and he laughed to himself. His laughter died away as he started thinking about what those two ghosts had in common. Suddenly the connection became clearer as he realized they had a common purpose in their actions. Both ghosts protected the individuals they represented. But why? Why were they doing this?

His efforts to solve this puzzle were interrupted by a low-pitched, demanding, and demeaning voice that grated on the nerves as it spoke—a voice that dominated the bar by its very arrogance and overwhelming indifference to the conversations of others. It was a voice that belonged to a very abrasive individual who had no regard for the rights of others or feelings of anyone else. This was a man who had no knowledge of common civilities of any kind—who believed it was his right to do whatever he wanted, regardless of how it impacted on anyone else. It was the voice of an individual he had only met once before, thirty-some years ago, and had hoped never to hear it again in his lifetime.

It was the voice of a much older Warner Barney.

Gerry went cold inside and hunched down inside his overcoat, turning slightly to keep his back to the voice from his past. Warner had sent in his money, plus a lot more, but so far as Gerry was aware, his son hadn't sent any notice for him to come on out. But then, he reflected, Warner didn't believe in waiting his turn for anything.

Although he had told his son almost everything about that night, he was confident his son was still going to give that man a chance to get that elk—and a chance to hurt many others in the process.

But maybe it is just a coincidence Warner is here—maybe he is in town for the skiing, Gerry told himself.

But Warner's next words dispelled his faint hope.

"I hear you people up here in the backwoods have something of a record animal running around that no one can bag. Well, I'm here to take him down. My name is Warner Barney, and I've never seen an animal I can't track and kill. I'm going out with one of the best trackers in this state next week, and we are going to find and bring that elusive red-coated animal back here—and I'll put his head up over that bar for everyone to see!" he boasted.

"Who's yer tracker?" someone called out from the back of the bar.

"Mr. Gerry Bruce, tracker supreme," Warner called out to the man at the back.

"You mean Gerry Junior or Gerry Senior?"

Warner started looking around as the recognition set in that his old tracker was still alive. Warner had never told anyone of his part in the disaster thirty years ago, because that would have put him at risk. As he quickly scanned the entire room, he saw a door closing in the back and recognized his old tracker making his own tracks out of the bar—probably ashamed to show his face after his scurrilous and cowardly behavior some thirty years ago. No matter. He would be able to find him later.

For now, he just wanted to make his name known and create a

situation where he couldn't be refused his participation in that hunt. He would call the younger Bruce tomorrow and set up the details of his hunt. This was turning out to be the best adventure of his life, and it was certain to be better than the last time he was here. That had been a real troubled hunt, although it did end well—with him getting his target at the end, in spite of Gerry.

A tap on his shoulder interrupted his reverie, and he turned to see a very pretty, slender brunette with short hair, standing behind him. Beside her was a mousey-looking young man with a video camera. Never one to shun publicity, Warner focused his attention on her and presented his best side to the cameraman.

"Yes, young lady, what can I do for you?" he asked with all the charm he could show.

"Mr. Barney, my name is April Martens, and this is Adam Jacobs. I am a reporter for *The Galleton Chronicle*. I've heard of your records and wonder if I might get an interview with you." This was a lie— April hadn't heard of him until he announced himself, but she could recognize another self-promoter instantly, being one herself. He wasn't here for the skier, but she had been thinking about the animal ever since Adam brought it up, and Barney's arrival had tipped the scale in favor of exploring this angle as well.

"I understand from what you said that you are here to catch—"

"Not catch, as in catch and release, my dear, but hunt. *Hunt*, as in track and kill, and then mount and display," he corrected her.

"... here to *kill* the Red Elk. May I ask you why you want to do that?"

"Because, my dear young lady, that is what men do. We catch and kill our food. It is the fair challenge of the hunt: the mind and superior thinking of man against the instincts and speed of the animal. It is nature at its best, my dear."

"Does the animal get a high-powered rifle with a scope too?" Adam muttered under his breath. April knew that Adam was an animal rights man, and hunting for sport was just murder to him.

She ignored him, focusing on the large and powerful man in front of her, hoping he hadn't heard Adam.

Warner hadn't heard, or he just ignored him. He continued to explain his position. "I am here to find and kill that magnificent animal, because I am the only one who can. I will follow his trail, no matter where it takes me, no matter how long it takes, because that is my destiny. Would you care to come along and document the hunt, young lady?"

"Whether she does or doesn't isn't up to her, Mr. Barney, but we have some rules that you need to know about first," someone said to his left. "Allow me to introduce myself, Mr. Barney. My name is Oliver Barry, and I am the head of the park safety patrol. Anything that happens here to put any of my guests at risk is my concern, and your statement that you will go anywhere the trail takes you concerns me a great deal. Before you can get any permit to hunt anywhere on this mountain, you will come to my office tomorrow, and we will talk about it. I know you are thinking you are going to be hiring a guide, and he will take care of all that, but you would be very wrong in thinking that. His ability to get the necessary permits needed to hunt on this mountain depends upon getting my approval—and right now, he doesn't have it. So I will see you tomorrow, and we will see if he gets them after we have talked. Good night, Mr. Barney, I hope you have a nice evening," Oliver said stiffly.

As he turned to walk away, April attached herself to him, Barney totally forgotten for the moment. "Mr. Barry, my name is April Martens, and I am a reporter for *the Galleton Chronicle* ..."

Oliver listened to the reporter as she demanded, "As head of the safety patrol, surely you're aware of the stories about this phantom skier who comes out of the snow to help people in danger. What is your opinion of these stories and the people spreading them?"

Oliver was just about to say something flippant when he saw her pencil poised over a notebook and the man beside her targeting him with his camera. He wisely decided to tone down his reply and give a more official-sounding statement, one in keeping with his overall plan for dealing with this legend.

"Miss Martens, I am aware of these stories, and while I do not say any of the people making these reports are doing so out of a desire for publicity, it is my belief they are simply mistaken or have fallen victim to some form of mass hysteria," Oliver said in his best "public-official" voice. "While this spirit appears to be a benevolent one, we are preparing a full statement we will be releasing in the coming week. Our paramount concern is always the safety and enjoyment of our guests on our mountain. I'm not a believer in ghosts and I have yet to see any concrete proof that such apparition does exist, but I try to keep an open mind on such things, and—"

"That's because you are not a novice or beginning skier, Mr. Barry," Fred called out. "Because if you were, you might see him and be damn glad you did! I did!"

April's head spun around, and she motioned for Adam to get the speaker's picture, which he did without being too obvious about it.

"What are you saying, sir?" Oliver and April asked at the same time. The man looked at both of them, shook his head, and continued with his story.

"My three friends and I were coming down the slopes this morning—early afternoon, actually—when he intervened for all of us. We were in twos, and my partner and I were just about to hit a big tree with a low-hanging, jagged branch sticking out into our way. We got tangled up with each other and couldn't separate when he came up out of nowhere and diverted us to the side. My other friends were heading for a small jump when they lost their balance and fell into an out-of-control, headfirst slide right for a rock that would have killed them, when he appeared and saved them as well. He was gone in an instant, and all I saw was a flash of red and the forest. I saw the forest right through him! Do you understand me? I saw the forest right through him!" Fred said excitedly.

"Mr. Barry, what do you say about this eyewitness report? Does this change your official position at all?" April asked provocatively.

Oliver realized he was being baited to make an injudicious statement, but he didn't react to it.

"Miss Martens, I would remind you that people up here have been seeing this apparition for almost thirty years, and one more opinion, pro or con, is not going to change anything or anyone's beliefs. We are very happy that these gentlemen were able to avoid injury today. We at the patrol are always focused on safety on the mountain—safety for everyone—so I would ask this gentleman and his friends to come see us tomorrow at the main station so we can pinpoint where these obstacles and skiing hazards are, and deal with them to prevent any further injuries. Now, if you will excuse me, I have some work to do before tomorrow comes. Miss Martens, Mr. Barney, gentlemen; I will see all of you tomorrow," Oliver said as he left.

The next morning, Oliver was complaining to Eileen about the evening before. "I tell you, that man is trouble. He is the sort that ignores rules and safety when it is convenient and insists on them when it is to his benefit," he said angrily.

"Now, Oliver, you can't make that kind of judgment about someone you just met," Eileen said soothingly.

"Yes, I can, particularly when I hear him say he doesn't care about boundaries or limits if it prevents him from getting his quarry."

"He said that?"

"He most certainly did. I'm telling you, Eileen, I don't trust him. I've a good mind not to give Gerry a permit for the damn hunt. The more I think about it, the more that it seems to me that elk is bad for this mountain. It draws more hunters here willing to take chances and go far deeper into the forest than is safe. It draws hunters like that Barney, who don't obey the safety rules and put everyone in danger. And that damn ghost skier, it gives people a false sense of security and draws more people here than we can safely handle. Everyone is relying on the ghost to protect them, rather than on their own good judgment and common sense.

"Maybe we're making a mistake promoting those two legends, Eileen. Maybe we should be downplaying them, instead," Oliver said pensively. "And on top of that, there's this newspaper reporter sniffing all around here, looking to make something out of all this. I didn't mention the four men who are claiming they saw the skier too yesterday afternoon. I think they were on a closed run, but I didn't want to say anything in front of that damn reporter who could use it to make us look bad," Oliver grumbled. "These four men are saying they saw the ghost themselves, and that it rescued them from certain death in two separate incidents.

"And, of course, they had to say this in the bar in front of that reporter. She's probably pumping those four idiots right now for all the details they can make up about their accident and that damn ghost story. She's going to turn it into something atrocious, I just know it," Oliver muttered negatively.

"You don't know any such thing, Oliver. Quit being so damned dramatic and calm down and just think about what you're saying. You already have a plan in place for dealing with these stories, so just stay with your plan and don't let this throw you. You've never allowed anything to upset your plans before—you always found a way around every little setback and this shouldn't be any different," Eileen said encouragingly.

Oliver stood at the window and listened to her words, his mind turning over options for making the most out of this situation.

With his back to Eileen, Oliver didn't see her face suddenly brighten up, but he turned around when he heard her call out excitedly. "Oliver, I've got it!" Eileen blurted out. "Okay, tell me about it."

"I used to date a psychotherapist, and he—"

"A what?"

"A psychotherapist. You know, a shrink. Anyway, he once told me about a problem he had with a competitor who was always complaining about him and his style of working. He said the man constantly complained that he was doing things in an unethical manner and driving away his business."

"So what did he do, sue the man?"

"No, he did something much more clever: he gave the man a job with his office."

"What! He gave the man who was complaining about him a job in his office? Where's the sense in that?" Oliver asked disgustedly.

"He said it is called 'co-opting,' and it works like this: if the person who is complaining about you works for you, then they are complaining about themselves. By giving his attacker a job, he took away his power to complain," Eileen explained.

"Let me see if I have this right, Eileen. By taking the complainer into his office, he turned him from a threat into an asset, right?"

"That's it, Oliver. So we can do the same thing with this reporter and the four men who are saying they saw the ghost and turn them into our advantage in promoting the mountain."

"I see …" He stood, looking out the window at the landscape and the other mountain in the distance, and then he whirled around. "I want you to find those four men and tell them we want to make it up to them. Find Barney and tell him he needs to be here as well, but don't make their appointments consecutive. I want to see Mr. Barney first. And place a call to Gerry Bruce and tell him to bring any information he has on that man, Barney. This isn't going to turn into a fiasco like it did for my predecessor. With your help, Eileen, I'm going to get out in front and stay in front of this mess."

"I know you will, Oliver. You always do," Eileen said confidently.

Gerry Bruce Jr. hung up the telephone and turned to his father. "That was Oliver Barry, the head of the safety patrol for the mountain. You'll never believe what he just told me," he said slowly, his anger starting to build.

"Okay, tell me and surprise me, son," his father said absently as he worked on oiling his saddle and rifle scabbard.

"He said that he has the right to deny us any permits to pack or hunt on the mountain if, in his opinion, it creates a risk to the safety of anyone on the mountain. Can he really do that?"

Gerry Senior stopped what he was doing and looked over at his son. "You know, I'm not sure. I know he's never done it before, and I don't recall Arthur or Will ever doing it to Dad during their administration, but I really don't know if he can do that or not. I'd have to look at the regulations, but I will say this about Oliver: he's not one to rush off without thinking of the consequences of his decisions," he said thoughtfully. "I know this is his first year as head of the department, but he spent several years as Will's second-in-command, and things always ran very smoothly and efficiently. He never lied to me, and he never promised me anything he couldn't deliver ... so, all in all, I don't think I'd bet against it being in the rules somewhere or him not having the authority to do it if he thinks it is in the best interest of the safety of everyone on the mountain. Did he give you any options, or is it a done deal?" he asked his son.

"No, he said he wants me to come in on Tuesday morning and talk with him about it. You want to go in my place?" Gerry Junior asked hopefully.

"No, but I'll go with you if you want me to," his father offered. "What time do you want to meet at his office?"

"How about nine a.m.; would that work for you?"

"Sure, son, that will work. Right now, we need talk about something else. We need to talk about Warner Barney, son. He's a very dangerous man. I told you what happened when I took him out, and I told you what he is like. You still want to take him along, even though he is dangerous and unstable, just for the money. I'm telling you, son, he's not worth the money he's paying you. He is more trouble than he's worth, you'll see. But it's your business now, so you make the decisions. But know this, son: you are my boy, and I'll never let anyone hurt you if I can prevent it. I'll do whatever I have to in order to keep you safe," he said solemnly.

Gerry Junior just hugged his father in response—and he couldn't see the look in his father's eyes as he did.

"I'm telling you, this is going to be a big story," April said excitedly to Adam, who was placidly cleaning his cameras again. He spent a lot of time cleaning his camera equipment because it was his business, and he wanted to take the very best pictures he could.

April was busy packing a small backpack with the minimum she could live on for three or five days up in the mountains, and she seemed to be having difficulty making a choice between her thermal shirts and her more visually appealing clothes. Adam had already filled his backpack with the warmest and most comfortable clothes he could. He had a separate bag for his cameras, and he was wrapping them up in towels to keep them and the film, warm and safe. He looked over at what April was laying out to pack, and he stopped wrapping his cameras.

"April, those thin and revealing clothes won't help you much where we are going, but you will look nice. Everyone will be very impressed by your ice blue boobs, I am sure," he said encouragingly, and then went back to wrapping up his cameras.

April looked at what she had laid out and said something rude to Adam, who just smiled and continued with what he was doing. She pulled everything out of the backpack and started over, throwing her heavy socks and sweaters and all her thermal shirts and pants into the bag instead. She picked up a handful of pencils, a sharpener, and three notepads, and stuffed them into the side pocket. She had told him how she planned on getting a lot of insight into all the principals of the story before this was over.

"April, I'm not sure it is a good idea for us to go on this hunt. This man, Barney, he doesn't seem to have his head on straight. I've got a bad feeling about him. Maybe we should sit this out and wait for them to come back?" he asked hopefully.

April stood up straight up, sighed, and turned on him with fire in her eyes. "Adam, I don't want to go through this all over again. This is our big chance to move up the line—and to do that, we need pictures of this elk, we need pictures of the people going after it, and we need the pictures of them getting it. I can't take the damn pictures; that's your job, so you have to come along. I'm going to get this story, Adam, and you're going to help me. Understand? Now relax, this is going to be fine. The activity will do you good, anyway," she gaily assured him.

Adam didn't believe her, but he wasn't interested in fighting with April. And he was rather curious about how this was all going to play out.

Warner couldn't believe the insolence of this man, telling him he might not give a permit for the hunt.

"Who the hell does he think he is? This is a public mountain, and anyone who wants to can hunt or ski here. He has no legal right to prohibit me from doing anything I want to do. No one has ever been able to prevent me from reaching my goals once I make up my mind to do something," he growled. "All my life, I've been taking what I wanted when I wanted it, and I see no reason this ponytailed windbag and overgrown boy scout can prevent me from taking what I want this time, either," he slurred. He reached out to the bottle of bourbon sitting on the nightstand and, ignoring the glass beside it, drank heavily.

"There's no one who can catch this animal as easily I can. I know this mountain, I've been up here before, and even though my old guide didn't want to acknowledge me, I know my money will get me what I want, just as it always has. I've got to meet with that interfering idiot on Wednesday, and at that time, I'll make it perfectly clear who he's dealing with and what's expected of him," he said confidently.

He took another healthy swig from the bottle and turned it upside down. A couple of drops fell onto the soiled rug in the cheap hotel room. He dropped the bottle in the trash and stood up. He lurched over to the suitcase on the other bed, opened it, and rummaged through it until he found his spare. He broke the seal and took a long swig from it. He sat down hard on the chair and resumed his ruminations about the impositions he was being forced to endure.

"At least that reporter recognized my name, and she obviously knows where her bread is buttered. She wants to get my story in print and give me all the credit I so rightly deserve. All over the world, people will know my name and they will recognize me as the ultimate hunter when this one is done," Warner boosted himself. "That reporter, she was nice-looking, even if she is a bit young for me, and I'm sure I can get her where I want when this is over."

He sat down in the chair by the window, looking up the mountain and wondering where the magnificent animal was. "I'm coming for you, my friend. You can run, but you can't hide. It is my destiny to find you and take you down, as it is yours to run from me in panic until you can't run any longer. But I will make it quick, my friend, befitting such a magnificent opponent." He took another long drink from the half-empty bottle of bourbon, lifted it in a salute to his distant opponent, and finished it off. He turned out the light and went to bed, supremely confident of his absolute success in the coming meeting, as well as in the hunt.

Oliver sat in his chair, looking at the two men in front of him. "Gerry," he said to the senior Bruce, "why are you here? This meeting was with your son, since he is the man running the company now. I thought you were retired and relaxing?"

"Well, Oliver, here's how it is: my son is running the company, that's true, but he's still my son, and I worry about him. This hunt, while it seemed like a good idea at the time, there are aspects about it that have me worried about his safety. I have some experience with this man, Warner Barney, and I don't like him or trust him one bit. I know he'll bend and break the rules to serve his own needs. But, on the other hand, he is willing to put a lot of money in our pockets for a chance to catch this elusive animal. You obviously have some concerns about this, so I'd really like to know where you stand, Oliver," Gerry Senior responded calmly.

Oliver sat back, wondering how to answer that question, since he didn't really know himself what he wanted. He decided the truth was the best response. "Well, now, here's the thing. Initially, I was thinking the best plan was to play down the ghost stories, but then I decided the best bet would be to embrace these stories and make them part of our appeal to the public. After a while, though, I started to see some drawbacks to that approach.

"For one, when I started hearing about all the people trying to do stupid things just to draw the ghost skier out to help them, I realized that was just going to create more hazards on the slopes for everyone. When I first heard about the elk, I thought it was a good thing, and I planned to promote that; but then it started to attract too many hunters, some of whom are no better than your Mr. Barney. So when I first read about your hunt idea, Gerry—" He nodded to Gerry Junior. "—it seemed like a great idea. Then I started listening to the people in town and reading some of the editorials in the local papers, and I realized public sentiment was not with a hunt.

"People are saying that animal is a symbol of this mountain and should be protected and allowed to live out its days in safety. So I have made a decision. I will not be allowing a trophy hunt on this mountain for that elk. I will, however, be issuing a permit for a collection hunt, for the purpose of relocating him to an animal preserve," he said calmly, although this idea had only come to him as he was talking. "I will be issuing the permit to your ranch, Mr. Bruce, as it was your idea to hold the hunt. Although, I do wish you had talked to me about that idea first," Oliver said, frowning.

"Well, since it's my business, Mr. Barry, I didn't think I had to clear how I run my business with you," the younger Bruce replied stiffly. His father put his hand on his son's knee, and Gerry Junior reluctantly sat back in his chair.

Oliver didn't respond to the open hostility and continued as if he hadn't spoken at all. "Of course, I understand you're under no obligation to do so, but it has always been my desire to work closely with everyone who has a stake in this mountain. We'll never know, but perhaps we could have found a way to promote this for you in way that didn't raise the risk of danger to everyone else on the mountain," Oliver said suavely.

"Perhaps it still isn't too late to do that, Oliver," the elder Bruce suggested diplomatically. "I was thinking, what if you came with us to oversee what happens? We will be in charge of the hunt itself, of course, because that's our area of expertise. I think you had a really good idea, Oliver—the goal of not killing the elk, but putting him into a preserve to save his life. With your contacts, you can bring along a conservationist and someone from the preserve to oversee the transfer of the elk to the preserve. I know that reporter wants to write up the story; how about bringing her along to write it up our way? We limit the party to one or two shooters, and that way we don't look like mindless, bloodthirsty hunters to the general public. What do you think?" Gerry Senior asked him innocently.

Oliver particularly didn't like this idea, because he had never been on a horse. For all his fitness programs and other activities, riding a horse was one activity he had never been into. The closest he had ever been was when his father put a quarter into the slot for him. He wanted to decline this offer, but he realized he had been outmaneuvered by the older man. He wanted to keep this deer or elk, or whatever it was, safe and alive to preserve the mountain's environmentally friendly and people-friendly face, so he couldn't very well turn down the conciliatory offer to meet in the middle on this situation.

He did know several people in the organizations Gerry had mentioned, and he was reasonably sure he could get one of them to go along for the ride. They were much more into horses than he was, and he felt sure they wouldn't turn down the free positive publicity. They had already been calling him about the hunt, ever since they heard about it, and this could improve his relationship with them as well. Still, having to ride a horse for three or four days …

But he hadn't heard from the other Bruce about the issue of the man he would be taking along.

"Gerry," he said, turning to the younger Bruce, "what is your position on this? I haven't heard from you yet."

Gerry Junior just stared at him, not responding for several minutes. "My father and I have talked about this man, Barney, and he has some serious concerns about his reliability, as you heard. He has already paid for the trip, and he paid very well. If I cancel his outing, or any of the others I advertised for, I am at risk of being sued or shut down for false advertising. I can't cancel it now, even if I wanted to … and if you deny the permit to do it, he will still sue me—and you too."

"How do you know that, Gerry?"

"Because he told me so," was the reply. Oliver sat back in his chair, reflecting that this was getting complicated.

"Okay, so we have to allow it to go on, but I will do so only on the proviso that it is a tag-and-capture operation for the expedition. If you two are in agreement, then the next step is for me to talk to Mr. Barney and explain our agreement to him. I will tell him you fought me on this issue and didn't want to give in. I will make sure he understands you agreed to the arrangement, only in order to be able to keep your deal with him. He's coming in tomorrow morning, and I will talk to him about his options, so if the deal falls through, it will be on his head.

"You get the trip lined up; I will talk to Barney and get him in line and the reporter and get her on board. When do you want to leave, Gerry?" Oliver said, looking at Gerry Junior.

"I figure to be outbound in about a week. I need to make a pack list, buy the supplies I don't have on hand, and I need to see the riding ability of this diverse group you're saddling me with," he said wryly.

"Well, speaking for myself, on a scale of zero to ten, with ten being a rodeo rider, I'm probably a minus ten," Oliver said sheepishly.

"Lucky me," Gerry Junior said tiredly.

April and Adam sat down in front of Oliver, Adam more concerned than April about why the head of mountain ski patrol would want to talk to him, and what would come out of this talk—no matter how "friendly" the man said this was supposed to be. As April was the person in charge of this journey, he decided to defer to her and allow her to do all the talking.

"I understand, Miss Martens, that you have talked with Mr. Barney and that he has agreed to allow you to accompany us on the hunt and document his success or failure?" Oliver asked.

"I'm very sure Mr. Barney doesn't anticipate failure in this adventure, Mr. Barry," she said sweetly.

"Yes ... well, that may be—my Ouija board is in the shop today. Here is the problem, Miss Martens, and I'm going to tell you what the deal is now. I have several concerns about the safety of this outing as it stands, and I am using the authority given me under the regulations concerning public safety to either cancel that hunt or to amend the conditions of it. To protect our working partners in this area, I chose to amend the conditions it will be conducted under.

"This will no longer be a hunt with the end being the killing of that animal," he said casually as her eyebrows went up. "No, we are no longer interested in killing that animal; we are going to trap him and transport him to a regional animal preserve, where he will live out the rest of his days in safety and peace. We feel it is a more humane approach to this issue, and it eliminates the danger created by having untold numbers of hunters in the woods shooting at every moving shadow, and not looking where they are shooting," Oliver explained. "Now, I have talked with the guides, Gerry Bruce Senior and Junior, and they have reluctantly agreed to my amendments. They have only agreed to avoid disappointing Mr. Barney and the other applicants by not fulfilling their contract with them.

"I am offering you a chance to document this outing and record the particulars for your paper. Would you be interested in doing this? You would be the only one authorized to come along," Oliver added.

"Well, that's not really why I'm here, so I think I'll pass on that invitation. I thank you, though. I've got a different story to work on here, so we'll say good-bye and get on with our work. Hope you have a good hunt, though," April replied. She stood up to leave, shook hands with Oliver, and motioned to Adam to join her.

Oliver called out to her as she started to leave, curious about her reasons for turning his offer down. "Miss Martens, just exactly what are you looking for here, if I might ask?"

Apparently sensing a door opening in her search, April turned around. "What I am looking for, Mr. Barry, is a story on your ghost skier. I want to know where he comes from, what he is looking for, and why he is haunting your mountain. I've heard all the stories about what he does, and my readers want to understand what drives him too. I don't really care much about the animal Mr. Barney is after; so while I like to ride and be outdoors, right now my attention is on the ghost skier, not some dumb animal who is outwitting every hunter on this mountain.

"So, you see, while it is interesting, it really isn't what I am here for and would be a waste of my time. If you could help me find the ghost skier, I would be most appreciative and perhaps we could work out something about that deer later on," April offered.

"Let me think about that, Miss Martens. I'll get back to you on it. Have a good day and enjoy your stay on our mountain," Oliver said to her.

Oliver walked both of them to the doorway, turned around, and returned to his desk to wait on Warner Barney's arrival. This was going to be the hard meeting, because Warner Barney wasn't used to being told "No" by anyone. He had to keep a firm grip on his temper, and Eileen wasn't going to be able to help him with that.

"Just keep your mind on what you are doing and what it is you need to say. He can either accept the terms or not—either way, you win," Oliver said to himself as he swiveled in his chair to relax.

CHAPTER 3

Eileen knocked on the doorframe of Oliver's office to announce Warner Barney. This knock was drowned out by Warner's loud and grating voice announcing himself in a tone suitable for an emcee's introduction at a boxing match.

Bypassing the amenities of even a minimal degree of sincerity, Warner went right to the point immediately. "What's the game, Barry? What are you after? What's it going to take to get the permit from you? What do you expect to make off this?" he asked with his typical, undiplomatic, heavy-handed directness.

Oliver bit his tongue and took a slow, deep breath to collect himself before responding. Looking past Barney's shoulder, he saw Eileen slowly moving her hands apart in a stretching motion, signaling him to take his time in responding and stay in control of the conversation and situation. With a pleased smile, he ignored the rude implications of his guest's hostile questions and offered him a beverage. "Mr. Barney, please have a seat. Would you like a drink or some other refreshment?"

"How about a bourbon and branch water?" Barney asked with a bored and ungracious air.

"I think I should explain, Mr. Barney. Alcoholic beverages are only provided in the restaurant and bar in the lodge proper, not in the administrative offices. May my assistant bring you a water, juice, or soda?"

"Nothing, then. Let's get on with this farce. I want to know about the permit for the hunt. I demand to know why you're not giving my guide the permit. I've paid for this trip, and I have every right to go. You can't stop me from this hunt—this is public land, and I represent the public," Warner said in a loud, blustering voice.

"I don't recall saying that I wasn't giving the permit to the Bruces, Mr. Barney. I only said I had some concerns, but I have found a way to address those concerns to everyone's satisfaction. A compromise is a far better way to resolve a conflict than a fight, Mr. Barney. You want to be the one who finds this mysterious animal; I understand, because it represents something of a challenge to you. I have no problem with that, Mr. Barney. In fact, I want the animal off the mountain as well. You have paid a considerable sum to be the one to do this, according to Mr. Bruce. I have no wish to prevent you from reaching your objective, Mr. Barney," Oliver said, calmly and pleasantly. So far, he was holding the high cards and allowing Barney to feel he was the winner. Oliver was very pleased with himself.

Warner was being given what he wanted, but it was obvious that he felt the tug of invisible strings all over the gift. "Why are you being so agreeable now, Barry? You were all set to close this hunt down last night. Why the change of heart?" Warner asked suspiciously.

Here it comes, Oliver thought to himself. He took a deep breath and dropped the other shoe on Warner Barney. "The reason I am changing my mind is we are changing the conditions of the hunt. I am giving Mr. Bruce the permit for the hunt under three conditions. One, that he limit the party to no more than six hunters. Two, that I will accompany him on this hunt with three of my special friends, including the young reporter you met the other day, to document this hunt," he said pleasantly.

"You said three conditions. That's only two. What's the third?" Barney asked him, distrust evident in his eyes.

"Oh yes, the third condition. The third condition is simply this, Mr. Barney: This will no longer be a track-and-kill hunt, but is now a tag-and-trap expedition—and the elk will not be killed, but safely transported to a no-kill preserve, where he will live out his days as the elegant and noble symbol of this mountain. My friends who will be accompanying us are representatives of that preserve who will help us transport him safely back to his new home," Oliver said, and he watched the rage growing in Barney's eyes as he talked. He had been expecting Barney to show his temper, and he could see it was building up quickly.

"I don't know what you're talking about, Barry. I paid for a week-long hunt with a trophy and, by God, that is what I intend to take part in. Neither you nor Gerry Bruce is going to cheat me—"

"Mr. Barney." Oliver jumped to his feet and slammed his hand on his desk. "Mr. Barney, no one is trying to cheat you, and if you do not keep a civil tongue, I will rescind this permit immediately! Neither of the Bruces willingly agreed to this compromise and only did so to be able keep their contract with you and the other hunters. It was their choice to accept this compromise rather than default on their arrangement with you and the others—only because of their high professional ethics," Oliver said in a clipped tone, trying to keep his own temper under control. "I think you need to understand something here. Everything on this mountain is under the protection of this department, and that includes both the skiers and every animal, feathered or furred, that lives here. Any hunting that is done will be done with the required permits in place, and with the appropriate care used in the process of the hunt. The rules of hunting guides and packers *will* be obeyed by every man on that hunt. Anyone who disobeys any of the rules will be given just one warning, and then they will be relieved of their firearms for the second offense."

Warner stood up and leaned over the desk, challenging Oliver in a face-to-face stare-down. "What gives you the idea that you can get away with that crap? You have no authority over the hunters on this mountain—you can't tell them what to do! You can't tell me what I can or can't do! I won't stand for it!" Warner blustered at him.

Knowing what would push him further over the edge, Oliver just sat back down, leaned back, and smiled at him. "I believe you didn't hear me correctly, Mr. Barney. I'm not trying to tell you what you can't do—I'm merely telling you how it will work out here. I am merely explaining that, according to local law, the guides run the trips, and you buy a place on the trip. According to this same law, the guides are accountable to the area authorities for the right to run their trips. I am the local authority; I outrank the guides, and I set the terms by which that hunt will be run. So if you are still interested in participating in this rather special hunt, Mr. Barney, I am happy to have you go along and lend your expertise in the interest of achieving our special needs—as long as you are willing to comply with the rules we have set out for this outing," Oliver responded calmly.

Warner stood there silently—not in fear, but from the shock of someone standing up to him. Oliver could see him thinking very hard for a way he could get around those rules and get what he wanted in spite of their interference. Suddenly, he began to smile and sat back down.

Although he recognized that Barney's smile meant trouble, Oliver didn't change his expression or indicate in any way that he was aware it meant he would comply with the rules only when it suited him.

"So, Mr. Barney, are you willing to follow our rules for this hunt, or will you be leaving town?" Oliver asked him innocently.

"Well, Mr. Barry. You seem to hold all the aces in this game right now, so I think I'll play along for now. I want to go along on this hunt, so I guess I'll accept your terms. When will this farce start out, Mr. Barry?" Warner sneered.

Ignoring his open hostility, Oliver consulted a slip of paper on his desk before he responded with the utmost courtesy. "Mr. Barney, Mr. Bruce has informed me he will need at least a week to get his supplies and personnel together, and I will need a few days to get my arrangements made. This will also allow the other hunters to arrive and get ready, so I anticipate we will set out on the fifteenth, which will be next Monday. So you have until then to make your arrangements, and we will meet at nine a.m. on the fifteenth at the Four Firs Ranch. That is where Mr. Bruce will be starting the hunt. Will you be needing the directions to the ranch, Mr. Barney?" Oliver asked courteously.

"I think not, Mr. Barry. I reckon I can find my way out to where I've been before. I'll see you next Monday. Have a nice week." Warner got up and left the office without any further effort to be sociable, including a handshake. He stormed by Eileen without acknowledging her and left the building.

As Eileen watched him leave, she turned to look at Oliver, who was swiveling in his chair again. "What did you say to him, Oliver?" she asked with a scowl.

"I didn't raise my voice once, my dear. All I did was explain the rules we were going to follow and ask him if he wanted to come along or stay behind. He made the decision that worked for him," Oliver said with a smile … a smile that quickly faded. "But I don't for a minute believe he will comply with the rules any longer than it will take him to find a way around them," he added, reflecting on the man's obvious character flaws. "Well, I'll worry about that when the time comes. Eileen, I have a bunch of calls I need you to make for me as soon as you can. Get your pad, and I'll give you a list."

She ran to her desk and returned while Oliver went for a stress-reducing swivel. When she came back to his office, he was spinning himself back and forth, but he put out a hand to stop the rotation when he saw her.

"First thing, call Kevin McGivern at the Open Range Preserve and tell him we want to move the Red Elk to his property. I need to know what he needs from us to transport the elk, and would he like to come along. Next, call Marcie at the Freed Animal Rights Movement and tell her I need someone to come with us to oversee the handling of this animal once we get him down." He thought for a moment and continued. "Then call Dr. Gill at the veterinary clinic and tell him I need about thirty tranquilizer darts and a couple of tranquilizer rifles. I know thirty sounds like a lot of them, but I expect several of these big hunters aren't as good as they think they are and will likely miss most of their shots. I'd like it if he would come along too—but if he can't make it, can he recommend someone who would be able to come along for a week? Finally, call Gerry Bruce and let him know Barney accepted the changes. Tell him to bring whatever information he has on Barney and to hand-deliver it to me. I want to know what kind of person I'm dealing with here," Oliver said.

"Are you expecting any trouble?" Eileen asked him, concern for his safety in her voice.

"Oh, yes, I anticipate trouble. I expect Mr. Barney to cause as much trouble as he can, as soon as he can find a way to get away with it. But I am prepared for that, so this gives me an advantage over him. An advantage I will sure need to use, Eileen."

April and Adam stood at the bottom of the mountain, watching the people ride the lift to the top and ski down. While most of the people they watched were fair to good skiers, occasionally Adam saw some who were complete beginners or woefully inadequate. From time to time, he witnessed some of the people on the slopes take a tumble and slide down. He didn't see anyone get seriously hurt, but he did see a few broken legs. This did nothing to inspire confidence or reassure him of the wisdom of his own effort to learn to ski.

"April, I don't really think I should do this. I don't feel comfortable with the idea of being on skis, and I really don't want to go up this mountain and come down on them. I don't see why it's really necessary for me to learn to ski, April; I'm not going to ever do it after we leave here," Adam told her.

"I told you, Adam, you do need to learn how to ski if we are going to get the pictures of the runs from the skiers' points of view. You don't have to do it a lot, but you need to learn how to stand up on them if we're going to get the shots we need to sell this article. Now, I'm tired of arguing with you about this. You take some lessons and then you'll feel a lot better about it. I tell you what, I'll pay for them. You won't have to spend a nickel of your own on the lessons.

"You don't have to be a pro or even take a jump—you just have to be able to walk on them. You can use them to walk across the hills and runs from the top of the runs, Adam. You don't have to ski downhill at all. You just need to be able to move about, okay?" April countered. "Now come on, I see the instructor's shack over there. Let's get you started on these lessons so we can go looking for our ghost … partner," April said, putting out her hand in a friendship gesture.

Reluctantly, Adam took her hand, and they shook on the agreement. After walking over to the shack, April paid for ten lessons for Adam, putting them on her credit card. April hadn't suddenly developed a soft spot in her heart—or her head. She was thinking, like she always did, about what was good for April Martens. And what was in April Martens's best interest was getting a good picture of the ghost skier in action. Although Adam was the best photographer, he was also her best chance to lure the ghost out of the mist and into action.

Although she never talked about it or showed off her work, April was a better-than-average photographer herself. While she had never won any awards or had any shows, she had regularly sold some of her work to help pay for her schooling. Her landscapes were always popular, but never as much as her self-portraits. These always seemed to sell the best, she had very quickly discovered, in part because of the artistry of her light work, and partly because they were always nudes. April knew how to promote what she had, and she wasn't shy about doing it. She was very confident she could get a good shot of the skier if he would just present himself to her, and she believed putting Adam on skis would be her best chance of getting that to happen.

During his lessons, which consumed the better part of the day, April kept telling Adam how good he was doing and cheering his efforts. To her surprise, he did better than she had expected of him. This encouraged her greatly, and she responded by cheering Adam on. He heard her, and he seemed surprised that she was as invested in his progress as she was.

The time passed very quickly, and when it was over, she couldn't believe that he asked her if she would take a turn or two on the bunny slopes with him. To his great surprise, she readily agreed. They spent the rest of the day gliding down the easy hills together, so when the light finally failed, Adam told her how much he found himself looking forward to the next day when he would tackle one of the less challenging intermediate slopes. That night as they ate dinner in the restaurant, Adam was excited and talked nonstop about the feelings and sensations he had experienced in his first day of skiing.

April sat and listened to Adam rave on, partly in amusement about the complete turnaround he had made, and partly in anticipation as a result of the plans she was making to use Adam as bait. She had told Adam all about the information she had obtained from the library on their second day in the town, and how the ghost was reported to be the spirit of a ski patrolman who was killed in an avalanche while on a rescue mission long ago.

She had told him there were a number of theories for why he was coming back, based upon all of the typical beliefs one had for these sort of things, ranging from revenge to remorse for things done badly—or not done, as one chose to believe. The one thing April was sure of was that the ghost seemed benevolent more than malevolent. This meant he was far less likely to represent a threat to Adam than he was to be a protector.

She wasn't sure how to draw the ghost out, other than to place Adam in a slight position of risk. She really didn't want to hurt Adam; she just wanted him to appear endangered so that the ghost would want to protect him. The one thing she wasn't sure about was where to place him for the best results. All the research she had done on this mysterious phantom said that he was never reported on the beginner slopes, only the advanced or intermediate ones. What had made her happy was Adam's request to try one of those intermediate slopes tomorrow. She was very willing to go and make sure he had a good run or two.

April wanted Adam to feel the glow of success in his efforts tomorrow, because that would make it so much easier afterward to lure him onto trying one of the harder intermediate slopes, where the ghost had been reported in most of the prior sightings.

"April, I have to confess that I enjoyed today much more than I ever imagined I would. I never thought that skiing would be so much fun. It isn't as hard as I thought it was going to be, and the few times I fell, it didn't hurt at all. It was cold and wet, to be sure, but it was actually a lot of fun. I owe you an apology for putting up such a fuss about it. Maybe I can make it up to you by allowing you to take me out on some of the more advanced courses later tomorrow," Adam, in a buoyant mood, offered. His fourth glass of wine was helping him keep those spirits uplifted. "What about the hunt, April? Why did you decline to go with that Barry fellow on the hunt? He was very cordial about inviting you to go along. That Barney fellow, the one who's so full of himself and his hunting prowess, he seemed interested in having you do a story on him."

"Yes, I'm sure he would like a story on himself. He seems to think he's the most important person on the mountain. He comes across to me as a man who will do whatever serves his own ends," April said with scorn.

"Sort of like looking in a mirror, one could say," Adam said to himself.

"What did you say, Adam?"

"I said he probably likes looking in the mirror," Adam said smoothly. "Say, I forgot to tell you something that I heard from the instructor," he said excitedly. "He was really very interesting. He said he used to work here a long time ago, and he knew some of the people who were here back when all of this started."

April was very alert now, and keenly interested. "What else did your instructor say, Adam?"

"Well, he said he knew the other two men who were working the slopes that day—Evan Winston and Parker Woodson. He said he didn't know the one who got killed, but he was supposed to be the best skier of the three of them. He said the three of them had been sent out to find a party that had gotten lost, and there were reports of hunters moving into the area reserved for the skiers. There was a front moving in as well, and the weather forecast was for a freezing snow at the top of the mountain. It was a situation guaranteeing a disaster or worse, he told me," Adam said with a conspiratorial air. Their conversation paused when the waiter brought their steaks, and after he left the table, Adam resumed his story between bites.

"I asked him about those hunters, and he told me they were taken out by a man named Amos. I asked what Amos's last name was and he said that Amos had a son. His son had a son also."

"Did he say what Amos's last name was?"

Adam ignored her question to continue with his story. "He said that Amos's son used to go out on these hunts with him most of the time, up to the point of this event. After this tragedy happened, his son never went hunting again. Amos's grandson runs the family business now," Adam said casually as he cut his steak. "Wow! This steak is really fantastic. How's yours?" he asked interestedly.

"Forget the damn steak, Adam. Did your new friend tell you what Amos's last name was?" April queried intently.

"It seems that something really threw Amos's son off his footing, and he wouldn't go back up the mountain with a gun anymore. He would take pack trips of people sightseeing or on photo tours, but no more hunting trips. He left that to his son when he got old enough to do it, and now Amos's grandson does all the hunting trips. Amos passed away about ten years ago, or I would have wrangled an invitation to talk with him," Adam said conversationally, relishing the look of frustration growing on April's face as he slowly gave up the details of his conversation.

April picked up her knife and pointed it at Adam. "If you don't tell me what Amos's last name was right now, I am going to cut you up like this steak, Adam," April threatened him through clenched teeth.

With an innocent air, he looked up at her with his eyebrows raised. "Oh, didn't I tell you what his name was? My apologies, April. I didn't mean to leave you in the dark. It was—"

"The name, Adam. What was Amos's name?" April said through her clenched teeth.

"I took the liberty of inviting Amos's son and grandson to join us later for a drink to talk about the history of the mountain. I didn't think you'd mind that, April," Adam said as he avoided her question once more.

"Adam. No offense, but I'm going to kill you now," April gritted out.

"Not in front of our guests, April. Play nice. May I introduce Mr. Gerry V. Bruce, and his son, Mr. Gerry A. Bruce. These gentlemen will be conducting the hunt for the Red Elk."

Oliver was sitting back in his chair, twisting from one side to the other, just relaxing and playing with it. The four men sitting on the couch to his left were not as relaxed. Eileen was sitting in her chair to the right of Oliver, with her notebook in her lap and her pen in her hand. There was a red folder on his desk with their permit photos clipped to the front, and several sheets of paper visible inside.

After keeping them on a hook for ten minutes while he said nothing, and looked over the sheets of paper in the folder, looking occasionally over at each of them in turn, their anxiety was visible and palpable. Unknown to the men, the sheets of paper they could see had nothing to do with them; they were there only for effect. Oliver had no real information about them other than what he had gleaned from talking to the sales and hotel staff the day before.

Oliver put down the folder, leaned back, and turned to look out at the mountain.

"Gentlemen, let me first say that I'm not looking to cause you any legal woes. I'm quite sure I know what run you were on the other day when you reported seeing our mysterious Red Skier, so I'm not looking for you to spin me a lot of fairy tales about where you weren't. I am not interested in prosecuting you—and, believe it or not, I'm not interested in banning you from our mountain resort. What I do want to know, however, is where on the run you were when you saw him, and how it happened.

"I want you to tell me exactly what happened, from the moment you stepped out of the lift on the top until you walked into the lodge at the bottom of the run. Please do not make up anything; please do not leave anything out. You will go into that office"—he pointed to a small office on the left just outside of his doorway—"and you will give your story, without omissions, to my assistant, Ms. Gayle. You will do this one at a time, and you will be completely honest with us. This is *not* about assigning blame, so don't feel you have to protect yourself or your friends. The only way you can hurt yourselves is to tell me a story, make something up that didn't happen, or lie about what run you were on. If you are completely truthful and leave nothing out, you will only have to give me your promise you will stay between the marked runs, and you can finish your vacation in peace. Otherwise, I will be forced to reopen this file and take the appropriate action. Do we understand each other clearly, gentlemen?" he asked in a very soft voice, carefully placing a hand on the bogus but very effectively intimidating folder in front of him. The four men looked at each other and nodded so quickly and enthusiastically that, for a moment, Oliver thought their heads would fly off.

Keeping a serious expression on his face, he pointed to Fred and waved him off with Eileen.

Three hours later, when all four were finished and had left the building, Eileen came to him with her notepad. "You know, I think the young one, Fred, he was about to have an accident right there on the couch." She laughed. "You scared those poor kids half to death, Oliver. You should be ashamed of yourself. And just what was in that red folder, anyway? What did you have on them?" she scolded him.

"All I had is that they are four kids from college, University of Montana, and that's it. The rest of the paper was just a menu for our open house and banquet next month. Now, enough about me and my folder; let's talk about them. What run were they on, and where on the run were they when he appeared?"

"Well, as you suspected, they were on the old Mosquito Run. This is really interesting. Apparently, he appeared to Pete and Gene first, about two-thirds of the way down. They were going to make a jump out of a rock outcropping, and the snow had been taken off the approach-face by the time they got there.

"Gene said he lost his balance and fell, rolling into Pete, which sent them both rolling toward the rock ledge. Pete said the skier came from the trees across the run and pushed them aside. Pete is the one who saw him, and all he saw was a red blur and felt something cold and hard nudge him off the path away from the rock. Gene was tangled up with him, and he didn't see anything.

"Now, with Fred and Ed, it really gets interesting, because apparently, he went back up the mountain to rescue them after he saved Pete and Gene. I don't think he's ever done that before—gone backward up the mountain for a second save in the same event, I mean. How could he do that in just a matter of seconds? No real person could go up two hundred feet so fast, Oliver.

"Fred and Pete were doing something many college students try to do—they were going for the old 'both-sides-of-the-tree' stunt," Eileen explained.

Oliver just groaned and shook his head. "How long is it going to take before someone gets killed trying that damn fool trick?"

"Well, it almost happened here, and it would have if it wasn't for … him," Eileen responded. "Fred said they were headed for the tree, and when they went to separate, he got his watch caught on Pete's sweater, and they couldn't get separated, and were heading right for a low, broken branch on Pete's side of the tree."

"Okay, how did he make his appearance in their situation?"

"Fred said he thought he saw something before they began their downhill run, but he figured he was just seeing the wind. And that's another thing. Three of them said they saw the wind pick up and blow the snow around, and it seemed to come out of the trees. Gene did see the snow swirl before the skier appeared, but didn't see him appear or disappear. Fred and Ed agreed that he came out of the swirling snow, and they lost him when he went back into it on the other side of the run.

"Fred claims he saw the trees on the other side of the mountain, right through the skier. He seems to be very credible, Oliver. Actually, all four of the boys seem very sincere, and I believe them—I don't think they are making this stuff up for attention or anything else. They all seemed scared of what they saw, or at least that's how they appeared to me," Eileen said.

A few seconds of silence followed her report, while Oliver turned in his chair and looked out the window at the mountain. "What do we have going on here, Eileen? Is he waiting for something to happen? Is it something we need to prevent, or something we have to let happen?

Or is it something we can't prevent, even if we tried to?" he asked her softly, not really expecting an answer.

"Oliver, what if it isn't a something, but a someone? What if he is waiting for someone to come back?"

He turned around to look at her. "If he is waiting for someone, what's going to happen when that someone gets here? And who is that someone?" Oliver asked the mountain.

By eight in the morning the next day, Adam and April were standing at the bottom of the lift to the intermediate runs. Adam looked up the lift to see the height of the mountain he would have to come back down, a twinge of anxiety on his face.

"I don't know, April. This looks a lot harder than it did at dinner last night. I'm not sure about my skill level. I know I felt good and up to it then, but now this is morning, and I can see it is a big piece of real estate. If I get hurt, or if I freeze up, I can't take the lift back down. The instructor said I should stay on the easier slopes for the first week or two, and I've only been doing this for three days. Maybe I shouldn't be here just yet. If you want to go, go ahead, and I'll wait for you down here. This may be more than I'm really able to handle at this point," Adam said nervously. He was looking around at the people lining up for a seat on the chairlift.

April was silently praying that he wouldn't see any falls until after he was up at the top—or on the way up, at the least.

"Come on, Adam, you did fine yesterday; you never fell once. And the instructor, he showed you how to snowplow, didn't he? If you start to come down too fast, that's what you do to slow your speed. Here, look at me: see?" April pointed the tips of her skis together to form the safety move.

"When you do this, Adam, it cuts your speed down to a stop. That's the trick: tips are parallel, you go fast; tips touch, you slow to a stop. You want to go faster, lean forward and bend your knees, like this." She demonstrated the proper posture for increasing her speed. "I'll be right beside you all the way so if you feel nervous, just snowplow, and I'll be right there beside you in a second," April assured him.

To herself, she thought that it wouldn't be smart to push him too far too fast. He needed to have a good run or two before she suggested one of the others, where the ghost had been seen before. Besides, considering what she had learned last night, she didn't want to be too much like the unnamed hunter who had caused the problems so long ago.

The elder Bruce had very skillfully avoided all her questions about his client from back then, even the minor questions about his background. He wouldn't give anything away, she had soon discovered—although he had talked at length about everything else.

He was hiding something, she was sure, and this only made her more determined to look behind the veil of secrecy he was drawing over that hunt. This was turning out to be a bigger story than she had imagined it could be. If she was still here when they got back from their hunt, she made a mental note to call on the man and try to get the goods on this story as well.

The younger Bruce was willing to talk about his business, but had nothing much to say about anything else. He had made it clear that this big hunt was his idea, and he was in charge of every aspect of it. His father was only along to help out. She had gotten him to admit that the *A* in his middle name stood for Amos, his grandfather. The younger Bruce had idolized Amos and had learned much of what he knew from him.

The relationship with his father was still developing, she sensed, but wasn't sure whether it was a new or old rift between them; neither of them would talk about it at dinner. The older Bruce seemed more hesitant than the younger.

She had been surprised by how good an interviewer Adam was, and gradually she had allowed him to conduct the interview of both men. She only needed to get one or two details for her story, as Adam had done a very good job of getting both of them to talk. He had actually been able to get the older man to discuss some really interesting history of the mountain, facts that she had been totally unaware of, in spite of all her research.

April suspected Adam was a more faceted person than she had previously imagined he was, and she wondered what else he was holding out on her. She realized she was starting to be interested in him as more than just a photojournalist.

After spending most of the day watching him slowly make his way down the runs, April was faced with a dilemma. Her plan to draw the ghost's attention wasn't working out as she had anticipated—Adam was messing up her carefully laid plans by doing much better than she had expected. This was causing her to experience a conflict she'd never experienced before. Part of her was happy that he was doing so well, and part of her was frustrated that he was doing so well. April had never allowed her feelings for anyone to get in her way up the ladder of success, and here was the last person she ever expected to be in her way, taking over her thoughts.

Damn it, Adam, what are you doing to me? April thought to herself. *This isn't working out like I had planned. I need to regroup and figure out how to do this. Do I push you to the intermediate runs now and risk you getting hurt in case our ghost doesn't come out like I want, or do I look for another bait for him? What to do, what to do?* she mused.

From her vantage point on the top of the hill, April watched Adam cleanly make his way down for the fifth time. She turned to the right to look over the intermediate runs and assess their levels of difficulty in relation to Adam's newly developed skills. They didn't look too different from the run he was currently on, except they had slightly steeper downward angles. She could see three people making their way down the line of one of the slopes, but they were very faint and small from that distance.

April reached into her pack and pulled out her field glasses. She never shorted herself on the quality of anything she wanted, and these had been no different. She had spent weeks researching the best pair she could find, comparing the quality and distance and special features each model offered, and eventually she had decided upon the Zeiss model. It had the best range and autofocus feature she wanted. She put them to her eyes and started scanning the mountain. She was very pleased with her choice, as it brought each skier so close she could almost see their faces in enough detail to see the color of their eyes. April watched them glide down the slope with apparent ease and felt a tinge of jealousy, as she wanted to be out there with them instead of babysitting Adam.

Sighing with disappointment, she shifted her direction to the next hill. No one was on that run, so she moved on to the next one and refocused her glasses to the farther distance. She dialed in the longer and more powerful lenses in order to make out the details, but all she saw was snow. There was no sign of her target, so she turned back to Adam.

After an hour more of watching Adam come down the hill in a smooth flow, she felt he was ready for the next level. She turned back to the intermediate runs to find one that would be a challenge for him without being too dangerous. She looked at three of them without finding one with a clear view.

She then remembered that the stories said the Red Skier came out of the woods, so she turned back to the second one she had looked at, as it was next to the woods. She started scanning the run from the top of the hill and saw only skiers having fun. As she panned down the hill, she suddenly stopped and lowered the binoculars. She picked them up again and backed up about thirty feet or so to focus in on something she had seen only briefly.

It was a growing cloud of snow. At first she had thought it was from someone sliding, but when she looked again, there were no tracks. That cause ruled out, she assumed it was just a result of the slowly deteriorating weather conditions. She decided to keep an eye on the cloud to see what happened. As she looked around the field, she saw several skiers coming down the slope. Something then moved into her line of vision, so she lowered the binoculars to see what it was. There it was again—a cloud of snow ... moving uphill?

"Clouds don't move uphill," April said to herself. She started to feel a chill and tingle all over, a sensation she knew had nothing to do with the ambient temperature.

She locked onto the cloud, not daring to take her eyes off of it. She wanted to see where it was going and what was attracting it, but she didn't want to lose her visual contact, because she had a feeling she was going to get what she came here for. She suddenly wished she had paid a little more for the more expensive model of binoculars that contained a camera, or that she had one of Adam's telephoto lens cameras with her now.

As she watched the top of the hill, she saw the skiers separate and speed up, until one of them suddenly fell over and started sliding down the run. The skier tried to get his balance, and April thought he had made it until his skis crossed at the tips, his poles went flying, and he started to roll downhill.

Taking a quick look down the slope, she could see a shadow farther down the mountain. She increased the binoculars' power, and the shadow became a ravine. A skier could easily jump that small gully, but someone rolling down the hill would certainly fall into it. From where April was positioned, she couldn't get a clear view of what was inside, but she was certain it wouldn't be a safe fall, and that whoever landed in there was very likely to get badly injured.

She quickly moved her gaze back to the skier, who was rolling helplessly down toward that ravine and certain harm. April held her breath as she saw the cloud *change direction* and suddenly begin to move back down the hill, just behind the out-of-control skier. It began to change shape and color, and out of it came someone in a red parka, heading in a straight line right for the out-of-control skier. She tried to zoom in on his face, but he was moving too fast for her to be able to keep her focus on him.

April couldn't take her eyes off him, watching as he closed the distance to the skier rolling down the hill. *He isn't going to make it in time,* April thought in horror as she watched the helpless skier approach the edge of the ravine. He was only ten feet from the ravine when the red coat disappeared from view and suddenly reappeared beside the helpless man and nudged him to the side, where he slowed to a stop. The fallen man slowly got to his feet, looked into the ravine, and quickly stepped away from it. She looked at his feet, and it slowly dawned on April that there was only one set of tracks in the snow, made not by skis, but by the man's body as he had rolled down the hill. There was no visible trace of the ghost's skis anywhere on the slope.

The ghost! Where was he?

She looked across to the edge of the woods and almost fell over. There he was, just moving back into the woods on the left. April could see the cloud begin to swirl around him again, but this time there was something else going on. As April watched him head into the center of the cloud, she knew she had seen something she couldn't begin to explain or understand. April could not believe her eyes, and she knew no one else would believe her story either—and she didn't have any way to prove it later.

As she watched the ghost skier, he moved into a rapidly developing snow cloud that seemed to come up around him. April quickly looked back down the slope to check on the downed skier and saw him slowly getting to his feet. She turned her glasses to search for the cloud again, but couldn't find it. As she looked for it, she saw a large red elk running up the slope toward the edge of the tree line. As it faded into the woods, Adam came up behind her and pointed excitedly.

"That's him, April! Did you see him? Isn't he just magnificent? Too bad I didn't get here sooner, I could have taken his picture ..." Adam's voice trailed off as he saw that April wasn't listening to him, but just staring at the spot where the animal had entered the woods. "What is it, April? What's the matter?" he asked curiously, looking at the dazed expression on her face.

April slowly turned to face him, her binoculars falling out of her hand, forgotten, as she put her hand on his arm. In a quavering voice that had never before come out of her mouth, she tried to explain what she had seen in the last few minutes. "Adam, I saw him. The ghost, I mean. I was looking over the mountain, testing out my new binoculars." She looked down to see the binoculars lying in the snow and stooped down to pick them up.

Breathlessly, she described in compelling detail everything she had just seen.

When April paused to catch her breath, Adam asked a question. "Do we need to notify the authorities about the man being injured?"

April shook her head, looking back at the slope behind her. "No, we don't. The man was about ten feet from the edge of the ravine when the skier vanished and then reappeared beside him, and then he nudged him off the course he was on and out onto the flat, where he slowed and stopped," April said in an awed voice.

"Wait up a minute, April. You're saying the skier just vanished from sight, and then he reappeared ten feet closer to the man heading for the ravine? Maybe he just moved too fast for you to catch it in the glasses?" Adam suggested.

"No, Adam, I saw him just blip out of sight and then blip back in my sight right beside the man in danger, and then he kind of nudged him out of danger. I saw the man come to a stop and get up, and then he went over to look in the ravine. I looked for the skier, and then ... Oh, God, Adam, you're going to think I'm crazy. I saw him at the edge of the woods, and the snow was beginning to swirl around him. He skied into the cloud, and he faded out of sight. And then I—or, rather, we—saw that animal come out of the snow and run into the woods. I didn't see him run into the cloud, Adam, did you?"

"No, but I wasn't really looking for him. I was focusing on climbing up here and looking for you. I wanted to tell you about my last run downhill," he said excitedly.

"I am talking about the purpose of our trip here, Adam, so try to stay focused. I saw the mysterious Red Skier save a man's life, and then I saw him go into a cloud and disappear. I think he has something to do with that Red Elk everyone is talking about. I think he turns into the elk, somehow," she said excitedly.

"April, don't be ridiculous. How can a man turn into an animal? And why would he do that anyway?" Adam asked her. "Why would he be protecting the skiers and the animals? Why not just protect one or the other? Something is missing in this equation, April. There is something to this we don't know about, or don't know we know. And I'll tell you this, April, I don't think we should be pursuing him ... or it. I've got a very bad feeling about this situation. I think we should get in our car and go home now. I think this is more than we think it is, and I really think we're in way over our heads here, April. I don't know what's going on here, but clearly it's beyond my understanding and I'll bet it's beyond yours too, if you're honest with me."

"Adam, I admit this is more than I anticipated, but we can't stop now," she said entreatingly. She suddenly smiled and, taking Adam by the hand, headed for the top of the run. "Pack up all your warmest clothing, Adam. We are going on a tag-and-capture hunt."

"What? You said we weren't going on that stupid outing, April! Now you want to go? Oh, I see. You want to go because you're hoping I get pictures of the skier turning into an elk, don't you? You aren't thinking clearly, April. There are a lot of questions about this situation we don't have any answers for. With all these hunters coming to kill—"

"Catch, Adam."

"Fine, coming to *catch* the elk. All these people are carrying guns, a lot of guns, and we have one über-macho, trigger-happy fanatic to contend with as well. He's a loose cannon, so to speak, and I don't trust him to play by the rules! And I don't want you to get hurt, April," Adam said softly.

April turned to face him and lost her footing in the loose snow. She fell, dragging Adam down on top of her. As they pulled themselves up to a sitting position, Adam found himself inches from April's face, and he decided impulsively to go for it. Expecting her to slap his face, but deciding it was worth the risk, he kissed her.

To his great surprise, she responded by putting her arms around his neck and kissing him back. He held on for several minutes, not wanting it to end. Finally, she drew back and looked at him.

"My oh my! Those still waters, they do run deep, don't they?" she said with a smile.

Adam took a deep breath and looked at her. With a sigh, he admitted defeat. "How do we get back on the hunt, April? I guess we're going along after all. I suppose our next stop is seeing that Mr. Barry again, right?" Adam asked as he pulled April to her feet.

She took his hand and rose to her feet. "Yes, dear, I think that is exactly what we should do. Just as soon as we get off the mountain and back to the lodge so we can warm up and change clothes. Do you have any ideas on how we can warm up?" she asked him innocently.

Adam looked at her, and said, "I do believe I can think of something."

When the man had come in to report his encounter with the phantom, he'd left out the last thing he had seen, because he had been certain no one would believe him. After making his report, he'd gone to the bar, where he had proceeded to get totally drunk. His wife had been on the slope with him. She hadn't seen the ghost skier intervene to save his life, but she wasn't going to give him a hard time about his drinking tonight. He had earned the right.

"Oliver, we have another report of our phantom skier," Eileen said, interrupting his afternoon swivel.

"Damn, now what is it?"

"Basically the same thing, Oliver. Someone coming down the run gets into trouble and starts falling down the mountain," she read from his statement.

"Okay, Eileen, what are we going to do about him? Do we keep silent about him and let him remain a secret and have it come out later from that reporter we were hiding something? What if he makes an appearance and scares someone into an accident or a heart attack? Can we be sued for not publicizing we're haunted? Goddamn, this is turning into a public relations nightmare. I wanted to avoid this kind of press during my administration, and here I'm caught between two of them! You may have hitched your wagon to a falling star instead of a rising one, Eileen. If you want to leave while the getting's good, I'll understand. The same thing goes for everyone out there," Oliver said morosely.

"You big baby! Who do you think you're talking to? Do you really think I'd run out on you, or that anyone out there in the office would run out on you, just because we hit a bump? I came along with you because I believe in you, just as everyone who works for you believes in you. Stop feeling sorry for yourself and do what you do best: make the best of a bad situation.

"Okay, there are some things going on that defy rational thought, but you're the man who always tells everyone to think outside of the box, so let's see you do some of that and lead us like you always have," Eileen said scathingly. To emphasize her words, she leaned over and put her hands on the arms of his chair and gave it a push, sending it in a slow spin.

They both began to laugh, and Oliver reached up to pull her down into his lap and gave her a big hug. "I don't know what I'd do without you here beside me, Eileen. You always make me feel better. Now go get that reporter and have her come over here," he said as he pushed her to her feet and turned back to his desk. "We have a resort to rescue. Did you call those people, and are they going to come with me?" he asked, reenergized.

"Yes, I did. Dr. Gill will be coming himself; he said he needed the time away from people. He asked if you were going to use the tranquilizers on an elephant or the hunters. He said he needs to know how big an animal we are talking about, because that will dictate the dose he puts in the darts. He said he would bring a couple dozen darts—that's all he has on hand right now—and he'll be here tomorrow morning.

"I spoke with Kevin, and he said he will fax you the particulars today. He said he can't make it himself, but he'll send someone to supervise the transport down the mountain to a staging area where he can get the animal in the truck. He said this is a bit unusual for him, but he thinks he can do it safely.

"Then Dr. Gill called back and said he couldn't go, but he'll send someone to oversee the hunt and make sure the animal isn't hurt in any way. And the reporter is outside right now, waiting for you," she read from her notepad.

"I've got a hell of a lot of chiefs and damn few Indians on this completely insane trip," Oliver muttered. "I don't suppose you'd like to come along too?"

"Who would watch the store if I left?"

"Oh, come on. Rodney can do what little needs to be done, and you know you like to be where the action is. You probably already have a bag packed and hidden in this office somewhere and your long johns on, if I know you," Oliver retorted as he made a show of looking around.

"That just shows how much you know, Mr. Smarty. I'll have to go home and put my long johns on. I'll be back in twenty minutes, love," she said sweetly as she walked out. As she left, he heard her tell the reporter to go on in.

"Okay, Miss Martens, what can I do for you today?" Oliver asked curiously.

"Mr. Barry, a lot has happened in the last two days, and I've had a chance to think about your offer. I've decided to take you up on it. I think I rushed my decision the other day and, after talking with my photographer here"—She indicated the young man sitting beside her— "we have decided that your hunt-and-catch trip represents the new face of hunting and preservation of our natural resources, and we need to promote that. You put together a very comprehensive group of animal rights and conservationists to save the life of a very noble animal, and I—that is, we—feel you deserve proper recognition for this. You are demonstrating the new face of balance between the needs of the animals and the rights of the people and how to peacefully coexist in the same space. I want to document that accomplishment for the world," April told him with mock sincerity.

Oliver had not said a word, but was jotting down some thoughts while she was speaking. When she finished, he put down his pencil and turned to look out the window at the mountain. After a moment, he turned back to April and stood up. Oliver smiled and held out his hand and spoke in an equally sincere manner.

"Miss Martens, Mr. Jacobs, I would be very happy to have both of you coming along with us. It will help to keep this a nonviolent mission, and to help keep the rest of the group focused on what we are there for if you are documenting this openly." He looked down at the pad in front of him and scribbled off a quick note to the owner of the outfitter's store. Oliver didn't miss the quick look the two of them exchanged when they thought he was looking down, and he smiled to himself, confident he had read the attractive reporter accurately. This one was a climber, and she was willing to do whatever she had to in order to get her story and make her name. He knew she would bear watching on this trip, which was why he had decided to bring her along.

He had read the famous quotation attributed to Sun Tzu, a Chinese general and military strategist from 400 BCE and used in the *Godfather* movies: "Keep your friends close, and your enemies closer." He believed it certainly applied in this situation. He figured it would be a lot easier to keep an eye on her—and Mr. Barney—when they were close by. Oliver knew it was asking for trouble, but figured he could contain the damage if he kept all of them in his sight all the time.

"I will make arrangements for you and Mr. Jacobs to obtain the supplies and clothing you will need from a store downtown, and, within reason, we will take care of the cost. The store is called Uphill Climb, and it's down on the intersection of Sugarloaf and Walker's Run. You can get all the gear you will need for this journey in one place, and they'll know what to recommend. Keep the cost down, and we will pay for it up to three hundred dollars apiece. We will be ready to go in three days, so you better get down there today. I have another appointment to keep with another member of the journey to explain the rules of this expedition to him. I expect this to be a rather acrimonious conversation, so I'll not detain you, nor subject you to the rather heated words that I am very sure are going to come. You two get out of here now, and I'll see you in three days up at the base camp. You can get the directions for the camp and the store from my assistant, Eileen," he said helpfully.

He walked them to the side door out of his office, just in case his next appointment was sitting in the waiting room. As they left, he noticed the photographer casually brushing the back of her hand with his. Oliver smiled, noticing she failed to respond to him, and thought to himself that the young man was on a cold trail. He turned, closed his door, went back to his chair, and began absently swinging from side to side as he looked out the big picture window. He hoped he was making the right choices—he wasn't nearly as confident as he wanted everyone to think he was. With a sigh, Oliver swung back to the desk and made note on the pad in front of him to check on how much they had spent of his money so he could factor it into his budget for this trip. He thought to himself that he needed to talk to Gerry Senior and find out some more about Warner Barney and that long-ago hunting trip. Something didn't feel right about their relationship, and Oliver was worried about what he didn't know and even more worried just how and when it all was going to come up.

CHAPTER 4

"Adam, we have a golden opportunity here to get ourselves a real story that can get us the byline we are looking for," she said excitedly in the elevator after they had left Oliver's office.

"April, we both know that you are thinking about yourself here," Adam said sadly.

April put a pained look onto her face and sounded innocently hurt. "What do you mean, Adam? I thought this was something we both wanted to achieve. Back there on the slopes, when I told you what I saw, you were just as excited as I was. Back in the room, didn't we share a magical moment together? Now you are saying I'm not thinking of you and just thinking of myself? How can you be so mean and insensitive?"

Adam looked at her and almost believed he had misjudged her. As he started to apologize, her cell phone rang. She quickly pulled it out of her purse and opened it up, her voice now back to her usual bright and cheery lilt.

At that moment Adam realized their shared intimacy was really just another ploy by April to get what she wanted from him. He felt himself moving farther away from her thoughts as she spoke on the phone, totally oblivious to his presence next to her in the elevator. He wasn't sure who she was talking to, as she didn't use any names and very coyly turned away from him. He realized she didn't want him to know what she was saying, or risk him hearing what was being said to her.

He now understood just how much they really were not a team, as she was making plans without asking him anything. He was just a photographer to her, a tool to be used in her climb to the top. Adam felt used, and he made up his mind that he was quitting the paper when they got back. His personal ethics wouldn't allow him to quit in the middle of a job, but he was determined not to get pulled into any further schemes she might dream up, as it was already starting to look far more dangerous than he had ever anticipated.

When April was finished with her call, she turned back to him and put her hand on his arm. She was excited—it was in her face. Her eyes were aglow, her cheeks were flushed, and her words were coming like a machine gun. The conversation about him "misunderstanding" her was forgotten, as if it had never happened. She was on the trail of a byline, and Adam could see there was nothing else on her mind—certainly not him.

"You'll never guess who that was, Adam!" Before he could guess, she went on as if his response was unimportant. "It was Edward Willis! The publisher of our paper. Apparently he heard about my story on the ghost skier and ghost elk, and he is interested in what I write. He said that if I can do a real good human-interest angle on my story, he'll push it and promote it across the wires, and maybe I can earn a Pulitzer out of it somehow! That's just fantastic!" April was so excited and worked up over this possibility, she didn't notice she hadn't said "our story" but had reverted back to "my story."

This slip wasn't overlooked by Adam, who took this as confirmation he really was only an accessory to April and meant no more to her than a stepping stone to her big chance.

"That's great, April," he said sincerely, but without enthusiasm. "I hope you get it."

"It's my big chance, Adam, and I'll need your help to make it happen. You won't let me down, will you?"

"No, April, I'll do whatever I can without risking my life to get you the photos you need. I will do my part in this, but I have one condition."

"What do you mean, you have one condition?" April asked in a cold voice. "This is my story we're talking about here, Adam. What kind of conditions are you trying to set for my story—and what gives you the right to set conditions, anyway?"

"The condition I want, April, is for you not to lie to me or withhold information from me or put me in any real danger. I understand how important this story is to you, and I know that you are so focused on getting this story that you might be willing to take unnecessary risks to get it. You can be very single-minded, April, which is great for a reporter, but a little hazardous for a photographer.

"This story is taking over your normally good judgment, April. You are willing to put yourself—and me—in great danger just for the sake of the story. This is your story, April, not mine. I don't want to get any posthumous awards for it. I need to be certain I'll be able to read the story when it goes into print. I just need to know that you are not going to lead me blindfolded into a situation we can't get out of," he said calmly and softly. "I'm not trying to undermine your story, April, but I do intend to be alive to read it later on," he said firmly.

April stood there for a moment, angry and stiff. She then relaxed and turned on the charm to lower the tension between them. "Of course, Adam. That only makes sense. I want to be able to write the story, and I certainly understand the need for caution. I want us to work well together so we can get the best story we can. I would never put you in danger on purpose, and I certainly wouldn't take reckless chances by ignoring the advice of the professionals on this outing. We are going to take their advice all the way down the line, Adam, and we won't do anything they tell us not to do. I promise you this, cross my heart," April said earnestly, crossing her heart with her left hand as she raised her right hand, as if taking an oath, smiling as she did it.

Adam wanted to believe her, and he accepted she meant what she said—at the moment she was saying it. But even as she was saying it, he knew she wouldn't be able to keep her word if the situation changed enough or if something required her immediate reaction and there was no time to check with anyone else. Adam reluctantly accepted the realization that his place with April would always be second to her byline of the moment, and resolved to keep his eyes open and stay close to the guide and ask questions whenever he had a concern.

The elevator stopped, and the doors opened. They headed for the exit, out into the sunlight. As they walked out of the building, April suddenly whirled around and put her hand on his arm. Her face lit up with excitement, and she had a glow in her eyes that Adam knew could only mean that she had figured out a new way to put them at risk. It didn't take long for him to learn he was right.

"You know what we should do, Adam?" she asked excitedly, before going on to answer her own question without hearing his response. "I think what we should do is go see that hunter, what's his name, that is so determined to be the one who finds that deer!"

"His name is Warner Barney, April, and I'm not sure that's such a good idea. He didn't seem like such a friendly person when we met him. There's something wrong with him—I don't know what it is, but I have a bad feeling about him," Adam said cautiously.

"Nonsense, it's just your imagination," April said, dismissing his concerns as groundless. "I've been Googling his name, and he has quite a reputation as a hunter. He seems very confident of his ability to bag this animal, and I think it would be a good human-interest angle to track this story from both sides of the hunt," she said enthusiastically.

Adam recognized that talking to April about the risk of anything she wanted to do was going to be a major waste of his time and breath, so he made the decision to call and talk with the park overseer upstairs as soon as he could get away. He allowed April to get a step ahead of him and then reached into his jacket pocket. He had picked one of the man's cards off the desk as they were leaving, just in case he needed to talk to him later. Adam weighed the risks of talking behind April's back versus telling her he was talking to him, and came to the conclusion it was safer for him to do the second one, because, if he told her, she would just keep him in the dark even more. No, he had to find a way to speak to the ranger by himself.

"So, are you going to interview the elk too? You might find his conversation somewhat limited, April," Adam said sarcastically.

"No, silly. I'm not going to talk to the elk; I'm going to talk to the park ranger and the naturalists coming along with us," April said with a laugh.

After a moment thinking about this, Adam saw his opportunity. "April, how about this idea: you deal with the naturalists and Barney, and I'll keep the ranger busy. That way, you can get the information you need for your story, and I can keep the boy scout out of your hair," he suggested.

Suspiciously, she asked him, "What's in this for you, Adam? Why are you offering to do this?"

"Well, April, if you want to try to talk to everyone all by yourself, I'm sure you can do it without my help. Would you like to take the pictures too? I thought that this was something I could do for you to help, so that you could focus on the heart of the story. But no matter—I'll just stick with what I know," he said placidly and turned to walk away.

April grabbed his arm, laughing. "Don't mind me, I'm just being silly. I appreciate that, Adam, I really do appreciate it. Sure, that would be great. I'll write down a few questions for you to ask him, and some questions to build on, depending upon his answers. Do you have a tape recorder?"

"No, but I figure I can get one in town. You want me to record the interviews with him, I suppose?"

"Yes, dear, record them. Then I can play them back and get it direct from the horse's mouth. And if there is anything else I need to know from him, I can give you some more questions. Yes, that'll work out fine. Now let's go get outfitted. I'll drive," April gave him a quick hug and grabbed the car keys from his hand as they walked to their car.

Warner Barney was in a bad mood again, and he was drinking heavily to relieve it. "Who the hell does that glorified trail guide think he is, telling me what I can do and what I can't?" he muttered to himself. He glared out the window at the falling snow that was delaying his big adventure even more. "What gives him the right to tell me what I can do and what I can't? I paid my fee to be on this hunt, and I'm the best damn hunter in the world—there's nothing I can't track and kill, no matter how wily the damn animal might be. I have been all over this damn world, and nothing has ever escaped my sights.

"I don't want a bunch of fool amateurs tromping around scaring this buck off. I wonder if that fool Bruce is behind this. He's never gotten over that accident back in '63, and it took all the spine out of him. He's afraid I'll make him look bad because he can't track anymore. I'll bet he's the one who talked that overgrown trail guide into stopping this hunt, just to spite me.

"Well, he can't stop me. I don't need his permission to do this. I can get my own guide and go up there without their stupid and ridiculous rules. It's a public mountain, and I can find some other packer to go up there with me." He smiled to himself, pleased he had figured a way out of the box the ranger and his former guide had tried to put him in. "I won't get someone from the town, because they might not be willing to go against the ranger's authority, but I figure I can find someone from the area who needs money badly enough. Money always talks the loudest," Barney said to himself.

It always had. He had plenty of it and he had used it like a weapon many times before to prevent anything from getting in his way. He had paid off the policeman who wanted to give him a ticket for driving too fast, and he had bought his way out of that little thing with the waitress. That had been easy because she had been cheap and hungry for the money.

He had used his money to fix things many times over the years, and he knew it was always a tool that would work. He had never met anyone he couldn't buy; it was a simple issue of negotiation to find just the right price.

He was feeling pleased with himself, so he fixed himself another drink and pulled the telephone book out of the drawer of the cheap bedside table. As he looked at the tiny directory, he thought to himself that it fit the size of the town. "This is a really small town, both in its size and in the thinking of the locals," he sneered to himself. He turned to the yellow pages to look for guides and packers, and found this to be the largest section of the meager offerings for this hick village.

Unconsciously, he downgraded the town while building himself up as the liquor took hold of his judgment. He scanned the ads and looked for a name that inspired him, and then his eyes fell on a small box on the page. There was a quote in the box, but the page was torn, so he couldn't read the name of the author. "There are no small ideas, only small men," it said. He stared at it for a long time; something about that phrase giving him a strange feeling.

He quickly turned the page, and the quote disappeared from sight and fell away from his thoughts. He called several before he was able to find one who was hungry enough to make a deal. Barney knew that he had found his man when he hesitated when he heard where Barney wanted to go. The others had told him immediately they weren't willing to cross the ranger, no matter how much he paid them, so he had acted contrite and said he wouldn't do it either. This man was hungry—Barney knew that when he didn't set a price, but instead asked how much it was worth and what his goal was.

Barney had always been able to tell what the right price was for everyone; it was his gift, and it didn't fail him now. An hour later, he had made his arrangements, and the man knew what he was to do. Barney counted on the other packers to tell the ranger he had tried to go behind his back, so he was planning on joining the expedition as agreed upon.

His new guide was to head for the first campsite and wait for him there with the horses and the supplies. Barney would slip away at night and meet him farther up the mountain, at a place the man had designated on the map. Barney was counting on the rangers looking for him to slow the other group down and interfere with the success of their hunt. He wasn't going to be bothered by any such obligations and he would find this big red buck and have him in the camp, gutted and caped, before those others knew what had happened to their precious animal. If they wanted to make an issue of it then, so be it. He would deal with that if and when it ever came up.

Feeling pleased with himself, Barney poured himself another drink and stretched out on the lumpy mattress in his cheap room. Just then there was a knock at the door, and he sat up quickly.

"Who is it?" he asked brusquely.

"Mr. Barney, it's me, April Martens. We met a few days ago. I'm a reporter for—"

"Yes, yes. What do you want?"

"I was hoping to do a story on you, Mr. Barney. I wanted—" She stopped as the door opened suddenly.

"Come on in, Miss Martens," Barney said with an oily graciousness. "And your assistant too," he added, as he saw Adam standing there. "Now then, Miss Martens, what's this about doing a story on me?" he asked with a smile.

"Mr. Barney, you have quite a reputation as a hunter—and, of course, it is common knowledge that you're here to get that mysterious elk everyone talks about. I was thinking—what if we teamed up to provide an in-depth story about you and your hunt for this animal? Adam here is a fantastic photographer, and his skill at taking action shots is unparalleled by anyone I know. I think that the three of us could make a very wonderful story that would really sell," April gushed.

Adam wasn't paying attention to her sales pitch, because he had heard it before. He was more interested in the telephone book that he saw lying on the bed. It was open to the yellow pages, and Adam could just barely make out the heading. He took out his camera with the telephoto lens to take a picture of it, but first he moved to place Barney in the foreground of the shot to cover his actions.

"Mr. Barney, if you wouldn't mind moving a bit to the left, I'd like to get a shot of you and April talking. No, that's not going to work. Let me get around here … yes, that's better. Hold it … okay." Adam could see the headlines in his viewfinder very clearly now and he could see they were for hunting guides. He took two shots, trying to get the best and clearest picture. He could see one of the ads was circled, so he took one more shot of that ad.

"Thank you, Mr. Barney. That's exactly what I'm looking for. I won't bother you again."

He sat back and reviewed the picture in his camera. Barney was contacting another hunting guide. What he was doing that for was unknown, but Adam had a feeling this man wasn't to be trusted. And what made matters worse was that Adam didn't really trust April either. This meeting was looking more and more like a bad idea—but, of course, no one was asking for his opinion, Adam thought silently. He sat there listening as both April and Barney discussed the documentary she wanted to make.

"Well, Miss Martens, what's in this for me? Why should I cooperate at all with you in this thing? I have a lot to do in preparation for the hunt, so why should I give up any of my time for your benefit?" Barney asked her.

"Mr. Barney, I hope to make this a front-page story in newspapers across the world—and, in the process, I hope to make your name a household word as well," April said enthusiastically.

"But what if I don't want to be a household name, Miss Martens?"

"Well, what do you want, Mr. Barney? Is there anything I can do to get your cooperation in this? It really means a lot to me to get this story, Mr. Barney. My future career is riding on this; I would do just about anything to get it. I would really appreciate your help on this, Mr. Barney."

Adam watched as April began to pour on the charm and put her hand on Barney's knee to sell her point. He watched as she batted her eyes, and he saw a light in Barney's eyes that worried him. He hoped April wasn't getting herself—or him, either—in over their collective heads.

He decided not to say anything about the circled ad until he had a chance to blow it up, look it over, and decide what it meant. April continued to smooth-talk Warner Barney.

"Mr. Barney, this is a once-in-a-lifetime opportunity for all of us. This fabled Red Deer—"

"Elk," Barney said curtly.

"Yes, I meant *elk*, Mr. Barney. It is my plan to provide a full documentary approach to this magnificent humanitarian hunt and to record the impressions and actions of each member of this team, including the ranger and the animal-rights people, and even the guides. But mostly I want to focus on the mind and skill of the primary hunter, and that would be you, Mr. Barney. I want to show the world what it takes to be a champion hunter—the trials and the challenges, the hardships, and the tricks and crafts of the art of tracking. I want everyone to know you as the greatest tracker of all time. Adam will be there to provide the photographic record, so the world will see you in your element."

Adam was amazed at how easily the words flowed out of her, and he also thought about how easily they had flowed when she was trying to sell him on coming along. This confirmed his suspicions that he really didn't mean anything to her; all that affection was just part of selling him. With that realization, the last traces of any affection he had for her faded away.

She was all business, and that was how he was going to deal with her from now on. He thought about what she was saying to Barney and contemplated how many ways that it could go wrong, deciding there were, indeed, many.

"I understand quite clearly what you want, Miss Martens, but what I don't get is what I am getting out of it. Please don't take up anymore of my time—unless you are prepared to state plainly what I am going to receive in return for allowing you to accompany me on this hunt. I don't need someone underfoot and in the way, making a lot of damn noise, and scaring my quarry off. I don't need someone shooting off flashbulbs and scaring the crap out of the game," Barney said coldly. "If I were to agree to this proposal, my terms are these: you take my orders, I tell you what pictures to take, and I choose the pose. You don't spend a lot of time with the boy scout, and you don't get in my way. And, above all else, you don't tell anyone what I am doing until this is over. You agree to these terms, I'll make sure you get the story you want out of this," Barney said evenly.

He stared April right in the eyes until she nodded and agreed to his terms. His mood changed immediately—from cold and controlling to that of friend and coworker, as if the preceding conversation had never happened. April was happy now that she had her story and knew it would be the prizewinner she wanted. If she had any doubts about the agreement she had made, she never showed them in her face or her attitude.

She turned to Adam and, with a sweet smile, told him to take some more pictures of Barney in various poses with his weapons. As Adam did so, he couldn't help but notice that the only time Warner Barney's eyes looked alive was when he was holding one of his several rifles. When he looked at Adam or April, there was a cold and lifeless look in his eyes.

Adam liked the water, and he had done some scuba diving in the past. One of his best underwater pictures had come about accidentally when a big fish swam up to him for a closer look one day. The fish had that same look in its eyes—lifeless black circles on the sides of its large pointed snout. Those eyes were very scary, almost as scary as the fake smile and the large serrated teeth in its mouth.

Adam had felt very lucky to get away with a picture and all his appendages, and he was getting that same feeling in the presence of this man.

After saying their good nights, April and Adam drove to their rooms. In the car, Adam sat silently, thinking about the conversation that he had heard. He'd had a very bad feeling about this assignment from the start, and that feeling was growing stronger every minute. April only had eyes for the prize, and she wasn't the least bit interested in the path she had to follow to get there—or who she had to walk over to reach her goal.

Adam made up his mind that he was going to talk to that ranger as soon as he could get him alone. He wasn't sure what he was going to say, but he knew he needed to show him the picture he had taken in the room with April and Barney.

He interrupted her midstream. "April, hold up a minute. I want to say something to you."

"What is it, Adam?"

"I think we need to be careful here, April. There's something about that man I don't trust. I think you ought to be very leery of putting your faith in him; I think he has his own agenda for this hunt, April. I don't think he's the kind of man who plays fair, not when he's used to getting his own way in everything. I think he'll cheat you, and I think he'll leave you out on a limb and cut the tree off behind you, April. I have a really bad feeling about him, and I don't think I'm going to go with you if you're going to be working with him that way," Adam said sadly.

April didn't turn her head, but her voice became as cold as ice. "Adam, you were hired by the paper to do the photography that goes with the story, and you were assigned to go with me. If you're going to let this job or any other assignment conflict with your ethics and moral compass, then you don't belong in this business. This job is about reporting—showing the public what is going on in the world, and that means both the good and the bad in it, as well as working with both the good and bad people who make up this world. A good reporter doesn't judge the story—she tells it, and she tells all of it. She doesn't let her personal bias get in the way of that telling, either. Now, if you want to be a documentarian—"

"A docu-what?"

"A documentarian. Someone who makes a documentary ... someone who makes only documentaries."

"I'm not sure there is such a word as—"

"Whatever. If you want to be known as someone who makes an award-quality documentary, then you need to learn how to put your biases aside and focus on the story. If you think Barney is bad news, then you show it. You use your photographic skills to tell the story of why he is bad, and then you can expose him to the world for what he is. If you don't want to do that, that's fine with me, but I'm going to tell the story as I see it and how I see the players in it. That's what a reporter does, Adam," April said coldly.

The silence that followed filled the car for the last ten minutes of the drive, neither having anything else to say on the subject. When they arrived at the motel, both of them got out without saying a word to the other, and they managed to do it without locking eyes on the other. Not a word was exchanged as both of them pulled their room keys out of their pockets and entered their adjoining rooms. The entire night passed without any further contact between them.

Across town and up the mountain road, the Bruce family was talking about the coming hunt and what it would mean for all of them.

"Look, Dad, we're coming out of a dry summer and a bad winter. The hay crop hardly fed the horses, and we had to buy most of the fodder for the cows from Edgar Calvin, and you know he don't give nothin' away. This trip, with all the publicity it's gonna bring us, will put us back in the black and then some. I've already paid for the cow feed with the advances in these entries." Gerry Junior held up a stack of envelopes and waved them in his father's face.

"I know it is a lot of money, son, but there's a lot more at stake here than just a pile of cash. I told you what he did before and how he reacted. I doubt that man's changed one iota in all this time, and that worries me more than you can possibly imagine. I know what's important to him, and it isn't conservation or safety. It isn't you, and it won't be anyone else on that adventure, and I can guarantee you it damn sure won't be me.

"The only thing Warner Barney cares a damn thing for is what Warner Barney wants. He will do whatever gets him what he wants, regardless of the danger or problems it causes anyone else. Gerry, son, I am pleading with you—I don't think you should do this. Back out of it, say you can't get away from the ranch, say you are worried about me, say anything you want to—please, just don't go," Gerry Senior implored.

"I understand what you are saying, Dad, but you raised me to never run from anything. I grew up on stories of you and Grandpa Amos fighting for what you believed in and not backing down to anyone. You taught me about honor and paying your debts, and about giving your word and how much that means to be a man. I remember you giving your word to Wilbur Brackman when I was fifteen. Do you remember that? He helped you fight a fire in the bottomland down around Beavertail Hollow. You were so grateful, you told him to call on you anytime he needed help. And do you remember when he called on you? Where you were then, do you remember? I do. It was the night Mom died.

"You were with Wilbur helping him with his cows when they got out of the high pasture. You could've said you couldn't make it, you could've told him about Mom, he would have understood—he told you that at the funeral. But you had given your word and that was that. I was so damn mad at you, but Mom, she said I had no right to be mad, because you'd given your word, and she was proud of you for being someone whose word was gold. Someone whose word was his honor. She said it wasn't anything serious that wouldn't keep, so I shouldn't be mad at you. When you finally came home about four in the morning, she was gone. So now you are telling me that giving my word means nothing?" His anger spent, Gerry Junior just sat there and stared at his father.

Gerry Senior looked back sadly, understanding for the first time where the gulf between them over the years had come from. "Son, I'm sorry. I'm truly sorry. I never knew you felt that way. I always regretted that decision to go out that night. I lost someone that night that was very important to me too. I would have stayed if I had known she was sick—but, son, your mother never told me she was sick or in pain. She hid it from me too. She told all the doctors that I knew and that I didn't want to talk to them so they wouldn't call me and spill the beans. She knew we were just hanging on by our teeth during that period; it was the insurance money from after she passed that enabled us to get back on our feet at all. That was her gift to us, something she couldn't give while she was alive.

"She knew how much the ranch meant to all of us, coming down from your great-grandfather as it did. She knew I would have stayed home if she asked me to, but she also knew that helping Wilbur was the key to getting access to the range we needed to grow. She made that choice for us, for you and for me, so that we could keep the ranch. She left me a letter—I'll show it to you if you want to see it and ..."

Gerry Junior just shook his head.

"... she said I had to buy the range Wilbur was offering me so we could grow and survive into the next generation. She's the one who ..." Gerry Senior stopped talking.

"She's the one who what, Dad?" Gerry Junior said, slowly but curiously, his anger quickly turning to sadness.

His father didn't answer at first, but then he gave a long sigh and turned to face his son. "Your mother is the one who came up with the idea of me being a guide. She knew I wasn't happy at a desk, son. I grew up in the saddle, in a different time, in a different world. I was too late to be a real cowboy, and too soon to be a businessman. Think about it for a minute, son, who helped you with your homework? Who helped you study? Your mom did, I was no good at that. Hell, I never finished high school, son. I went back years later, at your mom's insistence, and squeaked by just to get my GED. I'm no great shakes in a contest of smarts, son," Gerry Senior said, with shame evident in his voice.

"But, Dad, you made this ranch work. If something broke, you fixed it or made a replacement for it. I saw you pick up stuff and make it into working machinery when all of us thought it was just junk or time to replace it. Don't say you're not smart, Dad, you're very smart," Gerry Junior said with pride.

His father put a big, rough callused hand on his son's shoulder and smiled. "No, you're the smart one, son. I'm just a big old farmhand mechanic who can fix some things. It was your mother, and then it was you that kept this place running. You understood how to make the deals that kept this old place going during our lean years. You brought in the business that paid the bills, or kept them from taking it away from us when the money wasn't there. I'm good in a saddle, working with the stock, and keeping things running, but you are the real heart of this ranch now. I'm sorry I put you in this position, son.

"So here's what we'll do. We'll do it together. I'll take this hunt out for you—you stay here and keep things going like they should be. How about that?" he asked hopefully, knowing his offer wasn't going to be accepted. He knew this because he wouldn't have accepted it in his son's place either. So he wasn't really surprised then when his son stood up and shook his head.

"Nope, it's not going to be that way, Dad. We'll do this one together, then we'll stop the guide business and focus on doing what we do best, and that is ranching together." He put out his own rough, callused hand and took his father's in a silent, strong—but loving—embrace. These were two men who didn't talk about their feelings openly, but there was no mistaking the love that existed between them.

Both men looked at each other for a long moment, and then Gerry Senior looked away and sniffed. "That damn cat hair; it gets my allergies every time."

"Me too, Dad; it must be hereditary or something," Gerry Junior said as he wiped his eye. They both then laughed together. The last time there was a cat in the house had been well over twenty years ago.

Oliver hung up the telephone and sat back in his chair, staring out the window overlooking the mountain. "Eileen, is everything ready to go on Wednesday?" he called out.

"I've got everything written out for you, Oliver. Just look on your desk, please," she called back.

Oliver started shuffling the papers, becoming frustrated when what he wanted didn't instantly appear on the top of the pile. "What do they look like, Eileen? What am I looking for here—a folder, a piece of paper, or a needle in a haystack?" he called out in frustration.

"You're looking for a folder that is red in color and labeled 'Red Elk Hunt.' Just work slowly from one side of your desk to the other; you will find it," she called out to him. When he didn't say anything for several minutes, she probably thought he had found it—but then he called out again, and Eileen straightened up and excused herself from the telephone conversation she was in, sighing in exasperation.

She walked into Oliver's office and over to where he stood, his hands full of papers, and folders of every color spread all over. Eileen looked at the pile of papers on the desktop, and put out her hand to touch the pile. She reached into the middle and, without a word, pulled out the red folder he'd requested, handing it to him.

As she quickly walked out of the room, Oliver called after her, "How did you do that? I looked all over for it—how'd you pull it out of the pile without even seeing it?"

"That's what you pay me for, Oliver," she called back to him with a laugh.

"That's not much of an answer," he muttered to himself as he sat back down and opened the folder. "What in the world have I got myself into?" he said softly to himself. Oliver turned around in his chair to pick up a box lying on the floor. He dumped the contents and then, turning back to his desk, waved his arm across his desk, sweeping everything into the box. He then tossed it all behind him and spread out the contents of the folder on the newly cleaned desktop.

He picked up a bill from the outfitters for the reporter and her photographer. The reporter had apparently spared no expense in outfitting herself, while the photographer had been much more respectful and hadn't bought the most costly of items, settling for mid-range quality—except for two items—he had purchased the best thermal jacket and gloves that could be had. Oliver thought this was reasonable. He started to put the receipts away when he saw there was a second receipt attached to it. He looked at it and saw it was a copy of a second credit card charge in the name of Adam Jacobs. The photographer had paid part of the cost himself, a behavior that impressed Oliver very much, and his opinion of the young man rose, equal to how his opinion of the female reporter had declined. He sat back and thought about the young man's attitude in their meeting, and then he called out to Eileen.

"Eileen, did we ever fill that position left open when that jerk Kevin quit last month?"

"Kevin? The geek who was working on our Internet?"

"No, the geek who was taking pictures for our—"

"Oh, I know who you mean now. His name wasn't Kevin, it was Connor."

"Kevin, Connor, Clyde, whatever. Did we fill that position yet?"

"No, but I have a couple of résumés to go over."

"Well, hold off on them for now. I have an idea that we might already have our man right under our noses."

"Are you thinking about that news photographer?" she asked.

"Yes, I am. I have a hunch he might be a good fit for us. I'd like to talk to him about it and see how he'd feel signing on."

There was no response, so he keyed the intercom again. "Eileen?" No answer. Oliver got up and walked out to her desk, only to find her engaged in conversation with the very person they had been talking about.

"Mr. Jacobs, what can I do for you?"

"Mr. Barry, I need to talk with you. It's very important, and I really need it to be confidential. Can I talk with you … in private?" the young man asked anxiously.

"Well, I don't see why not, but I always have my assistant in meetings with me—it's policy. But you can trust Eileen; she hears all and says nothing. Come on in, Mr. Jacobs. Do you want to leave your camera on her desk?"

"No, sir, I think you might want to see some of my pictures."

Oliver looked past him at Eileen, who just shook her head, indicating she didn't know what was going on. As she closed the door behind them, she sat down on the sofa to the side of Oliver's desk.

"Okay, Mr. Jacobs. What can I do for you today?" Oliver asked, curious about what was coming.

"Mr. Barry, I am here on my own, and it could cost me my job. I am, in a way, acting against the wishes of my supervisor. I want it very clear that this is my decision to do this, and if there are any repercussions of this decision, they should fall on me, not Miss Martens," Adam said solemnly.

Oliver glanced at Eileen, who was taking notes behind Adam. "I understand what you're saying, Mr. Jacobs, I just don't understand why you're saying it. Could you possibly be a little clearer?"

"Two nights ago, April—that is, Miss Martens—and I met with Mr. Barney to talk about his participation in this expedition. Miss Martens wanted to make a deal with Mr. Barney to allow her to document his role in the hunt, both as a story and to allow me to photograph the hunt with a focus on his participation."

"I don't have a problem with either of you doing that, Mr. Jacobs. That would actually help me in my efforts to protect the elk."

"I know, Mr. Barry. I was interested in that as well. But while we were there, I was taking some shots of Mr. Barry and his weapons, and I saw he had been making some telephone calls. The telephone book was open, and I took a picture of the page he was looking at. Here it is." Adam reached into his bag and pulled out a set of black and white photographs. He looked through them and handed one to Oliver, who looked at it for a minute without seeing anything significant.

"Okay, so he was making some calls. So what?"

"Look a little closer, sir, in the upper-left-hand corner. Or you can look at this one; I blew it up a little for you," Adam said. He handed Oliver a second photograph, and Oliver could see very clearly the heading on the page of the phonebook in the picture. It was hunting guides and pack trips.

Oliver turned around in his chair and pulled the phone book off the shelf behind him. He turned to the page shown in the picture and ran his finger down the listings. The Bruce ranch was not on that page. He looked at the picture again and then back to the telephone book.

"I see that Mr. Barney is interested in some of our hunting guides, but that doesn't indicate anything sinister, Mr. Jacobs. Is there something else you want me to see?" Oliver asked Adam politely, hoping the reply was going to be negative.

"Well, there's this …" He handed Oliver the third photograph.

Reluctantly, Oliver took the picture as eagerly as he would a live scorpion. "What am I looking at here?" he asked.

"It's a copy of a check. I sort of saw Mr. Barney's checkbook while he and Miss Martens were talking. I wasn't prying into his affairs, honest," Adam said quickly in response to the dark look Oliver gave him. "His checkbook was on the desk behind him, and I saw it through my close-up lens to get the pictures Miss Martens wanted, and this was in the background. I just happened to get it in the frame. When I printed it out, I saw he had written a check to one of them in the last two days. At first it didn't make sense to me, because he had already paid for this trip. I decided to do a little detective work, and I didn't like what I learned, so I decided to come to you with it," Adam said as if he wanted to get the words out before he changed his mind.

"Okay, Mr. Jacobs, I will take the next step. What did you learn?" Oliver asked warily.

"I didn't learn a lot, which is what bothered me. I called the name on that check, and the minute I mentioned Mr. Barney, the man suddenly got busy and didn't have time to talk. What they did tell me is that they run hunting parties up in the mountains. I asked around town about the business, and what everyone who would say anything about them said is they wouldn't hire them. I have a theory, Mr. Barry, and I hope I'm wrong, but I decided to come to you and let you know what I've found. If you do not think there's anything to worry about, I'll let it go. I just ask that you don't mention any of this to Miss Martens; I don't think she'd be very happy with my doing this. Well, this is all I have to tell you, but …"

"Mr. Jacobs, there is one more thing you can tell me. You can tell me why you came to me about this," Oliver said politely.

"I guess I respect what you do, Mr. Barry. I want to save that animal, and I don't think that's what Mr. Barney is intending to do. I don't trust him, Mr. Barry, and I don't think you should either. I think he wants a trophy, and I don't think he cares very much what he has to do to get it. So I guess I'm hoping you'll be able to stop him and save that elk. He deserves to be saved."

After Adam had left, leaving the pictures behind, Oliver sat and looked at the photographs for a time before picking up the telephone. He dialed a number, but hung up the receiver before it began to ring. Looking at the phone for a long minute, he dialed it again, but this time he didn't hang up. There was no answer at the other end, and didn't leave a message. He turned to look out the window at the mountain and then walked over to his doorway and looked out in the waiting room. There was no one but Eileen in the office, who looked up as he stood there.

"Eileen, why don't you go down and get a cup of coffee in the lounge? And would you mind taking about fifteen minutes to drink it?" he asked. He went back to his desk and sat down, taking out his personal cell phone and looking up a number from his call list. Turning back to his phone, he dialed a different number, and this time it was picked up at the other end. After a brief exchange of pleasantries, Oliver began explaining just why he was calling to the person on the other end. The conversation lasted ten minutes, and he was promised that the package would be sent out that afternoon.

When it was done, Oliver sat back in his chair and turned to look out at the mountains. He thought about the call he had just made, and what the consequences of that call might be. He reminded himself he had a job to do and an obligation to everyone and all who lived on the mountain. Regardless of the outcome, he knew he had made the right decision.

When Eileen came back in, he told her to expect delivery of a small package by messenger before the day was over, and not to open it but bring it to him. When she asked what was in it, he just looked out the window and said, "Insurance."

The day began with a shiver, as if it knew something bad was going to happen. The temperature was unusually low for the season, and the clouds were moving about fitfully, as if they weren't sure where they wanted to be. This had the effect of creating numerous drifting shadows on the mountains that seemed to be hiding something from the sight of the observer. The clouds were mostly white, but there was a tinge of red that, to the eye of the old-timer Charley Weeks, seemed to be a warning to stay off the mountain. Most, however, believed it came from the sunrise.

Everyone was gathering at the Bruce ranch, where the hunt was to begin. Oliver looked around at the group, recognizing most of the people standing there. It was a larger than usual crowd, with a diverse group of riders. Eileen was standing beside him, looking and right at home in her denim jeans and high-top boots. She wasn't wearing a Hollywood outfit, but a set of real working clothes. Her hair was tied back with a rawhide cord, and her hands were enclosed in a pair of well-worn leather riding gloves. She had no makeup on today, but, nevertheless, she looked even more alive and glowing than usual.

Standing off to the side he saw the reporter and her photographer. April was wearing a riding outfit that was designed for looks more than comfort, and even Oliver could see she was going to be very sore well before this day was over. She was wearing tennis shoes instead of boots and jeans that were thinner than regular Levi's. They were tight on her, and Oliver knew she was going to be uncomfortable riding in them after a few hours. They were sure to ride up on her and leave her legs subject to severe chafing on the stirrup leather. Her shirt appeared to be heavy and woolen, and she had nothing but a thin T-shirt on underneath it. It was open at the neck and it revealed pale skin beneath. She had on light, skintight gloves, not the heavier, lined ones favored by the ranchers for the higher elevations. He could see a fringed coat tied on behind her saddle, and knew that, while it would keep her warm at night, it would be too warm to wear during the day. Oliver knew the people at the outfitters, and he was sure they had advised her to go for the layered approach, so that she could take off or put on clothes as needed. He was also positive that the reporter was dressing for effect— the effect of her appearance on the other men—more than she was for her own comfort in the cold. He smiled to himself, recognizing she had completely underestimated the weather and was very likely going to be one cold girl before the trip was over. Her hat was a baseball cap, with her sunglasses on a cord hanging around her neck. This would not protect her neck or her face from the sun. Oliver hoped she had brought along plenty of sunscreen.

Her photographer, however, appeared to have taken the outfitters' advice all the way. He had on black jeans and high-top boots with a good riding heel. The height of the boots would help protect his legs against chafing in the stirrups, and the riding heels would help keep his feet secure in the stirrups. He had on what appeared to be a thermal underwear top, and Oliver suspected he had the bottoms on as well. Over the thermal shirt he was wearing a new red plaid flannel shirt and a light, lined jacket over that. Behind his saddle was a long, lined duster that looked to be oiled. Oliver nodded to himself, thinking this young man was going to be okay. That duster would double as his blanket or pillow at night and as a raincoat if it did rain. He had on a wide-brimmed, flat crown Resistol hat to protect his eyes and keep the rain off his neck and a pair of lined gloves to keep his hands warm and protected. If he could ride as well as he came prepared, then he would be okay.

Standing off by the pack string he saw old Charley Weeks, who had volunteered to be the cook. Charley looked to be on the north side of sixty-five; Oliver knew he was closer to fifty, but the years of heavy drinking had taken their toll on his skin and his middle, which was showing a considerable paunch. But Charley Weeks was a damn good cook, and Oliver had attended many a barbecue hosted by ranchers who had eagerly sought out old Charley to do what he did best. His berry cobblers were as legendary as was his thirst. To the unknowing, Charley looked like he had come right off a movie set, and he had spent many a summer playing just that role for the movie companies who filmed up in these mountains.

His long, white moustache was kept in peak condition, and he always used either wax or some other noxious substance to keep it rolled and shaped, no matter what he was eating. His eyes were a watery blue, but he didn't miss much of what was going on around him. His hat was dark brown, sweat-stained, and chewed up—he always called it "air-conditioned." When someone would suggest he replace it with a new one, he always said he had spent too much time giving this one its honorable character to replace it. His skin was leathery and seamed, and there was a small scar over one eye.

Charley was overseeing the packing of the panniers on the mules, so he was busy, and Oliver didn't want to disturb him.

Standing together in a small knot were three people Oliver knew only slightly.

The closest of the three was a short man, about five-foot-four, with a clipboard under his arm. He was wearing aviator-style sunglasses, a denim shirt, green denim pants, and a flannel-lined jacket, and had a pair of riding gloves tucked into his belt. On his feet were high-top hiking boots. He was Ed Baxter, who was the representative of FARM, the Freed Animal Rights Movement, the conservation group that was to oversee the capture and eventual transport of the large animal to the preserve for its future care. Ed had a short gray beard, and what hair showed under his straw cowboy hat was also gray and clipped short.

Standing to his left was Arnold Wilcox, the representative of Open Range Preserve property, who was going to take possession of the elk. Arnold could easily be taken to be a local rancher, which he was. He was wearing a pair of worn cowboy boots, run down at the heels. His flannel shirt was worn, and the pocket was torn. His jeans were faded and threadbare in places, and he was wearing a long duster over his flannel shirt. His face was thin and browned, almost the color of the saddle he was leaning on, and his hat was silver, neatly curled on the sides and held in place by a horsehair stampede string hanging down the back of his neck. Arnold was known to have a long fuse for most situations, but a quick reaction was known to occur when he saw any acts of animal cruelty. Arnold wasn't a big man, but his strength was well known. He would often entertain friends by tearing the Great Falls telephone book in half with his bare hands. He had, on occasion, been able to straighten out a horseshoe with his bare hands, wearing only gloves to protect his hands from any possible metal fragments.

The third member of the group was a woman. She was thin and

very plain. She was wearing what looked to be a medical jumpsuit, which was to be expected, as she was the veterinarian, Dr. Wanda Fleming, who was to supervise the tranquilizing of the animal and its care until it arrived at the preserve. She was wearing a light jacket and high-top hiking boots as well. Her hair was cut short in a very mannish style, and she had a camera hanging around her neck.

The three of them were engaged in a heated discussion, and Baxter looked annoyed, as did Dr. Fleming. With a sigh, Oliver nudged Eileen and pointed in their direction. "We're not even out of the gate and we have a problem. I guess I best get on this right away and head off the stampede. You find the hunter, Barney. I don't see him anywhere, and that bothers me," he said in a low voice.

"I'll find him, boss. Go get 'em, cowboy," she replied with a smile.

Oliver put on a smile and sauntered over to the little group, which was quickly heating up. "What's the problem, people?" Oliver asked cordially.

"I was just telling Dr. Fleming here that we may have a problem transporting the animal back to the preserve, depending upon where we finally corner it. We won't really know how to get him out until we see where we find him. It's possible that we may not be able to take him in the best location and will just have to steer him to a place where we can ..." Ed explained.

"And my position is that there is no way we can carry him out off the mountain easily without stressing him out or hurting him, without tranquilizing him ..." Arnold added.

"And I can't do that safely without knowing precisely how much this animal weighs," Dr. Fleming put in.

"And we don't know just how much he weighs because no one has ever seen him up close or for very long. I get it," Oliver finished sadly. "The thing is, folks, we all knew this when we put this venture together. So does anyone have any suggestions on how we can get this done and not waste everyone's time and effort?" Oliver asked. "I mean, why didn't one of you raise these issues when I called all of you a few days ago?"

"Well, son, you didn't exactly give us a lot of time to work out all the kinks of the transfer," Arnold said kindly.

"I didn't have the time to work out the logistics of transportation on anything but a simple carryout," Ed said icily.

"Mr. Barry, I will not be responsible for risking the welfare and safety of this magnificent animal. I want to help you, I really do, but I have rules I have to work with, and there are laws I have to obey. We can't break any laws to get him out, and we can't hurt him doing it. I am sure we can't expect him to be cooperative with us, of course, so his fear level will have to be considered," Dr. Fleming added.

"And I don't care to add any cold water to this bath, Oliver, but I do need to point out that we don't have any way to get him down off the mountain when we get him," Arnold added gently.

"May I make a suggestion?" came a voice from behind them. They all turned to see the photographer standing there.

"Who are you?" asked Ed brusquely. "We don't have time for this distraction. We are trying to solve a serious problem here."

"Well, I'm not trying to cause any, sir; I just have a suggestion," Adam said respectfully.

"This is Adam Jacobs, folks; he's the official photographer on this event," Oliver explained to them.

"Mr. Jacobs, we are trying to figure out, somewhat belatedly, I must admit, how we are going to get the elk off the mountain and into the preserve. You say you have a suggestion? I, for one, would like to hear it," Arnold said courteously.

"Well, I don't know if this is feasible or not, but what about putting him in a sling and lifting him out by helicopter?" Adam asked.

There was a pregnant silence among the group, broken only when Arnold began laughing. He had a very deep and full-bodied laugh, coming from way down in his chest. "Out of the mouths of babes, so to speak," he managed to get out, while clapping a ham-sized hand on Adam's back that nearly knocked him over. "That's a damn good idea, son. You can come and work for me anytime with a mind like that. This here boy's got a good quick eye for the shortest route. You ride much, son?" Arnold asked Adam.

"No, sir, not very often. I like horses, though. I just don't get much time to do it," Adam said, getting his breath back slowly.

April stood off to the side, a scowl on her face. Even though Adam hadn't wanted to come along initially, he was stealing her thunder now.

She moved in closer, with the intention of putting the focus back on her.

"Excuse me, gentlemen, can my photographer get back to work now and take your pictures for my story? I have a lot to do before we move out, and I need him to get busy. While he is doing that, I would like to interview each of you to get your perspectives on this adventure," she said in a friendly manner, while sending a subtle message to Adam that she didn't appreciate him getting more of their attention than she. She shot Adam a stern glance to make sure he understood and was relieved to see him unpacking his camera as she was talking. She began interviewing the big man first—the one who had shown an interest in the suggestion Adam had made, with the intent of making him forget all about him.

"Sir, may I have your name for my story?"

"Yes, ma'am. My name is Arnold Wilcox—and just what might your name be, miss?" he asked, sweeping his hat off in his big paw with a surprising speed.

"My name is April Martens, Mr. Wilcox, and I represent *The Galleton Chronicle.* Can you tell me just what your role is in this operation, Mr. Wilcox?" she asked him, pencil poised over her notepad.

"Well, Miss Martens, I am the representative of Open Range Preserve property, which is going to take possession of the elk. It will be our pleasure to provide him with a permanent safe home and free medical care for the rest of his life," he said with a smile.

"That's going to cost a lot, won't it?"

His smile dimmed a little as he answered her question. "Well, Miss Martens, out here we take our land management issues very seriously, and that means taking care of the wildlife that lives on the land as well. We work hard to keep the various herds in a proper balance for the ground cover and food sources available. We monitor the health of all our animals using GPS that tracks their ID tags. Each animal is given a small tag, here is his …" He handed her a small, green, metallic square, about the size of a large postage stamp. "It is encoded with his or her name, the date they are tagged, where they were tagged, and an estimate of their age. This tag is fastened to their ear, and this …" He showed her a small pellet the size of a bean. "This is inserted under the skin, and it is a duplicate tag and is capable of transmitting a signal to a transponder that bounces it off a satellite and is picked up back in Whitehorse at the center.

"I can track him—or any animal wearing this tag—for thirty years before it gives out. By the way, if the signal doesn't move for more than twenty-four hours, we go looking for him. And, as for the cost, every rancher who registers a brand or buys and sells a cow, and every tourist permit or license sold—all of these and a few other things all contribute to the maintenance and upkeep of the preserve," Arnold explained. "Plus, we have a few wealthy contributors who help out every year if we have an emergency in our funding. Many of us contribute a sizeable number of man-hours each year to the daily maintenance of the property in their areas. Now, I have some things to attend to before we leave, so if you will excuse me?" With a bow, he walked off toward the horses.

April called out, "Thank you," to his rapidly retreating back and received a friendly wave over his head in return. She turned to interview the other man and the woman, only to find they had walked off as well. She turned around and walked back to her pack, pushing her pad back into the side pocket. As she did, she looked around for Adam and saw him walking around the camp, taking pictures of the people involved in the venture.

He was framing the portraits in front of the mountain, using the snowcapped peaks as his backdrop. She could not help but admire his professionalism and the way he was staging his scenes and the pictures. A high-pitched nasal voice spoke behind her, startling her.

"Excuse me—are you the reporter for this potential screw-up?"

She turned around to see the second man of the group she wanted to talk to. "Yes, sir, I am. And you are?"

"My name is Ed Baxter, and I want to go on record as saying this is a major mess already, and I don't see any way it's going to get better. I've got a long of list of problems with the project and no sign of any solutions!" He was waving his clipboard in her face and getting more and more excited as he talked. Because he was two inches shorter than April, the clipboard was getting dangerously close to her nose, so she slowly shifted her weight to her back foot to give herself a little room.

Ed Baxter was getting redder as he wound himself up, so April pulled her mini-recorder from her backpack, and held it up for him to talk into, and asked him to explain his concerns to her.

"Let me tell you, miss, this is going to end badly for this animal, and it is going to be a major setback for conservation efforts everywhere! For one thing, no one here has ever seen the animal with their own eyes, so we have no real idea how big it is."

April decided this wasn't the time to mention she had seen it, because that would only invite the question of how she happened to see it and under what circumstances. "Just how this going to set conservation back, Mr. Baxter?" she asked in her best professional interviewer's voice.

"The act of hunting this animal is going to stress it out beyond belief! Then, trying to get a tranquilizer dart into him and transport him back to the bottom of the mountain from wherever we find him—if we even can find him—is just going to pile on even more stress!"

"Mr. Baxter, I've heard stories that this animal is very capable of avoiding capture or being killed. Is it possible—"

"Miss, we are talking about an animal working off instinct, not a human with a brain. There is no possible way this animal, as wary and alert as it is, can possibly outwit any human for very long. It will tire and it will panic, and when it does, it will be caught. My job in this disorganized venture is to supervise the capture of the animal, and make sure that he is not mishandled or in any way mistreated during his forced contact with us. I will be using that rifle"—he pointed to the rifle leaning against the fence on his left—"to sedate him. I will be using these tranquilizer darts"—he gave one to her for her inspection—"to administer a prescribed dose of methotrimeprazine into his hide—not enough to kill him, but enough to render him unconscious for a time.

"This is when it gets risky, because to give him too much could stop his heart. And it is this very issue that could bring this haphazardly coordinated tragedy to an untimely end. No one knows what the right dosage should be. Dr. Fleming over there—hey! Dr. Fleming!" Baxter called out to the tall and painfully thin woman standing near the corral.

Dr. Wanda Fleming walked over to Baxter and, with an air of annoyance, looked at April.

"Who is this, Ed? What is she doing here? Where is the head wrangler? I have a complaint about the way he is treating those animals in the corral. Who are you?" The questions came rapid-fire, and April didn't realize the last one was directed at her until the silence was deafening. April decided she didn't like Dr. Fleming, who seemed almost as dried up as the landscape and as cold as the horseshoe she was holding in her bony hand.

"My name is April Martens, Dr. Fleming, and I am a reporter for—"

"A reporter, you say? And just what are you going to report on? How this magnificent animal is going to be driven from its home to be placed in a safer but foreign territory? How this hunt is being botched by a lack of proper preparation? Or how the people of this state watch out for the wildlife and try to keep the hunters from killing off the very best of our native animals? Are you going to write about how everyone works together for a common good in these parts, to preserve the balance of nature and people?" Dr. Fleming said angrily. "I've never seen a reporter yet who was willing to speak out about how hunting serves a beneficial purpose for the ecology of the area.

"I don't mean indiscriminate killing of any animal in sight, Miss Martens; I mean the careful and selective hunting of a limited surplus population to prevent overgrazing and the starvation of the entire herd. Hunting has a purpose, Miss Martens, and it always has. Out here, we do it for food and to protect our crops and our livestock. We don't do it for fun or to prove how big and bad we are, and we don't do it to put heads up on the wall. Those are not hunters by our definition, Miss Martens, although there are many who see it that way. No, out here hunting is for a purpose and it is a licensed procedure. No one is allowed unlimited killing—not for an elk, not for a deer, and not even for a fish. That is how hunting is done out here by responsible westerners, Miss Martens, if you care to report that too," Dr. Fleming said coldly.

"I am here to report on the story, Dr. Fleming, whatever that story is. I am not trying to support hunting or write against it either. I am here to cover a story about ..."

She paused, no longer certain just what she was covering. She was supposed to be here for the story on the mysterious skier, but only she knew they were connected. She didn't want to tip her hand just yet, because she was no closer to one over the other. If she said she was here to cover the Red Skier, which was her original intention, they would ask why she was here now. If she said she was here to cover the hunt, she would likely be killing the story on the skier when the elk was taken by Warner Barney, and no one would know the really big story. April had never anticipated being put in this position. What was she to do?

"… about a mysterious skier, but this is a very compelling story as well, Dr. Fleming. It is a story about the balance of nature versus the wants of man, and the people who want to keep that balance strong. It is a good story, Dr. Fleming, and one that needs to be told from the perspective of the caretakers. I would like to tell it, and with your help, and the help of Mr. Baxter and Mr. Wilcox and even Mr. Barry, it can be told. But Mr. Barney, he has a place too. I may not like his story, and it may not be as warm and fuzzy as other parts, but it represents many others and they have an equal right to be heard as well," April said.

"Well." Dr. Fleming sniffed again. "I suppose you have a point … maybe. Well, I have a lot of details to take care of, and I want to see the wrangler about this horseshoe, so I need to join Mr. Wilcox and Mr. Baxter. Perhaps I will have a few words for you later. If you will excuse me." Without another word, she turned and walked off, the horseshoe in her hand.

"That was quite a speech, Miss Martens," Oliver said, coming up behind her. "Just how much of it do you really believe?"

"I really believe all of what I said, Mr. Barry,"

"That's good, Miss Martens. That should make for some good reading, then. I certainly hope you will have a lot to write about by the time we are finished with this relocation project."

"Mr. Barry, I am certain that, by the time we are finished, I will have more than enough to write about," she assured him.

With a bow, Oliver smiled at her and walked away to look for Warner Barney.

Also going along on this adventure was Bern Justner and his brother, Axel, who were the wranglers for the Bruce ranch. They were in charge of the livestock, the horses, and the mules to be used on the hunt. It was their responsibility to match everyone to the appropriate horse for the trip to ensure each rider wasn't overwhelmed by their mount or vice versa. Both men had been with the Bruce ranch for many years, and they thought of it as their home too.

They were natural horsemen, and could size up a rider, or a man, with great accuracy in just a few minutes. They both took to the young photographer as soon as they saw him get a brush and curry comb without being told. He spent time brushing each horse, taking care to handle its tail and mane with great care and attention, kept one hand on the horse's rump and on its neck, getting all the knots out without yanking and hurting the horse. Both men looked at each other and back at him, and speaking one word at the same time.

"Cinnamon."

Axel nodded and went to go get a different horse for Adam. As he walked away, he saw the reporter talking to people. Noting what she was wearing, he shook his head and smiled to himself. He could hardly wait until they reached the higher altitudes and that reporter got colder. This sure was turning out to be a much more interesting ride than he had expected. Maybe he would just volunteer to keep an eye on that young lady, to make sure she didn't fall off her horse or anything unpleasant like that along the way. Of course, there was always the possibility of a cougar or two—even though the last one had been seen well before his time, one could never be too sure.

As he passed by the bunkhouse, he impulsively ducked inside, ran to his footlocker, and opened it to paw through the contents, looking for something he hadn't used in a long while. He came out a few minutes later, buckling his gun belt around his waist. *Just for safety reasons,* he told himself as he headed for the corral to get Cinnamon—somehow managing to walk in front of April along the way.

Across the corral, Bern had been watching his younger brother very carefully, because he knew how Axel could get when there was a pretty girl around. Sure enough, he saw him scoot into the bunkhouse, and he wasn't surprised to see him come out again with the gun belt. He sighed as he moved to head Axel off, and then he stopped. *What the hell,* he decided. *Let my brother have his fun.*

This was going to be a tedious outing, and he had heard through the grapevine that there were going to be a lot of tenderfeet and difficult personalities to contend with, so if Axel found a way to make it somewhat more enjoyable, then let the kid have a good time. Axel was only twenty-five, he reflected, still a youngster. Bern was much more mature, almost thirty-two, and more experienced than his younger brother. He was good with animals, while Axel had more charm and was better with people—specifically women. He knew Axel was going to try and sweet-talk that young reporter into snipe hunting, but he didn't think she was going to fall for his brother's siren song.

With a sigh, Bern turned his attention back to his task, choosing the pack string and the mounts for the riders. He had a long list to fill—there were to be eighteen riders, not counting him and Axel and the two bosses and the cook. That meant at least twenty-three horses and ten pack mules for the supplies. Bern shook his head, thinking of the logistics of this trip and how it was already out of hand and no one had set foot in a stirrup yet. He looked around for Gerry Junior, deciding he needed to talk to his boss about this setup and how long they were supposed to be wandering around on the mountain.

As he headed for the office in the barn, he nodded to Oliver as he passed by him.

Oliver was looking around at the hive of activity, and he was amazed by the progress. Although everyone was busy doing something—and he wasn't sure what they were doing—he could see that the expedition was quickly coming together. He had been here for only three hours, and the men who worked for Gerry were getting everything in order in what could only be some sort of record time. The horses were being saddled, and the mules were being loaded. Everything was getting ready, except that there were no hunters here. He looked around and couldn't see them anywhere. He saw Eileen talking to one of the wranglers and hurried over to her.

As he approached them, she looked up, saw him, and waved. "Oliver, Gene needs to know your riding experience so he can pick out a good horse for you."

"Gene, I can ride any horse you can put a quarter in its ear," Oliver said with a straight face.

Gene looked puzzled, "You can't put a … oh … I get it. No experience. Okay. I've got just the mount for you. I'll put you on Sleepy.

He likes to just walk. But since you are here, let me ask, have you seen anything of the hunters we are supposed to be taking out? I can account for everyone except them, and I need to ask them what their riding abilities are," he said, looking around for them.

"I don't know, Gene. They were supposed to be here about an hour ago, and I've heard no word from any of them. Eileen, can you call back to the office for me and—"

Just then, a dark green Land Rover pulled up to the parking area and stopped. A man got out of the car and went to the back of the vehicle, opening up the cargo area. He began unloading several large boxes, just as another man got out of the side of the vehicle, stepped to the back door, and opened it. That man leaned in, took out three large rifle cases, and hung a pair of field glasses around his neck. When he turned to the corral, Oliver saw it was Warner Barney. Oliver walked over and put out his hand to Barney, who looked at it and ignored it.

"When are we leaving for the hunt, Barry? I'm ready to get started as soon as I get mounted," Barney said brusquely.

Oliver allowed his hand to drop to his side and pointed to a man who was silently observing this exchange. "See that man there? His name is Bern Justner, and he is the head wrangler. You want a horse, go see him," he said calmly, and walked away to join Eileen, who was getting mounted.

Fuming inside at the insulting and disrespectful snub, he took the reins from Gene, who just walked away and mounted up. "I can't believe the arrogance of that man, Eileen. He just infuriates me at every encounter I have with him. I don't want to have anything else to do with him; I'll ignore him and talk to the other hunters. I wonder where they are."

"I called Rodney, and he said he had heard from—"

"Barry! What's the delay here? Why aren't we leaving?" Barney demanded.

"We have to wait for the other hunters, Mr. Barney. We are not leaving without them," Oliver said with restraint.

"Oliver," Eileen said. He turned to look at her. "Oliver, Rodney said the others called in, and they aren't going to be coming. Warner Barney bought them off."

He looked at Warner Barney, who just smiled smugly and turned his mount away. "We're all here, so let's get started," Barney called back.

Oliver looked over at Eileen as Barney trotted away and their eyes met in silent agreement. This man was definitely going to be trouble, and he had wasted no time throwing his weight around. Oliver was furious. Although he didn't say a word. Eileen was able to read him as clearly as if he had his feelings printed all over his face.

"Oliver, take a deep breath. Don't say or do anything to create a scene," she said in a low voice, one hand on his arm. They watched Warner Barney ride off, looking for the head of the column to ride at the front of the parade. Oliver lagged back to allow the others to form up ahead of him, intending on speaking with Gerry Junior as he rode by.

"Mr. Barry," came the voice behind him. He turned to see the photographer sitting there. "Mr. Barry, I saw what he did. I am sorry you were treated so rudely, sir. I hope he doesn't cause anymore trouble for you, but I want to assure you that I will not do anything to cause you any trouble, Mr. Barry, and that you can call on me for any help you might need."

"Adam, I am quite certain that you had nothing to do with that man's behavior, and I know you will be an asset to this venture. I sincerely appreciate the warning you gave me, and it will remain between us. For now, however, I need to treat you as if you are the enemy, if only to protect your relationship with your boss. So don't take anything I say for real, Adam. When I have something real to say to you, I'll say it to you in private or have Eileen get word to you.

"Now, you get on up there with your boss and keep your eyes and ears open, 'cause I have a feeling things are going to be happening on this trip, and when they do, they'll be coming fast and furious, and you may not have time to think about your options," Oliver warned him.

Nodding, Adam dug his heels into his horse, flicked the reins, and his mount went from first to third gear instantly.

"He's a nice young man, Oliver," Eileen said approvingly.

"I agree, Eileen. It's nice to know I've got a friend in the enemy's camp. I have a feeling I'm going to need it. I need to think about this a little more. This changes ... ouch!"

"What happened, Oliver?"

"Oh, nothing, I just sat on something hard in my pocket. Like I was saying, I need to think about this a little more. Keep a lookout for Gerry Junior, if you will; I want to talk to him," he said and lapsed back into a deep silence.

CHAPTER 5

The next three hours passed without a word spoken between any of them. The entire party worked its way slowly up the mountain, each person lost in their own thoughts. At the head of the line was Bern Justner, who was looking for the signs of the elk. He would ride off a ways, get down and look at the ground and the surroundings, and try to pick up any trace of the animal's passing that way.

Riding beside him was the senior Bruce, who hadn't been up this high in the mountain for many years. While many things looked much the same to Gerry, he was well aware things were always changing in the mountains. Seasons turned, landscapes shifted, animals lived and died, but the one constant was that the weather was always unpredictable. He also knew he was riding into danger being around Warner Barney, who didn't care about anyone or anything else, as long as he got what he wanted. Gerry was worried about how Warner's single-minded obsession with this animal was going to impact his son's safety.

He knew somehow he had to stop Warner, no matter what the cost to himself. In another part of his mind was the question about that phantom skier, and how he figured into all of this. But that question would just have to wait until he had Barney under control. His obsession with the animal came first, and Gerry had to keep an eye out for the elk to keep ahead of Barney.

Riding behind Gerry Senior were the three naturalists, and they were enjoying the early winter snows and smells of the mountain. This was new scenery for them, and, since they didn't expect to come across the elk at the lower altitudes, they were just taking in the opportunity to be outside for a time. Their jobs usually kept them tied to desks inside buildings. Only Arnold was frequently outside, so this was a real change of pace for them.

Dr. Fleming was particularly enchanted with the variety of the trees. She had a hard time telling one from another, so she kept asking questions of the other two men. She pestered Ed and Arnold about every one of them she saw, asking about the shape of the leaves and the texture of the bark, and what kind of nuts or seeds they produced, often writing down in her notebook everything they said.

Arnold was amused by her inquisitiveness and interest in learning, while Ed was annoyed and frustrated, and he finally rode off down the line to join up with the reporter and explain his concerns to her. Arnold wasn't bothered by Fleming's incessant questions, because he wasn't really listening; his mind was really focused on what he was going to do with the elk when they found it. That photographer had given him the idea to airlift the animal off the mountain and down to the ground, where he would have a truck waiting. The only problem was how to get the animal to a space where they could lift him out. That was going to require some handling of the animal, and he wasn't sure how much stress it would create on the animal's nervous system. The key factor would be the elk's size, something none on them knew with certainty.

Well, that would be the doctor's call when they found him, and he could call for an airlift from an opening in the trees once they had him cornered. He could call for the truck as they came off the mountain, and they would meet the helicopter at the bottom. He reached for his cell phone so he could make the initial calls and get the helicopter and truck on standby basis, but his hand on his cell phone found it open and empty. He looked down and saw that it was indeed gone and let out a mild oath.

"Son of a ... b—biscuit!"

Dr. Fleming looked at him in dismay. "What on earth is the matter, Mr. Wilcox? Are you okay?"

"No, damn it! I've lost my cell phone. It must have fallen out during that last patch of brush we went through. I felt something brush my leg, and I thought it was a branch. Now I can't call my office and arrange for the airlift or the truck when we get him. This is the fourth one I've lost in the last three months too."

"You can use mine, Mr. Wilcox—here." She handed him her phone, which he gratefully took.

He made his call to the home office, explaining the plan. He told his assistant they didn't know just when they would need the helicopter and the truck, but to have them ready to go on a moment's notice, when he would call back with a location and directions.

He gave the cell phone back to Dr. Fleming with a smile. "I surely do appreciate the loan, Dr. Fleming. I'll pay for the call if you'll tell me how much it was."

"No need for that … Arnold." She smiled at him.

"Well. I surely do thank you for that kindness … Wanda." He smiled back at her.

As they rode along, saying nothing else of importance, Arnold slowly pressed his right leg against the side of his horse, causing it to move slightly closer to Wanda's own Appaloosa.

Behind them, Ed Baxter watched with amusement. He knew that Arnold was a widower of ten years; they had been friends since long before that. He didn't know Dr. Fleming all that well, although he knew her type: lonely, devoted to her work and nothing else, homely as a mud fence and half as interesting to talk with, no social life and no prospects for one. He could see what she was thinking, although he was surprised that Arnold was responding to her. Still, maybe he was tired of being by himself, and he was interested in her for her mind. Baxter laughed to himself, not sure which one of them was getting the best of the bargain.

He looked around as they climbed the faint path up the mountain, admiring the growth and snow-covered branches. Putting the beauty of his surroundings aside, he couldn't help but notice how little clearance there was between the many trees that were growing so thickly on this particular side. This would make it very hard to track this animal, and even harder to get it off the slopes. Baxter raised his arms, aiming an imaginary rifle. Sighting down an invisible scope at an imaginary deer, he visualized the difficulties in making a clear shot.

"Damn," he said to himself. How the hell was he going to do this when he couldn't see around the damn trees, let alone shoot through them? He was going to have just a few seconds to sight it in and then get off the shot—with a dart gun, at that. He was going to have to shoot between branches and tree trunks, each of them with the potential to deflect or stop the dart. He was going to catch hell for this if he missed the elk and allowed it to get away, and he was going to catch even more hell if he accidentally hurt it. If he got really, really lucky and made his shot, his role in this would be minimized and forgotten in no time.

Somehow he had to make his the name that was associated with the success of this project, not the failure of it. He needed to be really accurate, and that required he get some practice in with the gun before he had to take the money shot. Maybe the good doctor cozying up to Arnold might be a good thing. If she was distracted by his friend, then so much the better. If his shot accidentally killed the elk, he could always pass it off as the fault of the dosage. The more he thought about it, the less responsibility he really had in this mess. He was there to make the shot to bring it down, so it could be transported to Arnold's new happy home for the big elk.

He had no animosity for the animal; it was, of course, just an animal. True, it seemed to be smarter than most of the hunters after it, but he had no great opinion of their kind anyway. Most of them were just showing off their big guns and using hunting as an excuse to get together for a month without their wives giving them a hard time. They would meet up, drink until they were drunk, and then would shoot at anything that moved in the forest. They had no respect for nature or the balance of nature, and they just made Baxter's work harder. And this one, this super-smart elk that was making a fool out of every hunter on the mountain, was making his work harder yet. But there was something strange about it—something no one had ever mentioned or come up with an explanation for.

An elk lasts about twenty years in captivity, but only about fifteen years in the wild. This one was going on thirty years, and that didn't make any sense. He supposed it could be the offspring of the original elk, but that made even less sense. Baxter had volunteered for this duty because he wanted to know how this could be. Was this some new evidence that knowledge could be passed on genetically from generation to generation? If it was, he was going to be the man who published this proof. He was going to take a blood sample from the animal and tag it, just in case there was a male offspring that had acquired its skills and knowledge. He had to get the good doctor on his side, so he could talk her into doing some blood tests he would need to prove his theory. He hadn't talked about his theory with anyone yet; he wanted to get some information about this animal before he spoke, so as to avoid looking like an idiot.

But if he was correct, this animal's success was the proof he needed to demonstrate that animals communicated on their own level and were able to remember what they learned. How else could the knowledge one animal acquired from years of surviving hunters be carried over into the next generation of the species? He was going to prove it to the world and, not incidentally, become famous in the process. It was a win-win situation.

Ahead of him, Wanda Fleming was curiously excited, more so by the man riding beside her than she was by the cause she was supporting. She didn't understand what was going on within her, because she had never been interested in men before.

Even in graduate school, she had found her attention and focus was always on her studies more than on dating or even talking to boys. They were just not as interesting as her studies. Her grades were always at the top of her classes, and she knew how the other students viewed her—she was always the mousey one, the bookworm, the one who had "a good personality," although she really didn't. She didn't know how to flirt or wear pretty clothes. She was always plain, and she chose plain, serviceable clothes. Even her dreams and hopes, for the most part, were plain and functional.

She liked to be with animals, because animals didn't complain about her or make her feel less important than them. Animals always appreciated everything she did, and they were loyal and reciprocated her attention with their love. They were never ungrateful or spiteful; even when they hurt her, it was never out of maliciousness, but fear. She could understand their fear of her, because she felt the same fear of being hurt by the same animals that tormented her—other people. She could sense others' contempt of her, even though they might need her knowledge.

But she was always careful to never show her fear. Over time, she learned to mask it with coldness, and, after a while, it became her way of life. The dreams she had once enjoyed as a child and as a teenager—dreams of being loved and of having someone to love in return—had been packed away long ago into a box in a secret closet in her mind, and the door to that closet was kept locked and shuttered. Now, somehow, this man riding alongside her found a way to open that door. How and why, she didn't understand.

There was something about him … about his calm demeanor and his love of animals that had touched her. She had known his name for some time—they had similar interests, and that inevitably led to their having served on many of the same animal-rights campaigns, although never together until now. There was something about him—his voice and mannerisms, his gentleness and strength—that called out to her on some silent, long-forgotten signal. She looked down at his foot, which had accidentally bumped hers, and she noticed something.

"Arnold, I just noticed you aren't wearing spurs. Did you forget yours?" she asked curiously.

"No, ma'am," he answered with that delightful western-mountains accent in his voice. "I don't ever wear them. I figure if I gentle a horse the proper way, neither of us will ever have any use for them. I think they're mostly for show for most people, anyways. I don't think they're much use in an emergency, and if the horse can't get me out of whatever I'm in on his own, hurtin' him ain't gonna help me much. 'Sides, I can get Pablo here to do most anything I want with my knees and legs," he said, patting the big roan on the neck with his hand.

"What's your secret for breaking a horse, if I may ask, Arnold?" Wanda asked him, interested in anything he had to say.

"Well, first off, ma'am—"

"Wanda, please, Arnold."

He smiled and nodded. "Well, first off, Wanda. I don't 'break' horses; that's just an old-thinking saying. All 'breaking a horse' really means is that you've broken his spirit, Wanda. A good horse should be a horseman's partner, not his servant. You want him to help you because he wants to, not because he has to. If he is your partner, you watch out for each other and help each other. You do it right, he'll give you his all every time, and you owe him your full support and care for his needs in return. No, I don't 'break' horses, Wanda. I gentle them and teach them to be partners. No one knows this, but I trained those two Justner boys some time back. That's why Gerry Senior, he hired them away from me when I cut back my operations. He knows what those boys can do. The older one, Bern, he's just like a centaur when he's riding."

Wanda listened to this little speech with rapt attention, and a growing warmth throughout her body. This man was speaking to her about his own innermost thoughts and feelings. She had nothing to compare it to, but if it wasn't love, then it would certainly do for her. Her only fear now was that he was just being nice to her, and he didn't feel the same way for her. But no, he couldn't be saying those thing and not mean them—not him. He had to mean them.

Wanda felt a chill in the air, as if the night were coming. Wanda knew why she had come on this expedition now. She had felt some misgivings at the start of it, and that man Baxter was definitely annoying and rude. She hadn't liked the hunter either; there was something evil about that man. But this man—there was nothing but a good feeling about him, and she felt very safe around him.

Suddenly—and even strangely—that seemed to be very important, and she made the decision to stick close to him for the rest of this trip. That felt like a smart thing to do.

Arnold sensed the veterinarian was developing an interest in him. She wasn't attractive—not in the way he was used to women, but she was intelligent, and she liked animals. She was interested in what he had to say, and that was something he hadn't had much of lately. She wasn't his type, to be sure, but after this long in the barn, did he really have the right to have a "type"? She was a fair rider, he could see that, and she certainly was interested in the same things he was. She was very vulnerable, he could see that too; she probably lived alone all her life and had a cat for a connection to the world.

She would like the animals, Arnold thought. *They would respond to her too.*

"Wanda, just a question if you don't mind."

"Why, no, of course not, Arnold."

"Do you have a pet?"

"Yes, I do. An adorable Siamese cat. He's only three, but he's a very lovely and loving friend. Why do you ask?"

"Oh, I was just curious. Tell me a little bit about you. What are you doing on this trip, Wanda?"

As she began telling him her life story, Arnold listened and stored everything she said. Very few people knew he had this ability to remember everything he heard or saw. He had looked it up once—it was called eidetic, or photographic, memory, and it had gotten him through graduate school with a master's degree in business.

He listened to what she was saying and he could hear the sadness and the loneliness in her life; in some ways, it mirrored his own life since his wife died. He had thrown himself into his work, both on the ranch and at the preserve, in order to occupy his time. He had become very successful financially, as well as enhancing his reputation, but that was only during the daylight hours. At night, it was a different story.

He was either at a meeting for some cause or farm board or the preserve. He looked for ways to be out of the house at night, because his house was haunted—not with real transparent, sheet-wearing Hollywood ghosts, but the real ghosts of his mind and his past; the ghosts of all of his mistakes and could-have-beens that he had survived over the years. He had tried drowning them by drinking, but they had just swam to the surface and laughed at him. He had tried redecorating the house from top to bottom, but they showed up anyway. He thought about selling the ranch, but it was his home, and he had never run from any fight in his life.

He had eventually decided to live with them and just dive into his job headfirst and not leave himself any time to think. He had worked until he fell asleep, night after night, day after day. He hadn't dated, because that felt too much like cheating on Lorraine's memory, and the women he'd brought home didn't like seeing her picture over the bed. He would sometimes take it down when he was going to have someone come over, but this was very cumbersome, and eventually he gave up on it—and on dating as well.

Now, here he was, riding out on what had to be the most insane operation he had ever been involved with, and he was thinking more about this very plain woman beside him than what he was there for. Arnold suspected that she really was interested in him, and he was intrigued by this. He had known other women who were interested in what he owned and who he knew, but this woman seemed to be only interested in who *he* was inside. It was a strange feeling, and a welcome one, but he needed to be certain before he went out on a limb and took the risk of showing her who he was and what his faults were.

Just maybe, if the gods were smiling on him, his luck had turned, and he could find his future on this mountain. But he was too old a hand to jump into the river without knowing just how deep the water was. He was going to need to be very careful and take it slow.

"Wanda, you look a little chilly, young lady. Would you like me to get your coat off your saddle and put it on you?" he asked gallantly.

"Oh, would you, Arnold? That would be so nice of you; I am getting a little cold. I think it is the wind."

As he slowed down and leaned over to untie the cords holding her jacket, he heard Ed behind him snickering. He didn't say anything, but gave Ed a look that shut him up fast. Ed lost his smile and pulled up, dropping back in line to ride beside the photographer.

"Arnold, can I ask you a question?" she asked him in a little girl voice.

"Certainly you can, Wanda. What is it?"

"Well, I was just wondering, do you ever let anyone call you Arnie? I mean, if it isn't too personal or you aren't comfortable with that nickname …" she said hesitantly, as his reaction was one of definite hesitation.

"Well, Wanda, it's like this: someone used to call me that, but it has been a long time since I heard that name." His voice was soft and low, and the note of sadness in it was impossible to miss. There was a silence between them that seemed to go on for several minutes, but was in fact only a few seconds long. Suddenly, his tone improved, and he smiled at her, a heartfelt smile of great warmth, accompanied by a glow and a light in his eyes. "Wanda, I think I'd like that a lot. Yep. I'd be right pleased to have you call me Arnie."

He began to feel like something inside him was waking up—something that had been asleep for a long time. Maybe he would be going home with the hope of something more than he came with.

Farther back in the line, Axel Justner was trying his hardest to impress the pretty young reporter, but to no avail. She was busy talking into her tape recorder and not looking at him. He was determined to get her to notice him, but now it was becoming a challenge. She was a pretty thing—petite and blonde, with a trim figure and a perfect smile. She seemed to have no interest in that young fellow she was traveling with, although he was obviously sniffing hard on her trail. He wasn't in his element now, however—he was in Axel's.

Axel was determined to win her over—at least, for this trip, because there was always another pretty thing coming along later. He kind of liked the photographer; he was a good rider, and he seemed like a likable fellow. He was just in the way of Axel's plans. He decided to try and impress her with his riding skills, since that was his best talent. Slowly moving up to a trot alongside her, Axel swung a leg over his saddle and started riding, facing backward, looking at her, face to face.

Putting as much of a twang in his voice as he could, Axel tried to start up a conversation. "Howdy, ma'am. You look like you don't do too much ridin' to me. This year yore first time aboard a hoss?"

She smiled and looked right back at him, pressing the stop button on her recorder. "Mr. Justner, I heard you talking back at the corral, so I know that isn't how you really talk. You can drop the 'aw shucks' routine. It isn't going to impress me one bit," she said in a sugary tone.

With an embarrassed grin, Axel hesitated, and then he laughed at himself. "Well, it usually works on the less sophisticated and impressionable fillies. But I see it won't cut any ice with you, ma'am."

"No, it won't. If you want to talk to me, talk to me like the intelligent individual I expect you are, and we will get along just fine," April said, a little more naturally this time.

"Well, ma'am, it is going to be a long ride on this mountain, and I'd kinda like to talk with a reporter about what we are doing. If you wouldn't mind talking with me, that is."

"You're a good rider, Mister ...?"

"Oh, I'm sorry. It's Axel, Axel Justner. That's my brother, Bern, up front. He's the tracker and the real rider in the family. Put me on a horse, and I'm a good rider, and I can get the horse to do just about anything. But get Bern on a horse, and they become one and the same. Sometimes he amazes even me with what he can get a horse to do. But, hey, I wanted to talk about you and me, not Bern. What are you doing here on this ride? Are you doing a feature on this mysterious big elk, or are you just along for the atmosphere? Tell me about yourself," he invited her.

"I'd rather hear about you, Axel. You and this mountain you live on," April countered.

"Sure enough, ma'am, I'll be right glad to tell you anything you want to know." With an easy movement, he swung back around in the saddle, facing forward once more. As they talked, he was quick to point out the squirrels running through the trees and searching for hidden nuts for a meal, and the snowshoe rabbits that quietly munched on roots or the few leaves still green. They talked for several hours about the history of the mountain and of his childhood growing up in the valley. He talked about the lessons he had learned from the rancher, Arnold Wilcox, and how the older man had served as a substitute father after their own father had abandoned them when they were not yet in their teens. Axel talked about his mother and how she had worked for Mr. Wilcox as his cook until she passed away. He talked about his own dreams and hopes of owning his own ranch someday.

Axel told her of the frustration he often felt growing up in his brother's shadow, and he told her all the stories he had grown up with about the mountain and about the people who lived and played on it. This is when April started to really pay attention to what he was saying.

"Tell me more about the old days on the mountain, Axel. Tell me more of those old stories you grew up hearing—you know, the ones from the beginning of the legends," April urged.

"Why do you want to hear about those, miss?" Axel asked her.

"Call me April, Axel. I want to hear about them because that is why I'm here on this ride—to uncover the story behind the legends, that's what all good reporters do. They dig up old stories and ask questions to fit them to new theories," she said excitedly. "You can help me with this story, if you will just tell me all the stories you heard growing up around here!"

"Well, I'd much rather be talking about me, if you don't mind," he said with a grin.

"We can do that too, Axel, but I really need to hear about those early days on the mountain," she said entreatingly.

"I can do that too, April," Axel said eagerly.

"I think you need to go help your brother, Axel; he's having a hard time finding the animal's trail," came a stern voice from behind her.

April turned to see the guide, Gerry Bruce, Sr., sitting on his horse behind her. He wasn't exactly glaring at Axel, but he was the boss, so there was nothing for Axel to do but tip his hat to her and put his horse into a lope to the front of the line.

"You shouldn't distract the boy from his duties, miss. He has a job to do, you know, and it isn't to talk about gossip and rumors," Gerry told her, politely but firmly.

As he rode along in silence beside the reporter, his attitude conveyed a sense of peace and calm. He would smile at her and point out the sights as they walked along the trail, but inside, where no one could see, his mind was racing in search of answers.

Gerry wondered how this was going to end up. He had convinced himself many years ago that he was never going to think about that day again. Now, here he was, some thirty years later, retracing his steps with the same lunatic that had created his nightmare. *It is worse this time,* he thought, *because my son and a dozen or so more innocent people are being dragged into this mess. Would it be any different if I had done the right thing back then?* he wondered.

He couldn't say this with any certainty, but he knew he wouldn't be here now if he had. *This reporter is certain to turn up certain details I would like to keep buried if she keeps digging, but I know that trying to pressure her to lay off will only make her more determined to dig into it further.* Somehow, he had to take her focus off that skier and keep it on this trip.

I really can't avoid discussing the past—after all, that is where the legend of this super-smart elk comes from. But maybe I can do it in a way that keeps her looking where I want her to look. He wanted to get her to focus on Warner Barney, but without implicating himself and getting his son involved. *I know I can't point her in that direction; that would be too obvious. But what would her reaction be if she thought she was getting something out of me that I didn't intend to say? What if I dropped a little crumb and allowed her to pressure me into giving up the entire loaf? Okay, that could work,* he thought to himself. *While I look like I'm steering her away from the subject, I'll let slip some little detail that can lead her back to the person really responsible for this mess. I just hope his ego is still big enough to overrule my part in that fiasco years ago. But how to drop that crumb—and what should it look like?* he pondered.

Gerry was troubled, but he didn't want to let it show. There was no connection that anyone knew of between the elk and the other legend of the mountain—that mysterious phantom skier. Gerry believed there was a connection, but he couldn't prove it, nor did he care. What he wanted to do was protect his son from any harm that Barney might create with his obsession about catching the animal. He had to do it carefully, though; he couldn't look anything but reluctant in giving up information.

I know, I'll let her catch me in a contradiction, and then she will confront me about it. But what kind of a contradiction will work? It has to be something small but significant, something that will lead her where I want her to go.

Pleased with himself, he began to relax a little. He then began to smile as he realized he didn't have to let her catch him directly—he could tell her something that he knew Barney or someone else would say differently.

Yes, that will be better. Tell a lie, and let someone else catch the lie and tell her about it. That photographer—I could tell him something about Barney's behavior that ... no, not about Barney. That would be too direct and too dangerous. I could tell him something about the past hunts I have taken people on and how I had never run into the elk until after ... after ... after what? After someone killed an animal in a protected area? Yes, that will do nicely. Some hunter crossed the line and took an animal in a no-hunt zone. That's good; it doesn't name anyone, and it doesn't point any fingers at anyone. It also provides a positive theory for a ghost elk—but to really sell it, I'll have to talk it down ...

He would have to downplay this as just a smart animal, nothing more than that. That way he didn't look like he was blaming anyone or buying into the ghost story—either one of them.

His path decided, Gerry cleared his throat and got started on redirecting the reporter's attention. "Miss Martens, just why are you here, if you don't mind my asking?"

"Mr. Bruce, I am here to write the story of this hunt from everyone's point of view. I intend to let my readers know what it is like being on a hunt of this nature. I want to talk to everyone involved and get their perspective and contribution to the success of this venture," she said with enthusiasm.

"Miss, you surely don't believe in any of these stories of this animal being some sort of a ghost, do you?" he asked casually.

April laughed nervously and responded before he even finished his question. "Of course not, Mr. Bruce. There's no such thing as ghosts; they're just stories to explain coincidences."

He was a tracker by profession, and so he picked up on her hasty answer. April had answered quickly—much too quickly for Gerry's taste, meaning she was suspicious or had some knowledge he did not have about one or both of the legends. This could change his plans ...

or make them easier, perhaps … but he needed to find out what she knew before he went any further.

"Do you believe in ghosts, Mr. Bruce?"

"Well, miss, up here we have a lot of old legends and stories, and all of them come from something that someone saw or did—but they get so built up over time, it's often hard to know what's real and what's legend. Like they said in that old John Wayne movie, 'When the truth meets the legend, print the legend.' So to answer you real truthful-like, I try to keep an open mind on all of it.

"If you want to learn about the legends, you should spend some time talking with old Charley Weeks tonight at the fire. He knows them all, both the big and the small ones. Hell, he probably started most of them one way or another," he said with a laugh.

He was still laughing as he tipped his hat and turned away to ride to the back of the line, leaving her to wonder about his answer.

As he rode away, he wondered what she knew and how he was going to find out what she knew without tipping his own hand. He trotted his mount toward the back of the line, looking for the photographer as he passed the others, nodding and answering random questions about the landscape and the animals that were hiding from their passage through the trees. He spied the photographer about four riders back, talking with the ranger about something, and the ranger appeared to be annoyed. He decided not to break that up just now, and he pulled up beside the ranger's assistant, a real pretty thing who looked to be at home in a saddle.

"Having a nice ride, miss?" he asked.

"It's really beautiful and serene up here, Mr. Bruce," she responded.

"Just plain Gerry, miss, if you please. My dad, he was Mr. Bruce. Or you can call me G, that's what my friends call me."

"Well then, G, that's what I'll do too," Eileen said, flashing him a big smile. She was about to say something else when she was interrupted by a shot that came from the front of the line. Gerry threw his horse into a run and headed for the source.

Warner had been riding by himself all morning, and he was

building up a real resentment for anyone on this ride whose last name wasn't Barney. He was impatient for this day to end, because he was going to sneak away after dark to join up with his other guide at their prearranged location and get this damn animal all by himself. These damn bleeding hearts were slowing him down and were sure to get in his way. And that damn ranger, trying to box him into this stupid plan to save and preserve the animal. Well, he was going to preserve him, all right—preserve him right where he belongs, which was on his wall with his other trophy quality kills from over the years.

He hadn't counted on all the wranglers and the cook and the other inconveniences, so he was going to have to be careful slipping out of camp tonight. With all of those damn people milling about, someone might hear him and spoil things. He needed to be particularly stealthy as he collected his stuff when he left. He started to think about what he might have to leave behind, and immediately dismissed this line of thinking. Why should he forego any of his creature comforts just to avoid that ego-inflated boy scout? There was no law he was breaking, and even if he was posted off the mountain, there were a lot of other hunting ranges he could go to, and he didn't need this backwoods pile of rocks once he had taken down that magnificent animal. Let the boy scout see him leave—what could he do?

Turning his attention to the real issue, finding the animal, Warner began looking for some signs they were in its territory.

He scanned each tree they passed, looking for scarring to indicate that an animal had rubbed its antlers against it earlier in the year, but all he saw were bear scratches, moss, and old bird nests. He saw plenty of discarded antlers from past seasons, so he knew hunters had not been here for a long time, but there was no trace of the animal he was seeking. He didn't see the man in front of him, Gerry's son, making much of an effort to look for a sign, unless one counted him staring up in the trees and gazing at the ground now and then as tracking. Warner knew he was going to have to do this himself if it was going to get done. But he still had time; they weren't in the thick of the woods yet, although he could see the forest high above him to the left.

Right now he was thinking about his old guide and what had happened the last time he was here.

Gerry Bruce Sr. had let him down—had yellowed out on him just when he needed him most. Gerry used to be a good tracker, but now he was keeping himself apart, not even coming over to say hello when he had driven up. It was hard to understand that man; he seemed to be nursing a grudge of some sort, when it was really Warner's right to be carrying a grudge.

After all, it was Gerry who had almost cost him his trophy back then, all because he didn't want Warner to have a little drink. Of course, it had been the other boy scouts who had really tried to stop him. But Gerry hadn't helped him at all, and had even abandoned him after he got the buck. Now he was getting in his way again, just like before. Somehow, he had to get his "friend" out of the way before he left the camp to join up with his real guide later tonight. But now, he was getting …

Warner stopped. *There!* Off to the left, there was a movement in the trees.

He slowly pulled his rifle out of the scabbard, slowing his horse to drop back behind Gerry Junior and the wrangler in front of him. He slowly edged his way to the side of the trail, keeping his eye on where he had seen the movement. There was something there, he was sure of it, but he couldn't get a clear look at just what it was. Warner kept the rifle down at his side and out of sight of the two in front of him and the rest of the riders behind him. He kept his eyes on the tree line, looking for any movement that might give away the animal's position, whatever it was. He knew he would have one shot, so he had to make it a good one. He ignored the inane conversation between the two men in front of him, his attention focused on picking out the target to the side. He used an old trick of not staring right at the site of the movement, but at the general area, and allowing his peripheral vision to pick up any movement.

Suddenly, about six feet to the right of where he saw the first motion, Warner saw a shadow moving to the left. He eased the rifle up, keeping his eye on the motion and estimating the distance and angle needed to make the shot. He heard one of the men call out to him, but Warner ignored him as he brought the rifle to his shoulder and lined up his shot. He heard the man call out to him again, more urgently this time, but he ignored this call also. He heard the horse coming closer as he squeezed the trigger and felt the rifle recoil against his shoulder. He saw the animal, a big buck, but not a red-coated buck, jump and run for ten feet before falling down in the distance.

Before he could lower the rifle, a big hand grabbed the barrel and twisted it out of his hands. As he reacted to this, another big hand grabbed him by the shoulder and pulled him off his horse. When he got to his feet, Gerry Junior was standing inches from his face, rage stamped across his face. The wrangler was holding his rifle, barrel pointed down, and was jacking the remainder of his shells out of the magazine.

"What in the hell do you think you're doing?" Gerry Junior roared at Warner Barney.

"Just one shot fired, boss," said Bern, off to the left.

"Give me back my rifle! Right now!" Warner demanded as he reached for it. Bern just stepped back out of his arms length, and as Warner began to step toward him, Gerry Junior reached out and grabbed him by the shoulder of his coat, spinning him around.

"I'm talking to you, mister. Don't you turn away from me! We've got a problem here and we're not going one step farther until I am satisfied you understand what the rules are, and that they apply to you as well!" Gerry said, trying to get his temper under control as all of his father's warnings about Warner Barney came back into his thoughts.

Son of a bitch, I should have listened to the old man, he said to himself.

Warner was unfazed by this outburst, except to look disdainfully at him.

"What's your problem, Bruce? All I did was get us some fresh meat," he said casually, pointing toward the deer on the ground off in the distance.

When Gerry nodded at Bern, he nodded back and tossed the rifle to his boss. As Bern swung up into the saddle to go check on the deer, he heard hoof beats and looked over to see the ranger and the senior Bruce coming hard for the spot he was just leaving. Bern decided the situation was in hand, so he spun his mount and headed over to the deer. He decided this was as good a time as any to get away, and he spurred his horse to move out faster before the main fight really began.

Gerry Senior reined his horse up to a stop beside his son's horse, but he didn't dismount. He knew if he took a hand in this, he would be sending a message that his son wasn't in charge, and Gerry had no desire to undermine his authority here with his riders. He let his right hand slowly slide down to his side, not resting on the butt of his gun, but not resting far from it either. *I have to control myself,* he thought. *This isn't the 1890s—it's the 1990s, and I can't just shoot someone for being a problem.* Besides, if he was going to do that, then he wasn't any different than the skunk he was shooting. Besides, he had a better and more fitting end in mind for Barney. He relaxed and watched his son deal with the troublemaker.

"I'm talking to you, Mr. Barney, not my father," Gerry Junior said harshly as he saw Barney's eyes lock onto someone behind him. He hadn't seen his father arrive; he just knew he would be there, backing him up. "I'm telling you again, Mr. Barney, I am in charge here, and you *will* follow my rules, or you will be off this trip immediately! Do you understand me, mister? Now, what in the hell do you think you were doing, shooting into the woods like that? You had no authority to—"

"I don't need anyone's authority to shoot when I see my target, Mr. Bruce. I'm the real hunter here, and I will shoot when I damn well want to. This is my hunt, and I paid for it, so I will shoot whenever I damn well feel like it," Barney said contemptuously.

"Actually, Mr. Barney, you will not shoot whenever you feel like it, because although you may have paid for it, this trip is under the supervision of the park authority, which is me. And I must confess, Mr. Barney, you are wearing your welcome very thin on this mountain," Oliver said coldly. "Now, this time you didn't cause any real problems, so I will let you off with a warning. But I assure you, the next time you try to get around the rules, you will be off this mountain in an instant. You better not let me catch you trying anything like this again," Oliver warned him.

Gerry Junior looked over at Oliver with a glare, but he did not say anything.

"Mr. Barry," Warner said after a moment, "I give you my word, you will not catch me doing anything like this again," he said smugly.

To Gerry Senior, who knew Warner very well, this sounded like a promise only to not get caught. He decided that he would let his son handle this, but he needed to keep a closer eye on Barney from now on. Seeing the tension cooling down, he wheeled his horse around and headed back to the cluster of riders that had gathered thirty feet back.

"All over folks, nothing to see, except for Bern comin' in with fresh meat for tonight. Charley! Charley, Bern's coming in with a fresh buck; you want to give him a hand dressing it out? Then, when you are done, you two head for Small Creek Meadow. Take the Willoughby Cut, and you'll get there before us. We'll make our first camp there," he called out to the cook, who nodded and headed over to a nearby tree to tie up the pack string. Once there, Charley dismounted and began rummaging through his packs, looking for his skinning knife. Gerry Senior herded the rest of the riders toward Gerry Junior, the ranger, and Barney.

As he led them off, April just sat there, looking back at Charley and Bern. "I think I'd rather watch Mr. Weeks and Mr. Justner dress out the deer, Mr. Bruce. I think it would be interesting to see and write about, if you don't mind," April said.

"No, ma'am, I don't mind, but it's sure to be a mite bloody and messy, just so you know. You do what they tell you, and I'll see you later tonight." He tipped his hat and rode off behind the others, leaving her to walk over to Charley.

Adam held back, expecting her to call him to take pictures of the dressing out of the deer, even though he didn't want to see it. To his great relief—and to his even greater surprise—she just waved him off. Although he was relieved, he was very curious about why April didn't want him around while she talked to the cook and wrangler. She wasn't one to be nice without a good reason; he had learned that much about her. She had something on her mind, but he didn't know how to find out without asking her directly, and he didn't really think she would tell him the truth if he did. With a sigh, he turned and followed Gerry up the path without looking back, leaving her to her own plans.

April walked her horse over to where Charley was still digging around in his packs, muttering to himself as he did. Hearing another horse closing on him, he looked up to see April dismounting. Quickly, he moved over to her.

"Miss, don't tie up your horse next to my mules; these here mules don't get along with horses. Tie your horse over to that there tree." He pointed off to the left where there was a small stand of elms. "Then you can come along with me to the deer, iffen you want to see what it's like to field dress a deer. But I got to tell you, it's a mite messy and not for the faint of stomach," Charley warned her.

"Hell, it's good training for eatin' your cooking, Charley. This way, once she eats her venison, she'll know that it really is meat, no matter what it looks like then," Bern teased him. He had left the body of the deer in the clearing, about sixty feet from the mules and April. With an exclamation of glee, Charley turned around from the packs, holding a skinning knife in his hand.

"You be quiet, youngster, or I'll use this on you and serve you for dinner," he said with a laugh. Charley held out his hand to April, and she took it, noting how the roughness of his skin contrasted with the gentleness of his grip.

"Why didn't you bring the deer over here, Mr. Justner?"

"It would not have been a good idea, Miss Martens. The mules would not have liked it, miss; the smell of blood would have worried them some," Bern explained with a laugh as they walked over to where he had left the carcass of the deer.

"And the b'ars," Charley added with a snort.

"The bars?" she asked, puzzled by what *bars* he meant.

"He means bears, miss. If I bought the deer closer to the mules, and it attracted any attention by some bear who wants a last meal before he goes in for the winter, we could have a big problem. I'd rather have the bear come to the meat out there, where we can see him coming and give him room to be what he is, without giving him any challenge. This far away, miss, the mules can smell him coming, and we can get out of his way," Bern explained as he threw a rope over a nearby branch he had decided was thick enough to support the deer's weight.

He tied the end of the rope around the deer's hind feet and began hauling it up until its front feet cleared the ground, and then he tied the rope off to the trunk of the tree.

She watched as he walked over to the pack, took out a short-handled shovel, and returned to the deer. He steadied the swinging deer, held the shovel directly under it, and began digging a deep hole beneath the head

"Miss, you might better stand back a bit; this here work might get a trifle messy once we get to skinning and dressing it out, an' you won't be wantin' to git any of this hyar blood and guts over yore nice new clothes," Charley cautioned her.

April stepped back quickly, heeding his warning. "What are you doing that for?" she asked him.

"To catch the blood," was all he said.

As Charley took his skinning knife and cut the deer's throat, the blood began to pour out and into the hole.

As Charley and Bern began the dirty task of field dressing the deer, she watched as long as she could before she felt her stomach do a little flip as the blood began to fill the hole—but it passed as Bern went to work.

When the blood finally quit dripping, Charley began to fill in the hole with the dirt Bern had piled beside it and tamped it down with the shovel to make sure there was no seepage. Surveying the results, he turned and walked two feet away, where he cut out a square of sod from the ground and carried it back to the newly filled hole. He adjusted its position with his boot, and, after he was satisfied with his results, he patted it into place with the shovel.

Bern untied the rope from the tree trunk and slowly lowered the drained deer to the grass. He then took the knife and made a cut from just above the animal's genital area to just below the ribcage.

As Bern worked quickly and efficiently Charley explained what he was doing. "First thing you do, miss, is open the animal up. That's what he just did. Now he's got to be careful he doesn't cut into the intestines, because that would be a big problem."

"Because of the risk of contamination?" she asked.

"Yeah, and because of the smell too," Bern added. "If I was going to have this buck mounted, I wouldn't cut any further, but we are interested in the meat only, so …" He extended the cut up the middle and rolled the deer onto its side, allowing the guts to spill out. They stopped after a second, so he picked up his knife and removed the fat that held the intestines in. He was very careful to not puncture the deer's bladder in the cavity at the deer's hips to avoid contamination of the meat. He continued to slice away the rest of the abdominal cavity's contents and pulled out the heart and lungs.

By this time, April was facing Charley and talking to him about the mountain, no longer interested in what Bern was doing. Bern glanced back over his shoulder to see her engrossed in Charley's tall tales, so he smiled and went back to work. With no distractions, he had the deer dressed out in a short time. Bern stood up, stretched his legs and arms, and threw the rope around the deer's hind feet over the tree branch again and pulled it up in order to skin it.

April looked behind her and saw Bern. When she realized what he was about to do, she turned away quickly.

Charley explained this. "Bern, he knows how to turn a deer hide into the softest leather you can image. I 'spect he'll turn that into a vest or a coat by next year."

April had worn a doeskin vest before and had enjoyed the feel of other deerskin items, but this was far more information than she had wanted to know. She watched as Bern cut the remaining meat off the carcass into sections, including both of the legs, the hindquarters, the ribs, and every other usable part, before rolling them all up into the hide. He tied the pack up with a cord hanging from his back pocket and stood up, stretching his arms and legs once again.

Looking down at the remains of the deer, he leaned over, broke the antlers off, and put them on top of the pack. "Okay, Charley, I'm done here. I figure I'll leave everything for the animals to clean up, and that will help keep them away from us too. I'll load this on Beulah—she does the best with a fresh kill—and then we can get going," Bern told them.

April didn't respond, as she was deep into one of Charley's tall tales, but Charley nodded, never losing his place in his story or his position next to April. Bern just smiled and, lifting the heavy pack with a heave, threw it over his shoulder and walked the short distance back to the mules. Recognizing the tall tale Charley was spinning, Bern shook his head and dropped the pack onto the frame that was strapped onto Beulah's back. Holding it in place with one hand, he used the other to pull up the straps that tied the load securely in place. Once he had it in place, he used both hands to snug the straps up and tie them off.

"Okay, folks, we're ready to go," he called out to them.

"I'll finish this story once we gets going again, missy," Charley promised her.

Enthralled with his tales, April mounted her horse and moved over beside him. Bern untied his horse and, swinging up into the saddle from a standing position, took the lead rope and headed off into the trees, Charley and April falling in line behind him. None of them looked back at the meadow, their attention being focused on the trail in front of them and on catching up with the rest of the team. Had anyone turned around, they would have seen a large animal come out into the open from the other side of the meadow.

The big female bear with the silver hump on its back slowly walked out toward the remains of the deer. She stood over them, sniffed the air, and dropped down to feed. When she was finished, she stood up on her hind legs, sniffed the air again, dropped back to the ground, and slowly walked over to the spot where the deer had been drained of its blood. She pawed the ground where the new sod had been laid on top of the hole, threw back her head, and let out a roar, defying anyone to invade her territory. Her challenge going unanswered, she snorted and slowly followed the hunters into the woods.

As the bear shuffled off, its passage was observed by another large animal. This animal slowly walked toward the remains of the bear's meal, its head up, taking in the scent of the bear, the dead deer, and the mules. There was also another scent, fainter and fading, but still a warning—it was the scent of the dreaded and feared humans. The animal slowly followed the bear, pausing only to lower its head at the spot of the buried blood.

The bear was a survivor of many years, and her eyes weren't the best, but her nose and ears were still working fine. She stopped and stood up, turning around to sniff the air behind her for any trace of danger or food, but she heard and saw nothing of consequence behind her except a swirling dust cloud. She dropped down and continued on her way, following the scent of the fresh meat ahead of her.

At the back of the first group of riders, Oliver was talking with Eileen about Warner shooting the deer. "I'm telling you, Eileen, that man is dangerous. He doesn't care who he hurts to get what he wants. He's going to put someone at risk for sure before we're done. We're only on the first day, and already he's throwing his weight around. I'm going to have to keep a close eye on him if I want to get us out of this in one piece."

"I have confidence in you, Oliver. I know you'll do the right thing. I put my faith in you, sugar," she said with a pat on his arm.

"Thanks, Eileen. I need to go find Gerry and talk with him about this situation. We'll all need to work together on this if we hope to make a success of it, and everyone here seems to have their own agenda right now. I just don't trust that man worth a damn; he's poison, and I don't want anyone getting sick—particularly you. Hey! There's Gerry, come on," he said, urging his horse forward. "Gerry! Wait up a minute," he called out.

Oliver and Eileen rode up to Gerry Senior, who sat there, waiting for them. "Well, Oliver, I'll bet right about now you're wishing you hadn't come along on this party," he said sourly.

"Maybe, but I'm here now and I intend to do what I can to see that nothing else goes wrong," Oliver replied grimly.

"Well, just so you know, I expected this kind of behavior out of our man, and I have taken precautions to make sure he doesn't get away with anything on this trip," Gerry said, looking forward to a spot somewhere out of sight.

"I have to agree with you about him, but I didn't have any way to stop him from coming that I could defend in court without costing me more than I can afford. I have my own precautions, Gerry, and I will use them if I have to. What kind of precautions have you taken, if I may ask?"

Gerry changed the subject without answering him. "I have to protect my son, as well as the welfare of those who work for me, Oliver. They rely on me, and I will not let them down or put them at risk—not for money. Not ever."

There was a long silence between them, broken at last by Eileen's forced laugh. "Boys, we're sitting here, and the rest of the party is leaving us behind. I suggest we'll need to get caught up with them if we're going to prevent anything else from happening to anyone."

The two men looked at each other, and Gerry smiled, "I guess the little lady's got the right idea, Oliver. How do you feel about a little running?"

"After you, my friend." All three began urging their horses into a run, and they very quickly caught up with the group ahead.

At the front of the group, Axel glanced at his watch. He looked up at the sky and estimated the daylight remaining. He thought to himself that this was turning into something other than the good time he had anticipated. That man firing a rifle without warning or giving any notice was just plain stupid, and firing into a shadow without having a clear target was dangerous. It could have been anything ... or anyone. For someone who was supposed to be such an experienced hunter, it was a very boneheaded amateurish move. Anyone who would make those kinds of mistakes was capable of making other equally dangerous mistakes.

Axel decided he needed to concentrate on this matter and leave the flirting by the wayside for this trip. He had seen his brother's reaction to him, and he hadn't seen his brother that mad in many years. He remembered what had happened to Nelson when Bern lost his temper with him. He was certain Nelson was not going to forget it either. He had always steered clear of Bern after he came out of the hospital and had moved away shortly after that. Because Bern had been defending himself, no charges were ever filed against him, but no one ever trifled with him after that. No, he needed to keep his mind on the business at hand this trip; the temporary relationship with that cute reporter would just have to wait until this mess was over.

Farther back, the three conservationists were also uneasy. Arnold Wilcox was wondering what he had gotten himself into. He was very concerned—not just for himself, but for the others, and particularly for Wanda. He had felt a little spark from a fire he had long thought was nothing but cold ashes, and this fanatic Barney was quickly becoming a threat to it.

Aside from meeting Wanda, this venture seemed to be off to a bad start, encumbered as it was with the very unstable, unsavory specimen that was Warner Barney. Arnold was a hunter himself, and he knew the difference between a careless mistake and recklessness when he saw it—and he knew this was the more dangerous of the two. A man could get careless at times when his attention was drifting, but this usually disappeared when a close call occurred to get him to refocus.

Recklessness, however … that never went away. It was a part of the individual's personality, and it was a very dangerous character trait for everyone around him. Arnold was worried. This man, Warner Barney, showed a lot of that dangerous trait of recklessness, and that meant he would bear watching very carefully every single minute of this trip—for everyone's safety.

Ed Baxter wasn't worried; he was just annoyed. *That man has probably made our job harder with his reckless shooting, scaring the animals away. He's a troublemaker on top of that, not a very social person, and not interested in anything that I have to say about the animal. He's just a glory hunter looking for a new trophy, and not at all appreciative of our purpose in making this expedition. This man is definitely not someone I wanted to ever see or associate with again after this miserable trip is over,* Ed thought to himself. He sniffed in disdain as these thoughts ran through his mind. *This was what happens to me for agreeing to deal with riffraff like that hunter and spinster veterinarian. I never should have agreed to come on this trip.*

Wanda, of the three conservationists, was probably the least concerned about the purpose of their trip right now. She was wondering where her newfound relationship with the big rancher was going to lead. She had long given up on the idea of ever falling in love, and here she was, thinking about a man she had only really known for a few hours. She laughed to herself, thinking how her friends would never believe what was going on in her head—or her heart.

That unpleasant man with the rifle, she contemplated. *I don't trust him to do what he said he was going to do. I'm worried that ill-mannered man is going to do something that will upset Arnie, and maybe cause him some stress. I don't want anything to upset him, for purely selfish reasons. If he's upset, he won't be thinking about me and wouldn't have time to talk with me. Arnie is too professional to let personal feelings interfere with his work, and he said he would need to put all his energy into dealing with that threat to the animal we are here to save.*

She had to do something to show Arnie she could be useful to him. Somehow, she had to do something to keep that dreadful hunter from causing Arnie any problems on this trip. She vowed to keep her eyes open and look for an opening for her to do something to keep that evil man from hurting the elk or her precious Arnie. With a newfound sense of purpose in her life, Wanda sat up straighter in the saddle and made a mental note to herself to sign up for riding lessons when she got back. Or, even better, she would ask Arnie to give her the lessons himself. She began to smile at this idea.

The elder Bruce was thinking pretty much the same thing—but about someone else—as he felt a coldness in the air that had very little to do with the falling temperature. He looked around at the many leafless trees, thinking that their waving branches seemed to be warning him to stay out of their territory. He knew this was nonsense and just his imagination working overtime—his imagination for sure, or just possibly it was his guilty conscience coming back to life as he moved ever closer to the scene of his worst hour.

Camp was just a little farther; he would then have a talk with his son about this situation. In the meantime, there was nothing more he could do beyond what he had already done.

Payment in full past due, he thought.

He heard some noises to his left, and his head whipped around to see that it was just some birds taking flight, likely scared by the sounds of their horses and loud talking. *Just my chickens coming home to roost,* he thought ruefully to himself as his horse trotted steadily onward toward the site of the first night's camp.

Warner was very satisfied with himself. *My shot—and it was a snap shot at that—was a good one. I brought down the deer. That annoying boy scout tried to take the fun out of it for me by puffing himself up and threatening to send me home. Well, I'm not going to have to worry about him after tonight. Some time tonight, my real guide will meet up with me, and I'll get down to cases,* he thought to himself. *Brass cases, to be precise—.44 Magnum cases, ejected from my favorite Marlin Model '94 rifle, right after I put one through the animal's heart.* This witticism brought a smile to his face.

I'm here for one purpose and for one purpose only. That's to bag that trophy animal for my den. I don't give a damn what all those bleeding hearts think they're here for—they're not real men anyway. A real man takes what he wants and doesn't let anything get in his way. Let them go on spouting whatever nonsense they want to about this "noble beast," because when the morning comes, I'm going to be well on my way to getting what I want.

He'd show them all what he was made of and how a real man acted. Just let anyone try to stop him. He smiled to himself as he thought about the look on their faces when they saw him with the head of the elk. He would show all of those clowns who was the real big hunter on this mountain. He particularly was looking forward to showing that boy scout who had the real power in this world.

Adam was worried about April—not about her being alone with the wrangler and the cook, because he had no worries they would do anything, but because he was sure that lunatic they had brought along was certain to do something to put them all in danger somehow. He was worried April would say something to that madman to stir him up in the name of her story, and then there would be hell to pay. Adam didn't know if he would be able to protect her from herself. He had confidence in the ranchers, both father and son; and the big man, Wilcox—well, he seemed to be a decent person too. Of course, the ranger would be watching out for all of them, but they were no match for that crazy hunter. He was dangerous, Adam was dead certain.

Poor choice of words, he reflected.

The two wranglers would obviously do whatever their boss told them to do, so they would help if it came down to that. Adam decided he'd talk to the ranger about this later tonight after dinner and idly wondered what fresh deer steak would taste like cooked over an open flame.

Oliver was deep in thought as they approached the campsite, so at first he didn't notice that they weren't going into an empty camp. As he rode into it, however, he saw that the cook and wrangler were already setting up on the tents, and there was someone he didn't know sitting by the fire pit, tossing branches and kindling. The man never looked up, and he didn't speak, but by the time Oliver had dismounted and walked over to introduce himself, the man was gone. He looked around but didn't see him, so he shrugged his shoulders and made a mental note to keep an eye out at dinner.

He went back to the horses to look for Eileen and find out what tasks Gerry Junior wanted him to take care of. He found the younger Bruce in a deep conversation with his lead wrangler, Bern Justner. Both men looked somewhere between worried and angry.

"What's up, Gerry?" Oliver asked. Bern looked at Gerry, who just nodded.

"Mr. Barry, while I was working my way in here with the cook and that reporter, I came across the trail of another pack string, and it was headed in this direction."

"What's the problem with that?"

"Well, for one thing, there were six horses, but only one being ridden—the others were pack animals," Bern continued.

"And for another," Gerry added, "there's not supposed to be anyone else up here right now. Barry, did you give out any permits for hunting in the Wolverine or Bearclaw Ridge area?"

"No, I haven't."

"Then whoever's out there is there without anyone's permission or authority. It's an unknown element, and I've already got one out-of-control element to worry about. This doesn't make sense, and it worries me," Gerry said, clearly annoyed.

"What are you going to do about it?" Oliver asked, concerned about what this might mean to their project.

"For the moment, nothing. They could be innocent, or it could be trouble. I think we'll post a guard on the camp tonight; we'll say it's for animals. Don't say anything about this to the others, okay?" Gerry said. "I'll tell Dad what we've discovered. You have a good time at dinner. I think Charley is the entertainment tonight. This is likely to be the last easy day you have on this trip."

Oliver nodded and walked back to the main part of the camp, amazed at how fast it was coming together. He found the older Bruce unsaddling his horse, and he headed over to him.

"Can I do anything to help out, Gerry?" he asked.

"Nope, my boys will take care of everything. That's what they get paid for, you know. Right now, we need to set up for dinner. We'll talk more afterward, okay? Right now, I just want you all to relax and pick out a tent for yourselves."

"Okay, Gerry, you're the boss here. Oh, by the way, I saw someone sitting down at the fire when I came in, and I don't know where he came from or who he is. Do you have any idea who he is and what he's doing here?" Oliver asked him, the purpose of that mysterious pack train on his mind.

Gerry looked away for a brief moment, and then he answered casually. "He's just someone I know who has some experience in this area of the mountain. I called on him to help me out as a favor, and when I told him what I needed done, he said he'd be glad to help."

"Do you mind my asking what he is doing for you, Gerry? I'm supposed to know everyone who was coming on this trip, if you recall," Oliver said, slightly annoyed at the involvement of an unknown person.

"I'm sorry, Oliver. I didn't have time to get him cleared with you; the man I was going to use on this trip got sick, and I had to get someone to fill in for him at the last minute. You can call him Woody; I've known him for a long time. He's a good man, and he knows what he's doing on a horse. He's a volunteer like you, and I'll vouch for both his integrity and full cooperation, Oliver."

CHAPTER 6

Adam looked at his watch as he tied up his horse to the nearest tree and saw that it was nearing four thirty. He looked around to see what he could do and saw Axel walking over to him, his hand outstretched. Thinking he was coming to greet him, Adam walked out with his hand extended, but Axel just walked past him and took the reins off the tree branch.

"Never tie them by the reins, fella, because if they get spooked, they can snap them and run off. Always use the lead rope there, tied around his bridle."

"Sorry, Axel."

"No problem; it's a mistake a lot of new riders make. It comes from watching too many movies," Axel said with a smile. "Come on, you can help me with getting the stock fed and watered. Pick up the lead ropes from that group over there." He pointed out a tree to the right, where the three naturalists had tied up their horses to the branches just as he had, Adam noted with surprise.

He had just assumed they would know better, being more experienced at this; but anyone could make a mistake, he figured. He untied the reins from each horse, looped them around the saddle horn, and led all three back to where Axel was collecting another. "Now what, Axel?"

"Now we take them over to the others by the picket line, unsaddle and curry them out, put up the saddles and blankets, and feed and water them. Unless you're tired from the ride and want to rest."

Axel had just offered him a way to avoid doing any of the work, but Adam was more interested in learning than he was in sleeping.

"No, Axel, if you don't mind, I'd like to learn how to do it."

"Fine, just follow me and do what I do."

Adam noted they were headed around the encampment, and he asked Axel why they were taking the long way.

Axel just laughed. "These here hay burners. They ain't housebroke yet, so walking them through where we're gonna be sittin', eating, and sleepin', I don't figure that to help your sleep none," Axel said.

"I guess I wouldn't want to step in it on the way to the bathroom either," Adam said wryly.

"Nope, I reckon not."

With all the horses following along complacently, the two men walked around to the picket line, and tied the horses to the rope line. Once there, Adam watched as Axel released the cinch strap and pulled the saddle off the first horse. He then untied the bridle and slipped it over the horse's ears. With a shake of his head, the horse indicated his relief at having it removed. With the bit out of his mouth, it dropped his head to crop at the grass below.

Adam moved to the second animal as Axel moved to the third. Within twenty minutes, all fourteen saddles and bridles were removed and stacked. The saddles were turned upside down, and the wet saddle blanket and pad laid out to dry out overnight. Axel then produced two curry combs, a handle with a series of metal circles cut in a saw-tooth arrangement on one side. Axel took the first one and showed Adam how to use it on the horse to remove any dust or debris stuck to his coat. He held the brush in his left hand and, with the curry comb in his right, demonstrated how to clean and brush out the coat with a smooth routine.

Adam picked up the second curry comb and brush and began to work on the next animal. Although he had anticipated that this was going to be a chore, he was surprised to find that he was enjoying it. The animal was relaxing him as he was taking care of it. Adam was amazed at the experience he was having. He had ridden several times before, but he had always turned the task of taking care of the animal over to the wrangler or person whose job it was to care for it. He was enjoying the feel of this powerful and huge animal standing so close to him, and he could feel the muscles in this magnificent creature as he brushed her coat.

She gave a little reflex twitch and blew a breath of air out of her nose before turning her head, looking at him for a second, and then going back to chewing the grasses at her feet. Adam put a hand on her back and felt the warmth of her coat. She was beautiful, and he felt himself becoming very attached to her.

"How big is she, Axel?" Adam asked.

"Cinnamon is tall; she's fifteen-and-a-half hands." Seeing the look on Adam's face, he laughed. "A *hand* is four inches, so that means she is sixty-two inches from the ground to the top of her withers. That's right here," he said, placing his hand on the top of her shoulder. "She is about five years old, which puts her right at the beginning of her prime years. She's a good girl; she runs like the wind and is very sure-footed on the trail. She is very tolerant of a new rider and doesn't try to take control. That's why we gave her to you. You have some experience, and she will respond to that. You two are a good match; you'll have a good ride with her," Axel said approvingly.

Adam nodded in appreciation of the compliment and returned to brushing her.

"She's a good horse, Axel. Thank you, I'm enjoying being with her, Say, Axel, let me ask you—how smart do you figure this animal we're tracking is? Is it smarter than the usual animal of its kind? The things I've heard about it … are they normal behavior for this animal?" Adam asked in a rapid-fire delivery as he brushed out Cinnamon's tail.

"I thought you were the photographer, Adam; you sound more like the reporter."

"Well, I'm—"

"I'm just kidding you. Those are real good questions, and I'm not sure how to answer them, that's all. This here elk—I don't know of any other animal that seems to be getting away with what it is. It seems to be as elusive as any big animal I've ever seen, but there's something else. It seems to be bulletproof. We've had a lot of hunters up here looking for it, and no one seems to be able to hit it. It ducks behind a tree, it blends into the woods, it does something to avoid getting caught. I don't get it. And there's this: the normal life-span for this animal is about ten to twelve years, and this one's been talked about for nearly thirty years. That doesn't make any sense to me."

"Well, obviously it's not the same animal, Axel."

"I understand that, but that would mean this animal is teaching the others how to avoid capture, and they're learning and remembering their lessons. I don't believe I've ever heard of that before," Axel said in a puzzled voice.

Adam took this in, thinking about what it might mean to the story April was trying to write, and how that was going to work out with Barney on the hunt for a kill. As he thought about the possibilities, he was aware Axel was still speaking to him.

"I'm sorry, Axel, I was lost in thought. What did you say?"

"I said, if you want to learn more about that animal and what he can or can't do, you should go talk to that conservationist man, Mr. Baxter. He's right over there—in the shade with the red shirt. I'll finish up here if you want to go talk with him."

Adam looked over at Baxter, standing there looking bored, and decided to take him up on the offer. "If you don't mind, Axel, I would like to know some more about what that animal can do. I sure appreciate the offer."

Axel just nodded and moved on to the last horse and started to curry her coat. Adam put down the comb and brush and headed for Ed Baxter, intent on learning as much as he could about what to expect.

As Oliver and Eileen dismounted, they talked about the ride they had just finished. "Oliver, I have been with you for over twenty-five years, and I have been here with you by this mountain for almost ten, and I have never seen anything like this before! This is the most beautiful terrain and scenery that I have ever had the good fortune to walk through. How come we never came up here like this before?" she said, looking around.

"I suspect it was because we were busy making sure that it stayed looking like this for everyone else," Oliver responded. He was looking around for the senior Bruce, but he was already walking over to the picket line with his mount, so they took the reins and led their horses after him. When they arrived, Gerry Senior was talking with his son, so they hung back and allowed them their privacy.

"What do you need to talk with Gerry for?"

"I want to find out what the program is for tonight, and what's going to be the drill for tomorrow. I also need to talk to him about that loose cannon and find out what he is going to do about him. I don't want anyone getting hurt on this ride, and that man is going to be a handful to keep track of. I also need to sit down with the others and get an idea of how we are going to get him off the mountain," Oliver said, looking around and spotting the packs in a pile by the edge of the tents. "I guess we should get the tents up first, though. It's going to get dark pretty soon, and it'll be harder to get them up in the dark."

"How many tents do we have, Oliver?"

"I don't know, Eileen, that's another thing I need to ask Gerry about."

At that moment the two Bruces nodded, and the father clapped the son on the shoulder, while the son turned and headed over to his mount. As he walked to the horse, he called out to Bern, who also mounted up and came over.

"What's up, boss?"

"We're gonna take a look around, see what's out there that we don't know about. Get an idea of where to go tomorrow, and what's ahead of us."

"I haven't gotten the tents up yet, boss, and Charley's gonna need some help with the fire. Do you want me to take care of that first or ..."

"Tell Axel to take care of it; I need you with me. And one other thing, Bern," Gerry Junior said, looking at the wrangler's side. "You brought your pistol, right?"

"Yes, sir."

"Go get it. Wear it from now on," Gerry said curtly, before riding off up the hillside.

Bern looked a little surprised at the tone in his boss's voice, but he nodded and turned to reach into his saddlebag. He pulled out a gun belt wrapped around his holster and allowed it to unroll. He swung it around his waist, buckled it on, and took out the pistol, a nickel-plated, .45 caliber Ruger Vaquero. He opened the loading gate and he loaded it with five shells from the loops on the belt. Bern closed it up, pulled the hammer back, and then slowly eased it down. Once the pistol was back in the holster, Bern slipped a leather tie down over the hammer and he rode off after his boss.

Oliver noticed he hadn't loaded all six chambers, so he asked the senior Gerry about it.

"Mr. Barry, a smart shooter does not load one under the hammer in case of accidents. We—that is, all of us working on this ride—we are smart shooters. We don't take unnecessary risks, Mr. Barry," Gerry said.

That's what you think, Oliver thought to himself. *You're taking plenty of chances with that one, for sure.*

"What about the tents and the meals tonight?" he asked.

"I'll show you what to do, and I'll help you get all the tents put up. Let's go get started and get everyone situated, then we can talk about helping Charley get started with dinner," Gerry told him.

They started walking toward the center of the camp, and Gerry called out to the others. "Everybody, gather round. We have some details to take care of in order to get this camp set up tonight, and we all need to pitch in to help. Now, the first thing is that we need to assign sleeping arrangements. We are planning on using this camp as our base for a few days, and then we will move onto another location if we don't get lucky here. Now then, by my count, there are fourteen of us and only seven tents. We were supposed to have more, but, unfortunately, one of the pack mules got left behind at the last water stop. I'm going to send someone back later to pick it up and bring it forward, but for tonight, we are four tents short. Now, our two wranglers will be using a tent, and my son and I each will be using a tent, and someone can stay in with my son, but we will still be three tents short, and that means we will need to double up."

"Are you taking a tent to yourself?" Baxter asked suspiciously.

"No, I will be sharing my tent too. Now, we have three women with us, so that means two tents are taken off the top. What I would like to know first, folks, are any of you are comfortable being tent mates with another member of the party?"

Eileen looked at Oliver, who nodded slightly. "Oliver and I can share a tent, if that will be of any help to you, Mr. Bruce."

"Yes, ma'am, it will. That means I can put Dr. Fleming and Miss Martens in one tent. Okay, that's four tents. Now we have Dr. Baxter,

Mr. Wilcox, Mr. Barney, Charley, and Mr. Jacobs. Okay, anyone have any preferences?"

"Yes," Warner Barney spoke up, loudly and rudely. "My preference is to not share a tent with anyone."

"Mr. Barney, I'm afraid that's not going to be possible tonight. Tomorrow, when we get the other tents, I will make sure you get one by yourself. But for tonight, you will be sharing a tent," Gerry said politely, but with no room for discussion in his voice.

"You don't understand, Mr. Bruce. I refuse to share a tent. I brought my own sleeping tent, and I will not be sharing it with anyone," he said with a sneer, and then turned and walked away from the group.

"Charming piece of work, isn't he?" said Wanda to no one in particular, but loudly enough for Warner to hear. He stopped in his tracks and stiffened, but he didn't turn around. He then kept on walking to his pack, where he picked it up and carried it over to a spot near the fire, away from the others. He dug through it and pulled out a compactly folded canvas tent and began to set it up for himself. Everyone just watched him with clear contempt.

Gerry shook his head and turned back to the group. "As I was saying, who wants to be in with whom?"

Adam spoke up first, asking to partner up with Axel. Ed and Arnold volunteered to share one, and Charley and Bern jokingly said they could tolerate each other's snoring for a few nights. With the sleeping arrangements taken care of, Gerry took one of the tents and demonstrated how to set them up. Every couple took one and picked a place, and Gerry went from site to site, checking on their progress and helping them relocate when they had picked a bad spot.

He pointed out how Oliver and Eileen had picked a nice, low place where water would seek their tent as the place to pool, and he moved them two feet to the side where they would be higher and drier. Arnold was experienced at camping, so he had picked out a good spot for him and Ed. Adam relied on Axel's experience to help him secure a place where the smoke from the fire wouldn't drift into their tent. Gerry Senior took the time to set up for April and Wanda, noting that, while Wanda was watching him to see how he did it, April was busy watching Axel. He knew he wouldn't have to check on Charley, as he had been doing this for more years than he had, and knew more about setting up a camp than anyone here. He didn't bother to check on Warner Barney, because he wanted to keep his distance from him.

His own tent had been set up by his tent-mate before they arrived, and he knew Woody would stay inside as much as possible until he was really needed. He just hoped he wouldn't be needed, and this would be a vacation trip for him. He tried to convince himself this is how it would go, but Gerry instinctively knew he was just lying to himself.

Once all the tents were up, Gerry assigned tasks to everyone to help get the dinner ready. Adam volunteered to peel the small bag of potatoes for the stew, and April helped Axel gather the wood for the fire pits. Charley was cutting the meat into steaks, and Oliver was delegated the task of helping the elder Bruce clear out the brush for the second and third fire pits and collecting the burn control stones that were to ring the pits. Gerry explained they didn't usually have three pits, but because there were so many of them on this trip, cooking the steaks three at a time would take too long.

Ed was assigned the task of preparing the meat skewers out of branches. He insisted oak was best, because it would add flavor to the meat, so he went out looking for the proper size of branches from a stand of oak trees down the hill. Eileen volunteered to work with Charley to prepare the salads and the vegetables.

Charley asked Wanda and Arnold to look for some wild berries or wild onions that were known to be growing on the mountain. Although Arnold doubted they would find any in the dim light, he didn't turn down the opportunity when Wanda said she wanted to go along with him on the search. The night air was cool, and there was a slight breeze wafting through the camp, carrying with it the scent of pine and other trees into the mix. Gerry Senior and Oliver walked over the campsite, picking up some rocks from previous campfires that Gerry wanted to use to ring the fires.

"We'll need to clear a space of about three feet beyond the stones after we place them in the circle. We do this to help keep the rest of the mountain safe. It helps prevent forest fires by controlling the sparks that jump out, taking away their possible fuel."

Gerry studied the pattern of the breeze and moved the fire pits to the other side of the camp. "I know we don't know where the animals are, so it is just going to be luck that no one smells our fire—but I think we stand a better chance of not discouraging anyone's pattern of behavior by having the wind going back down the mountain rather than having our scent blow up the mountain," he explained to Oliver as they filled in the started holes. They picked up the big stones they had gathered, moving them to the other side, and rebuilt the circles in the fading daylight.

"We usually have this all done by the time we get the hunting party up here, but nothing about this trip is going according to Hoyle, so we will just have to adapt," Oliver said quietly. "Now that we're alone, what do you think that other trail means? Do you think it's trouble or a coincidence those horses are up here? I have reason to believe that Barney is planning something on his own that could be a real problem for all of us," he said in a low voice.

"Well, sir, I have to say that doesn't surprise me one bit. It's actually what I would expect from him. I guess it's time for me to tell you a story about Mr. Barney ... and me. You see, we go way back together. I brought him up here the first time—about thirty years ago. I was just a youngster then, 'bout the same age my son is now. I took him on a hunt that didn't go well. I don't reckon he has much use for me now 'cause of it. And to tell you God's own truth, I don't think so much of myself neither because of that trip. You want to know the real reason I don't do these trips any more, Oliver? It's him. And he's the reason I'm here on this one now. I think this will be my last trip, Oliver. I've felt it ever since I heard he was coming, and I'm sorta looking forward to it being over."

Oliver felt the pain in Gerry's voice as he made this confession, and while he didn't fully understand why, he recognized the man was talking at him more than he was talking to him, so he just listened without interruption or platitudes.

"Do you believe in karma, Oliver? I never did—leastways, I didn't until about a month ago. His letter came then, and I tried to talk the boy out of taking him up here, but he wouldn't have it. We needed the money—last season wasn't too good for us, and Mr. Barney was willing to pay more than we asked for what he wanted. I should have known then, but I thought I could talk it down. The boy got a full head of steam up, and you know how easy it is to change the mind of a Bruce once he's set on something. Well, it damn sure wasn't any easier for another Bruce to do it.

"Well, we talked, and I told the boy what was what and why I didn't want him to come, but he wasn't going to back out of it once he gave his word. I taught him that, and I guess I taught him real good. So here we are, and for all I know, we'll be chasing the devil until he catches us. I'm not real sure I'm gonna ride off this mountain, Oliver, and if I don't, I want you to keep an eye on my boy and steer him right.

"I know you well, better'n you might think, and I know you don't take the easy way on nothing. We've had our differences over the years, you and me, but I know you to be a man of your word and someone I trust. We've had our moments together, and we've accomplished a lot for this area. I know you put your heart into making this a safe area to work and play in. As my daddy would say, you're a man to ride the river with. I'd feel better about his future on this mountain if you give me your word you'll keep an eye out for him should something bad happen to me, Oliver," Gerry said to him.

"Gerry, I don't think anything's going to happen to you, but if it will make you feel at ease, you have my word on it," Oliver promised him. Gerry put out his hand and took Oliver's in his own.

"I thank you, Oliver," he said simply. He then changed the subject and started talking about dinner.

Wanda and Arnold were walking through the woods, looking for berries. Wanda stayed close to him, keeping her hand on his arm as she walked through the brush and the trees that densely populated this part of the mountain.

"Arnie, do you think we'll find any berries out here?" she asked.

"Well now, Wanda, it surely is possible. This is the season, and it's the right area for them to grow, but we might have a lot of competition for them between the deer, the chipmunks, certain birds, and even the bears."

"B-b-bears? What kind of bears, Arnie?" she asked nervously.

"Well, Wanda, up here we have black bears and even a few grizzly now and then," he informed her casually.

"I thought they were found just up in Alaska or Canada."

"No, ma'am. They're in our neck of the woods too. We just try to stay out of their way as much as possible—less trouble for all of us that way. You're not from this area, are you?"

"No, Arnie. I moved out here from Rhode Island about four years ago; it was much too crowded back there for me. I grew up in a small town on the coast. It's called Middletown, and it's about a mile right down the hill from Newport. You've heard of Newport, I'm sure. They have had a big-time jazz festival there for years, and sailboat races. It's a beautiful little place, Middletown is. But it was too busy and too crowded for me.

"I like the open spaces, and there are more animals to protect out here. I looked around for a place where I could make a difference in the quality of life for the animals, and an opportunity came up to come out here and open a veterinary practice where I could work with all kinds of animals besides the pampered and spoiled pets of pampered and spoiled owners. I bought the practice of a vet who had gotten cancer and wanted to retire.

"I think I saw you at a park fundraiser three months after I arrived. I saw you there, you were wearing a green bib-front shirt and black jeans, and a dark gray Stetson—I assume it was a Stetson, all cowboys wear a Stetson—and I thought you were the most magnificent man in the entire auditorium. I couldn't take my eyes off you ... Oh, God, I'm talking like a schoolgirl with a crush on her favorite teacher. I'm embarrassing myself beyond belief," she said.

"No, you're no schoolgirl, Wanda," Arnold replied warmly. "That was near onto four years ago; I'm astounded you remember any of those details about me from so long ago. I wish I could say the same thing to you, Wanda, but back then I wasn't seeing anyone or anything but my work. I had buried myself in work to hide my hurt from the world and from myself. This is my first time out into the real world since my wife died many years ago. I am just starting to come back to life, Wanda. It's kinda funny, really, but because of you and this animal we are working together to try to save, we are also saving me," he said with a laugh.

"Then we should celebrate tonight, Arnie. Let's see if we can find some berries and maybe we can get Charley to make us something special for a dessert," Wanda said excitedly.

Arnie smiled and held out his hand, saying, "Let's look over in that thicket over there. It looks like a blackberry patch to me, and I'll bet Charley knows how to make a mean berry pie."

April and Axel walked around the outskirts of the camp, looking for any suitable deadwood they could cut into firewood. April was getting frustrated because Axel kept rejecting everything she saw that was small enough for her to carry. Her only reason for volunteering for this duty was that she thought it would be quick and easy, meaning she could get back to her real job, which was interviewing the rest of the players in this backwoods drama so she could write her story.

This boy was growing tiresome, because he was so clumsy at flirting with her. He wanted to kiss her, but was afraid to take the risk of her reaction. He was cute, but so was a puppy, and she had no time for a pet right now. If he wasn't going to do anything to make this stupid search more interesting, then she was going to have to find a way out of this so she could get back to her interviews. Maybe she could get him to talk about the mountain and the ranger. Maybe he knew some dirt on the tree-huggers or the rancher. Maybe he could help her keep an eye on the hunter and whatever else was going on.

Okay, how could she get him to focus on what she wanted him to instead of his juvenile lust? *Well,* she sighed to herself, *it's worked for me in the past, and he's certainly a lot less sophisticated than the others were. It's time for me to get to work.*

Gerry Junior and Bern were out looking for signs of the mysterious pack string in the fading daylight hours.

"Boss, I see something over here," Bern called out.

"What is it, Bern?" Gerry called back as he walked his horse over to where Bern was kneeling under a low-hanging branch.

"It's a cigarette butt, boss, and it's fresh. There are a bunch of tracks over there." He pointed to a stand of trees off to the left.

"Bern, the grass over here looks cropped down tight, and the ends are fresh," Gerry said. "They were here, but *why* is the question. I can't see the camp from here, but I think it should be about five hundred yards over that way," he added as he pointed in the direction they had ridden from.

"So are they trailing us, leading us, or just going in the same direction, do you think?" Bern said, puzzled.

Gerry lay down and looked along the ground in every direction until he saw a faint path of bent-down grass and small clods of dirt heading eastward toward the saddle in the mountain. "Well, I'd like to think it's just a coincidence, but I gave up believing in the Easter Bunny some thirty years ago. No, Bern, someone is leading us. I don't know who they are or what they're out here for, but it concerns us and that worries me. I'd like to get a look at who it is; that might help me know whether or not to expect trouble. Let's go on a little farther and see if we can get a look at this traveler while the light is with us." Gerry swung up into the saddle and slowly walked alongside the faintly marked trail.

As they headed down the path, Gerry's horse put his ears forward and lifted his head, flaring his nostrils at the same time. As he did this, Bern's horse also shifted his ears forward and began to sidestep in his tracks.

"Hold up, Bern. Dusty hears or smells something he doesn't like. I don't know what it is, but we need to be careful here. I don't want us riding into something we're not prepared for," Gerry said cautiously.

"Boss, I don't know about you, but I only have my pistol on me. I left my rifle back in camp; I didn't think we'd be needing it tonight. I've got a full belt-load of cartridges, however, if you think that's all we might need."

Gerry continued to walk along the faint trail, thinking about the potential risks involved with the unknown. "Bern, I don't really know what we're getting into, so I'm not sure if that—"

Suddenly, they heard a low growl. The horses began to anxiously step back off the path and around in a circle, recognizing the scent of something they didn't like. As Dusty began to dance, a dark shape began moving toward him. Gerry's horse reared unexpectedly and, caught unprepared, Gerry went sailing off the saddle. As he hit the ground, he began to roll, and the dark shape came out of the shadows right for him. A gunshot came over his shoulder and hit the wolf in midflight, knocking it to the ground. A second shot quickly followed, causing the wolf to twitch once and be still.

A long moment paused, and then Gerry spoke. "Bern, have I complimented you on your marksmanship lately? If I haven't, then I think I should have."

"Well, boss, you know it's payday tomorrow, and you haven't signed our checks yet."

"Right. Good thinking there, Bern. Well, I think I've had enough excitement for the day, how about you?" he said calmly.

"It'll be suppertime when we get back, boss. I'm kinda hungry too," Bern added.

On the ride back to the camp, Gerry gave Bern new instructions. "Bern, I don't see any need to bother my father with any word of that last incident, do you?"

"No, boss, not if you don't."

"You can tell him what we found, and everything else you discovered, but the thing with the wolf we can just leave out. He probably would just worry needlessly about what's already done and over. I don't want to unnecessarily alarm him."

"Okay, boss, but what should I say if he says something about the gunshots?" Bern asked.

Gerry thought for a moment and smiled. "Tell him that we were taking a shot at some game, but missed in the bad light."

"Game. Bad light. Got it. There's the camp up ahead. Want me to keep a guard out tonight?"

"Yeah, Bern. That would be a real good idea. Don't say anything about any of this to any of the others." He thought a moment and added, "Not even to the ranger. There's nothing he can do about it right now, anyway. When it is time to worry, then I'll tell him what's up. For now, the fewer people who know, the less stress it will create for everyone," Gerry said sternly.

"Especially for us," Bern added sagely.

Dinner was a delightful combination of fresh venison, fresh vegetables, and two special pies made by Charley with the buckets of blackberries Wanda and Arnold had gathered. They all washed it down with sweet or plain tea—as each person chose—or just water. Ed Baxter, normally one to be grumpy, was quick to compliment Charley on his proficiency and the quality and flavor of their dinner. Everyone raved about the meal ... that is, everyone but Warner Barney.

He had taken his plate and cup without saying a word to anyone, and he walked back to his tent. He sat by himself, apart from the rest of the group, and spoke to no one. When others tried to engage him in conversation, he would just give them a cold, stony stare and turn away in silence. Even Eileen had attempted to engage him in a conversation about his role in the capture, but he just looked at her with his cold, dead eyes, and after a few tries, she got up and moved next to Oliver.

"He's not a very warm individual, Oliver. I think there's something very wrong, very evil about him. You watch yourself when he's behind you. In fact, I think you shouldn't ever let him get behind you," she warned him.

"That's good advice, Barry. I'd take it if I were you," Gerry Senior encouraged as he came up behind them. They were sitting on an old log that served as a bench, their plates in their laps and their cups on the ground at their feet. "I'd listen to the little lady, Barry. I always did trust a woman's intuition in these things. Women, dogs, and children—they always seem to know who's dangerous and who they can trust. I reckon we'd best keep an eye on him from now on, Barry, for everyone's sake."

Just then, Charley called out to the group, inviting them to gather round. "Folks, put yore plates and cups down and come on over here to enjoy some real cowboy entertainment. Now then, you all can have yore choice of performance: either I can tell you all some true tales—"

"That'll be the day, Charley, that you tell some true tales. Every time you tell them, they grow like weeds," Axel called out to him. "I tell you what, why don't you clean up this mess and spare them your windy tales, and I'll sing them a few songs so they'll all be relaxed," he said, laughing.

"Well, young feller, that's a good idea," Charley said, laughing back. "Then when yore done assaultin' their ears, I can send them to bed with a good, relaxin' yarn. Folks, you sit thar and listen to this here young feller try to coax a tune outten that overgrown banjo of his, and when you've had enough, I'll be ready to tell y'all some good night tales." With that, he bowed to Axel, who was tuning his guitar, and slipped away to clean up the "kitchen."

Axel began with a lively trail song and held their rapt attention for the next three hours as he played one after another, taking requests when offered, and giving the historical background of each one before he began playing. He mixed up his performance, playing a soft ballad and then a rousing sing-along, before ending on the soulful lament he called "Montana." When the last note had died away, the audience broke into a loud applause, mixed with cheers and whistles.

Eileen turned to Oliver and whispered, "He's really good! Maybe we could get him to come perform for the guests at the lodge sometime."

Oliver nodded, thinking the same thing. Before he could get up to approach Axel about this, however, Gerry Senior stood up and began to speak.

"Folks, we've all come here for the same reason, so maybe we should spend a little time getting to know each other. I'll start, since I am already up and talking. My name, as you know, is Gerry Bruce, and I own the ranch that's putting on this hunt. I used to be a guide and hunter myself, but I gave that up some years ago, and my son does most of the hunts now. I manage the ranch, but I wanted to come along on this one because I've never actually been out with him on one.

"Now I'm going to use the boss's prerogative and speak for my men. You just heard Axel sing, so you know why we keep him around." This was greeted with a round of laughter, as all of them knew that wasn't the real reason. "No, folks, Axel and his brother Bern, they have been with me for many years. I might add, they were taught to be real workers by one of the best ranchers in the state, that man sitting over there—" He pointed to Arnold Wilcox, who was sitting very close to Wanda. Arnold just smiled and nodded, while Wanda squeezed his hand. "They are good with the livestock, excellent trackers, and fantastic horsemen, the both of them.

"Axel, he graduated from Boise State University with his degree in marketing, and Bern graduated from Colorado State University with a degree in agribusiness management, and they help my son and me run our ranch. I would like to say that both boys graduated with honors, by the way." He paused while the others—except for Warner Barney—applauded their appreciation of the hard work the brothers had accomplished. Gerry continued, "Charley Weeks you've already met, and you know what he can do with a pot and fire. Charley has been around campfires, trail drives, and cattle drives as long as I can recall. Hell, he was old when I was a boy.

"Charley's a good man; he is a real genuine cowboy. He grew up at the tail end of the real cowboy era, so he can tell you some stories about the real people who built the West. Now, I'm not saying he knew them personally, although he says he knew a few of them at the end of their lives, and he heard some of the tales from them directly, but he definitely knew the men who knew them, so if you get him going, you will hear about the men of the real West, not the Hollywood nonsense they portrayed the men as being.

"Now, that's all of us, so let's all take turns and you tell us about you. Oliver, you're the next one up, I figure, as this is your mountain we are riding through." He nodded to Oliver and sat down.

Oliver stood up slowly and looked around. "I guess all of you know who I am, and I am sure you know what I do. I'm in charge of the safety and any rescue for every visitor on the mountain, and I'm the one who issues the permits for all hunting trips on this mountain. I oversee the ski lodge and lifts and maintain the safety patrols. If it goes wrong, I'm the one you talk to. If it goes right, I never hear from anyone. That sums it all up for me.

"Sitting next to me is my right-hand lady, Eileen Gayle. If there's anything I need to know, she probably knows it before I do. If there's something I need to do, she has it all laid out for me before I need to do it. If I have any problems with anyone, she pours the oil on the troubled waters. In truth, she probably is more the head of the department than I am. She is definitely smarter than I am, because she doesn't want my job, and I couldn't do hers." He sat down to applause and laughter and, looking over at her, invited her to stand up and talk.

Eileen stood and put her hand on his shoulder as she spoke. "My boss underestimates his value to this project and to this mountain. Every dollar that comes in through federal funding is because he has done the homework to find those dollars and apply for them. Despite the downturn in our economy, we have never laid anyone off, and he is the man who keeps it that way. When someone has a problem or an emergency in their family or anywhere, Oliver is the one who finds the funds to help them. It is always anonymously and it is always denied if he is ever asked about it. He is one of the most generous and goodhearted men I have ever worked for. He truly cares about his employees, and he will do anything he can for them. That's all I have to say, except I love my job and thank you for letting me come along with you on this adventure." She sat down to whistles and applause.

"How come I didn't get any whistles?" Oliver complained jokingly.

"'Cause you don't look like she does!" Charley called out from the edge of the camp, drawing more cheers and whistles. Oliver just hung his head and waved his hand in mock submission.

Ed Baxter stood and looked at the group. "I'll go next. My name is Edward Baxter, and I am the official representative of FARM, the Freed Animal Rights Movement—the group whose job it is to oversee the relocation of this animal. I am also here for another reason: I volunteered to come along because this'll give me a chance to prove out a theory I have about their intelligence and how it is passed on through successive generations.

"My theory is that evolution is not random. I believe that some species of animals are capable of retaining what they learn and somehow pass this knowledge along to other members of their unit. You see, the thing is, this particular animal doesn't live more than fifteen years at the most. Nature is not forgiving or tolerant of the old and weak or the very immature, and it is this particular age group that is often the first one killed for survival by predators.

"So here we have an animal that is demonstrating knowledge that is more than one animal could conceivably acquire in a lifetime— somehow. I mean to test this animal six ways from Sunday to find what it is in his blood that is different than all the other animals of its species. That this is the same animal that's being reported on for the last thirty years or so is utterly impossible. That would mean the animal is virtually indestructible and can live forever, and everyone knows that's not possible either.

"No, this is another generation that has somehow managed to retain all the knowledge of hunters and everything else the first animal ever experienced. Somehow—and this is what I intend to discover and prove—somehow that knowledge was inherited and passed on to succeeding generations. This ability, if I can identify it, will change everything we know about animal management and nature parks all over the world. So it is very important to me and to my research to find this great animal and to help move him to a safe environment where he can be studied at length and the secret to his passing on his knowledge identified and understood. That's what I am here for," Ed concluded.

He sat down to complete silence as everyone began to comprehend the enormity of what he was suggesting. The silence was broken by harsh and disrespectful laughter.

"You people make me laugh." Warner had approached the circle while the others were listening to Ed. "You people don't get it. It's just a dumb animal. It's not smart, it's not 'passing that knowledge along'; it's just been mighty damn lucky—lucky I didn't hear about it before now. But its luck has run out, because now I'm here, and I'm going to get him if I have to chase him all over this damn mountain."

"Barney, sit down now!" Oliver commanded him. "You're drunk or crazy, but in either case, you're out of line here," he warned sternly.

"I'm out of line? Who says? You? I'm just expressing my opinion. You let that man express his insane opinion that animals can learn and pass their knowledge on to others, so why can't I express my opinion his opinion is ridiculous?" Barney said with undisguised contempt.

"Actually," Wanda said hesitantly, "there are many documented studies that have proven certain mammals are quite capable of learning and teaching their young what they have learned, Mr. Barney," she continued. "And it's not just found in the higher primates, I mean. Squirrels are well known to be able to figure out complex engineering problems in order to raid bird feeders. It's been well-documented that, no matter how many baffles and gates or barriers someone puts into the feeder, if the squirrel wants the feed inside, he is quite capable of figuring out how to get it. They have even been observed working together so everyone in their group can get the feed out of the feeder. The truth is, Mr. Barney, there's no such thing as a squirrel-proof bird feeder; it's just that the squirrel wasn't interested in the food at that time," Wanda explained politely.

Barney just looked at her for a moment before dismissing her with a snort of derision and calling her a name. Arnold began to stand up to address his rudeness, but Wanda put her hand on his arm. He sat back down, clearly angry.

"All of you, just don't get in my way," Warner snarled at them. "You can think about this animal any way you want to, but the reality is that it's just a big dumb animal and nothing more. You'll see that I'm right. You will all soon see who's right, me … or them," he said coldly, pointing at Ed and Wanda. He then turned on his heel and walked away back to his tent, ignoring the looks and softly muttered comments that filled the air in his departure.

After a moment, Adam stood up to change the mood. "My name is Adam Jacobs, and I'm a photographer. I'm here with Miss Martens, who is here to do a story on this hunt and the relocation of the elk. I've been a photographer for many years, and this is a big story for me as well. I'm enjoying the outdoors, the riding, and the scenery, and I am also enjoying the camaraderie of the group … well, most of the group, anyway," he said to the laughter of the others. "I've learned to snow ski on this trip, and I'm doing more riding than I ever have, and I'm really loving it. I just had the best meal I've ever had in my life, and I can't wait to see what happens tomorrow. I'm looking forward to taking some great photos on this venture, and I'll be glad to take some group photos for everyone whenever you want."

He sat down to the applause of the group, and April stood up next.

"My name is April Martens, and I'm the reporter that Adam is working with. I heard about this elk back in Yankton, and I thought it would make a good story. I've done some investigative reporting in the past, but this is a feature story I'm on here, so there is more pressure. I want to talk to all of you individually before the trip is over to get your perspective and history, so I can put it all in the story in a meaningful way. I know some of you may be thinking I am taking one side or the other, but I want to assure all of you that I am completely neutral.

"I want to get the hunter's perspective as well as the conservationist's perspective. If I could get the animal to talk to me, I'd include his point of view as well," she said. April was aware the laughter that followed her remarks was more a polite response than it was a genuine appreciation of the joke. She told herself it was the result of Barney's rather rude exit and having to follow Adam's "aw shucks" speech than it was due to her own lack of genuine warmth.

It never occurred to April she might have alienated everyone by her lack of real friendliness and unwillingness to cooperate with everyone on the chores of setting up the camp—an attitude and behavior that had not gone unnoticed by everyone earlier in the evening.

Axel's report on her lack of effort on their firewood detail had made the rounds as well, and this didn't help her status in any positive way. She pushed on, attempting to sell her project to the others while downplaying Adam's role in the process.

"This story will go out on all the newswires, along with any photos that the editor feels will enhance the story. Adam will be shooting a lot of film on this ride, and we will select the best shots for the story, so any help you can provide will be greatly appreciated." She sat down to no more than polite applause.

Arnold deferred to Wanda, who stood up next. "My name is Wanda Fleming, and I'm a veterinarian. I've been a vet for twenty years, the last four of them out here. I'll be responsible for making sure we don't use any more tranquilizer than we need to in order to sedate him for traveling out of here. I'll need everyone's help to make the assessment of his height and weight so I can formulate the sedative accurately. I'll be responsible for making sure his trip to his new home is stress-free, or as stress-free as I can make it. I will be the person to take care of our new friend when he comes under our protection. I'll be his doctor for the rest of his life, which I will try to extend as much as I can."

She sat down to genuine applause, which did not go unnoticed by April, causing her to feel a resurgence of the resentment that she always experienced when others were jealous of her and her talents. How that dried-up old maid could possibly be more appealing than she was to the rest of this group was beyond her understanding.

Arnold stood up last, looking around as he gained his feet. "My name is Arnold Wilcox, and I'm a rancher here in this county. I represent the preserve where this animal is going to be living from now on. It's my job to make sure he gets there alive and in one piece, and I don't like to fail. I am a hunter too, but only for food, not for fun. I don't like people who hunt for the fun of it, or for the fun of killing." His meaning, and who he was referring to, was obvious to everyone. "I believe that everyone is entitled to the respect they choose to earn." He sat down, having said his piece.

There was another long silence before Gerry stood up again.

"Well now, folks. We have a long day tomorrow, so I suggest that everyone turn in for a good night's rest. We'll be up and starting breakfast at six in the morning, so you'll need to be ready to break camp by eight. Charley and Axel will clean up behind us and then meet us at the next camp higher up the mountain. My son and Bern will be finding a trail that will lead us to the animal, and we should be able to make contact in a day or so. Have all your things ready to go by seven thirty so Charley and Axel can get everything packed right away. See you all in the morning. Have a good night's rest."

He walked off, and the group slowly said their good nights and went to their respective tents.

As Wanda and Arnold walked toward their tents, she cleared her throat and she spoke, keeping her voice low. "He's not a very pleasant person, Arnie. He's not worth you getting upset."

"Wanda, out here a man never calls a lady a vile name like that. Any varmint who acts like he did deserves to have a real as—attitude adjustment. And I'm just the man to do it."

"Arnie, that's very sweet of you to stand up for me like that; you're a real gentleman."

"Wanda, I always protect the important people in my life."

"Arnie … am … I … someone important in your life?"

He paused a moment while she held her breath for a lifetime—and then he turned night into day. "Yes, Wanda. You are quickly becoming someone important in my life. After this is all over, and the animal is on the preserve, I hope you will allow me to continue to call on you."

"Arnie, I would like that very much." As they slowly walked back to her tent, both of them were oblivious to the smiles of Eileen and Oliver, who were standing nearby, watching with amusement.

"Looks like Mr. Wilcox has found something he wasn't expecting to find," Oliver said.

"Looks to me like he has found something he has needed for a long time," she countered.

"Well, either way, they look like they are going to be seeing a lot of each other from now on. On a serious note, Eileen, that man Barney leaves a bad taste in my mouth. I'll be glad when this is over, and he leaves my mountain. I just hope he never comes back here.

"I like that photographer, I'm thinking about trying to hire him away from the paper to work for us, photographing the mountain and putting together a magazine to promote our area. Do you think he'd be interested in doing that?" he asked.

"I don't know, Oliver, but I suspect he can tell you if he is if you ask him. How much are you thinking of paying him?"

"I don't have a number in mind, but I know how much my budget will allow me to spend. I think I'll speak to him about it tomorrow and see if he's interested. Well, I'm tired so I'm going to turn in and get some rest. You going to come in?"

"I'll be there in just a minute. I want to look at the stars for a few minutes. I never get to see them from my place; there's too much light out at night," Eileen responded.

Oliver came back out of the tent and he stood beside her, holding her hand as they gazed upward at the stars, both of them lost in their thoughts.

Also thinking very hard right then was Ed Baxter, who was fuming over the insult he had received from Warner Barney. He was more determined than ever to be the one that brought down the elk, if only to show up that blowhard. He had no desire to hurt the animal—far from it. Bringing it down safely was even more important for the insult it would give Barney.

That man was absolutely insufferable in his monumental conceit and ego. He didn't have a civil bone in his entire body, and was probably going to just mount the head and throw the rest away. Well, not if Ed Baxter had anything to do with it, he wouldn't! He opened the bottle he had rolled up in his sleeping bag and, taking a longing look at it, opened the back of the tent and poured it out on the ground. He hated to waste good rum, but he wasn't going to be tempted on this trip. If he had a nip, he would be sure to have more, and then it would be gone in no time. No, he needed to keep his head clear this time, if he was going to pull this off and best that braggart.

Proud of himself, he closed up the tent and got into his sleeping bag. Tomorrow the hunt would begin for real, and he'd be able to prove his theory and show that blowhard up for the conceited pig he was.

Adam was getting himself ready for a good night's sleep. He had really enjoyed this day, both the riding and the scenery, as well as the friendships he had made with the other men. He really liked the big man, Wilcox, and the cook, Charley. Charley was a real class act and a character right out of the old movies Adam had grown up on. He had listened to him telling tales the entire ride, and the man had never repeated himself once. And the meal! That was far and away the very best dinner he had ever had in his entire life, bar none! He had taken pictures of Charley preparing it at every step until Charley had chased him out from under his feet, telling him to go and take pictures of the crew and the guests and quit pestering him. It had been said with such mock ferocity, Adam had known he was just teasing.

He had gotten some good shots of everyone as they gathered around the fire and of Axel while he was singing. He would never have suspected Axel had a voice like that. He had gotten a really good picture of Mr. Wilcox and Dr. Fleming that he was going to give them for a wedding present.

He laughed to himself, wondering if anyone else could see where they were headed. *Sure,* he thought with a yawn. The assistant of Mr. Barry's was sharp and could probably see it. Maybe she could see herself with that Mr. Barry too. They were clearly a couple if anyone here was. Even Mr. Bruce, the older one, was nice and friendly. Adam yawned again as he considered how Mr. Bruce seemed to be sad about something. That thought led to another thought.

He had taken pictures of everyone in the camp, even the very disagreeable Mr. Barney, but the only one who had objected or tried to cover his face was that thin fellow who was in Mr. Bruce's tent with him. The man was pleasant, but evasive to talk with. What tickled Adam's mind was that he looked somewhat familiar. Adam knew he'd never met him, but there was something about his eyes. He looked strangely like someone Adam had seen before somewhere, but he didn't remember where—and he was sure he would have recognized the name if he had.

He would ask Mr. Bruce about him tomorrow. His name ... was ... Oh yes, Woody. Adam's eyes closed in sleep before he had a chance to think about what he'd just realized.

Gerry Junior and Bern came into camp quietly, so as not to disturb anyone. As they dismounted, Gerry pulled his rifle from the scabbard and handed the reins to Bern, who took them silently and led both horses to the picket line, where he took the saddles and pads off the tired animals. He fed and watered both of them, tipped the saddles on end, and draped the pads over them to dry in the cool mountain air. These chores done, he picked up a brush and curry comb and groomed both animals while they ate, earning a nicker of approval from both tired horses.

"You guys did a heap of work today; I guess we'll give you the day off tomorrow. Here—a special reward for both of you," Bern said fondly as he gave both horses a few pieces of what he called "horse mints" as a treat. He always carried some in his vest pocket for his friends. Bern led them out to the pasture he had created with a portable electric fence and turned them loose to graze. Stretching, he walked back to the camp where Charley was putting a plate out for him.

"Bern, Gerry, I saved you all some venison steak and salad, and I have some tea for you boys," he said without a trace of the drawl and "good-ol'-boy" accent he used when the guests were around him. Charley had worked in the movies for years, and he could turn that accent on whenever he wanted to. It was not a well-known fact, but Charley had a master's degree in communications from the University of Colorado. Gerry Senior walked over to them, relieved to see them back in the camp.

"See anything out there, son?"

"No, not really. Bern found a couple of cigarette butts on a ridge a few miles back, and tracks, but we lost them when it got dark. I can't tell if they're following us or just keeping out of sight or just going in the same direction. I have no reason for thinking this way, but I have an unpleasant feeling they are tracking us. Whoever it is has made sure we're separated by a ridge that we can't see over. It's like they know where we are, but we don't know where they are. I don't like it. I'm going to go out with Bern tomorrow to see if I can get an eye on them and maybe convince them to go somewhere else. Any trouble here?"

As Gerry began eating, his father began to report on the scene at dinner. When he had finished, father and son looked at each other for a moment, and Gerry Junior said softly, "Don't say it, Dad."

"Say what? I told you so? Not me, son." Then they began to discuss the route for the next day's ride.

April was furious. Adam was stealing the story away from her and deliberately putting her into a background position. No one on this stupid venture was talking to her, and that silly old man Weeks wasn't much help either. None of the stories he had told her had anything to do with the reason she was here, and when she asked him about the elk, he would start and then allow himself to get distracted by something else. She hadn't seen the younger Bruce or the older wrangler since the morning got started. And, although that man Baxter and his theory of an animal who had taught the younger ones how to avoid humans was interesting, he just wasn't relevant to why she was here.

No, she needed to get closer to the real story: Warner Barney. The problem was that he wasn't very likeable or approachable. He had made it very clear at dinner that he was here for himself, and he didn't care about saving the animal for life on a preserve. He was here to kill it anyway he could, so he could prove he was smarter, but according to Baxter's wild theory, he wasn't.

April began to think of another angle to her story and how she could make it work either way. She listened to the voices outside, hearing that dried-up Dr. Fleming and the big rancher speaking to each other. They were talking about seeing each other after this trip was over, which was fine for them, but of no interest to her. She then heard them talking about where the elk was likely to be and when they might come up to him. Suddenly, she saw something moving behind them, but before she was able to identify what it was, it disappeared into the trees. Dismissing it from her mind, April resumed her deliberation of her primary problem, which was how to take this tedious exercise and turn it into something her readers would be enthralled to hear about.

Perhaps, if she played her cards right, she could turn it into a cause that would stimulate more interest, and she could even make this big elk into a celebrity, like Smokey Bear. She started to get excited about this idea, but then she remembered that Barney was determined to kill the elk. The animal was a much bigger story alive than it was dead, and it had the potential to keep on growing if she managed it right. April thought about her options and decided now she had to help the ranger keep the animal alive, and so she had to prevent the hunter from succeeding at killing it. Tired, she sighed and thought to herself that this story was more complicated than she had expected it to be. She went to sleep, resolved that her path was clear and she knew what to do.

Warner Barney wasn't sleeping; he had too much to do in order to be ready when his man came. He was busy in his tent, putting his things in order and fixing the sleeping bag. He was furious at those idiots who were trying to prevent him from achieving his goal. That fool Baxter and his insane theory about an animal teaching others all it knew and passing it down from generation to generation—that crap was just pure science fiction, as anyone knew. He could understand those animal-rights whackos, but that meddling veterinarian butting in with her two cents worth … that really made him mad. They weren't even talking about squirrels, for god's sake.

He knew that squirrels could solve problems in order to get food, so what? He had seen a rat learn to navigate a maze, and cats and dogs learn to do tricks, and there were birds you could teach to talk, but it didn't mean anything. The birds were just repeating sounds—they didn't really know what they were saying, and they couldn't make appropriate responses out of the sounds they had learned to make. Even horses learned to repeat behaviors if properly rewarded, but they didn't know what they were doing, and they damn sure weren't counting. No, this animal was no smarter than any other of its species, and very shortly he would prove this to all of them. He did not suffer fools gladly, and, for the most part, he didn't tolerate anyone gladly.

That reminded him: he had a score to settle with the Bruces—both of them. When this was over in a day or so, he was going to settle his accounts with both of them. But that was later; right now he had to get things together for the rest of the trip.

He had to put all his gear together and decide what he would need for the next few days. He thought briefly about the reporter and whether or not to go talk to her about his plans. She had wanted to do a story on him, and he was certainly willing to let her—as long as it was the story he wanted her to tell. He didn't mind the world knowing how good he was; he just didn't want them to know how he did it. Those were his trade secrets, and, after all, Gimbels didn't tell Macys their secrets.

In the cool night air, crickets began to sing and, far away, a wolf began to howl a song. On a ridge ten miles away, the sow bear was now sleeping. She had spent the entire day following the scent of fresh blood on the ground. She was tired and her paws were sore, but she had found a big patch of blackberries and the river had provided her with a couple of fat fish, so she was full and ready for a good night's sleep. Tomorrow she would resume tracking of that wonderful scent.

She recognized the aroma as coming from a recent kill, and she was hungry and needed to add a little extra fat before she went into hibernation. This scent held the promise of what she needed before she went to her den for the winter, so she was determined to find it and take it for her own. She growled softly in her sleep, dreaming about whatever it was that bears will dream about.

She was alert even though she was sleeping, because she had learned to always be vigilant for danger or for a meal. But her sense of smell and hearing allowed her to continue sleeping as a large elk slowly walked by her cave. The animal cast a large shadow as it moved through the trees, stopping for a few minutes to look at the entrance to the cave as if to wish the occupant a good night's sleep before it moved on. The elk came to a clearing, softly lit by the moon's pale light, and, as it moved into the light, it stopped at the edge of the clearing.

It looked up at the mountain, staring far into the distance as if it could see the group of hunters farther up and was deciding what to do about them. Slowly, the elk walked into the clearing, stepping softly on the carpet of leaves on the ground, and, as it did so, it stepped on a fallen twig hidden beneath the leaves, breaking it with a sharp crack.

The sound carried back to the cave, waking up the bear. She roused herself, sniffing the air as she walked to the entrance of the cave. When she reached the front, a quick check of the air satisfied her there was no danger, and so she went back to sleep.

CHAPTER 7

The night air was cold, but everyone stayed warm in their sleeping bags. In the morning when he woke up, Adam was very glad he had taken the clerk's recommendation when they were getting outfitted. He hated to think about what these next few nights were going to be like, as he knew they were likely to be climbing even higher up the mountain. When he had finished getting dressed, he opened the tent flap and stood there looking out, because he couldn't believe his eyes—the entire camp was covered in white.

He walked out of the tent and looked around to see most of the others standing around, looking just as surprised as he was. He could see Oliver and his girlfriend, along with the vet and her new friend, throwing snowballs at each other. April wasn't up yet—or, at least, hadn't come out of her tent. The other conservationist was standing beside his tent, just watching them. The two wranglers were busy with the horses, and the two Bruces were standing by the cook area with Charley, deep in conversation. Adam thought about waking April so she could see the snow, but then he decided to pass on that option when he considered what her mood was likely to be.

He walked over to the ranger to chat with him. "Mr. Barry, isn't this wild? I'll bet you didn't expect to see any snow this morning."

"No, Adam, I didn't. And this will make our hunt a little easier, as we will be able to track him a little better now. The downside of this, I am afraid, is that it completely extinguished our campfires, so we are going to have to make do with a cold breakfast. Charley was just saying that he can fix us some fruit and sandwiches for the ride today, but there will be no hot meals until tonight when we camp."

Just then, the elder Bruce came over to their little group. "Well, this is an unexpected event, Oliver. I am a little surprised by it. I know we're in the snow season, but I hadn't really expected any at this level. I didn't figure we would run into it here. Oh, well, no real harm done. Let's get everyone together and have breakfast, then we can talk about what we're going to do today."

Gerry turned around and addressed the rest of the camp. "Good morning, everyone! It's six thirty—time to rise and shine, campers!" he called out. Everyone began to walk toward him, including April, who was the last one to come out of her tent. As they gathered around the snow-covered fire pits, Ed looked around and noticed that they were not all present.

"We're missing someone; Mr. Personality isn't here. Maybe he's too good to have a cold breakfast with us. Not that I care, mind you. He's as warm and friendly as this fire pit," Ed grumbled to Arnold, kicking snow into the hole.

"Well, you're right about that, Ed. He certainly isn't someone to hang out with. But he's here because we need his skill with a rifle," Arnold said.

"No, we don't need him, Arnold. I'm a good shot, and I can do this for us. I don't need him, and he isn't going to help us one bit. You all know what he is here for, and it isn't what we're here for. I say let him sleep or sulk or whatever he's doing and get on with our morning. Hell, I'm for not even waking him up when we leave, but I suppose we have to do that."

"Well, our trip would probably be a lot more enjoyable if we could leave him behind, Ed, you're right about that, but you're also right we can't just abandon him," Arnold said regretfully as he kneeled down to pick up a handful of snow and began to play with it. "But," he added brightly, "we don't need to bother him until it is time for us to get started." He quickly turned toward Wanda and threw a snowball at her. She let out a shriek of laughter as it hit her in the shoulder, and she quickly ducked to grab some snow herself and throw it back at him.

Ed just stared at them and turned to walk away in annoyance. They watched him start to leave, looked at each other for a moment, grabbed handfuls of snow, made quick snowballs, and threw them at his retreating back. They landed with accuracy, stopping him in his tracks. He stood there for a moment, shook his head, and walked on toward his tent with as much dignity as he could muster.

Wanda and Arnold laughed together and continued to play in the snow like two children. Watching them enjoy themselves, Oliver decided to join in, and he threw a snowball at Eileen, who responded by pelting him with one right back. Pretty soon, Adam was pulled into the fight.

April watched in dismay at the five of them playing like schoolchildren. Adam waved to her to join them, but she just shook her head and walked off to the cook tent to get something to eat. Adam shrugged and returned his attention to the battle going on around him.

"Your lady friend doesn't want to play with us?" Oliver called out as he threw another missile at Adam.

"Nope," Adam called back as he ducked, and tossed one back at Oliver. "I don't think April even knows how to play. She probably didn't get to play much as a child. Her loss," he called out before getting pelted.

April took a plate at the cook tent and picked up some fruit.

"Ma'am. Care for some fresh berries? I've got some left over from last night," Charley offered. "You ain't gonna git involved in that there snowball fight? Shore looks like fun to me. Yore picture feller, he seems to be enjoying hisself right smart," Charley observed.

"No, Charley. I don't have any interest in playing in the snow like a little girl. I'm here to do a story, and this is work, so I don't have time to play games like that," she said pompously.

Charley just looked at her for a moment and said casually "I don't know if you knew this, ma'am, but back in the days of the trail drives, them old boys, they would play jokes on each other all the time. The thing was, if a man didn't take a joke well, they knew they couldn't rely on him in a tight spot. The man who couldn't laugh or take a joke was soon on the outside looking in. The games and jokes, they were a way to relieve the boredom and the stress of their lives. Seems to me, those folks out there, they's doin' the same thing. Kinda wish I had the time to join in that fight, but I got to take care of my chores. 'Scuse me, ma'am. Got to get back to work," he told her before he got busy and said no more.

April had the distinct impression she had been scolded and dismissed, but she had no way to prove it. She slowly walked away, thinking about what he had said. After everyone had eaten and things were cleaned up, it was time to move on.

Gerry Senior walked around the camp, calling out to everyone. "Folks, it's time to fold our tents and move on. Everyone, pull your stakes, and let's all get this camp broken down and on the trail. We're burning daylight, folks." This was not quite true, as the sun had just broken the horizon.

As they scurried around, Gerry looked around and he saw every tent was coming down—except one. Warner Barney hadn't started doing anything. He scowled and walked over to where he was supposed to be, apart from the others, and stood outside, and called in. "Barney, did you hear me? I said we need to get these tents struck and packed. Get a move on."

When he didn't receive an answer, he called out again. "Barney, I said we need to get these tents pulled down. Are you going to do it, or do you plan on waiting until someone does it for you?" he called out again. When he didn't get a response to his question, the thought suddenly ran through his mind that perhaps Barney had died during the night. He hesitated, and then he pulled open the flap and looked inside.

It took just a moment for his eyes to get acclimated to the darkened interior before he realized why Barney hadn't responded to his question. It would have been very difficult for him to respond, particularly if he couldn't hear the question, and he couldn't hear the question because he wasn't there.

Miles away by that time, Warner was riding along with his guide, a fellow named Floyd Bergen. They had been on the trail of the big elk for the last three hours, ever since Floyd had crept up to the camp and contacted him while the others were distracted by their good nights and after-dinner conversations. He wasn't sleepy, but he was still tired from his short rest. He hadn't slept but a couple of hours after the meal, because he wanted to be awake when Floyd came for him.

He had made arrangements with the man before they left the lodge, and he had told the guide where to look for them after dark. Bergen had told him he would be shadowing the party for most of the way so he would be well aware of where he was.

"Are you positively certain none of them know you are out here, Bergen?" Warner asked.

"Pretty sure, Mr. Barney. I move like the wind, and no one can see me coming or going," Bergen boasted.

"I paid you good money to be certain, not 'pretty sure,'" Barney said coldly.

"Then yes, I am certain."

"Good. Have you come across any trace of that animal yet? You know—the one I'm paying you good money to find?" he asked sarcastically.

"Not yet, Mr. Barney, but I'll find him now for sure in the snow. He won't be able to hide his tracks now. We'll come across his trail pretty soon, I'm sure. We're real close to where he has been seen a number of times, so there are sure to be tracks we can follow. All I need is a starting point; then I'll be able to find his hiding place. Don't you worry none about that," Bergen assured him.

"I'll believe you when you find him, Bergen. Do you know why I picked you? I picked you because you were the one who wasn't afraid to go up against the ranger and come up here without his permission or approval—and because you had the worst reputation in the area and had the most to lose by double-dealing or disappointing me. I only have one chance to make this kill, so don't make me sorry that I picked you, Bergen. I have a long memory, and I promise you I won't forget you—either way this goes," he said threateningly.

Bergen just nodded.

"What do you mean, he's not here?" Gerry's son asked in a quiet voice that was more upsetting than if he had been yelling. Everyone was gathered in a circle to discuss the surprising and disturbing news.

"I'm just telling you, son, I went to get him moving, and his tent was empty. I don't know when he left, but he wasn't there just a few minutes ago when I went to get him. I don't know what he's up to, but I don't like it," Gerry said.

"I can tell you what he's up to, Gerry," Oliver said. "He isn't interested in saving this magnificent animal. Before we left the lodge, I was given information that he had contacted another guide, a man named Floyd Bergen—"

"That varmint? They's a good match, that's fer shure," Charley muttered. He quieted down when Gerry Junior glared at him.

"As I was saying, he hired a man named Floyd Bergen to help him find the Red Elk and kill it for a trophy for his wall. I wasn't sure he had actually done it before we left, but I suppose I should have told you about it before," he said apologetically.

"Yeah, that would have been nice of you," the younger Bruce said sarcastically. Oliver ignored this remark and continued to address the elder Bruce. "I was hoping that he was going to cooperate with the rules, but I guess I was hoping for too much of him."

"I guess that, since we are sharing secrets, I should share one of mine," Gerry Senior said slowly. He turned around and waved to a man who had been standing off to the side, trying to be as inconspicuous as he could. The man nodded and walked over.

Adam stared hard at him, trying to place his face in his memory. He knew the man's name; last night he had called himself Woody. The man reached the circle and stood beside Gerry Senior. At that moment, Adam decided to take a photo of the group and, as he did, he realized who the man was.

Gerry put his hand on the man's shoulder, and he introduced him to the rest of the group. "Folks, this is a friend of mine. You can call him Woody, but his name is—"

"Parker Woodson!" exclaimed Adam.

As the sun started to come up over the crest of the mountain, Warner was becoming irritated. He had expected to see some signs of the animal by now. The new snow should have shown the way to his target, but all he saw were a few snow hares and squirrel tracks. There was no sign of his quarry anywhere.

"Bergen! Where the hell is my animal? Why haven't you cut his trail yet?"

"Warner, I—"

"Mr. Barney to you, Bergen," Warner cut him off short.

"*Mr. Barney,* then. This is a big area we're searching, so it might take us a little while to cut his path. There's no simple way to find an animal if he doesn't want to be found. We're just going to—"

"I'll tell you what you're going to do, Bergen. You're going to find this damn animal without a lot of delay or excuses, like you told me you could." His face was flushed with rage, and his eyes were flashing. "I paid you good money for results, not for alibis or excuses, do you understand me? I want results, nothing else. Now get busy tracking and find me that animal."

Cowed by Barney's rage, Floyd Bergen just nodded and silently wondered if he had taken on more than he was ready for.

"Parker Woodson?" Oliver asked.

"Yes, Mr. Barry. Parker Woodson. Perhaps you know who I am?"

"Hell, yes, I know who you are! Your name is legendary here. How did you …"

"Mr. Bruce and I are old friends. He helped me get that job thirty years ago with the park system. He gave me the recommendation that got me my position."

Adam just stared at the man in front of him. *Parker Woodson.* The last man to see the heroic Max Phillips alive, and the only person to lay eyes on the man who started the avalanche that killed him. The man in front of him was slender, but aged. He had short, gray hair and hazel eyes and stood about five feet, ten inches tall. He had a lined face, burned by the sun, and, although he was in his late fifties, he still had the look of a man who was capable of great strength of character. There was sadness in his face, and Adam could only imagine the pain he had carried all those years after the death of his friend. But why was he here now?

"I expect some of you are wondering why Mr. Woodson is here, and why he was keeping in the background," Gerry said. "I'm going to let Parker explain to all of you why he is here. Parker?"

"Thank you, Gerry. Folks, I'm here to get justice for my friend Max. I am sure you all know the story of how he died—cut down in the path of an avalanche while trying to rescue some lost skiers." There was a lot of nodding and a murmur of understanding from the group as he spoke. "What may not be common knowledge is what caused the avalanche in the first place."

"It was fresh snow on a high point, and a vibration caused by some trees crashing down set it off—that's what I read," said April.

"Yes, ma'am, a lot of fresh snow and a vibration did set it off, but it wasn't caused by any trees crashing down. It was caused by some careless and ignorant hunter shooting his rifle in a no-hunting zone. I tried to stop him, but he hit me from behind and got away. When I came to, he was gone. I've carried the guilt for Max's death all these years, because I didn't stop the man who caused that tragedy and killed, not just Max, but those helpless skiers as well. When Gerry called me to tell me about this hunting trip, I couldn't stay away. Hell, he couldn't have kept me away with an army. I owe it to Max to make this man pay for his crimes," Parker said with controlled anger.

"Are you saying that the man who caused that avalanche and those people to die is on this trip?" April asked, incredulous at the story that just fell into her lap.

"Warner Barney!" came the excited recognition from Oliver, Eileen, and Arnold.

"Yes, Warner Barney. And now he is going to pay for what he did. I'm going to press the state to file charges for murder against him as soon as we return from this trip," Parker said.

"Well, that's all well and good, but we have a problem here and now," Gerry Junior said angrily. "We still have a job to accomplish, in spite of him, and he's out there somewhere with a rifle and a lot of ammunition, and apparently he doesn't care where he is aiming, so we have to be very careful. I don't want anyone getting hurt by this lunatic, and Bergen isn't exactly a responsible citizen either. This thing is getting out of hand faster than a wolf in a henhouse. We need to come up with a plan and to do this real smart. Bern, do you think you can find where he made contact with Bergen?"

"Don't know, boss. The tracks he made getting to Bergen will be covered by snow—but once we do, it will be a lot easier to follow him now."

"I thought I saw something moving around last night, while Mr. Wilcox and Dr. Fleming were talking," April interjected.

"Why didn't you say something about that last night, miss?" Gerry Junior demanded.

"I didn't say I saw this Bergen fellow; I just saw something moving in the woods behind those two when they were talking," April said, pointing at Wanda and Arnold. "I had no idea it was anything more than just an animal looking for a meal," she said defensively.

"Fair enough, Miss Martens. No one is accusing you of doing anything wrong," the elder Bruce said soothingly.

"Well, Dad, what do we do now?"

"We have to get that animal, and we have to collect Barney as well. He started with us—he has to finish with us," his father said, determination evident in his voice.

"Yeah, we do. But I don't think he's gonna want to come with us. And if he does come with us, can we keep him from killing that animal?" his son asked.

"I'm not sure, to be honest with you. I had planned on keeping an eye on him here, and I figured we would be able to keep him under surveillance the entire trip. I was going to assign either Bern or Axel to be at his elbow every minute, but now ..." he said.

"Seems to me, boss, our first duty is what we were hired to do, and that is to find the elk. After that, we are obligated to protect our guests, which are these fine folks," Bern said slowly, as he waved his arm at the rest of the circle. "Now, Mr. Barney, he joined us under false pretenses with no real intent to abide by our rules or the contract he signed with us. I'm no lawyer, but that seems to me to be grounds for a breach-of-contract suit on his part. We have a real fiduciary relationship with the rest of these people, however, including Mr. Barry here, who represents the authority on this mountain, as well as the others who represent a higher purpose than Mr. Barney. But that's just my point of view, boss," Bern said respectfully.

A long moment of silence followed this speech, in which Gerry looked at his son and Oliver, and Gerry Junior looked at Oliver and Bern, and it was broken by Arnold's hearty laugh. "Well, son, if you aren't a lawyer, you could sure pass yourself off as one!"

"Well, Mr. Wilcox, I did take a couple of law classes before I decided to go into agribusiness," he said shyly.

"Son, you would do well to consider going back into law. I once heard a saying that I think applies here. It goes something like this: 'The man who controls the river controls the land.' So, as long as you work for my good friend Gerry, and you work hard, I'll pay for you to attend law school in your spare time. Then, when you're done, you come see me, and you'll have your first client," he said encouragingly.

"Actually, you'll have your first client in your current employer, Bern. Arnold will be your second," Gerry Senior added.

"And if you come see me, you'll have your third," Oliver added.

"I really appreciate that, Mr. Wilcox, and I won't leave you in the lurch, boss, I promise."

"I know, Bern."

"This is all well and good, and I'm really happy for Bern, but we need to solve what's going wrong here *first*," the younger Bruce said in an effort to refocus their attention.

"My son is right; we need to get our heads back on the subject of here and now."

"Okay, Gerry, what do you propose we do first?" Oliver asked.

"Well, I say let's get packed up and ready to ride, then we can talk more about it as we move," Gerry Junior said.

"Boss, I can go out now and see if I can cut his trail while you all are getting ready to ride out; then you will know what direction to move," Axel volunteered.

"Actually, I'd rather have you scout ahead for the elk, Axel, and I'll have Bern look for Barney and Bergen," Gerry Junior said, looking out at the sky in front of them. "I figure we'll be ready to roll out in about thirty minutes?" he asked, looking at Charley and his father. Both men looked at each other and nodded.

Adam raised his hand and spoke up. "You just tell me what you need, Charley, and I'll get it done."

"I surely do appreciate that, youngster. Come on and give me a hand getting everything packed up for the mules," he said, clapping Adam on the shoulder as he did.

The other riders dispersed to get their tents folded and their things packed for riding. Axel and Bern headed for their horses to start scouting for their respective targets, stopping only to pick up their rifles.

❖

Farther up the mountain, Barney and Bergen were slowly crossing the hills, looking for some signs of their quarry. Warner's attitude was falling as fast as the thermometer, and Floyd's anxiety was increasing in an inversely proportional manner.

"Damn it, where the hell is that damn animal? Why haven't you found some track yet, Bergen? What am I paying you for if not to find him?" Barney cursed.

After five hours of this, Floyd had had enough. He reined up his horse and turned him around to face Warner Barney.

"What are you doing, Bergen? What are you stopping for?"

"Look here, Mr. Barney. You've done nothing but complain about me ever since I picked you up. We have to get something straight here before I go another foot with you," Floyd said, making an effort to keep his voice down and the rage out of it. "You say you are a hunter from all over, and maybe so. If you are, then you have to know that you don't walk out your door and find your target standing there waiting for you. You have to look for him, and he isn't going to be easy to find. In fact, the more valuable the target is, the wilier he probably is.

"Now, this here animal you are hunting, he's been besting the best hunters in this area for as long as I can recall; so he's pretty crafty, and, most likely, he spooks real easy. If we're going to get a shot at him, you're just going to have to be patient. Do you understand me, Mr. Barney? If you can't show a little more patience, I just might take my string and ride down off this mountain and leave you by yourself. I don't want you yelling at me anymore or callin' me names, or none of that behavior no more, or I'm gonna give you back your check and then ride out of this area and leave you to fend for yourself," Floyd said curtly and sat back in his saddle and waited to see which way his speech was going to go.

Warner Barney was astonished that someone of Bergen's caliber would have the courage to stand up to him, and he almost told him to get lost out of anger. But then he realized Bergen was absolutely correct. He did know this was a time-consuming task; he knew that very well. He wasn't going to gain anything by insulting the man and driving him off to go and worry the ranger or worse, say where he was. Warner could make better use of him as an ally—he had to bide his time for now.

Axel and Bern mounted up, nodded to each other, and rode out in opposite directions, each with a goal of finding what they needed to be helpful to the team. Axel was looking for any sign of the big Red Elk that was fueling this hunt. As he walked his horse across the snow, he couldn't help but notice there were no signs of any animal life around him. He stopped and listened, and was a little concerned about what he heard—or, to be accurate, what he *didn't* hear. There were no sounds at all. This was very unusual because there should have been a lot of sounds in the wind. He looked up in the sky and frowned. There were no birds flying anywhere he could see.

Axel sat back in the saddle and wondered what this meant. Even in the winter, he should have been able to see birds flying somewhere up here. There were no signs of animal life anywhere. This wasn't a good sign, and he made a note to talk to Bern and Gerry about it as soon as he caught up with them again. He thought to himself that somehow he needed to scare up some signs of this elk. He pulled his jacket closer and looked around at the trees ahead. There was something over that way, so he headed over to them, hopeful he was on to something.

As he approached them, he saw that what he had seen was just a tree stump, and he lost his enthusiasm. Suddenly Axel had an idea. Maybe there was a way he could scare up some signs for real. He opened his coat and pulled out his revolver. Looking around, he pointed the pistol at the ground away from his horse and pulled the trigger. His horse was used to such things, being used in hunting expeditions, so he barely moved. Axel looked around in all directions to see what else might have been scared by the shot and was very surprised that nothing else had reacted to his shot.

"This is definitely very odd and very wrong," Axel said softly to himself. "I don't know what's going on here, but there's something going wrong at every opportunity. It's a damn good thing I'm not superstitious," Axel said to his horse. His horse just nodded his agreement.

Axel turned his head and started to work outward in a circle, scanning the ground for some sign of anything having passed that way in the last few hours. He spent the rest of the morning and most of the afternoon in this manner, looking in vain for a trace of his extremely elusive quarry.

Bern was having much better luck in his efforts. He had taken April back to her tent, and had her stand there while he mounted up and rode over to where she had seen the movement. When he was in the right place, she waved to him, and that's where he began his search. He started out by walking the ground, looking for some telltale signs of Floyd Bergen. He'd almost missed it, but a scared rabbit darted out from under a low bush, and he turned around to see what was causing the sound. When he did, he saw a branch hanging down from the bush. Bern walked over to it and took a closer look at the end. It was a fresh break, as the sap was still sticky to the touch, and the leaves were still green and not yet curled up.

"This is our starting point, boy," Bern said to his horse, who signaled his agreement with him by a snort and bob of his head. Bern turned to his right and swung up into the saddle. He slowly walked around in an increasing circle until he saw something on the ground. It was a cigarette butt—the same brand as he had found the day before.

Well, it's a starting point, he thought to himself. He knelt down to get a better look at the ground and studied the surface of the snow. Seeing no imperfections on the surface, he stood up and looked around to see what direction would be the most likely for his quarry to have taken.

"Well, they wouldn't have ridden back by the camp, and there's a ravine over there, so I guess we'll go this way, boy," he said to his horse. Bern turned themselves in the direction of the open meadow in front of him and slowly walked along in a wide S-curve to cover the most area as he looked for a sign of the mysterious pack string or their elusive absconding hunter.

After two hours, he found tracks of two horses, one being ridden, and the other not. He followed them in the direction of the camp he had just left and, after a few minutes, saw that the horses had stopped. They milled around for a little while, and then they walked off in another direction, this time both of them were being ridden. He followed this track until he found the sign of their last night's camp.

He was walking in his slow curve when he saw a ring of stones in the middle of the snow. Something about it looked odd, but he couldn't identify what it was for a moment. And then it hit him: how did the stones appear uncovered when the snow fell after …? He shrugged. Whatever, it didn't matter. What really counted was that he had found their camp. He looked around the snow until he saw where their horses had been picketed, and from there, it was easy for him to pick up their trail. They were heading up the mountain in a gradual incline, also going in wide circles as he was.

"Trying to find the elk, no doubt," Bern told his horse. As he followed their trail, he noticed a lot of tracks of different animals coming and going, but nothing that looked like an elk track. He noticed they seemed to be going rather aimlessly, and he assumed they hadn't found any trace of it either.

"This is a smart critter," Bern said to his horse, which showed his opinion in the matter by shaking his head. Bern looked at his watch and, seeing the time, decided to head back to where the others were supposed to be heading. As he made his way, he noticed he was seeing fewer signs of animals and hearing fewer birds calling. He hadn't noticed this at first, but as he rode along, the silence became more pronounced. Bern stopped walking to take his bearings and listen.

Suddenly, he heard a shot in the distance, and he quickly put his horse into a run in that direction, fearing what he might find.

April was ecstatic. Just when she thought her story was falling apart, it had opened up into more than she had ever expected.

This animal is going to be my ticket to the big time for sure, and I know just how to keep it going. And for that matter, why do I need a lot of photographs in my story? she said to herself. *This is my story, and Adam isn't really adding anything to it. On the contrary, he's trying to sabotage me by sucking up to the ranger and everyone else, making me look bad. I try to give the kid a break, and this is how he repays me, by stealing my thunder on this trip?*

All I need to do is make this a first-person story, and the focus is off him entirely. The pictures become punctuation for the story, not the other way around. So, I can do this. I just have to stay in front of the story, and stay close to Axel and Bern, as they will likely see him first. Maybe I should give Axel a little encouragement to try harder, then he'll want me close by for his big victory.

April had it all worked out in her head, and she started to look for Axel, until she remembered he was out in front looking for a sign of their quarry. She made a mental note to be on the lookout for his return and to start giving him more attention when they were alone. She was so intent on planning her strategy that she wasn't watching where she was going—or rather, she wasn't watching where her horse was going. But her attention was refocused very abruptly by a shout from Eileen … just a moment too late.

"April! Duck!"

She turned her head just in time to see the branch right in front of her, and then … *crack*! She went rolling off the back of the horse onto the ground, landing with a thud in the middle of the trail.

"Rider down!" came the call down the line, and Gerry Senior came running up to where she was lying on her back, motionless. He jumped off his horse and ran over to her, Oliver and Eileen right behind him, with Adam coming from the other direction; all of them getting to her within a moment of each other. As Gerry bent down over her, she let out a little moan and tried sit up, but he put a hand on her shoulder and held her still.

"Wha … what happened?" she asked thickly.

Ed remained seated on his mount, but trotted over to her horse, who was contentedly munching on a patch of grass he had found. Ed leaned over, gathered up the dangling reins, and led her horse back to her.

"You looked like you were lost in your thoughts, miss," Gerry said to April as he looked in her eyes for any signs she had suffered a concussion. Finding none, he relaxed and continued. "A horse, miss, he knows just what he can walk over or under, but he don't take into account the rider on his back. You weren't watching where he was going and he walked you under a low-hanging branch.

"You hit your head a good one, and then you went backward head over heels and landed plumb on your back. I don't see any signs of a concussion to your head, but don't you move until I can check out your neck and back and make sure you didn't hurt anything."

"I'm fine, really," April protested as she tried to sit up.

"I think you should do whatever Mr. Bruce says, April," Adam urged her, concerned.

Gerry touched her gently along her sides and manipulated her arms and legs to see how she responded. Finding no reactions of pain, he stood up and held out his hand to help April get to her feet. "Let's see you walk a little, miss. Come toward me and stop when I say stop," he said. She wobbled a bit on her feet, and Adam rushed to her side, but she curtly brushed off his offer of help.

Eileen looked at Oliver as she did this, but Oliver was looking elsewhere. He was looking down at the ground at something, and when she pulled on his arm, he shook his head in an imperceptible move and whispered for her to bring Gerry over when he was done.

"Miss, I'd like you to walk your horse for a little bit before you get back up, if you don't mind. It might be more comfortable for you if you give yourself a few minutes before you get on again," he cautioned her.

"Nonsense, Mr. Bruce. I truly appreciate your concern, but I'm fine. I've had harder falls from much higher up than that. You're right, though. I was lost in my own thoughts and wasn't paying attention. That won't happen again, I assure you. Now, who will be willing to give me hand getting back up?" she asked, looking right at Oliver.

Eileen frowned at this clear overture, but Gerry Junior moved right over and, with a surprising show of strength, picked her up and swung her up onto the saddle with no apparent effort.

"There you go, miss. You be sure to keep an eye on what's ahead of you from now on; I don't want you or anyone else getting hurt on this ride," he said, as he looked around the group. As his gaze swung past Oliver, Oliver gave a little motion with his head to call Gerry Junior over.

"Arnold, you mind getting everyone started? We'll be there in just a moment," he called out.

Arnold gave a wave and led them out again in the direction they had been going before the interruption. As Charley came by, bringing up the rear, Oliver reached out and caught his foot.

"I think I need you here too, Mr. Weeks."

"What's up, young feller?" Charley asked.

"This," Oliver said as he stepped to the left and pointed down. All four looked at the ground at the track in the dirt. "Is that what I think it is, Gerry? I'd be just as happy if you said I was wrong."

Gerry examined the print, at the big spaces and the holes in the ground at the ends of the toes, and he measured them with his own hand. "That depends, Barry, on what you think this is. If you think it is a bear paw print, you'd be right. If you think it is the print of a large bear, you'd be right again. And if you thought it was the print of a black bear, well—this time you'd be wrong.

"But if you thought it was the track of *Ursus Arctos horribilis*, well then, you'd be right. And if you thought it was a recent print, you'd be right again. You have passed your merit badge test, Barry. I'd be obliged if none of you mentioned this to any of the others," he said as he stood up. "We'll be extra careful at camp tonight with the food refuse, Charley. Bury it extra deep, and farther from the camp. This is a big one, so we'll all need to be alert. We'll have guards out tonight anyway, but I'll tell Bern and Axel when they get back. I just hope nothing else goes wrong," Just then they heard the single shot ahead in the distance.

"Now what?" all four said at once as they quickly remounted and rode after the others.

Farther ahead and higher up the mountain, Warner heard the shot as well. He recognized it as a pistol shot and figured by now they had discovered he was gone. He wasn't sure of the purpose of that shot, but he wasn't concerned about it either. They were so far behind, he knew they wouldn't be able to stop him now. All he had to do was find that damn animal, and then in one shot it would all be over. He decided he would wait for them to catch up, and he would show them his kill and there wouldn't be a damn thing any of them could do to him. He didn't have a permit, but the maximum fine was worth it to wipe that smug expression off the boy scout's face.

He would have it out with Bruce as well; he would file a suit for false advertising and anything else his lawyer could come up with, and he would ruin them as well.

A sudden chill wind swept over him and he shivered. As he looked over at Bergen, he saw him open up his coat as if he were warm. Warner found this annoying, as if Bergen was trying to show him up. He felt himself resenting this gesture and decided that, if Bergen could take it, so could he. Warner opened his coat as well, and pushed ahead of Bergen on the trail.

"What's the hurry, Mr. Barney? We don't really have a place to be, and until we catch sight of him or cut his trail, we're really just wanderin' around lost," Floyd called out to him good-naturedly.

"You are paid to find his trail, Bergen. I strongly suggest you start earning your pay, if you hope to get a single red cent out of me later," Warner said coldly.

Floyd pulled up short again and stood there until Warner realized he wasn't behind him anymore.

"Mr. Barney," Floyd said calmly, controlling his rage. "I told you before. There is no certain way to track an animal on this mountain or any other mountain. It is often a matter of luck that one comes across game. Now I am a good tracker, and if *I see* a track, I can follow it anywhere it goes—across dirt, grass, and sometimes water. But I can't, and I don't really believe you can either, follow a track that isn't there.

"I will find this animal if he is still on this mountain, but I can't tell you when I will cut his trail. We have to wander around until we find it. Now, I am taking you to some of the more frequently used watering holes that I know about, and if he has been to any of them, we will find him. But until then, unless you have something constructive to add to the conversation, I'd rather you shut the hell up and not break my concentration on this hunt." Having said his piece, Floyd turned his horse's head and cut off to the right, leaving Warner behind.

Now seething with rage himself, Warner put his hand on the .45 that was sitting in the holster on his hip and started to pull it out—but then he collected himself and let it drop back into the holster. He turned his mount's head and followed Floyd, although he angled to the side so as to put ten yards between them so both could scan the ground. Warner saw plenty of game tracks, but nothing that resembled an elk. He saw the dainty footprint of the deer and the evidence of foxes, snakes, and a bear or two, but nothing that spoke of any elk. They had been riding since before dawn, and he was getting tired.

How could this damn animal be so elusive and hard to find? he asked himself. *Could there really be anything to that crazy theory of Baxter's? No, that's ridiculous. This is a big mountain, and we're just getting started.*

Bergen's right, he assured himself. *It's just going to take some time and luck to pick up his trail, then skill will take over and I won't need this lout, Bergen, any longer.*

"Mr. Barney! Up here, if you would," Floyd called out. Warner kicked his horse into a lope for the short distance to Bergen's side. "Look there." Floyd pointed at the ground. "A track. It's an elk—and a big one, from the size of that print. He's headed for the water hole I told you about. Up that way." He pointed up the mountain.

As Warner's eyes followed Floyd's pointing finger, he saw the clouds building over the crest of the mountain. They were dark clouds, and they seemed to be centered over the right side of the saddle pass. "Yep, looks like snow coming in," Floyd commented. "Maybe we ought to come back later on …" he started, but he stopped as Warner just glared at him.

"Let me explain this to you so even *you* can understand this, Bergen," Warner said from behind his tightly clenched teeth. "I have one chance to get this trophy, and I'm not going back without it. I hired you to find it, so you damn well better find it. If you are going to let a little snow get in your way, then you'd better go back now and I'll do it myself. And when I'm done, I will sue your business into the ground and take everything you've got or ever will have. Now, do you want to make yourself a lot of money here? Or would you rather lose everything you have? I'll just sit here and wait for your answer," Warner said, sarcasm dripping from his voice.

Floyd looked at him without blinking for several moments, no expression on his face. Finally, he turned his mount and began following the tracks up the mountain. Warner trailed behind him, a smug look on his face, knowing he had beaten the man down.

A chill wind swept down the mountain over him once more.

Axel saw Bern coming at him at a run and stood up in the stirrups to wave him down. "Hey, Bern, I wanted to talk about this trip a bit."

"Are you okay? Why did you fire that shot? Is anything wrong?" Bern asked anxiously.

"No, bro, everything's fine … except for one little odd thing."

Relieved his brother wasn't in any trouble, he sat back and looked around. "So what's the deal here, Axel?"

"Well, it's like this, Bern: I've been riding for several hours and I haven't seen any tracks. And I don't mean any elk—I mean anything! Nada, zip, nothing. No tracks of anything. And look up—there's no birds flying around either," Axel pointed. Both men looked at the sky.

There were a lot of clouds, some wispy, some full of water, and some full of snow. The sky had a lot of blue, but that was behind them. Ahead of them was the top of the mountain, and the darkest clouds were ahead. But nowhere ahead of them were there any birds.

"And there's this, Bern. That's where we have to go. Up there. I'm getting a bad feeling about this venture. There's something wrong with this whole thing, but I don't know what it is. That man, Barney, he gives me the creeps. And who's that guy boss snuck into this trip? You know, the man we weren't supposed to know about or talk about or talk to or have anything to do with?" Axel persisted.

"You heard what he said—his name is Parker Woodson, and he was with the ski patrol when your Mr. Barney—"

"He's not *my* Mr. Barney," Axel protested.

"Just teasin', brother. Anyway, he was here when that other patrol guy, Phillips, was killed, and he believes Barney's responsible. He's here to bring him to justice when this is over."

"Well, I just hope this is over real soon. Getting that animal down the mountain will be a real chore. I don't look forward to wrestling it down the slope," Axel said with feeling.

"We have to catch him before we talk about getting him down the hill, and I haven't seen a sign of him either. And now that I think about it …" Bern turned in his saddle to look around him.

"Now that you think about it, *what?*"

"Now that I think about it, I haven't seen the tracks of anything big around here. You have any ideas, little brother?" Bern asked.

"Yeah, I'm thinking about going home. But I suppose that isn't the idea you were hoping for. Maybe we should ride together for a time, okay?"

As they climbed higher and circled the side of the mountain,

Warner became more conscious of the cold, even though it didn't seem to be affecting Floyd. He looked at his watch; it was almost two o'clock. He gauged the light and estimated they had about three hours of light remaining before they would need to set up camp.

Floyd noticed him looking at his watch and called out, "Don't worry, Mr. Barney. We're headed for our first camp. I keep it up in the winter for my other hunts. We're only a mile or so from the site; I recognize that tree right over there." He pointed up ahead.

A victim of a lighting strike, the tree had been split down the middle by the bolt. It was burned all around the top, and the inside was burned black—although it was showing signs of new growth around the base of the tree.

"We have to go upward a bit and head east for a few hundred yards. It's well protected from the elements and from sight. Unless you know it's there, you'd ride right past it every time and never see it. It's got fresh water coming from a stream a little farther down the hillside. Come on, we'll get set up for the night, and I will find him for you tomorrow. We'll get a good night's rest and a good meal, and you'll feel better in the morning," Floyd advised.

Warner hesitated for a moment and, in that hesitation, he experienced something he had never known before. This puzzled him, and he looked up at the mountain as if he could see to the very top. As he did, he saw the clouds moving around, forming and reforming shapes ...

And he had the strange sensation the mountain was looking down at him.

Suddenly, the name of the earlier strange feeling came to him. It was *uncertainty.*

The group had reassembled on the trail, and, naturally, everyone wanted to know what the four of them had been talking about. Gerry just brushed the questions off with a laugh and said they had just been discussing the accident and how to proceed. Although this made sense to Adam, he had a feeling they were not being totally honest. He decided to ask the ranger about it later—in private.

"Mr. Bruce, how are we going to find the others?" he asked.

"Son, I reckon they'll find us when they are ready to. You don't have to worry about it none," Gerry Senior assured Adam with a confidence he didn't really feel. "We'll be heading upward now, so y'all hold onto the saddle horn if you need to. Lean forward when we climb—it'll make it easier for your horse to do the work—and lean back when we go down the hills. Keep your eyes open for any sign of our friends," he added and moved ahead to the front of the line.

"Which one does he mean?" Wanda asked Arnold.

"Both of them, I suspect," he answered her with a smile he didn't really feel.

Just then, Oliver and Eileen trotted up to join them.

"Dr. Fleming, I was just wondering something; would you mind answering a question for me? About what you told Warner Barney yesterday, about the squirrels, I mean. I was just wondering ..."

"You were wondering if what I said about teaching their young applied to this animal we are looking for?" she said with a knowing smile.

"Yes, that's it. You told him that it was possible the ..."

"I have to tell you the truth, Mr. Barry. I was just trying to make him upset. Yes, it's true that squirrels do teach their young survival skills, as do most animals, but that *any* animal could teach the skills this animal is reported to have? No, Mr. Barry, I was exaggerating the possibility just to make a point and to get back at him. I can't think of any animal that could do that. I doubt you could find any naturalist or wildlife expert anywhere who would subscribe to that theory," Wanda said thoughtfully. She was silent for a moment as she considered other possibilities. "No, Mr. Barry, what I suspect we will find is maybe several animals with a similar color that are being seen all over the mountain. It could be a natural adaptation to their environment or a result of a change in their food supply. Perhaps this coloration is the result of a molecular change in the grasses or vegetation in their grazing area. This would account for the color change, I think. It would also explain why there are other animals with a similar coloration, Mr. Barry," she said confidently.

"You're probably right, Wanda. I'm sure that's the explanation for this mystery," Oliver said with a confidence he didn't really feel.

Gerry Junior rode at the head of the group, looking for the trail to their next camp, and he was thinking about what had happened to his easy money.

"This damn trip has all gone to shit in front of my eyes, and it's all because of that man, Barney. Why didn't I listen to Dad? He warned me that Barney was bad news and poison; I should have listened to him. Now I've got one person injured, although not seriously, and that lunatic is out of my sight and running wild. I'll be pretty damn lucky if she and her damn newspaper don't sue the crap out of me for this fiasco. The ranger warned me this could be a problem, and I was too damn stubborn to listen to him. That damn Bruce stubborn streak—it's going to get me hurt someday, for sure," he muttered to himself.

How he was going to salvage any profit out of this, he didn't know. He'd be lucky if Barney didn't sue him for every penny he had, as well as the ones he didn't have.

He looked up at the sky as he rode on and noticed that it was looking as dark as his future. It was probably going to snow again tonight—that would make it a little easier to find the animal. Maybe he'd catch a break on this after all. He didn't know how good Baxter was with a rifle, but it was his show when they found the animal. He was content to let Ed Baxter take the shot—and, hit or miss, it wasn't his responsibility to bring the Red Elk down, just to find it. That was going to be hard enough.

As he walked along, something kept pulling his attention back to the clouds. He watched them swirling high above, and he realized what it was that was drawing him to them. They weren't just snow clouds—they were *angry* snow clouds. They held a lot of snow, and that meant risky going in the higher elevations. It could be a blizzard up there, and a lot of new snow meant that avalanches were likely … and they were going to be shooting up there.

Gerry suddenly felt he was in over his head, and he ought to turn the group around and go back down the mountain. He couldn't do that, of course, but he suddenly wanted to. He started thinking about his boys, and what his wife would do without him. Gerry shook himself to get those thoughts out of his mind. He told himself he needed to put his focus on the task at hand, or those thoughts could be coming true.

Suddenly, the hair on the back of his neck started to rise. His hand immediately went to the stag-horn grips of the Colt 45 on his hip, but he noticed his horse continuing to walk along, showing no signs of nervousness. He slid the thong off the hammer, giving him freedom to draw quickly if he needed to, but the fact that his horse didn't seem to detect any threat caused him to become very concerned. What could be out there that he could detect and his horse couldn't? This didn't make sense, and that worried him too.

Gerry stopped in his tracks and looked around. Goldie was unconcerned, and she kept nibbling at the weeds growing along the trail. He couldn't see anything out of place, but the feeling that something was wrong wasn't going away.

"What in the hell …?" he said quietly to himself. "Don't you hear anything, Goldie?" he asked his horse, but she just kept on eating. As he heard the others coming up behind him, the ominous feeling passed just as quickly as it had come. "That was definitely weird," Gerry said to Goldie, who just nodded her head and began walking again.

"Any problems, son?" his father said as he came up beside him.

"No, Dad. Just taking a look around," was all he said, not mentioning the weird feeling.

An hour later, Gerry and his son saw Axel and Bern riding toward them in an easy lope. They didn't appear to be excited, and when they pulled up to a halt in front of them, Bern asked if either of them had seen anything, and both of the men said they had. Bern looked at Axel and nodded to him.

"We saw a big elk, boss. He was up on the mountain above us. We were fanning out, looking for some sign of him when we heard him bugle and looked up the side of the mountain, and there he was. He has a huge rack, at least an eight-pointer—or maybe even a twelve-pointer. A magnificent animal. I've never seen an elk like this before. He just stood there, watching us, it seemed, while we were watching him. Oh. And did I mention that he was red?"

Higher up the mountain, but twenty miles away, Floyd was on the trail of the track he had found a little while earlier. He led Warner as he followed the tracks to the watering hole, a pool at the bottom of a little outflow from a rock outcropping.

When they arrived on the way to their camp, Warner suddenly felt like someone let the air out of his balloon. The animal they had been tracking was at the hole, drinking. He was a magnificent six-point buck with a beautiful dark brown coat. Warner raised his rifle and took careful aim but didn't squeeze the trigger.

"You gonna take the shot or not, Barney?" Floyd whispered beside him.

Warner lowered his rifle and snarled at Bergen. "Maybe you're color-blind, Bergen, but that animal out there is not even close to red. And if I shoot now, I might drive him farther away. Let's get to camp and start out fresh tomorrow," he snapped. As they turned to leave, he chanced a look up the mountain at an outcropping sticking out into the air and froze.

He slowly reached out to stop Bergen from moving. As Floyd looked down at the hand gripping his arm with an unexpected strength, he saw Barney looking away and pointing up the mountain. He looked in the direction he was pointing and saw the elk standing on the ledge.

"Well, I'll be damned. I've never seen him before, but I can understand your zeal now, Mr. Barney. He's absolutely incredible! I've never seen another like him up here or anywhere else. He'll make a championship mount! Now we have him! Tomorrow, I'll take you up there, and we'll start tracking him down. We have a starting point now, and I'll show you how to chase down a target," Bergen said eagerly.

Warner heard him talking, but he wasn't really listening. He couldn't take his eyes off the animal, and he had the strangest feeling it could see him too. The wind picked up as he stared at the elk standing far above him, and he could see the clouds swirling in the darkening sky above. He could feel the chill in the air that told him more snow was coming, and probably a lot of it. Finding it and bringing it down was his destiny; Warner knew it as sure as he knew his own name.

"You saw him?" Ed couldn't believe his ears.

"Yep, both of us saw him, Mr. Baxter. He was a long way off, mind you, but with the binoculars, we got a real good look at him. It was him, no doubt about it," Axel said excitedly.

"Describe him for me, if you would," April said, her pen in hand.

"Well, like Axel said, he's a big one. He's got to be at least four hundred pounds, if he's an ounce," Bern reported calmly.

"And his color!" Axel added. "Tell them about his color, Bern!"

"What my excitable young brother is trying to say is that we have never seen any elk the shade he is. He's been described for years as being red, but I've always thought it must be a dull, reddish brown with a slightly more reddish cast than usual. You know elk are reddish-brown in color naturally, right? Well, this elk is a bright red! I don't know what he's eating, and I don't know where he's finding it, but something has made him look like no other elk I've ever seen or heard of. It should make it very easy to spot him in the woods with the snow behind him.

"He was just standing on this ledge, like he was surveying his kingdom," Bern explained. "It was kind of strange too; he didn't seem concerned to be standing out there in plain sight and so easy to take a shot at. We didn't have a rifle that would have reached him, and it was like he knew it," he recalled. "While I was looking at him, he turned his head in my direction, and I had the weird feeling he was looking back at me. He looked right into my face from that mountain, and I couldn't put the binoculars down until he looked away. I blinked and picked them up again, but he was gone, and I couldn't find him anywhere on that ledge or nearby," Bern told them, slowly reliving the moment.

There was a silence among the group while they all absorbed Bern's experience.

"Horseshit!" exclaimed Ed Baxter. "I don't know what you think was going on up there, but he wasn't looking at you, and he wasn't scarlet in color either!" he challenged.

Axel started to say something, but Bern just put his hand on Axel's arm, and he sat back in his saddle.

"Mr. Baxter," Bern responded politely, "I know it is a difficult tale to believe, and I know you didn't see it, so I understand your skepticism. I was willing to accept your theory of how he has carried on all these years, so I ask you this: isn't it at all possible that whatever has allowed him to pass on his knowledge might have also affected his ability to adapt his color, much like a chameleon does?"

"That may be true, Mr. Justner, but he can't change the color of his hair at will. That just can't happen," Baxter assured him.

"Then I guess he stays scarlet, Mr. Baxter," Bern said softly.

"Dr. Fleming, this is your area of expertise—what do you think?" Ed asked her.

Wanda thought for a moment before she responded. "Gentlemen, I am not sure. I don't rule out a genetic mutation that might have created a new color strain—those things do happen from time to time whenever nature has a reason to make a change. But that the animal would be looking at you directly, well, to be honest, that is a lot harder for me to accept as a fact. I think it is far more likely he was looking in your direction, scanning for danger or something like that. I was talking with Mr. Barry about this earlier, and, as I told him, it could be the result of a change in their feeding patterns or what they're eating—or even a change in the nature or growth of what they're eating. I've been giving it some thought since then, and I'm leaning more toward that possibility. Perhaps you might have a thought on that, Mr. Baxter?" she asked courteously.

"As much as I hate to agree with you, Dr. Fleming, I would have to say that makes a lot of sense," Ed agreed reluctantly. "I could see a bacterial infestation or something mutating the grasses and causing this outcome. Perhaps something on the order of the shrimp in the diet of flamingos causing their signature pink color," Ed suggested, reflecting on possible causes for the change in the color of the elk's coat.

"But what about him looking right at us?" Axel protested.

"Which way was the wind blowing—toward him or toward you?" Ed asked curiously.

Bern and Axel looked at each other for a moment, and then they spoke at the same time.

"It was blowing toward me," Bern said positively.

"It was blowing toward him," Axel said, just as certain.

As they looked at each other again, Arnold spoke up with a grin. "Sounds like a mighty confused wind to me, boys. Maybe it was blowing in both directions, or maybe it was blowing around in a circle?"

"We saw what we saw, Mr. Arnold. I can't help it if you don't believe us. Maybe later on, we'll be able find a way to prove it to all of you," Bern said sadly.

As the riders began their ascent to the camp higher up the mountain, everyone felt the air temperature and the first snowflakes began to fall.

Both of the Bruces looked up at the sky and the top of the mountain far above them. "It's kind of early for this kind of snow, don't you think, Dad?"

"Yeah, son. I don't like it. It reminds me of another early winter, a long time ago."

Parker just looked ahead and said nothing, pulling his coat closer around him. Oliver looked at the white flakes and wondered just was lying ahead and in store for them on the mountain.

Farther down the hill, and behind the group trailing Warner Barney, the sow bear could feel the air getting colder, and she knew her remaining time for hunting was growing shorter. She felt the pull of nature, calling her to seek a place to sleep off the winter; but the hunger in her belly was calling with equal urgency. She could tell she was getting closer to the source of food—the scent was growing stronger. She could smell it in the distance, along with another scent she knew well: it was the scent of the dreaded and hated humans, and that always meant danger.

But her stomach was growling, and she needed one last meal before going to sleep. She could smell the food—it was calling her, and she was hungry. She stood up and roared out her challenge to anyone who might be thinking about entering her territory to take her meal. She looked around, but no one seemed interested in challenging her for the food she smelled up ahead.

Satisfied, she dropped to the ground and huffed her satisfaction that she didn't have to fight. She swung her great head around, testing the air for the scent she was following. After a few exploratory sniffs, she picked it up again on a westerly heading farther up the mountain. The problem was the humans were also farther up the mountain, and the scents appeared to be in the same place.

Her needs were simple, as was her method of addressing them. She followed her nose and dealt with the situation as she found it. As she started to follow the scent, the snow began to fall—a few flakes at first, but then faster. She knew she had to hurry if she was going to get her meal in before her need to hibernate took over.

CHAPTER 8

It wasn't as festive a mood at camp as it had been the night before. April was nursing a headache, Wanda was busy taking notes as she interviewed Axel and Bern about the elk, and Gerry Junior was standing at the edge of the camp and looking up the mountain through the binoculars in the dark. Arnold was sitting with Oliver, Eileen, and Gerry Senior, and they were all talking quietly with Parker Woodson. Ed Baxter was cleaning and assembling his rifle for the tenth time, while Adam was helping Charley tend to the cleaning up of the kitchen.

It had been a quiet dinner, with little conversation and no music. Everyone was deep into their own thoughts and concerns, so there was little interaction between any of them. Even the normally chipper Charley was somber and not into telling stories this night. The expedition had changed from a lark to a dreary chore, and everyone was quite aware of the element of danger around them as they hadn't been before. The continually falling snow didn't help either, as it kept smothering the fire, which took constant care to keep it going. It was piling up in big drifts all around them, and the cold they all felt was not simply because of the snow.

Something ominous was in the air, although none would speak of it aloud. It was as if they were all sitting on a keg of dynamite, waiting for the tiniest of sparks to ignite it. Tempers were short everywhere, and no one wanted to say the one thing to set everything off. Each was thinking about the things that had been said at dinner, some regretting the words chosen, and others the manner in which they were said. They were no longer a team, but thirteen individuals coexisting in an uneasy truce that couldn't last long.

It didn't.

It hadn't started out that way; everyone had been excited and eager to get on with the hunt. Someone had seen it, and it was real. Regardless of the shade of its coat, whether a reddish-brown or the brighter red that Bern and Axel insisted it was, the elk was real, and it was out there. It was just ahead of them, and they had a starting point to look from. It was no longer a wild goose chase, and even the normally dour Ed Baxter was excited and jovial. The minor disagreement over the exact shade of its coat didn't really matter; it could have been just atmospheric conditions making it look redder.

At dinner, everyone was happy and cheery and eager to make conversation with their neighbor. Wanda had pulled out her notebook and field guide for the area and was comparing what the field book said to what Axel and Bern had seen—or claimed to have seen—and she was making notations in her book about what they were saying they saw. She was prepared to take their word, as they were experienced hunters and were familiar with the wildlife in this area. What was interesting for her was that everything they described was consistent with what was known about this animal, except for the color of its coat. If they were going to exaggerate or make something up, why would they select the easiest point to dispute or disprove? No, there was something to this color change, and she intended to find out what it was.

"Bern, I don't mean to say you're wrong about the color of this animal because I didn't see it, but I am sure you are aware it is quite unusual for an animal to have a color or markings that would make it stand out in the forest. The natural thing in nature is for their coat or skin to help camouflage the animal for their safety and protection. Is there any possibility you could have been seeing some red leaves in front of him or a reflection of the sunset on his fur?" she asked him politely.

"Dr. Fleming, I appreciate your position and your desire for accuracy, but I am going to tell you one last time, he was as red as ... as ..." He looked around the camp for something to compare to, and his eye lighted on the can Charley used to store fuel for the camp stove. "… as red as that can over there by Charley."

While casually playing with a stick, Adam spoke up. "Bern, would you say it is as red as the colors in my flannel shirt … or maybe in a parka?"

Parker's head came up fast at this question, but he waited for Bern's response before he said anything. He wondered if the photographer suspected what he believed to be the answer to that question. Bern thought about it for a moment, and he looked at Adam's shirt, and then he looked at Axel, and both of them nodded in response.

Oliver saw Parker's reaction, and he had the feeling he was about to step off into "The Twilight Zone," as Rod Serling used to say.

"Why'd you make that comparison, Adam?" Parker asked, looking down at the snow.

"Just something I read somewhere, I guess," Adam responded vaguely.

"No, I don't think so. I've talked with you already, Adam, and you're a real smart and observant fellow. I think you've got something on your mind that you want to ask me or tell me. I'd like to know what it is, please," Parker said, looking Adam in the eye.

Oliver looked over at Adam, who was suddenly very interested in the stick he was playing with, and he added his request to the conversation.

"I think you should discuss your theory, Adam. I am sure the others would like to hear it, and I don't think it is as crazy as you might believe."

Eager to find out how her former assistant was selling her out with the ranger, April added her two cents' worth. "Yes, Adam, I'd like to hear about your theory too!" she said very sweetly—but Adam wasn't fooled. He knew there was going to be trouble with her, and he knew he might as well start working on his résumé when he got back.

Reluctantly, he began to explain his idea. "You are aware there is a story about a ghost skier on the mountain who rescues wayward skiers from danger, Mr. Woodson?" Adam asked.

"I have heard of this skier a time or two," Parker admitted.

"Are you aware he is always seen in a bright red parka, and he never speaks, and comes and goes out of a cloud of snow?"

"I have heard that as well, Adam," Parker acknowledged.

Oliver spoke up in support of Adam. "I have a file back at the office that has about fifty sightings of him, including two just before we left on this trip. I have never seen him myself, but all of the sightings have been consistent with what Adam is saying, Mr. Woodson."

"Please, just Parker will do, Mr. Barry."

"Then I insist you call me Oliver."

"Anyway, the story is that is your friend, Max Phillips, is still doing his job of guarding the guests," Adam explained.

"I see," Parker said solemnly. "Well, that sure sounds like Max," he said with a laugh. "But how does that figure in to this red animal we're looking for?" he asked.

"Well, I'm not sure, but it's my suspicion that it's your friend Max Phillips again."

Ed let out a hoot of ridicule and began to laugh at the idea Adam was proposing. "I've never heard of such utter drivel in all of my life! There is a ghost haunting the mountain and the same ghost is this mysterious elk that we're all chasing? That's rich!" He bent over, still laughing, but stopped when he realized he was the only one who was.

"I can't believe any of you are taking this seriously," he said in complete amazement, only to be greeted by stony silence. "Come on, people, think about it. Even if you accept there is a ghost skiing on the mountain, rescuing idiots who shouldn't be skiing, how does that translate into a big animal?" Ed argued.

"Well, I, for one, do believe in spirits, Mr. Baxter," Wanda said stiffly. "I believe that each of us has a God-given spirit, and if an individual's life is ended abruptly, sometimes the spirit remains behind to complete the task assigned to it. I've seen things back in Newport that do not make sense or logic, but are explainable only by accepting sometimes we have to operate on faith and trust, and not just what our eyes or minds tell us."

"Well said, Wanda," Arnold said heartily, and then he turned to look right at Ed. "Ed, I know you read Shakespeare a lot, so perhaps you remember the famous quote from *Hamlet?* 'There are more things in heaven and earth, Horatio, than are dreamt of in your philosophy.' This just means we have to keep an open mind to all things, Ed. Remember, what we know now as fact was just science fiction for our grandparents.

"Do you remember reading *20,000 Leagues Under the Sea* in school,

Ed? Jules Verne wrote about nuclear-powered submarines, scuba gear, and dozens of other things he couldn't have known about in 1869, but we take them for granted now," Arnold added. "You think Custer could have used a few Uzis or flamethrowers? We don't know everything there is to know, Ed. And I, for one, would like to hear the rest of this young man's idea. Unless you have an alternate theory you'd like to present?"

"Fine," Ed responded in a surly tone, signaling his submission to Arnold.

"Go on, son. We'd like to hear the rest of your theory," Arnold encouraged Adam.

April didn't say anything; she was busy writing all of this down, along with notes to herself about what she was going to do to Adam for stealing her story.

"Well, it seems to be this animal is sort of doing the same thing as the skier, in a way, for the animals. And since that hunter from before—"

"Warner Barney," Parker added coldly.

"Yes, since Mr. Barney was involved in your friend's death, this animal may be trying to draw him out to bring some sort of closure. Maybe ..." Adam offered, uncertainly. There was another silence, broken by the sound of Ed whistling the theme from the old series *The Twilight Zone*, showing plainly what he thought of what he was hearing.

Defensively, Adam started to say something to Baxter, but he caught himself.

Eileen spoke at last. "Well, it is a possibility. If you can accept what Wanda said, then what Adam is suggesting could make sense. I kind of like the idea of a ghost protecting the skiers and the wildlife. It has a nice feel to it, and it's kind of folksy," she said as she looked around the group.

Wanda nodded, and Arnold didn't say anything to indicate he disagreed. Ed stood up and addressed the entire group.

"I think you're all nuts. It's just an animal—a big one with an unusual coat color, but it's nothing more and nothing less. When we get it back to the preserve, you'll see just how supernatural it really is," he said confidently.

Bern cleared his throat to get attention. "Well, for me, I don't believe in ghosts or any supernatural incidents, but this critter doesn't act like any other of its kind. I'm not sure just yet what I do or don't believe about him, other than he's tricky. I suggest everyone keep their eyes open," he said.

Gerry Junior stood up and stretched. "I'm going to take the first watch, Bern. You wake me in three hours. 'Night folks." And he walked off to the edge of the camp, picking up his rifle as he passed by his saddle and gear.

April stood up and walked over to sit down next to Gerry Senior, in an effort to start a conversation with him. "Mr. Bruce, what is your opinion of Adam's idea? Do you think it's as crazy as it sounds?" She said it loud enough for Adam to hear her, her intent being to make him look foolish and embarrass him back into taking orders, as he was supposed to be doing. She never expected the response that she got.

Gerry looked up at the mountaintop and spoke very carefully. "Miss, I have to say, I've been considering that for a while now. I've heard the stories about the skier and this big elk for a number of years, and I've got to say that I'm not ruling it out. Both of these stories began being told a short time after that man Phillips was killed. Both of them have a lot in common, just as your young man has suggested."

"He's not my young man, Mr. Bruce. He works at the paper with me, and he takes the photographs for my story," April said defensively.

"Yes, ma'am. Just as Adam has suggested, is what I meant to say. The other thing is, you see, both of these legends—and they have become legends around here, make no mistake about that—both of these legends have been described as being red. Now Woody here, he says that they used to wear a red parka on the ski patrol back then. Isn't that right, Woody?" he asked.

"Yes, Gerry. We used to use red because it would stand out in the snow and make it a lot easier for the skiers to see us coming and allow us to see each other from a long distance. That was before we had GPS and good radios. The radios we had then would go out without warning, and they were cumbersome to carry while skiing. Mine went out while I was looking for Max—I wanted to warn him about the snow and Barney, but he never heard me," Parker said sadly.

April was stunned; she hadn't anticipated that Adam's insane idea would have been taken so seriously by these people. Surely the veterinarian would have more sense than to buy into this ridiculous nonsense. Ghosts. April believed in what she could see and touch, and there was no room in her practical world for this mumbo-jumbo of spirits and ghosts and unresolved obligations carried on after life ended. You made the most of your time here, and when you died, you died. They buried you, and then the show was over, and that was that. How these supposedly intelligent people could believe this was beyond her comprehension. She turned to the rancher, but before she could even ask the question, he was answering it for her.

"Miss, out here we tend to be pretty open-minded about most everything. I've heard the stories about the ghost myself, just like Gerry has, just like everyone in this region has, and I even spent a couple of cold nights out here myself, looking for that Red Elk. Never came close to seeing him, though," he said with a laugh. Then his voice and expression turned very serious.

"I was here when that tragic event took place, and I was more than just friends with the late Max Phillips—I was his stepfather. Max used to talk a lot about his job and the sense of fulfillment it gave him. Max always liked helping people; he liked being needed and he lived for his time on the mountain.

"He was proud of his red parka; he felt he earned it the hard way, through hours of hard work and practice and dedication to the job. He would spend his off-time on the slope, learning every trail and every nuance of the mountain. He didn't have a steady girlfriend—he always said the mountain was his girlfriend."

No one said a word as Arnold spoke, the pain in his voice clear to everyone, even to April. Wanda held his hand as he spoke and gave it a squeeze, offering her silent support. He looked over at her and continued his story.

"Many times he would come over after his shift was over and talk about the events of the day. He used to say that he felt at home up on the mountain, and it was his calling to be on the safety patrol. He had offers of other jobs, but he always turned them down. That was where he wanted to be. After he was killed, we went out looking for his body, but we never found it. I think that's what killed his mother; she never got over losing her only son. We never had children ourselves; he was her child from an early relationship. She said he never knew he had a son—she never told the father about Max because he left her the moment she told him she was pregnant.

"She raised Max all by herself, until we met. He was twelve when I came into his life, and we got along from the start. She never told me who the father was, and I never asked. I found some letters in her closet after she died, and I looked through them for some clues to who he might have been, but all I found to identify the son of … the man was a photograph without any identification. So I never knew his name and I never looked any further.

"Even now, sometimes, when I am up on those slopes, I can feel Max near me. So do I believe, Miss Martens? The answer is yes, I do believe. Because I want to believe he is still up there, watching out for everyone on his mountain. Excuse me." He stood up and walked away, Wanda beside him.

April sat there, unsure of what to say or do. She started to make a joke, and Adam, who had been listening intently to every word Arnold said, spoke up.

"Shut up, April. There's a time to say something, and this isn't it." He got up and left the circle as well.

Parker looked at his retreating back and spoke to the fire. "Intense young man, isn't he?"

"I've known Arnold for five years now, and that's the first time he ever talked about himself in any way," said Ed, amazed by what he had heard.

"I've known him twenty-five years, and I never knew any of that," said Gerry with a hitch in his voice.

Oliver and Eileen just sat there, feeling the big man's pain and the frustration of not being able to help. Oliver made a decision and stood up.

"Folks, I'll be right back. Please wait for me," he said as he left to go to his tent, leaving everyone with puzzled looks on their faces.

Gerry looked over at Eileen, who just shook her head and shrugged her shoulders. Oliver was back in three minutes, and he had Arnold and Wanda behind him.

"Folks, it wasn't my intention to share this with anyone, but after hearing what Arnold and Parker have been through, I feel I have to do whatever I can to make things right." He handed Eileen the little box that had been delivered to his office before they left. She opened it up and looked inside. Looking back at Oliver, she handed it to Arnold.

He looked at it and then handed it to Parker, who took it out of the box for a better look.

"Where did you get this?" Parker asked calmly.

"A friend of mine has the authority to give me one. For special circumstances. I helped him with a problem once or twice, and he said I could always count on him for help if I needed it. I figured I might need it on this trip," Oliver said in a light manner. Just then, Adam rejoined them, as he had seen Oliver leave the group and return.

"Is this thing a secret or can anyone else see it?" he inquired.

Parker looked at Oliver, who nodded his assent. Parker handed it to Adam, who stared at it in complete surprise.

"Is this the real thing?" he asked in amazement. His question was understandable, as he had never seen a US Marshal's badge before, much less held one in his hand.

Farther up the mountain, Warner Barney was complaining bitterly. They had been unable to keep the fire lit due to the hard-blowing wind and steadily falling snow, so they were in a cold camp. Floyd wasn't feeling too good either, partly due to the elements, but mostly due to the company. He had tried to shut out his employer's harsh and nasal carping, but he was rapidly losing ground. Floyd counted in his head the money he was going to make off this trip, but it wouldn't drown the droning complaints.

After a couple of hours, he finally had enough. "Mr. Barney, don't nothing ever suit you none? You done nothing but complain the entire time we've been out. We got you away without any trouble and now we know where to start lookin' for your trophy kill. Don't you ever see the bright side of things, or do you always see the underside of the rock?" Floyd asked him, exasperation evident in his voice.

"Mr. Bergen," Warner replied coldly, "how I look at the world and the people in it isn't your problem. What I enjoy or do not enjoy isn't your problem, and neither is what makes me happy or unhappy. In short, any and all of my life issues are not your concern. You do not need to concern yourself with anything to do with me, other than making sure I get the shot I want of the animal I want before those other people find him. Do you think you can manage to do that, or have I overestimated your ability to do what you promised you could? If I have, tell me now, and you may leave and go back to your business of guiding the mewling little city-dwellers who want to see the big outdoors like real men do.

"You will, of course, be hearing from my attorney within a week of my finishing what I came here to do, and he will make sure that even that measly work will be beyond your reach from now on." The acid in his voice and the threat in his words were unmistakable. "Let me make myself perfectly clear to you, Mr. Bergen. I don't give a damn what you think or what you think about me. I haven't needed anyone's approval for anything I did since I was sixteen, and that isn't going to be changing anytime soon. When I want something, I go get it, and nothing stands in my way. I will go over it or through it—it doesn't matter to me. Success is all that counts in my world, and nothing and no one is going to hold me back from getting what I want. I don't need anyone hanging on to me to ride my coattails. I shake them off as quickly as they grab on," Warner continued coldly.

"Mr. Barney, you married?"

"Of course not!"

"Got any kids?"

"Are you listening to me at all? Of course not!"

"Didn't think so," was Floyd's closing statement as he rolled over in his sleeping bag and turned away from Warner Barney.

As he tried to get to sleep in the cold, he told himself he was done with this kind of business with this kind of person. Floyd thought about the men farther down the mountain. He had always sneered at the Bruces because he considered them "goody-goody" and suckers for allowing the regulations that the Park Service set up for them to dictate how they ran their business. He had had many a confrontation with Gerry Junior over this, laughing at him and calling him a chump for the way he jumped through all the hoops the park people made them jump through.

He had always skirted the rules as much as he could, doing whatever he wanted—under the table, as it were.

Now, here he was with a man who was just like himself, only meaner and with the money to make people do things they didn't want to do.

Is this what I am going to turn into in my later years? Floyd asked himself silently. *Am I going to become this man, who has no one to leave anything to, because no one wants to be near him except for his money? Those men down there—they have a good ranch, a thriving business, and no real worries. Everyone in town calls them mister, and me they just call Bergen. Maybe I'm the one who's the real chump here.*

What have I got to show for all my slick ways and corner-cutting, anyway? A broken-down string of over-the-hill horses, a broken-down ranch I can't afford to fix up or hire anyone to fix up for me, and an old, beat-up truck to haul a beat-up four-horse trailer with. I've got maybe about six hundred dollars in the bank, and I owe about six times that on the damn truck. I'm sleeping in the snow and bitter cold with a man who's even more miserable a person than I am, because I have to in order to make any money this month.

Sure, they're sleeping down there in the same snow and cold, but it is because they wanted to. So who's the real chump here?

Funny thing, Floyd, if anyone told you three days ago that you'd be thanking that mean SOB over there for showing you the light, you'd have spit in their eye.

And here's another funny thing, Floyd: remember the thing your old daddy used to say? He'd quote Ben Franklin and say, "It's an ill wind that blows nobody good." Bet you never knew what he meant by that, did you? Well, wherever he is, up or down, I'll bet he's laughing his ass off now, looking at you out here tonight. You know what he meant now, don't you, Floyd?

Well, it's pitch black out there and cold as can be, but I do believe I see a light in the darkness and a better future ahead, Floyd. You just remember this here conversation and don't weasel out in the morning, and get on the right path. A good time to start would be with this here client. You know what he is here for, don't you, Floyd? Well, maybe you need to think about your role in this mess. It's not too late for you to change, Floyd. It's not too late until the very end.

Having finished his silent conversation with himself, and having resolved to start on a higher path, Floyd felt strangely warm in his sleeping bag. Before he allowed himself to fall asleep, he called out, "Good night, Mr. Barney. Thanks for setting me straight and showing me what I need to do tomorrow."

If Warner Barney heard him, he didn't respond.

The morning came cold and clear—not counting the still-falling snow. It wasn't as deep as it could have been, but everyone still had to dig their way out from under a blanket of white. As they came alive out of the tents, everyone was glad they had their jackets, sweaters, and thermals on. There were no snowball fights this morning; there was work to do, and a sense of urgency in their movements.

Warner Barney was out there somewhere, with another equally unscrupulous individual serving as his guide. They were all after the same target, but for radically different reasons and with polar-opposite goals in mind.

Other than what was really needed, there was little conversation this morning, as if the friction and disclosures of last night were still on everyone's mind. Axel was already mounted and riding out when Oliver walked out of his tent, Eileen right behind him.

"Where you off to, Axel?" Oliver called out.

"Gonna look for his tracks, Mr. Barry. See you later!" Axel called out.

"Whose tracks did he mean, Oliver?" Eileen asked as he trotted off.

"I'm not sure, to be honest. I'm assuming he is going after the elk, because I think Bern is the more physical of the two, and I'm guessing Gerry will send him after Barney. I probably should go with him if that's where Bern is going," he said as he pointed to Bern, who was getting mounted as they spoke.

They watched as Bern slid his rifle into the scabbard and buckled on his pistol. Oliver couldn't help but notice that all of the bullet loops were filled, whereas on the day they left, he had only had a few in there. Bern was obviously taking no chance of being outmatched in his weapons. To further prove the accuracy of Oliver's deduction, they saw him pull another pistol out of his saddlebags. He opened the loading gate and slowly turned the cylinder; satisfied with what he saw, he closed it and tucked it behind his belt, into the small of his back. Oliver rushed over to him and put a hand out on his shoulder.

"Bern, you look like you're expecting trouble out there. Maybe I should go with you?"

Bern looked at him for a long moment before he answered. "Mr.

Barry," he said solemnly, "I do and I don't. I mean, sir, I do expect trouble and I don't think you should come along. First of all, this is my job, not yours. And secondly, you're not a good enough rider to do what I might have to do, so you might be more of a ..." He paused, looking for a tactful way to say what he knew would be hurtful any way he said it.

"More of a distraction and hindrance than a help. That's what you were going to say, isn't it?" Oliver finished for him.

"Yes, sir, that is exactly what I was going to say," Bern replied honestly. "Don't worry, Mr. Barry," Bern said as he swung up into the saddle. "I'm not going to start anything or have any confrontations if I can help it. I just want to know where they are so we can stay out of his line of fire," he continued.

"That's a very good idea, Mr. Justner," Parker said as he rode up to where Oliver and Bern were talking.

"What are you doing here?" Bern asked.

"I'm going with you. I have a vested interest in this man, and I know him better than anyone else in this group. Don't worry—I know how to ride as well as you do. I grew up on skis, that's true, but only when I wasn't on a horse. And you shouldn't be going out alone after this man, anyway. This is a two-man operation at least. If anything should go wrong, you'll need a second man to go for help. Right?" Parker said, confident about what Bern's answer would be.

Bern thought about it for a moment, and then nodded his head. "Do you want to ..." he started to ask. Parker shook his head.

"I don't want to have one on me if I do see him. I'm not sure I could trust myself," he said, looking up the mountain, as if he could see Warner Barney on the slopes.

"Does the boss know ...?" Bern started to ask.

"Gerry picked out the horse and woke me up to tell me you were going. He knows I'm going out with you."

"Good enough. Let's get to tracking," Bern said as he turned his horse's head uphill. The two men rode off at a ninety-degree angle from the direction Axel had taken, leaving Oliver and Eileen standing in the snow, watching them ride off.

"I feel I'm losing control of this situation real fast," Oliver complained to Eileen.

"You big baby. Don't you always say the really smart executives always know how and who to delegate work to?" she reminded him playfully.

"Yes, I do say that, Eileen. But this is a much more serious situation than just work. There are lives at stake here, and I—"

"And these men know that as well as you do, Oliver. None of these boys are just off the farm, you know," Arnold responded. He and Wanda had come up while they were standing there watching Bern and Parker ride off. "Judging from the hardware Bern was packing, I'd wager those two are going after your Mr. Barney," he added.

"Yes, they are. Bern said he was just going to find him and keep an eye on him. He said they aren't going to make contact with him," Oliver responded with a confidence he didn't feel.

"Oh, that's fine, but what if Mr. Barney decides he wants to make contact with them?" Arnold asked curiously.

Higher up the mountain, Floyd and Warner were just getting mounted themselves. It had been a cold camp that morning; the sun was out, but it had yet to warm the air. It was still snowing, although lightly, and they had had a cold breakfast because there was just enough snow to keep putting the fire out. It was also cold because they weren't speaking to each other—Warner wasn't speaking because he was angry at the delay in getting started, and Floyd wasn't speaking because he had nothing to say to the man who hired him.

He was thinking about the ride ahead, even if the maniac urging him to get going wasn't. This was more snow than he had ever seen up here for this time of year, and he was worried about the horses losing their footing. They couldn't see what was under it either, so there would be no way to tell where a hole was to be able to avoid it. He didn't want to lose any of his animals this high up the mountain, because it was a long way to walk to get down.

The ledge they had to get to was up another few hundred feet, and, while he wouldn't admit this to Barney, he was a little anxious about climbing up so high in this weather. He had only been up this high once before, and that had been in the summer, when he could see where he was going.

This was much more dangerous a trek because of all that wet snow piling up on the upper levels. Barney either didn't notice, or he just didn't care. Floyd wasn't sure which it was, but, either way, it wasn't healthy to ignore it. He hadn't forgotten his conversation with himself last night, but he wasn't sure what he could do about it at this point. Floyd reminded himself to keep his eyes open for any signs of danger from any direction.

As he mounted up, he called out to Barney in a soft voice. "All right, Mr. Barney. From here on out, we maintain a strict silence and communicate by hand signals. We don't know where he is, so we don't want to spook him none. You got to remember, his sense of hearing is far superior to ours."

"Thank you, Frank Buck," Warner sneered. "Don't you think I know that? His sense of smell is superior as well, so aren't you going to remind me of that and to stay downwind of him?" he asked sarcastically.

You're making my choice easier for me, you dumb son of a bitch, Floyd thought to himself, but he kept a calm tone as he responded to this dig. "I would, Mr. Barney, if I knew for certain which direction was downwind from him."

Barney didn't respond to this, as there was nothing he could say … yet.

They headed up the side of the mountain, this stage of their climb a much steeper angle than the day before. Floyd stopped to let Barney get beside him. "We're going to go around that rock up ahead, then to the left for about fifty yards, then turn uphill again. We might need to walk the horses for a while; it gets pretty steep up there. The ledge we saw him on should be about eighty yards ahead then. We will want to avoid the ledge itself because I will need to look for tracks around it, so we don't want the horses to step all over the tracks. Keep them back when I tell you to, and I will see if I can find a trace of him in all this snow."

Warner just nodded and followed him on the path. Neither man looked back, so neither of them saw the large elk fifty yards behind them. It just watched them climbing upward, its bright red coat dusted with snow.

Farther back down the mountain, April was in a good mood, her accident the previous day forgotten. She was eager to get this story and run with it—whatever that turned out to be. She was a little frustrated; this story seemed to have a mind of its own and wouldn't allow her to get ahead of it. Every time she started to compose it in her mind, it shifted its focus or something would happen to push her in a different direction. She wasn't going to allow the story to control her; she was in charge of it, and that was the way it was going to stay.

Not Adam, not that crazy hunter, not these animal rights people—no one was going to get in her way or prevent her from doing what she came here to do. She had wanted to interview that Parker fellow, but he had ridden out with Bern before she had the chance. She had seen him saddling up, but before she had a chance to get to him, the older Bruce had come over to show her how to fix the cinch and check her out for any signs of a concussion. For a moment, she allowed her attention to wander, wondering if it had been coincidental or more purposeful that he had come over just then, but then she remembered what had happened the last time she had allowed her attention to wander and refocused on the trail.

Maybe she could get some background from the rancher—him being the dead ranger's stepfather had been a fact that had never come out in anything she had read before. This could be an angle that would surely hook her readers. That hunter, Barney—his involvement in the old incident was an angle no one had reported on either. She realized she had no proof of that yet, so she would have to be careful and think about the risk of a slander suit if she linked him to the avalanche that had happened so long ago. No, she would have to wait until she had more to go on than just Parker's thirty-year-old memory. April had supreme confidence in her ability to get anyone to open up to her, so she started to think about how she could get closer to Barney when they caught up to him.

It really doesn't matter if he shoots the animal anymore, because it would be just as big a story either way. If I can get him to talk about his shot of the animal, or if I can get him to talk about the old days ... but how can I get that out of him? she thought. *Maybe if I ask him if he has ever been here before ... no, I'll ask him if he wants to comment about what Parker is accusing him of. Yeah, that'll work. I'll tell him I'm writing another story about that old avalanche, and that a former ranger has accused him of setting it off with a wild shot and would he like to present his side of the story before I write it up. Yes! That's it!*

April congratulated herself on her cleverness. She was no longer thinking about any pictures except as a window dressing. She never considered the risk to herself or to anyone else when she was on the hunt herself, and in this way she was very similar to Warner Barney. Of course, she didn't see this comparison and would likely have been very hurt to hear anyone suggest it to her.

For April, the goal is always the story, and everything and everyone else is always secondary. It never occurred to her that, if Barney had indeed acted as Parker was saying he had, he might not want that particular story written. It also never occurred to her that he might be willing to cause another "accident" to protect his name and liberty. It never occurred to April she might be risking the lives of everyone else in the group who had heard Parker tell them about that day. For now, she was in good spirits as she rode along, because her story was safe.

Oliver was deep in thought as he rode along. He was worrying about what was going to happen when they caught up to Warner Barney, and what Walter Barney would do when they did. He was starting to get the idea that Barney might not just fold up at the sight of a US Marshal's badge, and he might make a fight of it. That would mean the risk of others getting hurt. Oliver knew he could shoot a gun, but he didn't have one and didn't want to think about having to shoot someone.

This was spiraling out of control faster and faster. He figured he could count on both of the Bruces and Axel and Bern—and possibly Arnold—to be ready to handle a firefight if it came to that. He could count also on Arnold, maybe Adam, and most certainly Parker, if it were to be a matter of just physically controlling Barney. He wasn't sure what Ed Baxter would do or if he would help at all. And that didn't take into consideration the fact Barney had at least one other man with him, and he was an unknown factor. He didn't know what side, if any, Bergen would take in this matter.

He'd had some conflicts with Bergen in the past, and it was always a tense scene. Would he remember that and take Barney's side? Oliver was uncertain of what he could expect from Floyd Bergen now, and this only made him more anxious and concerned.

Adam rode along beside Eileen, hoping the ranger wouldn't object to him being there with his girlfriend. He needed to talk to someone about April, and Eileen seemed to be the best choice—particularly since she was the only other female he had spoken to on this trip. He didn't have any problem with the doctor, but she was pretty involved with the big rancher and didn't seem to have much time for anyone other than him.

"Miss Gayle, would you mind if I asked you a question? I've got a problem, and I don't know who else to talk to about it. But if you don't want to get involved with my ..." Adam paused.

"Not at all, Adam. I'm flattered you're asking me for my opinion. What's the problem?"

"Well, it's April, Miss Gayle," he started to explain.

"Adam, why don't we make this simple, and you just call me Eileen, okay?"

"Thank you, Eileen. Anyway, as I said, I've got a problem with April. I don't think she's very happy with me, and I've got a feeling she's gonna get me fired when we get back. She's so focused on getting her story, she doesn't care about anything or anyone else," he complained. "She can be real nice when she wants something from you, but she can turn on you real fast.

"I thought we were in love at first, but now I can see it was just an act to get me to go along with her plan," he said, disappointment in his voice. "I'm worried about what she's going to do now that she's heard Mr. Woodson's story. She's likely to do something stupid involving that Barney creep just to get her story. You tell Mr. Barry to be on guard and keep an eye on her; I'm going to try and stay as close to her as she'll let me, but I figure she's going to keep me in the dark as much as possible.

"Why would she do that to me, Eileen? What's wrong with her that she can't see what's right in front of her?" he asked sadly.

"Adam, sometimes people have needs that are more basic than

that, and they can't see anything else until those needs are met," she explained gently. "Did she ever talk about her childhood with you?"

"No, she always changed the subject whenever I'd ask her anything about that," he said.

"Well, Adam that says a lot to me. It says she has something she wants to hide or run away from, and, whatever it is, it probably has a lot to do with her drive to succeed at any cost. I can't tell you what to do about your relationship with her, Adam, but I think I can assure you that you won't have far to look for a new job if you want it."

His face brightened up instantly, and he asked her what she meant.

"I'm not the one to say, Adam, but if you ride up to Mr. Barry there and tell him you're interested in changing jobs, I wouldn't be surprised if he offered you something right here and now," she said with a confident smile.

"Are you sure? I don't want to put him on the spot if he has to turn me down. I'd like to work for him; he seems like a fair man," Adam mused.

"Adam, I think you ought to talk with him just as soon as you are ready to make a career change. Or maybe even sooner," she encouraged him.

"You think he'd talk to me about it now, with all he's got going on?"

"I'd be willing to bet on it, Adam." Standing up in her stirrups, she called out to Oliver, who was riding three spots ahead. "Oliver, can you come back here for a minute?"

He wheeled his horse around and dropped back, falling in step beside her mount.

"What's up?"

"Oliver, Adam is concerned he won't have a job when he gets back to his paper. He thinks Miss Martens is going to get him fired for helping us," she said.

Oliver looked over at Adam, who just nodded.

"Any other good news for me from our intrepid representative of the fourth estate?" Oliver asked sarcastically.

Adam looked at Eileen, who nodded at him to continue. "Well, Mr. Barry, I'm not sure, but I think she plans to play that Mr. Barney to get his input for her story."

"Great. How do you know this, Adam?"

"I heard her talking to herself while we were riding earlier. I couldn't get all the words, but I heard something about asking him for his comments on a story she was going to be writing. I can only assume she means …"

"She means to bring up the story about the avalanche of thirty years ago and try to tie him into it. Tell me, Adam. Miss Martens— does she work at being reckless, or does it just come naturally to her?" Oliver said sourly.

"It comes naturally to her *and* she works at it," Adam replied.

"Okay, I'll keep an eye on her. So what about your job there? Do you like it? Are you looking for a career change?" Oliver asked casually.

"I like photography, Mr. Barry. I always have. I'd like to stay in this line of work, and I wouldn't mind staying in this area to do it," Adam said as he looked around him.

"When you say this line of work, do you mean taking the pictures or what?"

"Well, I like taking pictures, but I wouldn't turn down something more challenging if it involved photography."

"I see. Well, chew on this. We are looking to start a small magazine about the mountain. Sort of like the one I have looked at a few times— *Arizona Highways*, I think it's called. I want to include pictures of the mountain in all seasons, showing the activities and the wildlife and flowers, and stuff like that. Would that sort of thing interest you any?" Oliver asked him.

Adam's eyes grew wide, and he almost came out of the saddle by turning so fast to face Oliver. "Mr. Barry, I'd love to be your photographer for that magazine!" he said excitedly.

Oliver turned to look in his offside saddlebag, keeping his face turned away so Adam wouldn't be able to see his expression, and he made his tone as casual as he could. "Well, here's the thing, Adam. I'm not really interested in having you be the lead photographer."

Adam's face fell.

"What I was really going to offer you was the editor's job. If you would like it, that is," Oliver continued evenly.

"The editor's job? Are you serious? You're not just jerking me around on this? I'd be in charge of putting it together and everything? For real?" Adam couldn't believe his ears, and he was sure that the ranger was just playing with him.

"Now the thing is, I can't afford to pay you a lot right now; we would have to see how the magazine did. But, yes, you would be in charge. You would have the responsibility for making it look as good as possible, all by yourself,"

"Oliver," Eileen jumped in. "You aren't serious, are you? All by himself? You aren't going to give him any staff to help him? That's not right!"

"All right, boss. I'll give him one assistant … two assistants … three … four assistants, but no more!" he grumbled at her, seeing her expression as he offered one assistant. "I suppose you want me to give him an office and a title as well?"

"Well, it's only right, Oliver. After all, he is going to put this magazine together for you." She winked at Adam. Adam wasn't fooled by the ranger's gruff exchange; he knew that he wouldn't be getting that deal if the ranger hadn't wanted to give it in the first place.

Adam was on air, and the rest of the ride was just a blur.

Arnold rode along in silence, his thoughts in great turmoil. After all this time, he knew the name of the man who was responsible for Max's needless death. Although it was a relief to know who it was, it was galling to think that he had been right beside him, and he hadn't known it. He would have liked to have gotten his hands on the man— but then he might not have been able to stop short of killing him. As much as that would have helped his frustration, it wouldn't have done anything to bring Max back. Connie wouldn't have wanted him to do that, he knew. At least he could finally put that hurt to rest.

"It's too bad you couldn't have been here to hear this, my dear."

He thought he had told that to himself, but Wanda leaned over and asked him what he said.

"I was just talking to myself, Wanda. I was just telling my late wife that it was too bad she couldn't have been here to learn who killed her son. That's what really killed her, you know— no, of course you don't. You couldn't possibly know.

"He was her world. She worked two or three jobs to pay for his private schooling—that was before we met, you see. When we met, it was at an auction—we were both bidding on the same item, and she was sitting in front of me. It was a scale model of a WWII bomber airplane. I remember how upset she was that she lost, and I saw her start to cry. She told the woman she was sitting with that it was the same kind of plane her father had flown before he was shot down, and she had wanted it to show her son.

"I tapped her on the shoulder and told her that if it was that important to her, then she should accept it as a gift from me on the condition she allowed me to take her out to dinner. We were married six months later and never apart for the next twenty-five years. The life went out of her after Max was killed, and it wasn't long after that that she just gave up on me."

Arnold was talking more to himself than to Wanda, and she knew it, but she also knew to not interrupt him. This was something he needed to get out—a cleansing of his guilt for not protecting his stepson and losing his wife. She could wait. She wasn't jealous of his late wife; they had had a long time together. So would they. Right now, she could help him most by just listening to him and being supportive.

"I don't need to be dumping all this on you, Wanda. You'd probably enjoy listening to Charley spin some tall tales more than listen to me feel sorry for myself," he said.

Wanda looked him right in the eyes and felt her heart skip a beat.

"Arnie, I'm right where I want to be. And you just say whatever it is you need to say. I'll listen, and I'll be here as long as you want me to. If you want me to keep silent, I can do that too. You just tell me what you need, Arnold Wilcox, and I'll do my damn best to do it for you. Understand?"

Arnold looked at her and he felt a great weight lifting from his heart. He put out his hand to take hers, and they both looked straight ahead as they rode on.

Charley was bringing up the rear of the group because he was leading the mules and the spare mounts. He was busy thinking about the last two days, and he was pleased that things had turned out as they had. He knew most of the people—or, at least, the important ones—on the outing, and he was very happy that Arnold had found someone he could connect with. He could see the light coming back into his eyes when he looked at that doctor woman. Charley had been real worried Arnold wasn't going to get back on the horse any time soon. Now it looked like he just might be okay. You couldn't predict those things, when two people would connect like he had with that doctor woman. Sometimes it worked and sometimes it didn't; you just never knew for sure.

And his friend Gerry, he had been real worried about him too. Charley had known there was something between Gerry and his son—naming your son a junior always did create problems. He wasn't sure what it was, but he had suspicions it might have had something to do with the loss of his wife and his son's mother so long ago. That last hunting trip up here had played a part in it too, somehow.

Charley had been busy on a movie set when that trip had come up, so he hadn't been able to go with Gerry when he'd called. He often wondered to himself if it would have made any difference if he had gone, but he was too long in the tooth to spend much time fretting about it. But here they were, working together again like a father and son should be.

Sometimes it just takes a common enemy to bring people together, he chuckled to himself. He liked the look of that photographer; he was willing to help out and no chore was beneath him. *He would make a good cowboy,* Charley thought.

Kinda reminds me of myself back in the old days, he said silently. *Boy, those were the real good old days,* he reflected sadly. His reverie was interrupted by the sudden nervousness of the entire pack string. All the ears on every mule and horse were turned backward, and they were all real jittery all of a sudden. Charley began looking around for some sign of what was bothering the animals, and he called out to Gerry Junior, who was riding about three spots ahead of him.

"Gerry! Something's spooking the string real bad! I don't know what it is, but it's close by, and they don't like it," he called out.

Gerry Junior came back on a run, and, as he approached, his own horse began to act antsy and prance around. "Mine too, Charley. I wonder if it is our lady friend coming to call?" he said quietly, so as to not upset the others. Charley knew who he meant, but he was hoping Gerry was wrong.

"How could she get up here so fast? We had a good day's head start on her, and what would she be wanting with us anyway?"

"I wish to hell I knew the answer to those questions, Charley. If I see her, I'll be sure to ask her for you."

"Hell, Gerry, you say that, but you won't do it. If you see her you'll be too damn busy to ask her anything of the sort!" he retorted.

"Think we should make a run for it?"

"Run where? Do you know where she is? I damn sure don't want to run *into* her. Charley, you got a weapon on you?"

"In my saddle bag."

"Give me the lead rope, and you get it out and put it on. Keep it on from now on, please. You're not the best cook in the camp, but you're all we got, and I don't want to lose you now," Gerry said with a straight face.

"Hell, you just don't want to deal with these mules. Don't try to bullshit me!" At that moment, the horses began to settle down, and Gerry and Charley looked at each other and then over at the pack string.

"She left or moved away," Gerry said.

"Not far enough," Charley said, as he pointed up the line at the horses ahead of them starting to dance. "You better get up there and keep an eye on that reporter lady, Gerry; the only ridin' she done is on them drugstore ponies what only goes 'round in a circle dance."

"You think?" Gerry called back over his shoulder as he spurred his horse to run ahead.

April was having quite a time controlling her ride, who suddenly wanted to run away with her. She heard Gerry Junior calling out for her to turn the horse's head and to pull the reins down and to the side. She had been holding them very loosely when the ruckus started, so that, when the roar came, she was totally unprepared. Her horse reared, and she went flying again, landing on her own back, like she did before. The other horses around her were becoming more panic-stricken every minute, and when they heard the noise, they all bolted in different directions, which led them back down the path they had come from.

April didn't know what made that dreadful and terrifying roar, but it didn't sound very friendly. She shakily stood up and looked around for her horse, who was long gone. She heard the sound again, and what made it stood up fifty feet in front of her. She wasn't sure what kind of a bear it was, but she could guess, and her guess didn't bring her any comfort.

She heard Gerry calling for her to back up slowly and then to one side or the other, but her feet wouldn't obey her brain. She could see the immense size of the bear and its dinner-plate-sized paws as it began to move toward her. She could smell the sour scent of its breath as it roared again; she could see the thick fur and the red mouth and curling lips as she tried to back up.

As it took another step toward her, she could see the red was blood from a very recent kill, and she recognized she was being seen as a threat to its meal. She watched in horror as the bear took another step toward her, roaring its displeasure at her presence. She vaguely heard the screams of the people and animals behind her as she tried to get her feet to move; but they refused to. She started to think her time had come and that she was going to die right here in this dirt.

In her mind, she was screaming for help, but no sounds came out of her mouth but a terrified squeak. The bear was almost within reach of her, and she closed her eyes to her imminent, agonizing death.

She heard the bear roar and actually felt the air move in front of her—and then there was a hiss of air and a sound of something crashing through the woods.

She held her breath, but nothing happened. She slowly opened one eye to see the bear lying on the ground in front of her. As she looked around, she saw Ed Baxter slowly lowering his rifle. At that moment, Gerry reached her side, followed by Adam, and the others surrounded her.

"Are you okay, miss? Did she hurt you?" The questions came fast from Gerry and the others. April just couldn't get herself to speak; she was crying and shaking too hard.

"I hope that drug holds for a while, Mr. Barry. But just in case, I think we should get out of here right now." Ed said while he took his time ejecting the shell from his rifle. He slid the gun back into the scabbard and remounted his horse.

"Mr. Baxter, you just saved that young lady's life. I thank you very much, and I am sure she will also want to express her thanks," Oliver said to him with heartfelt emotion.

"Yeah, well, that can wait until we're out of here. I'm telling you, we need to get out of here *now*. That was a very mild dose, so let's not press our luck."

Suddenly what he was saying registered in Oliver's mind. "Wait a minute! You're saying you didn't kill the bear? You only drugged it?" he asked incredulously.

"That's right; I saw no need to kill that bear. It wasn't doing anything but defending its meal, as any bear would do. So now I say again, let's get out of here, because it is sure to be a bit surly when it wakes up, and I don't want to have to shoot it again," Baxter insisted and began to trot to the front of the line.

"Gerry, he only tranquilized it! We need to get out of here now!" Oliver called out to the group. Charley came riding up with several horses he had picked up when they had run past him.

"Okay, everyone, get aboard, and let's light a shuck out of here. That's gonna be one angry bear when she wakes up, so let's be out of her sight when she does come around," Charley called out to the group.

Everyone scrambled to get to their horse. As she remounted, April never once looked at Adam, nor did she acknowledge his concern for her welfare. She rode up to Gerry and started to thank him for rescuing her.

"Wasn't me, miss. You want to thank someone, you go thank Mr. Baxter. He's the one got off that shot—my pistol would only have made the bear more dangerous, because I couldn't get off a head shot without risking hitting you. No, you feel a need to thank someone, you thank him. Now, let's get moving before she wakes up." He turned and headed for the front of the line to get the group moving again. As he did, he heard hoof beats coming at them hard. He reached for the pistol on his hip, but relaxed his hand when he saw it was Axel.

"Boss! I seen him! I seen him!" Axel exclaimed excitedly. "He was climbing the ... what happened here?" Axel stopped short, seeing the big bear on the ground. "Anybody hurt? Is everyone okay?" he asked anxiously.

"Yeah, everyone's okay, just scared the … devil out of Miss Martens here, is all," he said correcting himself midsentence.

"I think it scared a lot more than the devil out of me, Mr. Bruce. I need a change of clothes as soon as you think it's safe to do so," April said with a nervous laugh.

"We'll get you the time in a few minutes, miss, just as soon as we put a little space between us and that bear," Gerry said with a smile.

"Go on, Axel, you saw him where?"

"Oh yeah. Well, I was riding up toward the left up there, and I heard a noise, so I stopped. I waited for a few minutes, and then he stepped out into an opening in the trees. If I had had a rifle, I could have brought him down easy; he just stopped in between two firs and looked right at me. I guess he didn't see me, though, because he didn't move or run. He just stood there, looking around, and then he stared in my direction for a few minutes—then he walked off up the stream in the direction of Plum Run.

"The funny thing is, I don't know how he couldn't have seen me; we weren't that far apart," Axel said, puzzled. "We weren't no more than sixty yards apart, so he should've seen or smelled me. It was sorta like he recognized I was no threat to him at that moment, so he just slowly left the area. I took my eyes off him for just one minute to look around, and when I looked back, he was gone. I think he went back into the trees. I can take you right to where I saw him and we can pick up his tracks from there, I'm sure. We're getting closer to him, boss," Axel said excitedly.

"Dad!" Gerry called out, turning in his saddle to project his voice down the line.

"What's up, son?" Gerry Senior said as he rode up.

"Axel here saw him up a piece, heading for Plum Run along the stream. Let the lady here change her … socks and follow Axel and me up the hill. We'll leave a marked path for you to follow."

"Got it, son. Be careful."

"Right, Dad. Let's go, Axel, lead 'em out, and I'll leave Dad a trail. Come on, folks, the game's afoot!" he called out.

The others rode past April as they followed Axel up the hill. As Eileen came up, she motioned for Oliver to go ahead of her.

"I think I'll help April get changed. Mr. Bruce, why don't you ride just a little bit ahead of us, and we'll be along in just a few minutes," she suggested.

Gerry tipped his hat and smiled. "I'll be just up the path, ladies." He turned and walked just ahead enough to be out of sight, and then he sat and waited. He turned in his saddle to look up the mountain.

"Barney, I'm coming for you. We have a score to settle, and now it's time to settle it. You stole my self-respect—no, you didn't really steal it, I just allowed you to take it from me. Well, I'm coming to take it back. You're going down this time, Mr. Big White Hunter, and I'm going to help bring you down. You're going to pay for your crimes, you can bet on it."

He looked up, noticing the clouds moving again. They were heavy with snow and swirling around the top of the mountain as if they were waiting. But waiting for what? Or for whom?

CHAPTER 9

As the morning progressed, Warner Barney was growing more frustrated and more confused. He had definitely seen the animal, as had Floyd Bergen, standing right on that ledge. There was no way to get to it other than the path they were on now, certainly not from above. And it was unlikely it had passed them in the night. There was no way for them to fail to pick up its tracks or for it to lose them—except it had.

"All right, Bergen, you're the big expert tracker—where the hell is he?" Warner was in a particularly foul mood and was in no mood for excuses. They had spent three hours climbing through thick forest to get to a point only one hundred yards above them, as the crow flies. The fact that neither them nor their horses were crows only meant they had to take a more roundabout and indirect route to this point.

It hadn't been without its hazards, and, by the time they reached the ledge, both men were sporting several scrapes and bruises and were sweating, despite the cold air. Thankfully the snow had stopped falling, so their visibility was much improved. This only meant they could see very clearly that their quarry had left no tracks in the snow.

Floyd was just as perplexed as Warner was and, like Warner, had no explanation for this situation. "Damn it, Mr. Barney, I don't know where he is. We both saw him up here—you pointed him out to me, remember? I stayed awake during my time on watch, so I know he didn't go past us during the night. I assume you stayed awake during your time, so I have no damn idea where he is, but I'll take any suggestions you have," Floyd responded testily.

Warner didn't reply to this, partially because he didn't have any ideas, and partially because he hadn't stayed awake during his watch, so he couldn't swear the animal didn't get past him. He decided to change the subject before Bergen started to question his staying awake.

"It stands to reason that it is above us rather than below us, right? Okay then," he continued, not allowing Floyd to speak, "we need to work our way upward and keep an eye out for him. He's got to be above us somewhere."

The obvious fact that it could have been anywhere on that side of the mountain was overlooked or ignored in Barney's obsession to find the animal he wanted to kill.

"Maybe we should split up? Cover more ground that way, and less likely he'll slip past us while we're searching for him," Floyd suggested.

"No! Absolutely not, Mr. Bergen. We stay together, or at least in sight of each other."

Floyd made a gesture of resignation, but secretly he was happy that Barney had rejected his idea. It was, in fact, the reason he had suggested it. He figured Barney wouldn't want to take a chance on anyone else getting his prize. Floyd was happier not separating, because this cut their chances of finding the animal in half and made it much easier for the critter to slip past them. He was puzzled as to how it managed to get off the ledge without leaving a track, however. He had estimated the jump as being over twenty-five feet, and he didn't think any deer or elk could manage a jump like that, even with a running start—and it certainly hadn't had the room to get a running start off that ledge. He was willing to bet his ranch that the animal didn't climb up the side of the mountain, so where in the hell did it go, and how did it do that? He had no answer for this question—no answer that made any sense, that is.

They mounted their horses and began to slowly walk up the mountain, looking for any trace of its passing. The hours passed with no trace of the big animal. There were no broken branches, no scat droppings—no anything that suggested it had passed that way. Warner kept his eyes to the ground, looking for some signs of the animal's trail, while Floyd kept his eyes on the clouds. They were starting to boil again and were getting darker. He could feel the breeze getting a little stronger and the air a little colder.

"Mr. Barney, just thought you should know, I think it's going to start snowing again. We're up pretty high, and it could get nasty."

"Bergen, I didn't hire you to give me the latest weather reports; I hired you to find me a specific animal. Please stop wasting my time with anything else."

"Yes, sir," Floyd said through his clenched teeth. The idea ran through his mind that he should just leave the son of a bitch up here by himself, but he knew he wouldn't do that to anyone. These mountains could kill anyone if they were taken for granted; it had happened before to unwary campers and hunters.

As he turned to look ahead again, he caught a flash of something a little ways ahead of him on the right. He called out softly, "Mr. Barney, ahead at the two o'clock position. I think I saw something up there …"

He wasn't prepared for Barney's reaction.

The loud report of his rifle went off just behind Floyd as Barney snapped a shot in the direction Floyd had pointed.

"What in the hell!" Floyd shouted, both angry and surprised at the same time. "Damn it, man! You don't shoot at something unless you are absolutely certain what you are shooting at! You should know that, damn it! You could have killed me or my damn horse, you idiot!"

"Shut up, Bergen. I shoot when I see my target. We haven't seen any trace of any other animals or hunters up here, have we? There's nothing else it could have been but him. So what's your problem? Let's go see if I got him. Come on," Barney replied, indifferent to anything Bergen was saying. As they rode toward the spot where Barney had fired, Floyd began to think about what he had said.

He's right, now that I think of it. We haven't seen any animals so far. Not a damn thing, not even a squirrel or a rabbit. He looked up, no longer at the clouds, but at the sky. *I don't even see a damn bird flying around here. Something's wrong with this picture.*

He pulled his binoculars out of his saddle bag and began to examine the sky. *There's nothing flying out here, not anywhere near us. There's definitely something wrong out here, and I don't know what it is or what it means, but I know I don't like it. There's no point telling this idiot about it, because he's got tunnel vision, and he don't want to know anything but where's his target,* he said to himself.

"You see anything, Bergen?" Barney called out, having seen him pull the field glasses out for a look. "Or are you just sightseeing on my dime?" he asked sarcastically.

I'll be damned if I give him the satisfaction of knowing he got to me. "Just looking around to see if he's gotten behind us, Mr. Barney. We don't want to assume anything and miss picking him up, now do we?"

"Well, did you see anything then?" Barney responded curtly, clearly annoyed that he hadn't caught Bergen slacking off.

"No, sir, nothing yet. I'll keep on looking for him though," Floyd replied pleasantly.

"You just do that," Barney said acidly.

Walter Barney was fuming inside, he couldn't figure out how that damn animal was avoiding his detection. He knew all about elk—what they ate and how they moved—but this one wasn't following any of the normal patterns he knew to expect. Warner knew he was being hard on Bergen, but he had to take his frustration out on someone, and Bergen was handy. He would make it up to him when the hunt was over and he had his kill.

In the meantime, where the hell is that damn animal?

Just a little way below Barney and Bergen, but several miles to the east, Parker and Bern were in a stand of trees, looking for any sign of where the two men had been. At this point in time, Bern wasn't really sure how many men he was tracking, and that unknown was a big worry for him. He had been given the responsibility of finding Barney, and Bern didn't like to fail. He had only a rough idea of what kind of man he was chasing; he knew Bergen's abilities, but he didn't know Barney's.

He turned to Parker and questioned him. "Parker, what do you really know about this man Barney? Not what you think or feel toward him, but what do you know of his thinking patterns?"

After a few seconds, Parker answered him. "Not a lot. I just know he doesn't respect rules or safety protocols, and that he'll do whatever he wants to do in order to get what he wants. I know he'll go straight after the animal, regardless of the cost or inconvenience. I actually feel sorry for whatever guide he hired to take him up the mountain. I certainly hope that man knows what he got himself into when he agreed to play guide for Barney."

"Wonderful. That helps me out no end. Okay, Parker, where do you think we should be looking for him then?"

Parker looked at the mountain and considered it. "Where did you say you saw the elk yesterday?"

"Actually, it was Axel who saw him first. It was up on that ridge over there." He pointed to the right. "And he slowly walked over in that direction"—he pointed his finger slightly eastward—"up toward Plum Ridge."

"Then I think we should go in that direction and follow in his steps. If we go in front of the elk, we run the risk of chasing him right into Barney. And we don't want to do that, do we?"

"No, we certainly don't. Let's get up there and start searching for Mr. Barney. And remember, Parker, we're only to find him and report back to Gerry where he is and where he's headed. *No contact.* Those are my orders, and I will follow them."

"No problem, Bern. I wouldn't trust myself to have any type of physical contact with him, although I doubt he would recognize me anyway."

They started climbing, heading eastward toward Plum Ridge.

Down below, everyone was excited. The Red Elk had been spotted, and they were on the way to meet it. Everyone was eager to see it in person—to marvel at its color and to praise its ability. Ed was ready to take his shot, but first they had to get a good look at the animal up close to be able to measure the sedative safely for his size. They hadn't heard from Bern and Parker since they'd left early in the morning, and Gerry Senior was getting worried.

He wouldn't say anything to anyone, but he was uncertain where they were and what was going on out there. He didn't want them to get hurt, but he needed to know what his opposition was doing. He rode forward in line, exchanging simple pleasantries with everyone until he reached his son, and, with a slight gesture, he rode ahead. His son followed, and they were quickly riding side by side.

Gerry spoke in a low voice to keep the others from overhearing. "Son, I'm a mite concerned about Bern and Parker and Axel. We have been riding all morning and for most of the afternoon, and we've heard nothing from any of them. We never should have allowed Axel to ride by himself. Parker went with Bern, but we let Axel go alone, son, and if anything happens to him, I'll never forgive myself."

"Well, in that case, Dad, you won't need to worry none. Look over there." His son pointed behind Gerry's shoulder, where Axel was riding in as if he had seen a ghost.

"Plum Ridge! Plum Ridge! He's climbing up Plum Ridge! Come on! We're burning daylight, boss!" Axel yelled.

"Just where are we now, Mr. Bergen?" Barney asked coldly.

"We're looping over a small, unnamed ridge. Plum Ridge is over there." He pointed to the east. "And over there is the edge of Hunter's Run and Mosquito Run. I think you should …"

"Should what, Mr. Bergen?"

"Should look over your right shoulder very slowly."

Warner turned and looked up the road to see his quarry standing there, just looking back at him. It stood a hundred yards away, in the middle of the trail, magnificently beautiful, with a scarlet coat and a huge rack of antlers. It showed no fear and, in fact, seemed to be challenging him to do something. The elk didn't move at all—he could have been made of stone for all the difference that made to Warner.

He heard Bergen call to him to pull his rifle, but he couldn't get his eyes to leave the sight of that incredible animal or to make his body react to his mental commands. Finally, as if in a trance, Warner forced his hand to slowly reach back for his gun, but he felt like he was moving through mud. As his fingers made contact with the stock, the elk slowly turned and walked back into the woods. By the time Warner was able to get the rifle to his shoulder, the animal had disappeared into the forest again.

"Did you see him?" Warner asked excitedly.

"Hell yes, I seen him! I told you to look, didn't I? Why didn't you shoot when you had the chance? He was just looking at you, almost daring you to take a shot, and you just sat there, doing nothing. You've been talking about nothing but how much you wanted him, and here you get a perfect shot and you sat there like you were in a trance!" Floyd jeered, expecting an explosive response—but unwilling to pass up the chance to needle Barney.

To his great surprise, Barney did not react, but simply sat there. "You're right. I don't know what came over me; I just couldn't get my hands to move. He had me hypnotized. But don't you worry, it won't happen again. Now, which way did he go? Let's go get him once and for all," he said with force.

"He headed out toward Mosquito Run, up that way," Floyd said, looking up the trail that led up to the top of the ridge, where the clouds seemed to be settling down onto the trail.

They were gathering over the top of the mountain—dark, ugly clouds that were gray with snow in their bellies. They weren't moving around like clouds normally did; they were just hanging there, waiting for something. The air was getting colder as the temperature dropped, but Floyd and Warner kept climbing up the mountain, searching for the elusive elk.

They saw it briefly several times, but never where Barney could get a shot. It was always going behind a tree or rock, and he was never able to get a bead in time. Once in the trees, it would disappear into the shadows, despite the brilliance of its color.

It grew later and later, and they hadn't seen it for hours. Warner was getting very frustrated, and his mean nature was starting to come out again. "Where the hell is he, Bergen? We've been climbing for hours and there's no sign of him. I thought you said he came up this way!"

"Mr. Barney, I can't see through trees, and I don't reckon you can either. I've been looking for his tracks the entire time we've been climbing, and I haven't seen a single one. I'm starting to think that maybe he's doubled back somewhere along the way. Maybe we should turn around and go the other way for a time?"

"You may be right, Bergen. I haven't seen anything either, and it's getting late. Where the hell are we, anyway?"

"Well, if I figure it right, we should be coming up to the Mosquito Creek area in an hour. We're getting pretty high up now. We'll be able to see all the way down to the bottom in a little while. If we're going to pick up his tracks, maybe we should head to where we saw him last."

At that moment, Warner felt something touch him, and he turned to see what it was. It was just a branch, but when he turned back around, he saw the elk again. It was back in the trees, watching him. Warner stood there watching him back.

He called out to Bergen, but didn't take his eyes off the animal. "Bergen, get over here! But come over slowly, and come in on my left, so you can pull my rifle out of the scabbard."

Even though he had raised his voice, the animal didn't budge. Warner thought this was curious, but he was glad it hadn't spooked and run off. As Bergen approached him, the animal seemed to be watching Bergen as well, but it wasn't making any motions that suggested it was getting ready to bolt. As Bergen put his hand on the stock, the animal took a step back.

"Hold it!" Warner whispered. Bergen froze, and the animal stopped moving. "Okay."

As Bergen started to slide the rifle out again, the elk took another step back. Warner was totally astonished. The animal seemed to be able to look right through his horse to see what Bergen was doing.

"Hold it—no, slowly slide it back into the scabbard," Warner said, curious.

Puzzled, Bergen slowly did as he was told. As he did, Warner watched the elk take a step forward.

"The hell with this crap!" Warner said suddenly and grabbed for his rifle. As he did, the elk turned and ran into the woods, quickly vanishing from sight as it blended into the shadows.

"Come on, Bergen! We've got him now!" Warner called as he booted his horse to get it into a run. "I'm tired of playing this stupid game with him!" Warner snarled. "I'm going to end this charade right now, just you watch and see!"

Down the mountain, Axel and the rest of the party were at the bottom of Plum Ridge, but they could find no trace of the elk now. Axel was walking his horse, looking for tracks in the snow where he had seen it standing, but not finding any sign.

"Axel! You sure you saw the one we're looking for over here? Maybe you just thought you saw him but it was a different one," Gerry Junior suggested.

"Boss, I know what I saw, and I know where I saw it. I don't know why his tracks aren't here, so maybe I'm a little off on his position, but I know that I saw him right around here. He has an unmistakable color, remember? I couldn't mistake him for anything else. Just let me keep looking a little longer, boss. I know he's here somewhere."

Oliver rode up behind them, studying the ground as well. "I don't see any tracks around here either, Gerry," he said.

"You won't find his tracks here," Gerry Senior, said with a sudden certainty.

"What are you talking about, Dad?"

"I'm saying there won't be any tracks here. If there are any tracks, which I am beginning to believe there won't be, I know where they will be. And if I am right, Bern and Parker will be in serious trouble in the middle of something they won't be expecting. I'm going after them. They'll be needing my help," Gerry Senior said sadly.

"Well, you can't go by yourself, Dad."

"I'll go with him, Gerry," Oliver volunteered. "I might be able to do something with my borrowed badge."

"Well, if you're going, then I'm going with you," Eileen said in a tone that didn't allow for any discussion.

"Going where?" asked Arnold.

Before Gerry could say a word, Eileen answered for him. "Oliver and Gerry Senior are going out to help Bern and Parker. Gerry feels they may have ridden into trouble with Barney, and he's going to help them."

"If you're going to ride out to deal with Mr. Barney, gentlemen, then I'm going to go with you," Arnold said.

Gerry Junior started to argue with him but he was interrupted by Wanda.

"If you're going, Arnie, then I'm going with you," Wanda said emphatically.

"Well, if you're all going, then I might as well go along with you," Ed said resignedly.

"I'd like to come along too, Mr. Barry. Maybe I can get some ideas for that magazine we're going to put out," Adam volunteered.

April's head spun around when she heard Adam say what he said. She didn't like the sound of it, but she wanted to find out more about it before she said anything.

"If everyone is going with you, Mr. Barry, I'd like to tag along too."

Gerry Senior looked at Oliver, who looked at Gerry Junior. Gerry Junior just shook his head and gave in. "All right, I guess we're all taking a ride and putting this hunt on hold. By the way, Dad, just where are we riding to anyway?"

"We're going over to the area of Hunter's and Mosquito Run, below Moosejaw Ridge, above Otter Creek. I think we'll find them over there," Gerry Senior said with a growing conviction.

"Why are you sure we'll find them in that area, Mr. Bruce?" Adam asked.

Gerry Senior looked away in the direction they were going to be riding in before he answered. "Because I've been there before, and I think that's the elk's home territory. I think that's where he'll go when he figures out someone's chasing him. That's where Barney will track him to, and that's where Bern and Parker will track Barney to." He looked up at the sky over where they were going to ride, and he saw the clouds boiling over the top of the ridge. "And judging from those clouds, we'd better get started and get moving fast," Gerry Senior said. "Charley, how quickly can you get those mules to moving?"

"My mules will be running long after your horses are fast asleep, big boss man," Charley answered him gruffly, but with obvious affection.

"Well then, Charley, get them moving—we're heading out to Hunter's Run. Come on, people, we're burning daylight," Gerry Senior called as he urged his mount into a run.

Farther up Plum Ridge, Bern looked behind him and saw that Parker was looking westward through his binoculars.

"Whatcha looking at, Mr. Woodson? You see something?" Bern asked.

"I … I'm not sure. I think I saw a flash over that way …" He pointed in that direction.

"That way? That's …"

"That's Hunter's Run. I know. I know that area pretty well, Bern. And I would rather you call me Parker instead of Mr. Woodson, if you don't mind. Yes, I know that … There! There it is again! Did you see it?" Parker asked excitedly.

"Yep, that time I did. What do you think it is?"

"Well, my guess is that it is either a reflection off another pair of binoculars or off a rifle scope. But either way, I think we need to head over there, because I'm willing to bet that the party we're looking for is over there already. I seem to remember a shortcut over to that area. You know it?" Parker asked.

"Yeah, I seem to recall it's over that way somewhere. I reckon I can find it if you can. After you, Parker," Bern said courteously, and then he spurred his horse to running down the slope toward the notch in the ridge, Parker running right behind him.

When the light failed them, the group made their camp near the bottom of Hunter's Run. Because Gerry was concerned about Barney spotting their fires, he kept them low and well-hidden. Charley made a cold meal for everyone, and they sat around talking in the rapidly descending darkness.

Adam raised a question that had been on his mind for a long time. "Mr. Barry, I'd like to ask you something. It's about this mountain we've been riding through," Adam explained.

"Well, I was wondering how long it would take for someone to raise the question," Oliver said with a laugh. "You want to know why it is called Redd Mountain when we seem to be riding over several mountains, am I right?"

"Yes, sir. That's it exactly."

"Well, the reason is that Redd Mountain isn't actually a single mountain, but a group of peaks all clustered together and separated by a series of ridges. I don't know for sure just how it came to be called

Redd Mountain, but the local story is that, a long time ago, someone named Redd gave it that name. Gerry, you or your son know the way it got its name?"

Gerry Junior deferred to his father, as he was the historian of the family.

"Well, as I got it from my father, Amos, it was Kenton Redd who gave it the name. He was the man, back in the late 1870s, who first got here, and he was the man who explored all the ridges and peaks, and he is supposed to have said he got red in the face from exertion trying to figure out where the top of the mountain was, so he just gave up and called the whole damn thing Redd Mountain. At least, that's the story my daddy told me about it, and he grew up hearing that story, so it's as good as any other explanation I've ever heard," Gerry Senior said.

The group had a good chuckle over this. As the laughter died away, April asked him another question. "Mr. Bruce, why do you think Mr. Barney and the elk are up on this side of the mountain?" Her pencil was poised to take down his reply.

Gerry just looked at her, and his smile faded away. "I'd rather not answer that question, miss. I have my opinions and beliefs, and I don't want to be made fun of," he said seriously.

"Mr. Bruce, no one is going to laugh at you. You are experienced in these woods, so I would expect you know what you're doing. For my story, I would just like to understand what clues suggested Mr. Barney and the elk would be in this part of the mountain," April persisted.

"Come on, Dad. I'd like to know as well why we're here when Axel said he saw the animal back where we were. What is it that makes you think we had to come in the opposite direction from where he was last seen?" Gerry Junior asked, his curiosity aroused.

"Does this change of direction have anything to do with my stepson's death, Gerry? Do you think the location of that avalanche may have something to do with this animal?" Arnold asked suspiciously.

"Come on, people. This isn't a supernatural phenomenon we're chasing here," Ed scoffed. Gerry Senior said nothing, but it was obvious to Eileen, who was sitting beside him, that he was biting his tongue to avoid saying anything he would be sorry for.

"Gerry, we've been friends for a long time, and if you know something, I think you owe it to me and to Max to tell us. You know me, I don't make fun of any ideas anyone has without exploring their merit first. Hell, I've even been to a séance once or twice, so you know I'm open to anything. Just what is it you don't want to say?" Arnold said entreatingly.

"Mr. Bruce," Adam said hesitantly, "back home in my little town, we have three haunted houses where some of our most leading citizens have sworn they've seen a ghost from time to time. Even the White House is reported to be haunted by President Lincoln himself. Speaking for myself, I've seen several things I couldn't explain by science. I read a book one time that suggested what we call ghosts are spirits trapped between Earth and whatever comes next, and I read one that suggests they are souls that died an untimely death and came back to finish some task they left undone." Adam heard Ed snickering to his left, but paid him no mind.

Wanda added her thoughts to the discussion. "There are religions that believe in reincarnation of the soul as a means of learning or achieving a higher level of consciousness on the path to enlightenment. I believe there could be something to this, myself," she said.

"You people are really crazier than I thought you were!" Ed laughed.

"Mr. Baxter," Oliver said quietly, "how many tracks have you seen of this animal? How many times, just in the time we've been on his trail, have we seen any physical tracks where he was standing? Sure, we've seen him." He looked around at the others. "But how many times have we seen his hoof prints in the snow or anywhere else? Even Axel and Bern haven't seen any real physical tracks, have you, Axel?" Axel just shook his head. "What about you, Gerry?" Oliver asked the younger Bruce. "Have you ever seen his physical tracks?"

"Never," Gerry slowly replied.

"Now, I'm not saying I believe in ghosts or spirits or anything like that," Oliver told all of them, "but I have to admit I have more questions than I have answers to this puzzle, so I'm not discounting anything at this point. Unless someone has a better explanation, I'm willing to consider what Gerry is suggesting, regardless of how unsettling or inconceivable it might seem on the face of it. And, I might say, it has a very romantic ring to it being a ghost."

"Okay, I've heard enough of this drivel," Ed said. "I'm going to turn in and get some rest. I've got to be rested for the finale to this circus tomorrow." He yawned as he stood up.

"I don't mean to be a buzz kill, Mr. Baxter, but how do you know it's going to end tomorrow?" Adam asked him.

"Because that's all the time I'm investing in this snipe hunt, son," Baxter replied curtly.

"And just how do you plan on getting back by yourself, Mr. Baxter?" Gerry Junior asked ominously.

"I'll ride my horse back to—"

"Ride whose horse back to where, Mr. Baxter? Did you bring your horse, Mr. Baxter? I don't think so, because all the horses I see here are mine or my father's, and if you take one, that would be horse theft, and I'm sure you are aware of the penalty for horse theft in this state, Mr. Baxter?" Gerry asked calmly.

Ed looked confused for a moment, and then his face darkened in the twilight. "Very well, Mr. Bruce. How much to buy one of—"

"They're not for sale at any price, Mr. Baxter. I rent the use of them, that's all. And I can refuse to rent the use of them to anyone at any time I choose. Am I correct in this assumption, Mr. Barry?"

"I believe you are, Mr. Bruce," Oliver responded solemnly.

"Well then, what would your official position be if Mr. Baxter decided to take one without first securing my permission, Mr. Barry?"

"I'd have no choice then but to arrest him for horse theft, Mr. Bruce," Oliver said evenly.

"You two are in this together, aren't you?" Ed accused Oliver.

"Mr. Baxter, you saw the badge I borrowed. I was given that badge on one condition, and that was that I enforce the laws with it. I do not have the luxury of picking which laws I uphold or enforce—I have to enforce any law I am aware of that is being broken. And I am quite aware of the laws against horse theft. Now, I know the penalty isn't immediate hanging anymore, but I would be obligated to bring you in for booking," Oliver responded tartly. He laid it out for him plain and simple. "Please don't add to my problems tonight or any other time—I'd much rather concentrate on one problem at a time, and the problem in front of me right now is Mr. Barney.

"We'd like to have your help in this, Mr. Baxter; your ability to shoot might become the means to saving a life, so we'd rather have you as a member of our team than a hostile hindrance." He waited for Baxter to think it over and make his decision, but just in case it wasn't the right one, Axel and Gerry Junior moved slightly to stand behind Ed on either side of him—not touching him, but close enough that he knew they were there.

After a few long and tense moments, Ed made the only decision he could make under the circumstances. "All right," he grumbled, "I guess when you put it that way, I don't have any reason to want to help that pompous ass—jerk—get his way. And if he is responsible for the death of Mr. Wilcox's stepson and those skiers, then I want him brought to justice too. So, okay. I'll be on the team like a good boy, but I don't like being pressured into it. Just so's you know."

"Understood, Ed. It won't happen again. We're glad you decided to be part of the team," Arnold said cheerfully as he clapped Ed on the shoulder. "Besides, Ed, it's a hell of a long walk back," he added, to the amusement of the others.

After a moment, even Ed joined in the laughter.

"If we are all back together now, perhaps we can talk about how we're going to find any of the others we're looking for?" Gerry Junior said angrily. "I've got a good man out there, looking around in the dark with no idea of where we are, because we're not where we left him or where we said we'd be going, and he has no way to find us. I can't send him an e-mail or anything, because he doesn't have a cell phone, and if he did, it wouldn't work in this forest. So how about we talk about that and get off this damn ghost nonsense?"

There was a silence that placed a pall on the group when Gerry stopped talking, because none of them had thought about that aspect of their shift in the search.

"Boss," Charley spoke up, "don't you think Bern might have expected us to move onto somewhere else by now? A group this big, we surely left signs of our passing and Bern, he ain't no tenderfoot when it comes to reading signs, you know that. Bern, he can find an ice cube in the desert if need be. I figure he'll find us a'fore we find him, boss."

Gerry pondered this for a moment, and then he relaxed. "I reckon you're right, Charley. I'm just worried about what he might come up against in Barney and that no-account Bergen."

"Gerry, Bergen may be a no-account guide, but I don't think he'd do anything to put anyone in harm's way," Oliver said to reassure him.

"He'd better not. Or there won't be any place on this mountain big enough for him to hide from me," Gerry threatened, and all of them knew he meant every word he had said.

A few miles away, on another ridge, Bern and Parker were sitting by their own small fire. They were making small talk, as men will do when they have a bigger issue on their mind but are unsure how to broach it.

"So, Parker, this man Barney … you think he's responsible for the death of your friend Max?" Bern asked him slowly.

"No, I don't think it. I know it. I was the one who found him when he was shooting at an animal in a no-hunting zone. I called to him to stop, but he ignored me. I could see the snow pack up top was fragile, and there were too many overhangs on the field. I could see him shooting into an area that could have … did, in fact, cause echo vibrations that collapsed the tops; and when they fell, it just picked up steam as it flowed downhill.

"When I caught up to him, he was getting ready to take another shot at his target, and I tried to stop him from shooting, but he turned as I got to him and ended up shooting right up into the snowpack. That was all it took. The avalanche started, and Max's radio didn't respond. We had been having problems with all of them—the cases weren't as sealed as tightly as they should have been, and moisture seeped in them whenever they were left sitting on or in the snow. We tried to keep them as dry as we could, but with the jobs we had …"

"The jobs you all had put you into the snow more than most people, I'm sure. So what happened when he fired the round?"

"I heard the avalanche start, and then the lights went out."

"You got caught in it?"

"No. That son of a bitch coldcocked me from behind with the rifle stock. I saw a flash of it just before I went down. At least the son of a bitch had the decency to turn me over, so I wouldn't suffocate in the snow. But before I went out, I saw the snow start to build up the wall as it went down, and Max and the party he was trying to get out were right in its path. That man never tried to get any of them help or do anything for them. We never found any of their bodies, not even when the spring came," Parker said sadly.

He sat there, head hanging down, thinking about his good friend and the tragedy that had taken him. Bern didn't say anything, knowing there was nothing to say, and that his silence said more than mere words would.

After a few minutes, Parker raised his head and began to talk about his friend. "He was a hell of a skier; he could go faster and farther with less effort than any man I've ever seen. He could ride one ski down a hill a professional would blanch at. And no matter what he did, he never had to work at it. It always seemed to come easy to him. It used to make me so damn jealous of him sometimes." He laughed at the memory, and then something struck him, and he laughed even harder. "But, you know, the funny thing was, take him off skis, and he was the biggest doofus you ever saw. He could trip over a shadow when he was walking." Parker began to laugh so hard he cried. But it only lasted a few seconds before the tears changed to real crying as he felt the loss of his friend.

Bern was uncomfortable around a man showing such pain, and he didn't know what to do for him. He just sat there, watching a grown man crying over a thirty-year hurt.

After a while, Parker was able to collect himself and sit up. "Sorry about that, Bern. Sometimes I get to missing him, and I just feel all empty inside. But you know something? This is the first time I've cried for him I can recall that I feel a little better after crying. Why's that, do you suppose?"

"I don't know, Parker, maybe because you're doing it here? You know, being in the area that it actually happened. Maybe something about that is helping you to feel better," Bern suggested.

"Maybe. I do feel a little better, though. Hey. Tell me a little about yourself and your brother. His name is Axel?" Parker asked, changing the subject.

"Yeah, Axel. He's my younger brother. Not much to tell; our parents died when we were young, and Mr. Wilcox took us in, and he and his missus kinda watched over us till she passed on. They did it all for us—scolded us when we done wrong, praised us when we did right, were there when we needed someone to lean on, and let us make our own mistakes to learn from. Mr. Wilcox, he taught us all about ranching, and when he saw we took to it, he encouraged us to go to school to get an education, and he saw to it we got a good one.

"Mr. Wilcox, he said it was what they would have done for her son—your friend Max, although we didn't know it then, on account of she never talked about him. Mr. Wilcox, he did talk about him some, for a little while, until he saw it made his missus sad to hear, then he stopped talking about him altogether. I kinda think he liked to talk about him, sorta kept your friend alive for him. After his missus died, he kinda shuttered up the ranch and himself, so there was no need for us to stay on. That's when we went to work for Mr. Bruce, on Mr. Wilcox's recommendation, and we've been there ever since.

"I reckon we best get some rest, Parker, it looks to be a hard day tomorrow."

"Thank you for listening to me go on, Bern. I appreciate it very much."

"No problem, Parker."

Back down below, April cornered Adam by his tent with the intention of manipulating him into spilling the beans about that magazine he had mentioned earlier.

"Adam," she purred, "did I hear you mention something about a magazine to the ranger? Are you going to do some freelance photography for him? Is that it?" she asked sweetly, her hand on his arm and her chin on his shoulder.

"No."

"Well, what is it that you're doing then? You can tell me, I won't spill the beans to anyone, I promise," she asked.

"I'm not at liberty to discuss it yet—it is just in the planning stages."

"Then it isn't definite?"

"No, it's very definite," Adam said; but he thought to himself, *I hope.*

"Don't you want to talk to me about it, Adam? I thought we were friends and partners—now you're excluding me from your good news. That's not very friendly," she pouted.

"This project has nothing to do with you, April, so I don't know why you are so interested in it."

"Anything that interests you interests me, Adam." April was getting annoyed because Adam wasn't responding like he should have been. *I'm going to have pull out all the stops for this one,* she thought to herself.

Because it was so dark, she was unable to see the amused expression that was beginning to creep over Adam's face as he realized he had the upper hand now, and she wanted something from him she couldn't get for herself. He was pretty sure the ranger wasn't going to talk to her about it, even if she asked him, so he decided to play with her a little.

"Why do you want to know about what I'm doing or going to be doing, April? I thought this story was all that interested you these days."

April gritted her teeth silently, put a purr back into her voice, and started playing with the hair on the back of Adam's neck as she tried another tack. "Adam, I just want to help you get this project of yours off the ground. I know a lot of people, and maybe I can get you some publicity to help you sell your pictures," she offered sweetly.

For a second, Adam was tempted to tell her all about it—then he remembered who he was talking to. "Well, it's like this, April. I'm not supposed to be talking about it to anyone until it is official, and then I'll be able to tell you all about it. So that's an interesting theory Mr. Bruce was talking about, wasn't it?" he said changing the subject.

But April didn't respond to him; she just stormed off to look for the ranger, determined to get the information she wanted. As she marched off in the snow, Adam just smiled.

On the other side of the camp, Wanda was talking to Arnold about his stepson and his reasons for going after Barney. "Arnie, if you would like to talk about Max a little more, I'd be happy to listen. I'm thinking you didn't have children of your own? I have never had any children either—of course, I wasn't married. He meant a lot to you, didn't he? You were close, weren't you," she said softly.

Arnold was sitting on a tree stump, looking at the moon and the slopes up ahead of them. He didn't respond to her, so she walked closer and stood behind him, her hand on his shoulder. "Arnie? Did you hear me? Would you rather be out here alone with your memories?"

Arnold didn't answer her with words, but he brought his hand up to his shoulder to take hers and bring her down beside him.

"No, Wanda, I'm tired of being alone with my memories and thoughts. They aren't much comfort to a lonely old man. I want to start living again in the time I have left. I don't know how much it is, but I want to enjoy whatever time it is. I think that's the problem for me. I stopped living a little when Max died and stopped living a lot when Connie died. I buried myself in my work and in helping those two young men that ride for Gerry now.

"They'd been working for me and Connie since their early teens, and when their parents died, we took them in. They were good boys, and now they're good men. I put everything I was going to do for Max into them, and when they didn't need me anymore, I think I lost my interest in living. Now, Wanda, I have a chance to make things right by him," Arnold explained.

"I can understand why you want to find Mr. Barney, but what will it accomplish? It won't bring your stepson back, it won't bring your wife back, and if you get hurt or killed, it won't help us build a new future," Wanda replied softly.

"I know that, Wanda. I truly do, but I have to go after him. I owe it to Max to see that he pays for his act. I can't expect you to understand that, and I don't expect you to wait for me to get back, seeing as how I can't really be certain what's going to happen when we do find him. I'm sure he's going to put up a fight, and there's no predicting what could go wrong with that. So, what I'm saying, Wanda, is that I'll understand if you want to back out of our relationship," he said, holding his breath against her response as she looked up at the top of the mountain in the darkness.

"Arnie. You be very careful out there and come back to me safe and in one piece."

Higher up the mountain, Warner and Floyd were talking about the next day's activities.

"We're no closer to him tonight than we were last week, Floyd," Warner said—in an uncharacteristically friendly mood. "It's like he's leading us around, Floyd. How can any dumb animal, no matter how clever it seems to be, stay so far ahead of us and out of sight unless he wants to be seen? I don't understand this at all. What's your take on this situation, Floyd?" Warner asked.

After a moment, he got his response. "I think there's something wrong here. I've been looking around since we've been on his trail, and while we haven't seen much of him, we also haven't seen much of anything else either," Floyd pointed out. "You think about it, Mr. Barney. We haven't seen any tracks of any kind of animal—not a fox or deer or anything since we left their camp two days ago. Hell, Mr. Barney, we haven't seen even so much as a damn bird flying overhead.

"That isn't normal up here, not now, not ever," Floyd complained. "And another thing—all this snow. This is awful early for this much snow up here, Mr. Barney. I've been here all my life, and I've never see this much snow at this time of year. It's really deep in some places, and we might step wrong and break a leg. Or, worse yet, one of the horses might step in a hole and break a leg. I'm thinking it might be kinda dangerous for us to go traipsing around up there with the intent to do some shooting. It might set off something. Maybe we should just look for him on these lower levels, Mr. Barney. I don't think we should climb any higher right now," Floyd said with obvious concern.

Warner just looked at him in the darkening evening. He didn't respond right away, and when he did, all traces of his previous friendly and relaxed attitude were gone. "Mr. Bergen," he said slowly in a very icy tone, "we are up here for one reason and for one reason only. And just in case you don't remember, the reason is for me to get a shot at this magnificent animal that is roaming this mountain. I'm not interested in the snow or in any other animal on this damn pile of rocks, and all I require of you, Mr. Bergen, is that you help me find him. That is all you have to do—find him for me. I'll do the rest. So tomorrow, you get on his trail and find him. Understand me?" Warner said in an ominously cold tone.

"Mr. Barney, I just don't think you've got the true picture of our situation. Have we ever really seen one single track? No, we haven't. We've seen him a couple of times, and we saw him running away, but we've never seen his tracks, now have we? Doesn't that seem just a bit odd to you? Hell, man, we're running in circles after him. Our one best hope for chasing him down is for him to show himself and us to get on his tail right away," Floyd suggested hopefully.

"I feel certain that we'll get a good look at him in the morning without him seeing us first," Warner said confidently, ignoring the message in Floyd's words.

Floyd just stared in his direction, the failing light being insufficient for Warner to see him shake his head in disbelief at the resistance to seeing the truth of his situation.

"Mr. Barney," Floyd said too quietly for Warner to hear, "You're never going to see that animal unless he wants you to see him and he sees you first."

He rolled over with the intent of going to sleep, but something didn't seem right, so he sat up again. He looked off into the dark and slowly scanned the horizon and lower levels. As his gaze passed over the lower landscape, he suddenly stopped and began to smile.

"Mr. Barney. Do you suppose that animal of yours knows how to build a small campfire?" he asked in a curious voice.

"What the hell are you talking about, Bergen? Are you an absolute idiot? Of course he can't build a damn campfire, he's an—"

"The reason I ask you, Mr. Barney, is that there is a campfire down below us. I suspect our colleagues and competitors are down there, looking for him, just as we are. I don't know why they're here or what brought them to this part of the mountain, but there they are and we have to avoid them now," Floyd said thoughtfully.

Warner stared down the slope until he found the tiny flicker of light Floyd had seen.

"Damn! How the hell did they get here? Do they know something I don't? How did they find him? How can they find him and you can't, Bergen?" Warner said suspiciously.

"Mr. Barney, you don't know they're following a trail any more than we are. I suspect they just saw him, just as we did, and then came on a tear after him. Mr. Barney, we could get an early start in the morning, get a jump on them, if you want," Floyd offered cautiously.

Warner thought about this for a short minute and blew up. "No, damn it! I don't want to get an early start in the morning—I want to get an early start right now! Pack up—we're moving out and looking for him now!"

"Now, Mr. Barney, how the hell are we going to find him in the dark? We won't be able to see him in the dark, and he can see us. We won't know what we're riding over or into, and the risk of either of us getting hurt is too great to move around in the dark, Mr. Barney. I know there's a full moon out—" He held up his hand to forestall any remark by Warner about the moon as he saw him look up. "But the moonlight creates shadows and makes it very difficult to gauge distance. The last thing you want to do is make a mistake with your shot and just wound him or scare him off," Floyd warned.

Floyd's words seemed to cut through Warner's excitement and anger, cooling his ardor to get moving. As much as he wanted to get started, he must have recognized that Floyd was right—they had to wait until first light to get started, as much as he wanted to jump now.

"Okay, Bergen, I guess you're right. We'll wait until first light to get moving," he said, frustrated with the delay.

"Fair enough, Mr. Barney. Best we get some sleep now, sir," They both turned over and, without saying another word to each other, fell asleep quickly.

April was furious. She was lying awake in her sleeping bag, staring at the top of her tent, and running through the situation to herself.

This story is getting away from me like I can't believe. The damn hunter I wanted to write about is off on his own, trying to bring down the animal we're all up here trying to save; the rancher and that dried-up old vet are mooning over each other like schoolchildren on a playground; the guides are all business; that damn old cook is off in la-la land, telling tall tales about the West that never was; and the ranger is making deals behind my back with Adam.

And that's another problem: what the hell is going on with Adam? He came up here a babe in the woods, and now he's making deals without talking to me—and cutting me out of it, besides. What the hell kind of deal did he make with that ranger, anyway? What kind of a magazine is he involved with, and what's he doing for it? He's being awfully closed-mouthed about it, whatever it is. And why won't he talk to me about it? I'll bet he's planning on selling his pictures from this story for more money than the paper was paying him.

He's selling me out, damn him! I brought him along on this outing to give him a chance to get known, and this is how he repays me? What nerve! Who the hell does he think he is?

April was livid, and she was working herself into a rage of frustration and resentment. Her own double-dealing and manipulations forgotten, she could only see her once-glowing future starting to dim in the growing darkness of the night.

I've got to get the ranger to tell me what's going on, but to do that, I've got to get the ranger by himself so I can apply some charm. That damn assistant of his won't let me near him; I don't know what her problem is. She must think I'm going to try to steal him away from her. I have to get him alone somehow so I can pry this information out of him.

He's a man, so he's not immune to a little skin-to-skin contact; that usually loosens most men's tongues. Tomorrow, when we get started, I'm going to ride next to him and find out what's going on here. But first, I think I'd better get someone to keep that damn assistant of his occupied. I know—I'll get Adam to keep her busy, and that will give me time to work on him. That will work; then I can get back to working on my story.

Satisfied she had figured out a way of the mess her story was becoming, she relaxed and turned over in her sleeping bag, quickly dropping off to sleep in the cool air.

Gerry Senior tapped his son on the shoulder and nodded to a point away from the camp. Gerry Junior got up and carefully followed his father to a spot a good distance from the tents. The fresh snow crunched crisply under their feet. Gerry Junior started to speak, but his father motioned him to silence until they were a distance from the tents.

Once out of earshot, Gerry Senior turned his back to camp and began to speak in a low voice. "Keep your voice down, son. In this clear air, sound carries a good distance. We need to talk about what's to come tomorrow. I've got a notion this isn't going to end well for everyone, and we need to have a clear head when we go into it. I want to be sure that we are on the same page in dealing with Barney. I'm not going to waste time telling you that I told you so about that man, but we need to have a plan on dealing with him," Gerry said softly. "Now, I have had some experience with him, as I told you, and I know Parker also has had experience with him too.

"Oliver showing up with a US Marshal's badge—now that was an unexpected piece of good luck. But that's when we find him. Finding him is going to be hard work, because we don't know where he's going to be. I was thinking that maybe we should divide up into two teams: I'll take Oliver, Axel, and Arnold with me; you take the two women, Ed, Charley, the reporter, and her photographer with you. You'll look for the animal, we'll look for Barney," Gerry offered.

"What are you talking about, Dad? I'm not taking any group anywhere without you, and you sure as hell aren't going after Barney with Oliver or anyone else. You take that bunch out after the animal, and I'll take Axel, Oliver, and Arnold with me. You're not a spring chicken anymore, Dad. You aren't a match physically for Barney, and you know your heart isn't what it used to be. No, I'll go after him. You take the others looking for the animal," he countered.

There was a long pause, and Gerry Senior sighed. "No, son, this is something I have to do. I have an obligation, you see—this is old business, and I have to close the book on it myself. I need you to understand that, son, please."

His son recognized the futility of arguing with his father when that tone came into his voice, and he just nodded his assent to his request.

Gerry Senior turned to face his son, and he put his big hand on his shoulder and looked him in the eye. "Son, I want you to know I'm very proud of you. You are a real man to be proud of—the ranch is the success because of you. I know I didn't tell you this very often while you were growing up, but it wasn't because I wasn't proud of you. It was because I didn't think I had the right to say it to you, since I hadn't always been there. Now, I don't know just how this is going to turn out, but, just in case, I wanted you to hear it from me. I've talked to Oliver, and he's agreed to stand in for me if you ever need a hand or advice on anything not ranch related, but—"

"Stop talking like that, Dad. You're sounding like you're saying good-bye, and I'm not ready to say good-bye just yet. We just got started being a team, so don't be planning on running out on me again."

"I'm not planning on that, son, but we have to face the fact that anything could happen up there. We both know what kind of a man that Barney is, and I know better than you what he's willing to do to get what he wants. I told you, I have to do this to get back my self-respect he took from me years ago. I owe it to the people who died as a result of his actions."

"Well, if there's no talking you out of it, then take this," his son said as he started to unbuckle his gun belt.

"No need for that, son," his father said with a smile as he unbuttoned his coat to show his own gun belt around his waist and the twin .44 Magnum Ruger Vaqueros nestled in their holsters. "I came better prepared for him this time. You know Axel is a good shot too. I'll be back—I just wanted to make sure I told you I was proud of you, son. You be careful out there while you're looking for that animal, and I'll see you when I get back to the ranch," his father said with a big smile he didn't really feel. He gave his son a big hug, and they stood there for a moment in an embrace; and then he pushed him away. "Go on now. Get some rest. We'll split up in the morning and get this job done together, okay?"

"Okay, Dad. You're the boss. You be careful too, okay? Watch out for Oliver; he isn't the best rider." After another long look at each other, as if memorizing the other's face, they walked back to their tent to get some rest for the long day they both knew was ahead of them.

Ed Baxter sat alone in the tent he shared with Arnold. He was thinking about the conversations of the evening, about Woodson's story, and of Arnold's disclosure about his stepson. He knew he wasn't an emotional person, or even a very likable one. Ed had no delusions about his reputation, or the fact that he had few real close friends. He wasn't exactly disagreeable; he just wasn't a particularly warm person. Being a functional alcoholic had a lot to do with this, because he had to keep people at a distance in order to protect his secret. He was starting to feel the effects of going without for a couple of days, and it was beginning to sour his thinking.

But, despite this, he was unable to escape the fact that several of the men on this joyless joyride were willing to risk their lives for a friend, even a long-dead friend, and that said a lot about the quality of their relationships.

Ed knew there was no one who would miss him if something went wrong. He sat there in the dark, wondering what he had to show for his life, even on his best day. He laughed humorlessly, realizing the reason he had sniped at Arnold was that he was jealous of him. He was jealous of the respect Arnold received from others, even when he wasn't trying to, and that people just naturally trusted him because he was reliable and his word was gold. It was the same for the Bruce men and that ranger. Hell, even the photographer had won the respect of everyone, because he was willing to do whatever was asked of him and never complained.

He started thinking about the others and, with an increasing level of self-reproach, he reluctantly realized he was behaving more like the two people he had no respect for—Barney and that sneaky reporter—than he was the people he did have respect for.

Whatever else he was, that ranger was willing to do what he thought was right to honor his obligations to his position. Yeah, he might be out of his element up here, but he hadn't let that stop him from coming to do what his job required him to do. And he had thought ahead—he had to hand it to him for being smart on that score. That was pretty slick, getting the US Marshal's badge and authority for this trip. What was the sign in the administrator's office, the one he had always made fun of? Oh, yeah.

"Today is the first day of the rest of your life."

Suddenly the sign made sense—a lot of sense. Ed crawled into his sleeping bag to get some rest. He had a big day tomorrow.

And he wasn't even thirsty.

As the stars twinkled overhead through the clouds, Bern and Parker stared at the sky. Both men were awake, despite the lateness of the hour—in part due to the coldness of the air.

Parker asked Bern something that had been on his mind. "Bern, can I ask you something?"

"Go ahead."

"I know you have a pistol and a rifle with you, and I assume you're a good shot with either. But—and I don't mean to imply anything by this question, but …"

"But you want to know if I'm willing to use it on a man. Willing and capable, I guess is your question?" The silence that followed told Bern he had guessed right. "Well, you can rest easy. I can."

"Well, I mean no disrespect to you, Bern, but it isn't an easy thing to point a gun at a man, and then it's an even harder thing to shoot a man," Parker said with sadness in his eyes.

"Yes, it is. And it changes a man when he does it, whatever his reason for doing it. I saw it change a lot of men who came home from the war—some men could deal with it, and some men couldn't. My pa couldn't. It changed him to someone we didn't know anymore. It killed him, and it killed my mother too, through him," Bern said with pain in his eyes.

"Bern, I understand what you're saying, but how do you know you can do it? If you feel it changes people, how do you know you can do it and live with it afterward?" Parker asked.

"Because I already have, Parker," Bern said evenly.

"What? You shot someone? How? When?" he asked incredulously.

Bern looked away before answering him. "It's not something I like talk about, Parker. Sorry. But there is something that I meant to ask you last night, Parker. We kinda got distracted, but I meant to ask you about it."

"What's that, Bern?"

"You said it was the winter that Barney was hunting, and he had a target. What was it he was hunting? Did you get a good look at the animal he was trying to kill? Just out of curiosity."

"Yes, I did. It was a big buck."

"Oh, he was hunting deer?"

"No. It was a buck elk."

CHAPTER 10

❖

The morning came early, and the air was cold and clear—if you didn't count the snow that was steadily falling. The camp woke up to the sound of Charley announcing breakfast.

"Rise up and come git it, children! We got fruit and coffee, but no eggs or anything hot today. The damn snow put out my fire, and I haven't got any dry wood to get a fire going or the time to start one. We got a lot of riding to do today and a lot to talk about first!"

As everyone started to pull themselves together and come out of their tents, they heard Gerry Senior's voice as well.

"Folks, we have a lot of things to talk about this morning, so everyone get a cup of coffee, and we'll get to it. I have some news to share, and you all need to hear it. Gather 'round and get comfortable, and I'll explain."

As everyone stood around him, Gerry Junior walked over and stood by his father. "As you all know, we started out on this trip with one purpose in mind; that was to find, trap, and relocate a specific large, red elk. We were going to relocate him down to the nature preserve at the base of the mountain, where he would live out his years in safety and good health. Well, we all know what happened to that plan."

"Yeah, it got scotched by a real—" muttered Ed.

"A real disagreeable person, that's right, Ed," Gerry continued. "Well, the fact is, he has complicated our task no end, and now he's become a real threat to both the elk and our safety."

"He is also a suspect in the death of a ski patrolman and several others thirty years ago," Oliver added.

"Yes, that's true. There's that as well. Well, we—that is, my son and I—have decided that, in order to protect all of you and achieve our primary task, we have to divide up and address both tasks at once. Therefore, I am going to take Oliver, Axel, and Arnold, and we are going after Warner Barney and Floyd Bergen. My son and Charley will be taking the rest of you on to look for the animal as we had originally planned. Right, son?"

"That's right. So, everyone, start getting packed up and ready to go; we've got a long way to go," the younger Bruce said flatly, not looking his father in the eye.

Oliver didn't miss this nonverbal cue, and he knew this wasn't going to be as easy as Gerry Senior implied.

Everyone hurried off to their tent to get their things together in as short a time as they could.

Eileen turned to Oliver, her concern written all over her face as she pulled him aside to talk. "Oliver, are you sure this is the way it has to be? No animal is worth anyone's life. This man is clearly dangerous and should be stopped, I know, but it's not your job! You're not a real lawman or US Marshal; let them handle it when we get back!" she urged him.

"Eileen, I know it's not my job, but it's my responsibility," he said quietly. "I allowed this man to be here, I gave my okay for this excursion, and now he's threatening the safety of everyone on my mountain. If cleaning up the mess I created isn't in my job description, then it damn sure should be, because I can't leave this mess for anyone else to clean up for me. I'd have no respect for anyone who did that to me, and that includes myself. So, you go with Gerry Junior and find that animal before Barney does. I'll be fine. I'm not a child, you know," he said lovingly.

She looked at him and gave him a big kiss and ran to her tent. He could hear her crying as she ran.

Wanda watched her run off, and then she turned to Arnold and gave him a kiss and ran after Eileen.

Ed watched both women without saying a word and slowly walked back to his tent. Adam turned to say something to April, but she turned and stormed off without saying a word. He shrugged and headed for his tent to pack.

Having already fed and watered the horses, Axel began to ready their saddles in place.

Gerry Junior walked over to Charley and spoke to him a moment. Charley looked at him, nodded, went over to a board in his pack saddle, and banged his hand against it. It popped off and revealed a small space. He reached in, pulled out a small bundle, and handed it to Gerry. Without a word, Charley began to pack up the kitchen gear as quickly as he could, shaking his head as he did.

Gerry walked over to Oliver and handed him the bundle. Oliver unwrapped it, knowing by the feel just what it was. Gerry looked at him for a moment, saying "Put it on. You might need it," he walked over to his own tent to get ready.

Inside the bundle was a black gun belt with a .45 caliber Ruger Blackhawk in the holster. Oliver looked at it for a minute, flipped it around his waist, and buckled it on. He slid the gun out of the holster and opened the loading gate, running the cylinder over his arm to check the loads. Satisfied that there were five rounds, he carefully positioned the hammer over the empty chamber for safety and dropped it into the holster. After looking around first to make sure no one was watching him, he pulled it in the Hollywood quick-draw fashion, just like he had practiced for many hours in front of the mirror at home. Oliver spun it and shoved it back in the holster, smiling in satisfaction as he headed for his tent.

Within two hours, everyone was in the saddle and ready to move out. Gerry Senior, with Axel, Oliver, and Arnold beside him, started to move up the mountain toward Hunter's Run.

Gerry Junior motioned for the other members of the group to follow him, and then he headed out in the other direction. After a few moments, he stopped when he didn't hear anything and then turned around in the saddle to see where they were. He saw they all hadn't moved.

"What's going on here?" he asked, clearly annoyed. They all looked at Ed, who walked his mount a few steps ahead of the group.

"It's a revolt, Mr. Bruce. We all talked a bit, and we decided we're not going after the animal until the bigger threat is taken care of," he said calmly.

"What the hell are you talking about, Baxter?"

"What I'm saying, Mr. Bruce, and I'm speaking for all of us"—he waved his hand at the others behind him, who nodded their agreement with his words—"is that we all agreed that you don't want to leave your father alone, and that you will need each of our respective talents to protect him and the others."

"I'm not hearing this for real—I can't be!" Gerry Junior exclaimed.

"Yes, actually you are, Mr. Bruce. I'm an expert with the rifle, Dr. Fleming is the *only* certified medic on this ride, and—"

"She's an animal doctor, for crying out loud!" Gerry protested.

"Nevertheless, Mr. Bruce, she is a trained medic, and you can't deny we might have need for her training when we catch up to Mr. Barney," Ed continued politely. "Miss Gayle has a cell phone and has access to many special emergency contacts should we have a need of them, and I am sure you are cognizant of the fact that the odds are very good we will have need of them before this is over. Mr. Jacobs will provide us with photographic proof of whatever we find, and that will certainly be invaluable in court," Ed pointed out. "Miss Martens is prepared to provide us with a detailed record or transcript of any confession Mr. Barney may make, as well as her notes from her conversations with him, providing his motivation and intent to deceive both the ranger and yourself as to his intent to kill the animal.

"This would clearly be a breach of the contract he signed on for, and a good lawyer could make a case for fraud. It's also possible he might make a statement about that other matter while he is confessing his sins," Ed said, looking him in the eye. "I am sure you know what Charley's contribution would be. And in any case, Charley's agreed to be our guide to track the quarry we are seeking. That we have changed our focus from an endangered animal to a dangerous one is simply a matter of fact that you will simply have to accept." Ed finished his speech and backed his horse into the line formed by the others.

As he did so, Eileen stepped her mount in front of the line, with Wanda right beside her. "Mr. Bruce, I am certain you feel as bad leaving your father to go on alone as I do about Oliver, and, if you're the man, I believe you to be, you were certainly planning to leave us with Charley and go after them yourself. We—that is, Wanda and I—can do no less for the ones we love, and I don't think you're going to ask us to do that."

She backed up, and Adam walked his horse forward.

"Mr. Bruce, I don't have anyone here I am in love with, other than this mountain of yours, but I have certainly come to respect Mr. Barry and your father, as well as Mr. Wilcox and Mr. Baxter—and, for that matter, Axel and Bern—and I want to help them however I can. I'm not a fighter, I admit that, but I can take a mean picture, and I want to help, and that has to count for something up here." He backed his horse into the line—although not without some difficulty.

Gerry just stared back at them, and then to where his father and the other men had disappeared in the snow trail ahead. He turned to look again at the group. "You people are in way over your heads, I hope you know that. You're probably all going to get frostbite or fall off your horses or some damn thing to make me sorry I'm doing this—but okay. You all want to play hero, then fine. Let's get going." He shook his head and turned his horse to follow the tracks of the first group. "And one more thing, just for the record," he called over his shoulder. "I was going to leave you with Charley as soon as I could."

Higher up the mountain and three miles to the west, Warner very was excited. He had seen the damn thing again, and he was following it at a safe distance. He couldn't seem to gain ground on the animal, no matter how careful he was. He was out of accurate range, and the damn animal always managed to have something between them so he couldn't get a good shot.

Bergen was prattling on about something again, but Warner had tuned him out to focus his full attention on his primary goal. He kept his eyes on the magnificent animal ahead of him, somehow always keeping pace. Warner paid scant attention to where he was or to the snow that was steadily falling around him; his eyes were on the elk ahead. There was no need to track the animal; he could see it very clearly through the falling snow. He was following it on foot, because he felt that being mounted limited his mobility and would interfere with taking his shot when it came.

Because Barney was on foot and able to walk around trees and over downed logs, he was slowly leaving Floyd behind.

This was okay with Floyd because he no longer wanted to be a part of this kill. He had been paying attention to the slowly receding figure, and he wasn't sure what Barney thought he was chasing. Things had started to fall apart for this guided hunt about an hour after first light.

They had been slowly walking upward toward the general direction of Hunter's Run when Barney stopped suddenly.

"Did you hear that?" Barney asked him.

"No, sir, I don't hear anything but the wind, branches breaking, and the snow and temperature falling," Floyd said sourly.

"I don't mean the wind, stupid, I mean the bugling. He's bugling a call out there. Surely you must hear him. It's coming from that direction over there." He pointed upward to the right, through the trees with branches bowed by the weight of the snow covering them.

"Mr. Barney, I didn't hear anything that sounded anything like an elk bugling. I don't know what you heard, but it wasn't no elk sounding off."

Warner just looked at him like he was an insect. He walked over to Bergen and threw him the reins. "Take these, Bergen. You follow me with the horses—not too closely, I don't want to spook him now. He's out here somewhere, I know it. Keep a sharp eye out for his tracks. Finger-snapping and hand signals only from now on, Bergen," Warner commanded him as he turned and moved away.

Floyd didn't reply, partly as a response to the irritating command, and partly because he didn't care to respond anyway. He pulled up his horse, allowing Warner to move past him. As he did, Floyd noticed that Barney's tracks were filling with fresh snow rather quickly. He looked behind him and saw his own tracks were still visible a good way behind him. He scratched his head as he pondered this curious contradiction, and then he looked up to see Barney moving farther ahead and becoming less visible in the falling snow. He put his horse into a fast walk to catch up before he lost him entirely.

"Without voice communication, I'm going to have a much harder time keeping this man in sight," Floyd said softly to himself. "I don't know just what he heard, but I know what it wasn't, and there's no point arguing with him. He's got this damned obsession with this frigging

Red Elk, or whatever, and he's letting it get the best of him," Floyd muttered to himself. He pulled his coat closer and turned the collar up on the coat to protect his neck from the wind that was coming up.

Floyd had never been this high up the mountain—not in this area, at least—and he wasn't exactly sure where they were. He knew the general area, of course, so he was confident he could get his man back down the mountain if the weather got much worse, and his sense of the matter was that it was indeed going to get much worse.

Gerry, Oliver, Axel, and Arnold were on a blind hunt. They knew what they were looking for, but they had no idea where to look for it, and they all knew it.

Arnold gave voice to this problem first. "Boys, we're searching for a small diamond in a big box of broken glass. Between this snow and the thick underbrush and old growth trees up here, they could be twenty feet away from us, and we'd not see them unless we fell over them or ran into them. I'm open to any suggestions you boys might have on how to narrow this search down some," Arnold said cheerily.

"Well, I'm a stranger to this part of the mountain, fellas, so I have no suggestions that would be workable," Oliver said, buttoning up his coat around him.

"Well, one thing we're *not* going to do is split up," Gerry said as he hunched into his coat. "It's getting harder and harder to see ten feet in front of us, so we stay together and within the sound of someone else's voice. No wandering off alone by anyone, understand?" he ordered.

"People have been lost up here before, Mr. Barry," Axel said quietly. "Took us near onto a week to find them."

"Did you get them in time, Axel?" Oliver asked.

"Depends," was his reply.

"Okay, I'll bite. Depends on what?"

"Depends on whether you mean alive or while they was intact," came the laconic reply.

"Oh," Oliver responded, and he nudged his horse a little closer to Arnold's.

A little while later, Axel spoke up again. "Boss, I'm not one to be telling the boss what to do—"

"Go ahead, Axel. I want you to say whatever you think I need to hear, you know that."

"Right, boss. Well, I'm just thinking out loud, mind you, but it seems to me that this here animal is a mighty cautious one, and he just may be more at home in the upper growth at the top of Hunter's Run. It's thicker up there, and that would give him more cover and protection from the weather. It's also got more new growth, and he might find that mighty tasty during the winter when the berries are out of season. It's just my opinion, mind you, not a rock-solid fact," Axel said casually.

"Axel, I think that's a damn good opinion. You keep on voicing them whenever you get one, you hear me?" Gerry said after a moment's consideration.

"Sure enough, boss," Axel said, clearly very pleased with Gerry's praise.

"Okay, men. Axel here has had a real good idea, so we're going to make a left up here and head for the top. Now I want you all to be very careful, because it's going to be a very steep trail. In fact, I think we're going to need to walk the horses for a while once we get to the start of the climb. With all this snow, they can't tell what they're stepping on, so we don't want them to be carrying anymore weight than is safe for them on this climb. We'll lead them up the ridge, so we will be taking several stops along the way. I hope you all brought along some spare socks." He laughed, his breath forming little clouds.

Arnold was cold—not just on the surface, but deep down on the inside. He hadn't anticipated that he would be up this high, and he wasn't dressed for the weather. He pulled his coat around himself as tightly as he could and felt around in his pockets for his gloves. He found the left but couldn't locate the right one, so he put it on, took the reins in his left hand, and jammed his right deep into his coat pocket.

He didn't say a word to anyone about his missing glove, but Oliver had noticed his search and that he had only put one on. He didn't say anything to Arnold, but began searching in his saddlebags to see if he had any spare gloves in there that he could offer the big man.

Gerry walked his horse toward the start of their uphill climb, thinking about what was ahead of him. He turned back to wave Oliver up to his side and slowed his walk to allow him to catch up.

"Gerry, you want to talk about something, I take it?" Oliver asked him in a low voice.

"I've been thinking some, Oliver, and I think this man is going to be mad as hell if we get him before he gets his shot off. Now, I don't expect you to pull on him when we catch up to him, but maybe your badge will convince him to give up quietly, although I doubt it. What I'm saying is, make sure you don't get between him and me if he's got a gun in his hands. Let me or Axel handle the shooting if need be, because I don't relish the idea of explaining to your lady friend how you got hurt or killed," Gerry cautioned him. "I know my son gave you a pistol—I can see the outline on your hip and the tie down on your leg—but I want you to remember you're not Wyatt Earp or Bat Masterson, and it's no small thing to point a gun at someone.

"Once you do, you change the rules of the engagement, and now they can shoot you in self-defense. One of the old-timers, they used to talk about the good old days and the men they called shooters. They never pulled iron unless they intended to fire, and then they shot first and asked questions later. Those rules still apply out here, Oliver. You don't pull that piece unless I tell you to, and you don't fire it unless you have to. In fact, I'd rather you give it to me or to Arnold and not carry it at all," he cautioned Oliver.

Oliver shook his head, saying, "No can do, Gerry. Arnold's not going to be able to handle the gun—he doesn't have a glove for his right hand and that's why he's keeping it in his coat. He'll be too cold to handle the metal safely. In fact, if you have any spare gloves, he can really use them. I hear what you're telling me about the gun, and I give you my word I'm no hero. I think I'll keep it, but I'll wait for your word to draw it, and I'll use good judgment on firing it. I promise. What do you think our chances are of finding him? Really, I mean."

Gerry looked ahead at the steep ascent in front of them and back at Oliver and Arnold, who had just joined them. "Boys, I figure the worst part of this trek is going to start right now. We are going to walk the horses up this patch, and then it will level out, and we'll be able to start really looking for him. There's a more gradual incline on the south side, but it would mean another day to get to it, and getting to it will be just as rough as this climb will be. So, I figure we might as well take the short way now.

"Now, here's how we're going to do it: Axel will take the lead, followed by Oliver, and then you, Arnie, then me. We going to put a short distance between each of us for safety—say about twenty feet—and if you feel you're losing your step, grab a handful of the tail and allow him to pull you up. Once you get to the top, lead your animal off to the side to make room for the next man. Once we're all up top, we'll get mounted again, and Axel will find our man if anyone on this range can. Any questions?"

No one spoke up, so Gerry turned to Axel and nodded to him. "See if you can find us an easy way up, Axel, if you would."

Axel nodded, dismounted, and, taking the reins in his hand, started walking toward the base of the climb, looking for the easiest path.

As Axel walked ahead, Gerry dismounted, opened one of his saddle bags, and rummaged around inside. Not finding what he was looking for, he closed the left-hand bag and went around to the right-hand side. He only looked for a few seconds before he let out an excited "Got 'em!" and closed the bag again.

"Arnie, I always carry a spare set of mittens, ever since I left a pair on a fence post in a snowstorm. You might find these useful." He handed them to Arnold, who gratefully pulled his one glove off and quickly slid his hands into the fur-lined ones Gerry handed him. He nodded his appreciation to Oliver and Gerry and, taking his reins in his newly gloved left hand, followed Axel's tracks to where he was starting to walk up the side of the mountain. The snow continued its steady fall, along with the temperature.

Parker and Bern were riding along in the direction of Moose Jaw Ridge when Parker stopped. "I think I know this area, Bern. There's a familiar look to that ridge over there ..." He pointed to the west. "There should be some water running a little ways below it, am I right?" He turned to look at Bern as he spoke and saw something moving out of the corner of his eye. "Look! Over there! What's that, Bern?" he said excitedly.

Bern quickly spun around to see what Parker was looking at, but he didn't see anything at first—but then he did catch something moving. It was too far off to make it out clearly, but it was an individual object, and it was walking very slowly past a single tree that stood alone and reached into the sky. It was very clearly not human, but they couldn't make out just what it was.

Parker reached for his binoculars, but when he put his hand back to where the strap had been tied, it was no longer there. "Damn!"

"What's the matter?"

"I lost the binoculars. I had them tied to the back of my saddle, and the straps must have worked loose, and they fell off in the snow. I never heard them hit the ground, the snow being soft and all, and now we don't have any long-range vision. Wait! What about your …"

His voice trailed off as Bern slid his rifle out of the scabbard to show he didn't have the scope attached.

"My scope? I took it off so it would fit better in this holster. I didn't expect to be doing any long-range shooting. Okay, we just have to rely on our own eyes. What do you think that thing was?"

"Well, it had a rack on it, so it was a male, whatever else it was. It had to have been a deer or an elk; the rack was the wrong shape for a moose."

"Well, it's all we've seen, so let's go get a closer look at its tracks. Maybe it'll lead us to our quarry," he suggested.

"Sounds good to me, Bern. Lead on."

They trotted toward the spot where they had seen the animal, but when they finally got there, there were no tracks. "Are you sure this is where we saw it, Bern?" Parker asked as they walked in a big circle, looking for signs of the animal.

"I'm pretty sure it is, Parker. Look back down there, in that saddle. That's where we were, and see that tall fir over there?" He pointed to a lone tree ten feet away. "It's the high tree we saw from down there, so this has to be the spot he was walking by. Now here's the part I don't get—it's not snowing up here right now, so where the hell are his tracks? We both saw him clear as day walking by here, so there should be some signs of his passing this way. I don't get this at all," Bern said, puzzled. He looked all around and then dismounted to get a closer look at the snow.

"Parker, dismount and come over here, please," Bern called out as he kneeled down in the snow. Parker got down and led his horse over to where Bern was kneeling and stood beside him, not sure what he was to be looking for. "Take a good look around us and tell me what you see, Parker."

"I see snow. Lots and lots of snow."

"Good eye. Now, what condition is this snow in, Parker?"

"It's white?"

"Yes, it's white. Very good. What else do you see?"

"I see it's kind of shiny." He looked around, not sure what he was seeing, or not seeing.

"Feel it, Parker. Put your hand on the snow and tell me how the surface is to the touch."

Parker did as he was told, but, just as he started to ask what he was looking for, he realized what Bern was talking about. "Bern, the snow is hard-packed and frozen on top. It has a crust to it." He stood up and took a second look around—a real hard look around—and when he did, he felt colder for more reasons than just the air temperature. "And anything that's heavier than a mouse would have left a track in this snow, but I don't see any tracks but our own in this snow," Parker said slowly.

Bern stood up and pulled a cartridge from his gun belt. "Watch where this lands, Parker," he said as he tossed it a few feet away from them.

Parker watched the brass twinkle in the air as it spun after leaving Bern's hand. It hit the snow, and he heard the soft crack as it broke the crust when it landed. He looked at Bern, and both men walked over to the cartridge lying there. They stood over it and then squatted down to look at the brass. What they saw did nothing to resolve their questions, because the shell had a spider web of light cracks emanating around where it was lying at an angle on a piece of broken, crusted snow. They looked back at their own footsteps leading back to where they had first stopped to look for the animal's tracks. Theirs were the only tracks to be seen in the snow. "What's this mean, Bern?"

"I wish to hell I knew, Parker. I wish to hell I knew."

As Axel started to climb up the steep ascent, he led his horse along the snow lines, feeling his way carefully. He didn't look back, as that would have diverted his attention and focus, and it would have likely scared the confidence out of him to see what was below. He knew he had three lives depending on him—actually, nine lives, if he counted the others with Gerry Junior; or ten if he counted himself. He had to get his party to the top in one piece. All the joking and clowning around was done with; he was all business now.

He had to push all his worries about his brother to the back of his mind and concentrate on where he was putting his feet. If his horse went down, it would likely take him and all three of the men behind him down the mountain in a mad tumble that, if they were lucky, would just kill them all. Axel didn't want to think about what would happen if they weren't lucky.

He stopped as he approached a dead tree and broke off a branch. He pulled his bowie knife from its sheath and hacked off the remaining stubs until he had a single pole about five feet long that he used as a probe to test the ground under the snow. Armed with this tool to make sure that what he was standing on would support his weight and that of his horse, Axel began to make his way up the mountainside.

Arnold watched Axel work his way up the slope, and he felt a tinge of concern as he saw the difficulty the wrangler was having. He then started worrying about his own ability to handle the climb.

As Oliver came up beside him, Arnold expressed his doubts. "I don't know about this, Oliver. I may have bitten off more than I can chew here."

"Nonsense, Arnold. You're in good condition, and I'll help you up this slope if you need it. Tell you what, I'll lead the horses up and you grab hold of both tails and let them pull you up," Oliver offered.

"I'm not so sure about that, son. What if they kick back or something? I sure don't want anything to happen to endanger anyone else because of me."

"I don't see anything bad happening, Arnold. You'll be fine. Now come on, we'll do this together."

It took almost an hour for all four men to make the climb up that steep and treacherous slope, but, at the end of the hour, all four were sitting in the snow, gasping for air before they made the top. It had been a hard hour, with several missteps and each man sporting a few scrapes and scratches from hidden branches and rocks under the snow. They were sitting on a small ledge below the top of the crest, the horses catching their breath on a more gentle slope two feet below them. The top of the crest, only two feet higher, was still out of their reach after the exertions they had all been through to get to this point.

Even Axel was showing the strain, his normally tan face looking ruddy in the cheeks and slightly redder at the neck.

The snow wasn't blowing any longer; it had stopped just after they began their climb. They were all greatly appreciative of that, as they had been dreading doing it in a blowing wind.

"I think ... that's about ... as much exercise ... as I've done ... all ... year," huffed Oliver, who was showing the strain more than Arnold was, to his great dismay. For all of his concern about making the climb, Arnold was breathing the best of all of them. Even Gerry was having trouble.

Arnold looked around at the other three and he couldn't believe his eyes. He was tempted to lean over and look down to see where they had started, but he decided not to press his luck and just leaned back against the rock face.

"I think I'll take up rock-climbing for a hobby," he said thoughtfully, but when everyone looked at him, he started laughing. It was contagious, and within a minute, all of them were, until tears were rolling down their faces.

Oliver started to lean over, and Gerry grabbed his arm and pulled him back into the center of the ledge.

"I don't think you want to be taking the shortcut down, Oliver. Best you go the long way, with all of us," he cautioned.

Oliver scooted back farther from the edge and laughed again. "If you say so, Gerry. I'm not in any hurry to get down to the bottom, not without seeing the top of this rock pile, that is."

At that moment, Axel suddenly sat up and said, "Everyone be quiet. I think I heard something above us." Everyone sat still, frozen in position, listening.

"I don't hear anything," Oliver whispered.

"Axel's got good ears—if he says he heard something, there's something up there," Gerry whispered back.

Arnold shook his head. "I don't hear anything either. Are you—"

At that moment, the noise came again, and this time everyone heard it.

"It could be him; I'll take a look and see what's up there. Everyone stay down." Axel took off his hat and eased himself along the ledge until he found a foothold which he could use to get into a position to look at what was on top without the risk of being spotted. When he saw what it was, the look on his face said he thought his eyes were playing tricks on him. He dropped down again to where the others were and leaned back against the rock face, shaking his head.

"What'd you see, Axel?"

"Is it Barney?"

"Is it the elk?"

All three men whispered their questions at him at the same time, but Axel just shook his head. "You guys aren't going to believe it unless you see it for yourself," he said. "If I told you what I just saw, you'd just think I'd gone crazy. I don't really believe it myself, and I saw it."

The three men sat back, puzzled and concerned.

Gerry put a hand out to touch Axel on the arm and get his attention. "Is it dangerous? Will we need our guns?" he softly asked him.

"No," Axel replied. "I don't think it's dangerous—and no, you won't need your guns. Just be careful—you don't want to spook what's up there."

Gerry nodded and quietly moved to where Axel had been and slowly climbed up to have a look. He clearly couldn't believe his eyes either.

They had dismounted for a brief rest period after riding for hours, and Ed wasn't in a good humor.

"Gerry! Where the hell are we? And just how big is this damn mountain? I thought we had one mountain to search, not the whole damn Rocky Mountain range!"

"Ed, weren't you there when I explained how this layout works?" Gerry Junior asked him patiently. "It isn't just one mountain; it's a series of several peaks all in one cluster, and the name Redd Mountain refers to all of them as a unit. The ski slopes are on the two outside north and west slopes, and the hunting range is on the two outside south and east slopes, and the four slopes on the inside are supposed to be for hiking and fishing, as that's where the lakes are located," Gerry explained. "All that trouble back in the sixties is because someone—and it hasn't been proven who, despite what you've heard from anyone here—violated that boundary and went into the north side to chase down game.

"We are closing in on the edge of the biggest of the two hunting slopes. That tree line over there—" He pointed to the line of dark trees the next slope over. "That line represents the beginning of the hunting range. From there, we ride up that slope to the right and we'll be in the heart of the hunting range," Gerry explained to the group.

Adam was looking at the trees through the viewfinder on his camera with the telescopic lens, taking pictures of the snowcapped mountain peaks and the dark clouds boiling over them—so he wasn't paying as much attention to Gerry's words as he could have been. He was just about to put the camera away when he spotted some movement. Adam adjusted the lens for the best focus he could get and looked hard at the object in his viewfinder. At first he couldn't make it out, and, just when he had the focus as sharp as he could, the object moved again, this time away from him. He let out a disappointed "Damn," and the others turned toward him.

"What's the matter, Adam?" Eileen asked.

"I had something in my lens, but it moved away and now I can't focus in on it—it's out of my range," he said, disappointed in his luck. As he hadn't yet lowered the camera, he was surprised to see the object stop. "Hold it! It's stopped! I can just see it, but it's too far away to get a clear look," he called out. As he said this, the object moved again, but this time toward him.

"That's it, come to me," Adam coaxed it.

"Probably just a bug on his lens," muttered Ed.

Wanda gave him a poke in the side with her elbow and told him to hush. Ed moved off to stand next to April, who moved to stand next to Adam.

"Come on, come on, just a little closer, please," Adam urged the speck, which obligingly moved in the desired direction. "That's weird," Adam said to himself.

"What's weird, Adam?" Eileen asked.

"Well, twice I've asked the mystery object to come closer to me so I could get a better look, and twice it's come closer."

"Well, maybe it hears you and it wants to get its picture taken," she suggested playfully.

Adam looked at her and realized she was joking, so he smiled and returned his attention to the viewfinder. "Where'd it go? I've lost it—no, there it is! It's come closer still. It's just standing there—" Adam lowered the camera again, looked at the front of his lens, and then back at the object across the way.

"Eileen, do you mind taking a look and telling me what you see?" he asked calmly.

"Sure, where do I look?" she asked.

"Over there—see that group of trees by the overhang? Just to the left of that, and pan down a little," he directed.

Eileen held the camera up, searched for the spot he was identifying, and stood there for a few seconds before handing the camera back. "I just see snow, Adam. I'm sorry, it must have moved away," she said.

"Damn." Adam raised the camera again and called out to Eileen as she was getting ready to mount. "Wait! It's still there, come try again."

He handed her the camera and she looked again. "Sorry, Adam. I don't see anything but snow."

"Let me try, please?" Wanda asked. Adam handed it over, and she looked where he had told Eileen to look.

"Adam, did you see an animal?"

"Yes!"

"Was that animal big?"

"Yes! You see it?"

"I see it, Adam. What color did you see, Adam?"

"What did you say?"

"I asked you, what color was it?"

"It was red, Wanda. What color do you see?" he asked hesitantly.

"I see a big red animal too, Adam. A big, bright red animal."

"Let me see that camera!" Ed barked. He took it from Wanda and pointed it where they were looking. "I don't see a damn thing! Where the hell is it?" he demanded.

Gerry reached over and took the camera out of Ed's hands to look for himself.

"Hey, guys! That's expensive! Take it easy!" Adam pleaded.

Gerry scanned the area where Adam and Wanda had said they had seen the animal, but he couldn't see it either. April asked if she might have a try, and Gerry reluctantly handed it to her, but she didn't see anything either.

The only one left who hadn't looked for it was Charley, and he just waved the camera off. "My eyes ain't so good; I'd just be wasting my time. You tell me what you see, sonny," he said.

Adam took his camera back and tried to find the animal again. In just a moment, he had it in the viewfinder.

"He's just standing there—no! He's moving again, toward me again!" Adam was very excited, and he felt a little colder as well. "Wanda! Go to my pack and look in the green box! I've got another camera there with a telephoto lens—maybe we can get some shots of him before he leaves the scene!" he called out.

She ran to his pack, April right on her heels. April found it first, knowing what to look for, and she ran back to Adam with it. She adjusted the focus and looked for the animal, but she couldn't see it.

Wanda reached her side and politely asked, "I believe that Adam asked me to look for the animal, Miss Martens."

April glared at her but gave her the camera.

"I see him, Adam! He's magnificent!" Wanda said.

"What the hell is going on here?" Gerry muttered to himself. "There's six people here, and only two of them can see this damn thing. I don't understand this at all. How the hell can the two of them see this thing and no one else? Adam, are you jerking my chain here with this sighting? I mean, how the hell can you and Dr. Fleming see it and no one else can? I couldn't see it, Miss Gayle can't see it, Ed can't see it, and your own partner can't see it. Can you explain that for me?" Gerry asked suspiciously.

Without taking his eyes off the viewfinder, Adam thought for a moment and responded. "Mr. Bruce, I can't explain it. I have no idea why no one else can see it. Maybe you're not looking in the right place?" he suggested.

"Well, there's an easy way to clear that up," Ed growled. "You two are using a camera to see him, aren't you? Why not just take a photo of him so we can all see it. Then we'll all know what you're looking at," he said as he smugly looked around at the others.

"Ed, that's a brilliant idea!" Gerry complimented him.

"I guess I got so caught up in looking at him, I forgot I was holding a camera," Adam apologized. "Hold on a moment, I'll get a good shot of him." He pressed the button and everyone heard the shutter whirring as it worked, but when he looked into the viewer, all he saw was snow and a dark blur. "Damn, he must have moved," Adam said.

"No, Adam," Wanda corrected him. "He hasn't moved an inch. He is just standing there with his head up—now he's looking in our direction. Can he see us from here, Mr. Bruce?"

"Not likely, and if he does, we are just a dark spot to him. We represent no danger to him from this distance," Gerry said, looking off in the direction the animal was supposed to be in, but seeing nothing but white snow.

"Wanda, let's exchange cameras," Adam suggested. "It might be I've got some water in the lens that's causing a problem. Let me try it with your camera, and you look through mine." They both quickly switched and located the animal, which was still standing across the way, almost as if he was looking at them. Adam took several pictures, the animal making no effort to move out of their line of sight.

"Wanda," called Eileen. "Is it still there?"

"It sure is, Eileen."

"What's it doing?"

"Just standing there. Maybe looking back at us, I think."

"Adam, did you say it moved up closer when you asked it to?"

"Sure did seem to, Eileen."

"Hmm. I think you should make another request, Adam." All heads turned in her direction when she said this.

"What are you suggesting, Miss Gayle?" asked Gerry, not believing his ears.

"Well, I am not certain about this, but if it was responding to Adam's request when he asked it to move a little closer ..."

Ed sneered. "Oh, come on! You aren't suggesting it's actually listening to him, are you?"

"Mr. Baxter," Eileen said coldly, "unless you have an idea that makes more sense, how about you keep quiet? You are becoming a very disagreeable person, knocking everything anyone says that you don't believe in. I don't know what's going on here anymore than you do, but I'm open to anything that helps us protect our men and that animal. What have you got to contribute to that?" she shot at him.

Behind her she heard Charley laughing. "She got you there, Ed!"

Ed just turned and walked to his horse to get his rifle.

"What are you doing, Baxter?" Gerry asked him.

"I'm going to get a shot at him, and then we'll see what's what," Ed said crossly as he started to slide his gun out of the scabbard.

Adam didn't take his camera off the animal as he called out to Baxter. "Just a question, Mr. Baxter. If you can't see it, how are you going to aim to shoot it?"

There was a long silence, and then Ed shoved the rifle back down into the boot and walked back to the group.

Finally, Adam spoke. "What sort of request do you want me to make, Eileen?"

"I am not certain, but what about asking it for directions?"

Ed didn't say anything, but they could hear him snicker off to the side. Wanda spoke up as Gerry gave Ed a sharp scowl.

"Now that's interesting."

"What happened?" everyone but Adam asked.

"Well, when you told Adam to ask it for directions, it began tossing its head up and down."

"Maybe it's trying to shake off some bees or something?" Ed ventured.

Gerry just looked at him. "Bees? In the dead of winter? Up this high? Are you drinking or smoking something?" he asked scornfully.

Ed went back to making a snowball and threw it against a dead tree stump.

"Adam. Go ahead and ask it for directions to the other men," Wanda urged him, keeping the camera trained on the animal.

"What about those pictures, Adam?" Gerry asked.

"They didn't come out," he said apologetically.

"Water in the lenses, animals no one can see—what in God's name did I get myself into?" Gerry muttered to himself as he walked away.

April was busy off to the side, writing all of this down. She had no idea what was going on, or what any of it meant, but the look on her face said she could see a big story in this as clearly as she could see the pencil in her hand in front of her. She was taking notes and flipping pages as fast as she could write, with a vision of her Pulitzer probably dancing in her head. This really was more than she and Adam had ever imagined it would be, and it just promised to get ever so much better by the time they were done.

"Adam, I think you should ask for the directions, just like Miss Gayle suggested," April encouraged him.

"That was just a coincidence, people. Just a coincidence," Ed tried again.

Adam took a deep breath to settle his nerves and started to speak. "I sure wish you could tell us what direction to take to find the rest of our party. You know, we're all out here to help you. So a little help from you would be real nice right now."

Wanda lowered her camera and turned to the others. "I don't believe it, and you won't either, but now he's tossing his head again."

Ed began to laugh. "See, I told you it was just a coincidence. You just wanted to make something supernatural out of it," he said, pleased with himself.

Adam hadn't lowered his camera, however, and he had kept his eyes on the animal. He started to walk to the left, stopped, stood there for ten seconds, and then walked back the other way. "Yeah, he's tossing his head again, but this time it looks like he's saying we go to the right."

Ed quit laughing abruptly, only to jump to his feet in anger. "What in the hell are you talking about, son? He's saying we go right? Have you lost your mind, or is the cold getting to you?" he asked in a sarcastic tone.

Adam looked at Eileen and shook his head in disbelief. "When I started to walk to the left, he swung his head from left to right over and over, as long as I was taking steps to the left. When I started to walk back to the right, he began to bob his head and walk to the right as well."

"Are you serious?" she asked excitedly. "Wanda, did you see him do this too?"

Wanda nodded her head; she couldn't speak.

Gerry threw up his hands, giving in. "I guess it's the altitude affecting everyone's thinking here. Everyone mount up; we're moving out now."

"What direction are we going to go in, Gerry?" Adam asked.

"I'm going the way that's easiest for us to travel," Gerry said as he turned his horse's head to the right.

As they started to move out, Adam took one last look behind him. The animal was gone. Adam assumed it had walked back into the trees, so he turned back to follow the horse in front of him. As they rode along, from time to time Adam or Wanda would see the elk off in the distance, always ahead of them—always moving in the direction they were going.

Adam whispered to Wanda, "Do you think he's following us?"

After a minute, she answered him. "No, I think he's leading us."

Two hours later, they were climbing up a gentle, sloping ridge.

"Where are we now, Mr. Bruce?" Adam called out. Gerry pulled up and turned around in the saddle to answer Adam and watch the others coming up behind him.

"We're coming up to a place we call Half Peak. This is the easy way and, for my money, the only way to take this climb. It's almost a thirty-degree angle on the other side, although it will feel like straight up when you do it. It's not too bad in the summer when you can see where you're going, but only an idiot would even consider attempting it in the winter. Someone tried to climb it a couple of years ago in the summer and got almost to the top. He hit some shale and fell all the way back down. He was a real mess when we found him. He was in the hospital a long time. It wasn't worth the risk, if you ask me." Gerry turned back around to lead the way up.

"What's up there?" Eileen asked.

"A really nice meadow—good grazing in the summer, but it's probably all snowed in now. We'll be there inside of ten minutes. It's a good place to rest the horses and the riders for a bit. Maybe we'll start a small fire for some coffee if you ask Charley nicely," he joked.

As they reached the top, Charley called out to him. "Boss, I hear something over toward the break off."

"What do you hear?"

"I know you'll say I'm crazy, but I think there's something on the slide. Maybe it's an animal or something, but there's something moving over there. I'll go take a look." He carefully walked over to the edge of the peak and looked down, and what he saw there made him take a step back in surprise. Charley had to take a second look; his eyes said it was too incredible to be true.

Three miles away to the west and farther up the mountain, Floyd was getting worried. The snow was falling harder, and it was getting more and more difficult to keep his man in sight. He could see him ahead, but just barely. Warner seemed to have no regard for the weather, or the time, or the season—or anything, as far as Floyd could tell.

"I'm no head doctor, but this bird seems to have a screw loose—or maybe it's too tight. If he's not obsessed with this damn animal, then I don't know what the word means," he said to himself. He didn't need to whisper anymore, as he could barely hear the words himself.

The wind was picking up some as well, and things weren't looking good for either of them. Floyd looked up at the sky to estimate the amount of daylight remaining, but he couldn't see anything more than heavy snow clouds that seemed to hover over them. He could see it was getting darker, but he wasn't sure if it was due to the clouds or the setting sun. He reached into his coat pocket to pull out his watch and look at the time, and he saw the sun would be going down soon. He had to set up the camp for them while there was still enough light to find a place, but he needed to corral his man before he got lost. He knew there was going to be no easy way to do this, but it had to be done.

He called out as he urged his horse forward. "Mr. Barney! Mr. Barney, we've got to make a camp now. Can you hear me? Mr. Barney! We have to stop and make camp for the night! Can you hear me?"

"Of course I can hear you, you damn fool. I'm standing right behind you!" Warner said angrily.

Floyd whirled around in his saddle so fast, he almost fell out. "How did you get behind me, Mr. Barney? I saw you ahead just a few minutes ago," Floyd asked, taken by surprise.

"I came back because I lost him and figured it was getting too dark to keep walking, or I'd walk smack into a tree or off this damn hunk of rock. So there's no need to shout and chase all the game out of the area; we'll just hunker down for the night and get an early start. With all this snow on the ground, I should have no trouble finding him again in the morning. Where do you want to set up the camp, Bergen?"

"I'm not sure about this area; I can't get my bearings in the dark with all this snow coming down. I think Half Peak should be about a mile or two to the east of us, if we're where I think we are."

"Well, you certainly aren't much of a guide if you don't know where you are all the time," Warner said in a sneering tone.

Floyd looked at him, deliberating in his mind the chances of getting away with walking off and leaving the arrogant bastard to fend for himself up here. He decided the risk was too great, so he just turned to avoid getting provoked into making another poor decision. Floyd contented himself with finding a place to make a camp that might provide them with some shelter for the night.

He looked around, but there were no caves to hole up in. He settled for making a tent for the horses from the canvas covers and set up the two tents for them. He was unable to fix them a hot meal or make coffee because of the blowing snow that kept putting his small fire out. Floyd tried to situate the tents to close out as much of the wind as he could, but no matter what angle he tried to set the openings, the chill seemed to find its way in, bringing a load of wet snow with each gust.

"Now this damn mountain is turning against me too," he grumbled to himself as he struggled to secure the tent. He looked around to see where Barney was and saw him sitting on a snow-covered stump just watching.

"Hey, how about helping me with the other tent while there's still a little light?"

"I hired you; you're the guide; this is your job. Hurry up, Bergen. I want to get out of this damn cold. Besides, the sooner you get my tent up, the sooner you can get to yours," Warner responded indifferently.

Floyd stared at him, clenching his fists in anger. He started to take a step toward Warner, who slowly raised his rifle to point it at Floyd's midsection. He didn't say a word, but gave a smile that was colder than the wind around them. His meaning was very clear, even through the snow, so Floyd stopped short and turned around to go fix the other tent.

As darkness fell, he finally got the other tent secured. He stood up again, and Warner came over and looked at both tents before stooping, crawling into the second one, and closing the flap behind him without a word of thanks. Floyd silently wished that snow would drop on Barney during the night and thoroughly soak him, but he knew he couldn't be that lucky. He sighed and headed for his tent and climbed in, then closed the flap.

Just as he rolled up in his sleeping bag, he heard a whooshing hiss and heard Barney yell. He turned around, poked his head outside, and saw Barney buried under a mound of snow that had just dropped from the branches overhead. Floyd closed the flap and rearranged himself and settled back into his sleeping bag, wearing a big smile.

What do you know, he thought to himself contentedly, *there really is a God.*

Three miles away to the east, Charley was looking over the edge, right into the eyes of the senior Gerry Bruce.

"What the hell are you doing up there?" Gerry asked, astounded to see a familiar face.

"Me? What in the hell you doing down there?" Charley retorted.

"I think we can discuss that a lot better once I get up there, so can you help me? Me and the other guys, we'd sort of like to get up there and off here," Gerry told him.

"Oh, yeah. Here." Charley held out his hand to Gerry and started to pull him up, but realized he wasn't in a good position to do it. "Gerry! Bring your rope and a horse. We got to rescue some pilgrims what took the long way up the hill!"

Gerry Junior jumped to his feet, grabbed his reins, and ran over to where Charley was looking over the edge.

"Damn it to hell, this better not be who I think it is!" he yelled as he ran.

"That depends on who you don't want it to be, boss! But was I you, I wouldn't dawdle none, lessen you want to run the ranch by yourself," Charley snickered as Gerry reached him.

"Dad! What in God's name are you doing there? Are you crazy? You could have been killed!" As he talked, he took the rope from his saddle and shook it out. He took the end of it and handed it down to his father. "Here, Dad, tie the end of this rope around your waist. Charley, take this end and dally it around the horn and let me know when you're ready."

Charley took the rope and trotted over to Gerry's horse, where he wrapped the rope around the saddle horn twice to tie it down and called back to Gerry, "All set, boss!"

"Okay, start backing him up slowly and I'll guide him up. Okay, Dad. Get ready to climb up." He held out his hand to his father, helped him negotiate the last few feet, and pulled him over the ledge, the horse providing the lifting power to bring him up. When Gerry Senior was standing on solid ground, Gerry Junior untied the rope and called Charley to bring the horse back over. He dropped the rope down to Arnold and had him tie it around his waist. The process was repeated for Oliver and Axel.

When all four were back on the top of Half Peak, they were met with open arms by their friends and loved ones. While Eileen scolded Oliver for taking such a risk, Wanda was just too happy to have Arnold back to scold him. Charley took Axel aside to tend to his scrapes, while Gerry marched his father off to the side to lecture him about the risk he had taken.

"I don't know what the hell you were thinking, Dad. Do you have any idea how dangerous that stunt was? What in the hell were you thinking? Why did you come up that cliff? Are you trying to kill yourself? Are you tired of living? I can understand Oliver trying that, but what were you doing subjecting Arnold to that climb? Answer me, Dad!"

"If you'll give me a chance to talk, son, perhaps I can answer some of your questions. To start with, we were looking for Barney, and Axel suggested the elk might be looking for food and would likely head for the Hunter's Run area, since it has good ground cover and the kind of vegetation he would like. We figured that Barney would be on his trail, and we thought we could head him off by coming up here. I told the guys it would be a tough climb, but we all agreed it would be the shortest route. Axel felt confident he could find us a path up to the top."

"I'll talk to Axel later about his role in this," Gerry Junior said angrily.

"No, you won't. Axel was following my orders, and you'll not take your anger at me out on him. I won't have that boy pay for my poor judgment," his father said with authority.

"Fine," Gerry Junior said sullenly.

"And, by the way, what are you people doing up here?" his father asked.

"Rescuing some fools from their delusions of competence."

"That's not what I meant, and you know it. Once more, what are you all doing up here—since you're supposed to be looking for the elk while we were searching for Barney?"

"Well, I'll tell you, but it isn't going to make any sense to you. We were looking for him when Adam over there, he saw him in his camera. I'll tell you what happened next, but I hope it makes more sense to you than it does to me. He and Dr. Fleming saw the damn animal in their viewfinders, but they couldn't get the camera to take a picture of it. Then, when everyone else looked for it, none of us could see it. We looked through the same damn camera where they were looking, and none of us could see anything that even remotely looked like an elk.

"Then—and this is the strangest part of this fairy tale—Adam insisted the elk was telling us to come to Half Peak. We were trying to decide what direction to go, and he said he saw the animal point with its head to the right. He said he started to walk to the left and the animal shook its head no, and when he went to the right, it nodded yes. Then, as we came this way, they saw him a few more times, and he was always in front of us. Now the thing is, Dad, no one but Adam and Dr. Fleming were ever able to see it. So here we are, all of us together again, guided by the delusional who are seeing illusions. Makes perfect sense to me," Gerry Junior said sarcastically.

"Well, it does sound strange, I give you that. But, as you said, he brought us all together again from different directions. I don't know anything about this animal, I've not seen him myself, but I've heard all the stories. Say, have you seen any sign of Barney along the way?"

"Nope—not a sight, not a sound, not one trace of that man."

"Well, he's got to be up here somewhere. Has anyone seen Parker or Bern?"

"No, Dad. There's been no word on where they are, and we haven't seen them all day. I don't have a clue where they are. I'm worried about them, and I don't even know where to look."

"Well, let's think positively about them, son. Both of those boys know their way around these woods, and they can take care of themselves."

"Well, maybe Adam can ask the elk to send them back to us. And while he's at it, maybe he can round up Warner Barney and herd him back to us too," Gerry Junior said snidely.

"Well, considering that he brought all of us back together, maybe he can do just that," his father said thoughtfully.

His son looked at him and shook his head as he walked away. Gerry Senior just looked around and headed for the campfire that was now heating up their coffee.

CHAPTER 11

Parker woke up to a feeling of something in the wind—not something he could see or taste, but something present nonetheless. The air was cold and clear, and he could see it was snowing a little higher up the mountain. He looked around as he climbed out of his sleeping roll and saw that Bern was already awake and tending to the horses.

"Have a good rest?" Bern called out when he saw Parker stand up.

"Pretty good—that was a good idea you had to put some pine boughs in the bag with me, they helped to insulate me pretty good. I wasn't too cold during the night, but this morning is as cold as a witch's tit," Parker said.

"Yeah, it's downright cold. We don't have a lot to eat this morning, and not much feed for the horses, so we're going to have to limit our time before we head back down to where the horses can graze a little. So if you have any ideas on where to look, I'm open to hearing them," Bern advised.

"I figured as much; we didn't really expect to be out more than a day or two, and now this is day three, I think," Parker replied.

"Maybe it's day four, I'm not sure. I'm not really sure where to look, but I have a feeling we need to head to the area around where the slide took place," Parker said.

"Why's that? You know something you haven't shared?" Bern asked suspiciously.

"No, Bern, I wouldn't hold out on you. I'm not sure, really—it's just a feeling I've been getting since we started out. I feel drawn to that area, and I couldn't tell you why. The closer we get to it, the more the feeling grows. Does that make any sense to you at all?"

"About as much as anything else has on this ride. Mount up; we have a lot of ground to cover if we're going to get where you want to go before dark. If you're hungry, I've got some beef jerky in my saddlebag. I'll be glad to share it with you. There's two ways to get there from here, Parker, the fast and hard way, or the long and easy way. Which one do you want?" Bern called back over his shoulder.

"What's the difference?" Parker asked as he came up beside Bern.

"It's straight up for about a hundred yards, and then through a ravine for another hundred while you cross from one part of the mountain to the other, and then back up the rest of the way to the top of Half Peak. It'll take us upward of four hours to do it, but it's a pleasant ride and easy on the mounts. I hope you brought a heavier coat, because we're going to get into some heavy snow along the way. And judging from those clouds," he pointed toward the boiling dark and angry heavy-bellied snow clouds above the peak, "I think we're going to get a lot more."

"And the hard way?"

"The hard way is only for desperate measures and idiots—we ride like hell for an hour to the back side of Half Peak and then walk the horses straight up the mountain and hope like hell we don't fall off," Bern responded, only half-joking.

Parker looked at him, at Half Peak in the near distance, and then up at the clouds. "Bern, I'll do whatever you think is the best way."

"How much do you ride, Parker? I don't mean in a ring, but out in the open. Not nose-to-tail trail rides, but real working riding. And be honest with me, Parker, 'cause our lives will depend on it," Bern said sternly.

Parker thought about what Bern was asking, and although he wanted to say he could make the hard route, he knew he couldn't. "I guess if I'm going to be honest, we'd better take the long route, Bern. I'm a good ride, but that might be beyond my skills, and I don't want to put any extra burden on you by having to babysit me," Parker said disappointedly.

Bern looked at him for a moment without speaking.

"Bern?" Parker asked finally.

"Just wondering."

"Wondering what?"

"Wondering how long it's going to take us to climb up that mountainside. Let's go do it, Parker. What the hell, you only live once, right? Let's go ride up that rock pile, Parker, and see what we can see," Bern said with determination. He swung his horse's head to the left and headed for the base of Half Peak, Parker riding behind him.

As they started to climb the ridge, neither man looked back. An hour later, they were at the base of the rock-face cliff. Parker looked up at the imposing climb ahead of him and swallowed hard. He was used to coming down the mountain on fast skis; this was something else. One of the traits that had made Parker a good rescue man was that he knew when he was in over his head—like he was right now.

"No, Bern. I can't do it. I can tell this is beyond my ability. I hate to ask you, but can we just ride around to the easy side?"

"I kind of thought you might say that, but I wanted you to see what the hard side was. Sure, we'll go the easy way. I don't particularly want to fall off either. And, I agree, safer is better. Besides, it's starting to get darker. We wouldn't be able to get all the way to the top in daylight, and there's no place to stop for the night. It would be a hell of a lot safer for us to go around, so that's what we'll do.

"I think I know a shortcut that can save us a little time. I was out here with Axel last year—we were hunting for a wolf that was stealing some chickens, and we tracked him for a long time. We ended up over this way as we were riding around, and Axel saw a rabbit come out of the ravine. Don't laugh, but my brother decided he wanted to rope the rabbit. So he turns Patsy around and started chasing this damn rabbit all over the floor of the ravine, and I'm following him to make sure he's okay.

"Well, we're chasing this damn rabbit for over an hour all over hell and gone without looking where we're going. Axel threw his loop at least a dozen times, never once coming close to that rabbit. Suddenly the damn thing pops down a hole and we lose him. So now we're sitting there, and the four of us are breathing hard—me and Axel and our horses—and we start looking around to see where we are. Now, mind you, we're laughing our asses off because of what we just got through doing, and Axel, he looks around and he sees we're on the back side of Half Peak. We weren't looking for any shortcuts or anything—just out having some fun.

"So we toss a coin to see who goes back by the ravine we came through and who goes around the base, and I lose. I have to ride the long way around, and when I get back to where we were, Axel's already there."

"Maybe he ran through the ravine?"

"No, we agreed to walk both routes so we could measure the distance in time more accurately. Axel said he had been waiting for me for almost an hour, and it took me about three and a half hours to walk around. So, if we take the shortcut, we can save an hour or two and maybe make it to the top before dark. If not, we camp at the bottom and then go up in the morning. Are you ready to go?"

"Right behind you, Bern."

As the light began to fade, they were about thirty feet from the top of the plateau.

"You know, I never realized how tiring riding all day can be, Bern. How do you do it, day in and day out?"

"I don't think about it, I just do it—it's my job. I like my job, and I like being outdoors. I guess I'm just used to it, Parker. How do you manage to stay up on those skinny sticks you use to come down the mountain?"

"Same thing, I guess, now that you explain it that way. So, now what do we do?"

"I guess we'll—what was that?"

"I didn't hear anything, Bern."

"Well, I did. I heard something up there. It was faint, but it sounded like—maybe horses."

"Horses? What would horses be doing up there?"

"What are we doing up here? No, Parker, I heard something up there. And now I'm going to go up and see what it is. I was prepared to stay here for the night, but not with someone or something above me that I can't identify. So we'll take a little rest and then start our way up."

"Bern, are we going to be able to do it safely in the dark?"

"I guess we'll find out, won't we?"

Parker just stared at Bern, who looked back at him without any indication of whether or not he was kidding. Finally, Bern began to smile, and then he laughed. "It'll be okay, Parker. It's not snowing, and we have a full moon to guide us. Anyway, we just give the horses their heads, and they'll pick their way up safely. We'll be fine."

After just fifteen minutes, they remounted and started their way up the side of the moderate slope to the top of Half Peak. After riding just twenty minutes, Bern held up his hand to stop Parker from making any noise or movement. "Did you hear that?" he whispered.

"Yes, that time I did hear it. What do you think it is, Bern? It sounded like a clink of something hitting metal, or metal hitting metal, I think."

"You're right, that was metal on metal. And now I think I smell something in the air. Can you tell what it is?" Parker looked around, sniffing the air in all directions, trying to locate the source that Bern had detected.

"I guess I'm not as good at this as you are, Bern, because I don't smell anything."

"You will, when we get a little closer. I guess I recognize it because I've been out here more and don't have a city nose, no disrespect intended."

"None taken. Shall we move up a little closer?"

Bern nodded and wheeled around, loosening the reins and allowing his horse to pick its way up the slope. As they closed on the last hundred yards of the switchback, Parker began to smell it too.

"It's coffee! Someone's got a pot of coffee on the fire, Bern. They're waiting for us! Let's go get some!" Parker said excitedly. He started to urge his horse into a trot, but stopped short when Bern grabbed his horse's bridle.

"Just a moment, Parker. Is your eyesight that good that you can see uphill a hundred yards in the dark and over the top of a plateau and make out details? What I'm saying is, how do you know who it is that's boiling the coffee? Did you forget who we're looking for? I don't think he's going to be so willing to share with us. Perhaps we should be sure of who we're going to find up there."

This thought sobered Parker quickly, and it effectively dampened his enthusiasm for rushing up the slope. "Who do you think it is, Bern?"

"I'm pretty sure it's safe to go on up, Parker," he said with a slight smile.

"If you're sure it's safe to go up, why'd you stop me from going on up?" Parker asked, annoyed by this response.

"I stopped you because I wanted to point out the dangers of rushing into a situation without knowing just what it is you are rushing into, Parker. Out here, that's a very dangerous behavior, and you don't always get a second chance. Don't forget that. Now in this situation, I think you'll be okay to ride on up there. Just follow me, and I'll show you the way."

Parker nodded, chastened by the words of caution—not because he hadn't known that what Bern was telling him was true, but because he had known and forgotten it over the years he had been away. He was ashamed of himself, because he had often given that same advice to others on the slopes when they wanted to do something careless or dangerous. He followed Bern as he ascended to the top of Half Peak and was astounded to see what was up there making those noises and smells.

Gerry Junior was sitting with his back to the fire, watching the stars and the horses when he saw them all tip their ears forward. Very slowly, he slid his hand back to the butt of the pistol on his hip and gently eased it out of the holster. He held it down low and out of sight, easing away from the fire toward the horses. One of them nickered softly, and he put a hand out to reassure it. Approaching them, he heard a horse that nickered back. Gerry moved in that direction, but he didn't want to give away his position, didn't call out. A voice from the dark did call out, and Gerry relaxed and reholstered his gun, smiling as he did.

"Hello, the camp. You all have any coffee, or is it just that sissy stuff your cook drinks?" the voice asked.

"Come on in, Bern. Grab a cup and get comfortable. Is Parker with you?"

"Yes, sir! I'm still here," Parker called out.

"I'm really glad to see you both again, boys; I wasn't sure how we were going to find you on this mountain," Gerry Junior said as he greeted them. "Axel, come get your brother's and Parker's horses and take the saddles off and feed them," Gerry called.

Axel came out of the darkness to give his brother a nod and Parker a quick hello, and then he took both sets of reins and walked the animals away toward the picket rope. Parker went to the fire and poured himself a cup of coffee. Bern and Gerry walked to the edge of the camp to talk.

"Bern, did you see any sign of Barney out there?"

"Not a trace, boss. It's like he's dropped off the mountain. But, to be fair, this is a mighty damn big mountain for two people to cover. How about you?"

"No, we haven't seen anything either. I don't know where the hell he is. I thought he might see our fire and maybe that would pressure him into doing something careless."

Gerry Senior walked over to join them. "How you doing, Bern? We were getting kinda worried about you, son."

"Thanks, boss. I'm fine. Just a little hungry and tired is all."

"Anything to report about our man?"

"No, boss. I was just saying that it's gonna be hard to find him; this is a big mountain and we don't really know where to look for him. We're going to need a miracle to find him up here, boss."

With a sigh, Gerry Senior nodded his head. "Bern's absolutely correct, son. We're going to need some kind of miracle here. I hope you have one in your saddlebag; I used all mine up getting up here."

Bern looked at him, and Gerry Junior just nodded. "Yeah. Dad, Oliver, Arnold, and Axel all came up the backside of Half Peak—in the snow and in the dark. Now he thinks he's invincible and a real old-time mountain man," Gerry Junior said with a snort of critical amusement. Suddenly they heard a ringing chime from the center of the camp.

"Sounds like Charley's ready for dinner, so let's go eat and worry about this in the morning with a clear head and eye," Gerry Senior said.

Higher up the mountain, Floyd heard the ringing of a dinner triangle somewhere below them. He couldn't tell where it was coming from, but he had a good idea who was being called to dinner. He debated whether he should inform Barney of the bell, but decided it wasn't what he had been hired for. He turned around in his tent and lifted the corner of the flap to look outside. He didn't see anything that caught his eye, but he knew the Bruce party was closing in on them. He hoped this would be over tomorrow so he could go home and get warm again.

"I've never seen it so damn cold up here before," Floyd grumbled to his lantern and then turned over and went to sleep.

The next morning, Floyd and Barney awoke to find themselves deep in new snow again, with the temperature falling once more. Because of the cold, neither man woke up until the sun had begun to warm the air. It took Floyd over ninety minutes to get everything packed up and ready to go, because he had to do it all himself. Warner Barney sat on the same stump and gave Floyd orders on what to do and how to do it. While he was putting everything together, Floyd tried to figure out some way to get him off his back without opening himself up to legal liability and decided, reluctantly, there wasn't any. He sighed to himself and began singing all the cowboy songs he could think of.

After a few minutes of Floyd's off-key singing, Warner got off the stump and went to gather his things and carry them to the horses. He didn't bother saddling them—that was Floyd's responsibility. As he stood there, he looked around. It had been dark when they set up the camp, so this was his first look at the area. It wasn't a very impressive part of the mountain; it was very rocky and densely forested. There were openings in the trees big enough for a man to walk through, but too tight for a mount. There were downed trees everywhere, too big for a horse to step over, and there was no room for it to get its speed up to make a jump. Even if he *was* able to jump, there was no room for him to slow down afterward.

All in all, Warner thought, *this is a pretty difficult part of the mountain to track in. On the other hand, he won't be able to run away from me. Once I get on his trail, he won't be able to go any faster than I can, and I should be able to keep up with him long enough to get a shot at him and bring him down. He can't escape me forever.*

Warner started laughing as he anticipated the outcome of their meeting, but the laughter died on his lips as he turned around to see what was taking Bergen so long to get ready. Bergen was just standing there, looking out at the clearing behind them. Floyd was looking at the biggest damn Red Elk Warner had ever seen in his entire life. And it was just standing there, staring right back at them.

Warner couldn't get himself to move—he was spellbound by the sight of the magnificent creature in front of him. Floyd just stood there as well; he made no move toward his rifle either. As they both watched the animal walk around the edge of their camp, they were amazed by its apparent indifference to them. It seemed to ignore the foodstuffs that Floyd hadn't packed up yet, but wandered among their possessions, which were lying around. It nosed around Floyd's pack only briefly and moved over to Warner's.

It seemed to be looking for something specific, although they couldn't imagine what it could be. It spent twice as long rummaging through Warner's things as it had Floyd's, but neither man could get himself to disturb it or interrupt its efforts. Finally, its explorations completed, the animal looked up at both of them, tossed its head a couple of times in the direction of the densely forested slope, and turned and walked slowly into the forest, quickly fading from their sight. As it disappeared into the shadows of the trees, neither man was aware that the snow had started to fall again.

Warner shook himself and reached for his rifle.

"Hold up there, Mr. Barney. We still have to pack up the camp before we can leave this spot," Floyd called out to him.

"Pack it up yourself; you're the guide. I'm going after him before he gets away," Warner snarled at him as he scrambled to pull a box of shells from his pack. He picked up his canteen and slung it over his shoulder and started to follow the elk into the woods.

"Mr. Barney! Mr. Barney, come on back here, you're in danger!" Floyd called at his retreating back, although he wasn't sure why he said that. He did know that Barney wasn't going to come back.

He hurried to get everything put together as fast as he could so that he could follow. He moved with a sense of urgency and threw together what he thought he might need as quickly as he could. Anything he couldn't carry with him, he put in a pile and threw a tarp over it for protection and then hurried to saddle the horses and go after Barney.

When he was all done, he looked at his watch and saw Barney had a thirty-minute head start. Taking the reins in his hands, Floyd turned and prepared to follow him into the woods, but stopped cold when he looked in the direction he'd seen him walking off. Although the snow was falling down steadily, not enough had fallen yet to cover his tracks into the woods.

The problem was, all he could see were Barney's tracks. There were no animal tracks of any kind. Floyd was spooked now, because he had seen the animal in their camp, and he had watched it nose around in their packs for several minutes.

"This doesn't make any sense!" he said to himself. "I saw the damn thing walking around our camp and I saw it walk off this way with Barney on its tail. I can see Barney's footprints—the snow hasn't covered them up—but where are the damn animal tracks? There should be tracks in the snow for that animal as well, but I don't see any. The freakin' snow can't selectively cover tracks—that's impossible! What's goin' on here?"

Floyd tried to figure it out, but nothing he came up with made any sense.

"I've got to find him—before he gets himself killed and I get blamed for it." He looked ahead and saw Barney struggling to walk through the mounting snow in his relentless pursuit of the animal he came to bring down. Floyd called out to him again, but either Barney didn't hear him or wasn't willing to stop, so Floyd cursed him and plunged into the snow to follow him.

Lower down the mountain and two miles behind them, the entire party was waking up to a white morning. Charley was trying to build a fire out of some dry wood he had put in the packs the day before.

Adam came over to see if he could help him and to talk. "Charley, where exactly are we? I've been trying to place our position on this map, but I'm having a hard time finding this place. I heard Mr. Bruce call it 'Half Peak,' I think. Can you show it to me on this map?"

"Sure thing, youngster. Lemme see that there map." He looked it over and smiled. "You ain't gonna find us on that side of that there map, son. It's for the other side of the mountain; turn that blamed thing over, and I'll show you right where we're at."

"See this here line of ridges?" He pointed at a spot. "That's back where we started from, right there. I figure we been climbing steadily the entire time we've been chasing this critter, and he's done led us off this side of the map. Now, we turn it over ..." He flipped it over and spread it out on his knee. "Let me see ..." He traced a line on the map until he located Half Peak. "Here we are, right here, son," Charley said gleefully, as he pointed to a spot.

"And just where is the place that major snow slide took place thirty years ago?" Adam asked him out of curiosity.

"Hanged if I know, but I know who does. Oliver!" Charley called out. "Hustle your hocks, son. Man over here needs to pick your brain a bit," Charley said as Oliver walked over.

"What's up, fellas? Hi, Adam. What's on your mind?" Oliver asked him as he approached.

"Youngster here wants to know where the big slide took place back in '63. You know, the one that killed all those people," Charley said, recognizing what was behind the question.

"Hey, I just asked where the slide was," Adam said defensively.

"No problem, Adam. I understand. Let me see the map, Charley. Can you show me where we are right now?"

"We're right here, Oliver," Charley said as he pointed again to the spot marked "Half Peak."

"And the slide took place over ..." Oliver said under his breath. He finally found the point he was looking for and, taking out his pen, made a small dot where the legendary slide took place. He stared, seeing something he hadn't seen before. He glanced up at the top of Half Peak, and then off to the left, and then back down at the map. Oliver felt his anxiety growing over what he saw.

Warner Barney was elated; he could clearly see the animal moving slowly through the woods, despite the falling snow. He was having no trouble keeping up with it, to his great surprise. Every time he fell behind, the animal stopped to rub its antlers on a tree or graze at a patch of moss it found. The thought ran through his mind that it was almost as if the animal was waiting for him to catch up, but he quickly dismissed this thought as being as ridiculous as it sounded.

He patted his coat pocket to make sure he had enough shells to last him until the idiot guide was able to catch him, and he was relieved to feel the fullness of that supply in his coat. He opened the breech of his rifle to make sure it was loaded and carefully closed it as silently as he could. He was aware of how well sound traveled in the cold air, and he knew the animal's hearing was very acute. He didn't want to take any chances.

"I see you, mister elk. You are a beauty, that's for sure. I think you'll look very nice in my trophy room back home. Hell, I might just take you back and have you mounted whole. It will be expensive, but I think you're worth it." Warner laughed to himself. He halted in his tracks, as he could see the animal had stopped again. He slowly eased himself behind the tree he had been about to walk in front of. He peeked around it to find the animal he had been chasing was no longer there in front of him where he had been.

"What the hell! Where'd you go, damn it?" Warner cursed. He looked around and could see nothing of his quarry. The snow was coming down a little harder, making it difficult to spot it in the whiteness, despite the brilliant color of its hide. He felt a little colder and buttoned up the collar of his coat to keep the rising wind out of his clothes.

Warner was furious at this sudden turn of events. He peered into the whiteness in front of him, looking for any sign of his quarry, but, no matter what direction he looked, there was no sign of his target. It had just vanished, almost right in front of his eyes. Warner leaned back against the tree, frustrated and cold, and kicked the helpless mound of snow in front of him. He heard a sound behind him and whirled around, snapping his rifle to his shoulder as he did. He squeezed the trigger as he saw a large, vague object taking shape in front of him and was rewarded with a string of loud cursing and terrified whinnying.

"What the hell is wrong with you, man?" Floyd yelled at him as he struggled to keep his hold on his own mount while not dropping the reins of the pack horses. "You don't fire at anything if you aren't sure what the hell you're shooting at! You nearly hit me! Are you out of your—"

"Calm down, Bergen. I missed you; that's all that matters. I'm sorry. I'll add a zero to your bill, and we'll call it even," Warner said casually.

"Calm down? Calm down? Calm down yourself, you goddamn jackass! Do you have any idea where the hell you are? Do you know how to get off this goddamn mountain if anything were to happen to me? Well, here's a newsflash for you, *Mister Barney.* I quit! I'm out of here now! You're on your own. Find that damn animal or don't find it, I don't give a flying—"

Bergen stopped yelling when he saw Barney wasn't paying him any attention. He was looking away, his head cocked.

"Did you hear that, Bergen?" Warner asked him excitedly.

"Hear what?" Floyd asked grudgingly. He didn't want to stay with the man because he was a fool—and a dangerous fool at that. But the hunt was on, and he was caught up in the excitement it created, in spite of himself.

"He's calling me. That beautiful creature is calling me," Warner said, looking away. "He's challenging me to find him! That's what he's doing. And I'm going to find him, and then I'm going to bring him down, Bergen. I'm the man who's going to bring down the fabled Red Elk!"

Floyd looked at him, not sure what he was dealing with, but reasonably certain the man was mad or obsessed with this hunt. He sighed, knowing he wasn't going to leave him alone up here. He was stuck, for better or worse, so he figured he might as well take the money and just not do business with the man ever again. He started to say something to Barney, but found himself talking to his horse. Barney was already moving, heading toward the sound of the elk's trumpeting call. It sounded like it was coming from higher up to the west.

"Come on, boys," Floyd said to his horses. "Let's go follow his dream and see where it takes us. I'm sorry he shot at you; I'll make sure you get something extra in your feed bucket when we get home— maybe an extra order of oats for each of you. How about that?" Floyd offered them.

Eileen saw Oliver and Adam looking at something, so she walked over to see for herself. They had spread out a map on a tree stump and Oliver was focused on part of it.

She stood next to Adam to find out if he knew what was going on.

"What's all the talking about, Adam? Is there something wrong?" she asked, worried.

"I don't know. I asked Charley where we are now, and then where the slide happened back in '63. He didn't know, so he called Oliver over, and I asked him. He took a look at the map, and then he went silent. Now he's just looking at the map and—uh-oh. He's calling Gerry over. Something's up. I hope I didn't do something wrong here," Adam said, equally worried now.

"What's going on here, you two?" April asked. Neither of them had noticed her walking over to where they were standing, so her sudden appearance was somewhat startling to them. "I said, what's going on over there with the brain trust?" she asked derisively.

"They're reading a map is all I know, April," Adam said politely, not giving away anything.

"If they're just reading a map, why are both of the Bruce men involved?" April asked, her curiosity piqued.

"If you want to know so badly, Miss Martens, I suggest you go ask them," Eileen said coldly.

"Thank you, Miss Gayle, I think I'll go and do just that," April responded, just as coldly.

She walked over to where Oliver and both of the Bruce men were standing. While she had been talking to Adam and Eileen, Arnold and Wanda had also made their way over to the men, and Ed was following them. April shouldered her way past all of them to stand in front of Oliver and both of the Bruces. She turned on her electric smile.

"Mr. Barry, is there something wrong? Are we lost? Is our way blocked? What's going on?"

"Miss Martens, the answer is no to all of your questions. We are just discussing our position and where we will be going from here.

There's nothing going on that you need to be concerned about or that would interest you, I'm afraid," Oliver said politely.

"Mr. Barry, my instincts tell me otherwise. Whenever the head man starts to tell me I've got nothing to worry or be concerned about or says that there's nothing interesting going on, it usually means something very interesting is going on, and I should be worried. So, what's going on, and do I need to be concerned about this nonevent that I don't need to be concerned about because it isn't really happening?" she asked sarcastically.

Oliver looked at Gerry Senior, who only shifted his eyes toward Arnold without April seeing him. Oliver then looked over to Gerry Junior, who did the same—but this time April caught him.

She turned her attention to Arnold, but he seemed to be unaware of the looks being passed between the others or what was going on, as he wasn't watching either Bruce or Oliver; he was watching the mountain. There was something about the way he was looking out that seemed a little more than just sightseeing to her, so she decided to talk to him instead. She nodded to Oliver and headed over to stand beside Arnold, who had his arm around Wanda's waist. Wanda saw her standing there and turned to face her, and in the process, April slid between her and Arnold.

"Mr. Wilcox, I couldn't help but notice you looking off into the distance like that. You seemed to be looking further away than just mere miles, if I may say," April said gently.

"Miss Martens, you are correct. I am looking at a spot a couple of miles and a lifetime ago," he said sadly. "Right over there." He pointed. "That's where it happened. Right over there. I'll never forget the location. He was down at the bottom of the hill and—" He saw her trying to find the location he was talking about. "You can't see it from here, Miss Martens. Just take my word for it—it's over there.

"I get over that way every year, take some flowers, a couple of cans of his favorite beer, and I sit wherever I can find a spot and look. You know, we never found his body. I guess we never will. We looked for it all over the slope, but never found a trace. Even after the snow melted, we couldn't find anything. Not even his skis." His voice shook a little, and he stopped talking, but continued to look away. Wanda moved closer to him, glaring at April as she did.

"Mr. Wilcox, are you saying we're going in the direction of that snowslide?" she asked, her reporter's intuition firing up again. Suddenly, she knew what that conference had been all about. She saw him nod, and, after getting another cutting look from Wanda, she backed away and headed for the knot of men standing around the stump.

That was where the story was coming from, she knew. She smiled to herself and applauded her own determination and resourcefulness in getting around the shutout they had tried to run on her. *They are just men,* she said to herself, *and they don't have any idea who they're dealing with here. Nothing can ever stop April Martens.*

Warner followed the sound of the trumpeting's echoes for a while, the sounds always staying ahead of him. He couldn't see his quarry anywhere, and he knew he wasn't following it because he didn't see any tracks.

"I must be closing in on him—he's off to one side or the other. I just have to listen carefully the next time he trumpets, so I can home in on him." Warner was talking to himself, since he had left Floyd far behind him. "Come on, damn you. Trumpet again, I dare you!" he said softly to himself.

As if the elk had heard him, it let out another long and loud call from ahead on the left.

"Gotcha! I'm coming, baby!" Warner called out softly. He started moving a little faster—as fast as he could in the snow that was piling up all around him. The temperature was falling, and he could see his breath forming little ice clouds as he spoke, but he was hot on the chase, and the excitement kept him going. He hadn't had an opportunity to take a shot yet, but he knew his chance would come very soon. He just had to be patient. Just a little longer … then it would be his turn.

Just as he was thinking this, he heard it bugle again, but this time ahead on the right.

"What the hell?" Warner said out loud. "What's he doing zigzagging like that? Is he lost or … just what is he doing? How did he get so far across the timber so fast? Where's he going?" Warner asked himself, confused and annoyed that this animal wasn't behaving like it was supposed to.

Suddenly Warner smiled to himself. "He's just scared, that's all.

I've got him on the run now, so he's running blind. He doesn't know where to go, so he's in a panic! I've got you now, boy!"

Warner felt his blood racing as he realized the chase had changed. He was in charge now. He found the energy to move faster—but, in his haste, he lost his footing and fell face-first into a snow pile, his rifle falling from his grasp. He rose to his feet, a fleeting panic coming to his brain, until he saw his rifle just a few feet away. He relaxed and went over to it, picking it up and shaking the snow out of the barrel. He opened the breech, pulled out the bullet, and blew out the barrel to clear out the balance of the snow.

He heard a noise behind him and called out over his shoulder. "About time you showed up, Bergen. What took you so long, you get lost?" he said as he turned around.

Bergen wasn't there, but the elk was. It was looking at Warner from fifteen feet away, as if he hadn't a care in the world. Warner snapped his rifle to his shoulder to fire the kill shot, but all he heard was a click. He knew instantly what was wrong—he hadn't put the bullet back in. He tried to open the breech quickly, but his hands were shaking with excitement, and he dropped the round into the snow. Rather than try to pick it up, he reached into his pocket for another one and watched the elk slowly trotting away into the timber.

He finally got a round into the breech and closed it, quickly raising the rifle to his shoulder and trying to get a good line of sight on the animal as it moved deeper into the trees.

"You can't get away from me that easily, mister," Warner snarled as he lined up his shot. He peered through the scope and, placing the crosshairs on the elk, slowly squeezed the trigger, feeling the familiar recoil against his shoulder.

Farther down, everyone's heads turned at the sound of the shot echoing across the mountain. They all knew what it was—and, even worse, who made it.

"On the positive side," said Ed from behind them, "at least now we know where he is."

"Everyone saddle up!" Gerry Senior barked. "We've got to get movin' now. Time's a wastin'."

Everyone scrambled to their horses. Axel and Bern helped April and Eileen, while Arnold helped Wanda get her mount saddled. Charley quickly got his area policed and ready to go, and then he went to help Adam, whose nervousness was making his horse jumpy as well.

"Gotta relax, youngster. These here animals, they can tell when you're excited and it kinda makes them excited too. You want them to always know you're in charge, and that helps them to relax. Unnerstan'?" he asked Adam.

Charley picked up a curry comb and began to brush off the horse's back before he laid the saddle pad in place.

"Always brush him off a' fore you put the pad on, son. That way you remove any sticks or burrs that might be lying there, and that could save your life. Iffen you sets yourself on him while there's a burr under the blanket, you could find yourself on the ground real fast." Satisfied the area was clean, he laid the pad and the blanket on the horse's back and settled the saddle in place on top of everything. He rocked it back and forth until it was centered, and then he stepped back to take a look from the front. Giving his work a critical eye, he moved back to the saddle, scooted it forward about an inch, rocked it to the left, and placed his hand underneath to feel the space underneath it.

"Always should have a little rocker room there, son. It should be close, but not so tight as to rub him raw. This is how you check for that," Charley instructed him as he removed his hand.

"Charley, is there anything about horses you don't know?" Adam asked him in admiration.

"Youngster, I know enough to know you can't know everything about a horse's thinking or what that critter might do. There's lots of men who don't like them none, even though they depend on them. You remember this—a horse is an animal, and they have fears and are a flight-or-fight creature. Never approach your horse with your hands up and away from your body; always come at them slow and easy, and with your hands down and fingers closed," he advised Adam.

"Why do you do that, Charley?" Adam asked curiously, looking at his own open hands.

"Because a horse's primary predator is a mountain lion, and, if you think about how the cat attacks, he jumps at the horse with his paws and claws extended and over its head," he said as he demonstrated the stance. "So when you come at him like that, he sees a cat coming at him so he runs off—or worse, maybe he rears and kicks your head in. The smart cowboys always walked up to their rides with their arms down until they got there. So you remember that, youngster. Always approach your mount with your hands down, and you won't scare him off," Charley explained patiently and confidently.

The others were talking among themselves, excited but worried about what they might be riding into. The reality of the danger ahead of them was suddenly very clear to everyone.

"Oliver, are you sure we should be going after him?" Eileen asked quietly.

"Eileen, he broke the law—and, besides, do you know where we are?" Oliver replied, cinching up his saddle as he spoke.

"Not for sure, Oliver. Should I?" she asked.

"Well, I wouldn't have known for sure myself if I hadn't looked at that map. But here's the problem, Eileen. In the three days we've been out, we've ridden around a lot, but we've been going all around the mountain. And I mean going around—we're coming up on the backside of the ski area. We're only a little ways from the edge of the old runs—you know which ones I mean, don't you?" he asked her.

"You mean the ones that were closed after that slide? The ones where the people died?" she asked, suddenly much colder than she could account for by temperature alone.

"Those are the ones I mean, Eileen," Oliver confirmed. "I'm starting to have a very strange feeling that we're not chasing him—we're being led by him," Oliver said as he looked ahead into the trees on the slope in front of him.

"Which 'him' do you mean, Oliver?" Eileen asked softly.

"I'm not sure I know anymore, to be honest with you," he answered very slowly.

Just then he saw Ed walking toward them, carrying his rifle, a determined scowl on his face.

"This ought to be interesting," Oliver said under his breath to Eileen.

"Barry. Let me talk to you a minute. I've been thinking about this, and I think I've got an idea that might work," Ed said gruffly as he looked around and saw Wanda and Arnold standing nearby. "We need them two over here too," he added as he waved them over.

"What's up, Ed?" Arnold asked as he and Wanda joined them.

"I've been doing some figuring and I think we need to change our tactics some. This man is a loose cannon, I think we can all agree on that." He looked at them and, seeing them nod, he continued, "What if I can get a shot off at him—"

"I don't want anyone killed, Mr. Baxter, not even him," Oliver interrupted him to say sternly.

"Relax, ranger, I don't want to kill anyone either. I'm not carrying live rounds, remember? This is a tranquilizer rifle, not a killing rifle. I'm talking about getting off a tranquilizer round into his backside to put him down—until we can get to him and secure him, just like we would any wild animal. I know we have to adjust the dose to avoid hurting him—that's why we need Dr. Fleming's input on this. What do you say, Doc? Can we do that?" Ed asked her.

Wanda looked at him to see if he was serious and realized he was indeed. She looked over at Arnold to gauge his reaction to that insane suggestion. To her great surprise, he was smiling as if he was actually considering it! She looked over at the ranger and he wasn't rejecting the idea either. She was astonished at both of them; this was the craziest thing she had ever been asked to consider doing. It was absolutely irresponsible … unrealistic … totally reckless … impractical … improbable … a long shot at best … he'd have to be a superb shot … an incredible challenge and feat of marksmanship …

But workable if she could figure out just the right amount to use.

Wanda began to smile in spite of herself. It was, after all, fittingly ironic that that beastly man be brought down by the tool wielded by the very man he ridiculed.

"Yes, I think I could work out the right amount to do that without hurting him. I would, of course, be figuring on the low side for safety reasons …" she continued.

"Of course, Dr. Fleming. I would expect no less of you," Oliver said seriously, although she could see the light dancing in his eyes.

"I'll need to know his height and weight, his age, and … oh, damn," she said, her voice showing her dismay at something not previously considered.

"What is it?" everyone asked her at once.

"Well, it's one of the things no one can possibly know. I need to know if he's on any medications or has any allergies. Those things could change the danger level significantly. It would be tantamount to murder if we did this without knowing those things and he died," Wanda cautioned.

"Gerry! You and your father come over here for a minute, please," Oliver called out to him as an idea occurred to him. He had remembered looking at one of the applications for this hunt before it went out into the papers. If Gerry hadn't changed it any before he'd had them printed …

"This better be good, Barry. We've got to get moving before he finds the animal. We don't have a lot of time to spare on chit-chat," Gerry Junior said brusquely.

"Do you have the papers with you?" Oliver asked him, ignoring his clearly unfriendly tone.

"I didn't expect to be reading the newspapers up here, Barry," Gerry said sarcastically.

"Take it down a notch, Bruce. I'm not in the mood right now. I'm talking about the applications everyone filled out when they sent in their money to come on this big game hunt," Oliver responded, his own temper beginning to fray.

"Everyone just take a step back here," Arnold said in his deep tone, as he tried to prevent any outbursts from the people who needed to keep their heads. "Gerry, Ed here has an idea that just might solve our problems, and Oliver is just looking to see if it's practical. There's no need for a contest of who's got more testosterone, boys," he joked as he tried to smooth things out.

"Son, there's no need to be defensive. We all had a hand in setting this up, so we all need to work together to make it work. In answer to your questions, Oliver, yes, we do have them with us. They're packed up, but we can get to them if you need them. What is it you're looking for, if I might ask?" Gerry Senior asked calmly, as he put a hand on his son's arm.

"Did you take out the part asking about their medical history? You know, illnesses and allergies and medications and what not?" Oliver asked him hopefully.

"No, that's all still there. But it's all confidential information. What's the idea, Ed?" Gerry Junior asked in a surly tone, although he was curious. "Why do you need to know that?"

"Well, I figured that if we can't find the elk, maybe we can let

Barney find it for us, and I can shoot him—Barney, I mean … with a tranquilizer dart, that is," Ed said hastily with a smug smile.

"That's why I need to look at his medical information, Mr. Bruce," Wanda explained. "If I am going to come up with the safe amount, I have to know his height, weight, and medical background to see what a safe level would be. We're going to put it below the safe level, to decrease the risk of injury to him. That way, even if it doesn't knock him out completely, it will make him so woozy, he won't be able to shoot straight enough to be able to hit the animal. Then Ed can make the real shot on the animal so we can take him back safely," Wanda said in a rush.

There was a silence. Everyone watched Gerry Junior as he thought about this. He looked over at his father, and then at Oliver, and back at Ed. He walked around for a minute, considering his options, and finally came to a decision he thought he could live with. He walked back to where everyone was standing, waiting for his answer. He looked over all of them, and in particular, at his father. He took a deep breath to give his decision, but was interrupted before he could speak.

At that moment, they all heard another shot, but this one seemed a little closer to them than before—and this wasn't the bark of a rifle. This one was a pistol shot. It was followed by another.

Floyd was trying to catch up to his man, and he was just starting to step over a log when the shot went off. He heard the explosion and the whine of the bullet leaving the gun, and then he heard the solid whack of it hitting something solid. He heard a crash behind him and felt himself suddenly pulled backward off his feet.

"What the hell?" Floyd yelled as he went down. As he fell, his boot caught in a branch that had been hidden by the snow. He knew it was bad. He could feel his knee give, and he heard the ugly sound of something breaking in his leg. He slowly and very painfully turned himself over to find his mount standing a few feet behind him, beside Barney's. He also found the pack horse on the ground, blood trickling out of its nose.

"That horse ain't going to be getting up again. Not in this life, anyway," Floyd muttered to himself. "I'm gonna kill that man myself," he swore, more in anger than with any real intent. He whistled to his horse, which slowly moved over to him. "Come here, you goddamn stupid nag," Floyd said in as soft a tone as he could manage.

The pain in his knee and leg was starting to make itself known, and he had to get to the pack and dig through the junk for the medical kit before he passed out. He knew he couldn't depend on Barney to help him; Barney didn't know where he was, or he wouldn't have been shooting in his direction—he hoped. Floyd reached out for the stirrup and pulled himself up, grabbing for the reins. He led the horse over to a nearby stump and, taking a firmer grip on the stirrup, tried to raise himself to stand on his one good leg.

"Son of a bitch, goddamn his eyes, he's left me in a hell of a fix. Just how much bad luck can one stupid son of a bitch bring me?" he cursed. He grabbed hold of the saddle horn and painfully lifted himself into the saddle from the right side instead of the left.

Floyd gritted out against the pain. "Dandy," he said, calling his horse by name, "when we see old man Bruce again, remind me to thank him for teaching you to let me mount from either side." When he was seated in the saddle, he reined Dandy over to the pack horse and sat there, looking down on the animal as it struggled to right himself. Floyd saw that the horse had his leg caught in the straps and couldn't get it under him. Leaning over as far as he could, he took out his bowie knife and tried to cut the strap away from its leg. As he did, Dandy caught the scent of blood and crow-hopped to the side, spilling Floyd on the ground again. As he fell, he threw the knife away from him to avoid falling on it.

"Dandy, you son of a bitch! I thought I could count on you to help me!" Floyd yelled in pain as he landed on his already traumatized leg. As he rolled over, he saw his luck getting worse by the second. The medical kit was trapped under the downed horse, and the only way he could get to it was if it stood up. Floyd knew that the second the horse was up, it would bolt, taking the pack as far away from him as if he were in another state. With another curse at his absentee client, Floyd slowly drew his pistol and cocked it. He reached out with his other hand for the remaining strap holding the horse immobile. He could unbuckle it from there, and the horse would be free.

"I'm sorry to do this to you, Diego, boy. You're a good horse and a good packer, and you always had heart. You deserved a lot better than this for your last minutes, Diego. Believe me, I'm really sorry to have to do this to you," Floyd said sadly. He unbuckled the strap and, as Diego struggled to his feet and started to move away, grabbed the pack with his left hand and fired a shot at Diego with his right. He looked with sadness at the body of his favorite pack horse—and then, hearing a muffled noise, he turned his head to see his own mount running away through the snow, scared by the closeness of the pistol shot.

"Dandy! Dandy, come back here, you stupid nag!" Floyd screamed in a mixture of rage and pain. Dandy never looked back.

"Well, Mr. Warner Barney, I reckon you done killed me too. If I ever get my hands on you, you stupid, egotistical bastard, I'll take that goddamn rifle of yours and shove it so far up your … Crap! How can one person have so much damned bad luck? First things first, I've got to get into that medical pack and get something for the pain, and then I've got to figure out how to put a splint on myself. That ought to be quite an experience to tell the fellas at the bar about, I'm friggin' sure," Floyd muttered to himself.

He began rummaging through the pack to see what supplies he had put in there he could use to save his leg. Finding what he needed, he reached for his knife on his belt and remembered he had thrown it off to the side.

"At least it's early in the day; I've got some time to work with." Floyd sighed as he crawled to his knife, which was lying six feet away from him in the snow.

Warner heard the pistol shot, but he was puzzled to hear it coming from ahead of him—about the same direction he had fired. He quickly looked around him for some recognizable signs, but he saw nothing that looked in any way familiar. With all the snow coming down, he wasn't too surprised. He listened for another shot, but none came.

"I guess that's Bergen, trying to find me. The damn fool is going to scare that animal off if he doesn't stop that stupid behavior. This is the last time I use him for a guide," Warner muttered to himself. "It's my own fault for trying someone with the reputation he has."

Bergen was quickly pushed to the back of his mind when he looked up and saw the elk again.

It was standing in front of him, about twenty yards away, but

Warner didn't have a clear shot at him for all the trees and the snow that was still falling. It was just looking at him, not showing any anxiety or fear—and, more curiously, not moving. Its coat was a brilliant red, so it stood out in the snow very clearly. From this distance, Warner could see it was a magnificent specimen of its breed, with fine lines and strong shoulders and legs. It had a deep chest, showing it was quite a runner. Warner peered through the snow at his quarry and noticed there was something odd about it that he couldn't quite distinguish.

"What the hell do you have on your face, boy? Is that some sort of scar, or are you looking through some branches? I don't remember ever seeing that on you before—is that something new just for me?" Warner playfully said to his distant foe.

Keeping an eye on the elk, he slowly raised his rifle and, as quietly as he could, opened the breech to insert a round. Moving slowly to muffle the sound of the bolt closing, he brought the stock to his shoulder and sighted through his scope. Just as he began to squeeze the trigger, the elk turned away and walked back into the trees, showing only the outside edges of its rump as it faded back into the trees and snow.

"Damn! You're teasing me, aren't you?" Warner said, annoyed and frustrated by the lack of a good shot. "This animal is good! He's a worthy opponent, the best I've ever had," Warner said with grudging respect. "But, ultimately, he's only an animal, and I'm a man, and I'll outthink him eventually," Warner said confidently and looked around to get a fix on his position.

"Where the hell is Bergen? He should have been here by now. All the idiot had to do was follow my ..." His voice trailed off as he looked behind him to see that he'd left no tracks for Bergen to follow as far as he could see. The snow had filled all of them in already during the short time he was talking to the elk. He quickly looked back to where he had last seen it, but it too had already been filled in by the snow.

He had to make a choice: go forward or fall back to find Bergen. For a man of Warner Barney's abilities and temperament, the choice was very clear. He had to push on to find his quarry before he got away completely.

"I can always fire a shot to bring him to me with the horses. I've got plenty of ammunition, and I won't be wasting it on poor shots. I'll go on for a little while longer; I've plenty of daylight to work with. All I need is one good shot, and I'll bring him down, and this game will all be over.

Those clowns back there will be left to sing their sad songs about the glorious Red Elk, and there will be nothing they can do to me about it." He chuckled to himself as he walked carefully through the rising snow. "Bergen will be along soon, and he will have the supplies and extra ammunition. If I don't get him today, I'll close on him tomorrow and finish it then," he said confidently to himself.

He had no doubt about the eventual outcome of this chase.

"This just ain't my day, and that's for damn sure." Floyd was starting to feel very weak from the loss of blood. He had found the materials to make a splint, but he hadn't been able to get himself to set the break. He figured it wasn't going to matter in the long run, anyway. He had found some penicillin and painkillers in the med-pack and had taken them after putting on the splint as best he could. He was starting to feel the painkillers working, and his thinking was slowing down. Snow started to cover him in a warm blanket, and he knew his end was near.

He picked up his pistol and, with numb fingers, cocked and lifted it, and then fired it.

CHAPTER 12

"I heard another shot!" Adam called out.

This was met with a chorus of "Me too" all along the line of riders. Gerry Junior didn't say a word, but nodded at Bern, who nodded back and swung out of line and up the mountain in the direction of the shot. Parker hesitated only briefly, and then he turned his horse's head and followed Bern.

"Those two sure are getting along well, aren't they?" Eileen asked Oliver as she pointed to them as they rode away.

"A lot better than those two," Oliver responded, nodding at April and Adam, who were ahead of them in line. It was very apparent from their animation they were in the midst of an argument.

"April, I've already told you, I'm not discussing what my project is until it is nailed down," Adam said tiredly. "There's no reason for you to be jealous or—"

"Jealous? Me? Don't flatter yourself, Adam," she said coldly. "I've never been jealous of anyone or anything in my life! I'm only asking you what you're up to as a matter of friendship. We started out on this trip as coworkers, and I thought we had become real friends as time went by. I certainly won't pry into your business if you don't want me to know what you're going to be doing. I just thought I might be able to help you with it somehow. I was offering you my experience in journalism to help you in whatever way I could. You know, maybe I could help you come up with an eye-catching brochure or something like that," she said, putting on an air of injured innocence that didn't fool Adam for one minute.

"April, I really appreciate your offer, but it won't be necessary. I think I can handle whatever it is that comes up. And if not, my staff will."

"You're going to have a staff working under you?" she asked, disbelief in her eyes.

"Well, yes. It's only two or three people, I think. Not really more than five," Adam said, annoyed with himself for even dropping that single clue. He knew she wasn't going to rest until she had the whole story lined out. He hoped she wouldn't bother Oliver to the point that she screwed things up for him with the ranger. He had to distract her somehow—to give her another thing to be focused on until he could talk to the ranger. "Hey, April. Did you hear what we're up to now? I don't really mean us, but Mr. Barry and Mr. Baxter? Do you know where we're headed?" he asked her excitedly.

"That's old news, Adam. We're after a mysterious big Red Elk, and Baxter is going to shoot it with a tranquilizer gun. But now we have to find that other hunter first, Barney, and that's where we're going now," April said in a tired and bored voice. She clearly wanted to get to the bottom of his new deal so she could figure out how she could get a piece of it for herself.

"No, that's not it, April," Adam said conspiratorially. He leaned over to speak in a lowered voice, and he knew he had her when she leaned over to hear him.

"There's something new?" she asked him, interested at once.

Adam looked up and around at everyone in line. He knew this would get her off his trail and onto someone else's shoulders. "No. We're going to follow Barney to the elk, and then Mr. Baxter's going to shoot Barney with the tranquilizer gun. When he's out cold, Gerry and the other men will tie him up and *then* Baxter will shoot the elk. Dr. Fleming is going to make sure the dose is safe. They're all in on it!" he continued.

He sat back to watch her reaction to his outlandish story. He was a bit proud of himself, making all that up as he went along, and he figured Oliver would have a real good laugh too when he told him about it later. As he watched her face, he could see the wheels turning in her head, so he wasn't surprised when she started talking a moment later.

"Look, Adam, I'm sorry I've been such a pest to you. That wasn't right for me to press you like that. Whatever you've got going on, I wish you nothing but the best. I'll talk to you later."

"But, April, I thought you wanted to talk to me?" he asked her innocently.

"I do, Adam, dear. But I haven't been paying enough attention to the others on this trip. I do need to get some background history from Mr. Wilcox, Mr. Baxter, and Dr. Fleming. I'll catch up to you later on, I promise. Bye-bye." She hurried up the line to catch up to Ed Baxter, who was positioned two riders ahead of Adam.

Adam dropped back to talk with Oliver and Eileen, who had been respecting his privacy during his conversation with April by allowing him more space between them.

"What's so funny, Adam?" Oliver asked, amused.

"It's April, Mr. Barry. She's been after me like a hound to find out what I'm doing with you, and I haven't told her anything. Well, that's not true. I did let slip I will have a staff of two or three, but nothing else. I didn't tell her anything else, and she's very determined to find out what I'm doing for you. I needed to throw her off the track, so I made up a real tall tale, like Charley does, and she fell for it hook, line, and sinker." He started laughing again at the recollection of her face when he told her his fish story, and at the way she rode after Ed Baxter after giving him the brush-off.

"That's quick thinking, Adam. But won't she be mad at you when she finds out you were just stringing her along?" Eileen asked him, her radar working overtime.

"Just what kind of a tall tale did you tell her, anyway?" Oliver asked politely. He seemed to be distracted by watching Wanda play with her pocket calculator.

"Well, sir, it came to me while I was watching you and Mr. Baxter talking back at camp. I saw him go over to you and then everyone else joined in. I was busy so I couldn't get there before you broke up, but I saw that Mr. Baxter had his rifle with him. I figured he was telling you something was wrong with it, since he had a sour look on his face. So what I told April was that we were going to chase Barney, and then Mr. Baxter was going to tranquilize him instead of the elk. Then all of you were going to hog-tie him, and then Mr. Baxter was going to get his chance to capture the elk safely.

"Because I knew she'd immediately suspect that was just a story, I told her that Dr. Fleming was going to figure out the right amount to use on a human. Since Dr. Fleming is a doctor, I hoped that would sell it to her, and boy did it!" Adam said, now laughing so hard that tears appeared in his eyes. After a few seconds, he realized he was laughing alone and looked at Oliver's face. What he saw there wiped away his smile.

"Of all the—" Oliver started to say, anger clearly stamped on his expression.

"Oliver, it was just a wild random hit. There's no way he could have known," Eileen said to him. "Just calm down and don't get mad at Adam. How was he to know?" she said soothingly.

"You mean … you mean you *are* going to do that?" Adam asked in astonishment. "Honest, Mr. Barry, I was just making up a story, I had no idea … I'm so sorry …" Adam stammered out.

"It's all right, Adam. Eileen's right. You couldn't have known what we were up to. You just happened to hit the nail right squarely on the head with your tall tale. But it wasn't a tall tale. It was Ed's idea and Dr. Fleming's working up the right dose right now. It's just that this is something very risky for all of us, and for it to come out in the papers would damage everyone who is involved. I've got to get that story killed before it kills all of us.

"I don't blame you, Adam, and I'm not really mad at you. You just caught me by surprise, that's all. Don't worry, this doesn't change anything between us," Oliver said as he accurately read the worry in Adam's face. "I guess that anything that wild was certainly fair game for an educated guess by someone who is as observant as you are. I just trust you'll use that keen intuition for us on the magazine, okay?"

"Yes, sir! And again, Mr. Barry, I'm sure real sorry I messed up your plan. But—" he said as he paused to work something out in his head.

"I see the wheels turning again, Adam. What are you thinking?" Oliver asked.

"Well, it's just that I could say it was just a tall tale anyway, and if no one else ever admitted to their part, there's no way April can prove it wasn't anything but a story. Maybe Mr. Baxter could start sniffling like he has a cold, and then when he takes his shot at Mr. Barney, he could pretend to sneeze and that would explain his faulty aim?" Adam suggested.

"This boy has a good head on his shoulders, Eileen. We better watch ourselves around him," Oliver said with a laugh. "Okay, Adam, I'm going to leave you here with Eileen while I go tell everyone what's up and tell Ed he has a cold. If April comes back at you, you tell her you were just teasing, and the real story is the magazine. Tell her that you're going to be the editor. That should keep her focus on you and off Ed and Wanda," Oliver said as he rode forward to talk to Wanda and both of the Bruce men.

"I think everything's gone wrong that can so far. We're due for some good luck, don't you think?" Oliver said to his horse. The horse just shook his head in total disagreement.

"What do you think we're going to find up here, Bern?" Parker asked anxiously.

"Who we're going to find is more my concern," Bern replied tersely. "I don't understand the reason for those two shots. The first was a rifle, but the second a pistol. Why would Barney use a pistol when he has a rifle? A pistol is for close range, a rifle for long range. A pistol won't bring down the big animal he's after. No, that pistol means trouble … for someone."

"Couldn't he have used it to finish off the animal if he only wounded it?" Parker asked him.

"That's not consistent with this man, Parker. You've dealt with him before, remember? Did he show you concern or compassion then? Or maybe you think he's changed over the years?"

"Okay, I see your point. What then? Who fired that shot and why?" Parker asked him again.

"I reckon we'll find out when we find whatever it is we're after up here," Bern said flatly.

Just then, something flashed by the corner of Parker's eye, and he turned to try to get a better look at it. He called out to Bern as he did.

"Bern! Hold up. I just saw something over there," he pointed uphill a few yards away.

"What was it? Did you get a good look at it? I don't want to waste a lot of time on a snipe hunt, Parker," Bern said cautiously.

"I didn't get a good look, but it seemed to me it was something brightly colored," Parker said slowly. "I'm not sure, because it went by fast, but I think it might have been red." He looked at Bern, who looked back at him in silence. Both the men headed to the spot Parker had pointed at.

"Okay, we're here. Now what?" Bern asked impatiently.

"I don't know, Bern, but let's look around a little. Whatever it was, it should leave a track of some kind, and when we see it we'll know what we're looking for," Parker replied as he studied the area around him. All he could see were trees—a lot of trees. And they were all the same—white.

"There! On the right! Damn, it's gone now. Come on, Parker, it was over there," Bern called out as he headed after it. They moved deeper into the forest, following the flashes of something both had seen only out of the corner of their eye.

"There! Over to the left! Did you see it, Bern?" Parker said excitedly.

"Yes, that time I did. What did it look like to you, Parker?" Bern asked him cautiously.

"I didn't get a good look—it was just there, and then gone again between the trees—but it kinda looked like it might have been a cross-country skier ... maybe," he said reluctantly.

"Yeah. A cross-country skier. Maybe," Bern responded, equally reluctantly. "We're both spooked out of our common sense right now, Parker. Let's not let our imaginations run away with us," he said, with a laugh he didn't feel. It had looked like someone on skis to him too. He continued to ride in the direction in which he had seen the flash of red, looking all around him as he did.

"There is it is again, Parker. Over there." Bern pointed to the right, where the red was barely visible, but obviously present, as it stood out so clearly against the white snow. "It's not moving this time, though. It's standing still."

"Maybe he's waiting for us to catch up," Parker said, only half-joking, because it did look that way.

"If he's waiting for us, Parker, why isn't it getting bigger as we get closer? To me, it looks like it's getting smaller as we get closer," Bern said as they approached the shrinking red object.

When they reached the place they had seen the spot, there was nothing red to be seen in the snow. What was there to be seen were two large mounds separated by several feet. Bern went to the bigger one and looked at it for a minute from his saddle. He climbed down and used his gloved hand to brush the snow away to reveal the frozen body of a dead horse. He stood up to look at the other mound where Parker was standing. He turned to open his saddle bag as Parker called out with urgency in his voice.

"Bern! It's a man! He's ice cold, and I've barely got a heartbeat, but he's still alive. We've got to dig him out before he dies!" he called out as he started to pull the man to his feet.

"Hold it, Parker. Let's be smart. There's a reason he's lying there and his horse is over here. I think we ought to just uncover him first. Brush the snow off of him while I get a blanket to cover him with. You get started, I'll be right there," Bern advised.

He turned back to his saddle bags, opened up the left pouch, reached in, and pulled out a bottle. He quickly buckled the strap again and then untied his bedroll from the back of the saddle. He walked over to where Parker was uncovering the man's legs and whistled when he saw them.

"Boy, you really called the turn on this guy, Bern. Looks like his leg is broken and splinted together. If I had tried to pick him up, I would have ruined it beyond fixing. Thank God you stopped me in time, Bern," Parker said. He finished brushing the snow off the man and wrapped the blanket around him as best he could. He picked up the man's arms and began rubbing them in an effort to restore their circulation.

"Here." Bern handed him the bottle. "See if you can get a few drops into him; it will help him warm up. I'm going to look for some saplings we can make a travois out of. He'll never make it riding, and we can't leave him here." He turned to look for poles he could lash together in a hurry, before it started snowing again, but he stopped when Parker called out to him.

"What do you think he's doing out here, Bern? Is he lost?"

"He's not lost, Parker. I think he's out cold right now, and when he comes to—if he comes to—he's going to be sorry as hell that he took his last job. This is Floyd Bergen. Or what's left of him. That means Warner Barney is out here by himself. And we don't have a clue where to look for him. We can't take the time to look for him, either. We have to get this man back to the others so Dr. Fleming can try to save that leg if it's at all possible, and we have to do it quickly."

"Do you think we can save his leg, Bern? It looks pretty bad to me," Parker asked anxiously.

"To be honest with you, Parker, I don't know. The only thing keeping him alive is the cold—it kept him from bleeding out, and probably slowed his heart down enough to keep him alive. It's a damn good thing for him we found him in time," Bern said thoughtfully as he looked around.

"Bern," Parker asked him slowly, "did we find him ... or were we led to him?"

"I don't know, Parker. It really doesn't matter now, does it?" Bern said evasively. He didn't really want to answer that question, because he wasn't really sure just what the right answer was.

Warner was getting colder as the snow kept coming down, along with the temperature. He hadn't seen his quarry for a while, and he wasn't sure where it was. He had followed it for a time, catching just a glimpse through the trees, but the last sighting had been over an hour ago. He was getting ready to turn back and look for Bergen when he saw the elk again.

"There you are! Where have you been, fella? You tried to lose me, didn't you? You did your best, but I was just too smart for you. You can't get away from me, boy, I'll guarantee that!" His enthusiasm for the chase renewed, Barney forged ahead. As he was forced to high step through the snow, he couldn't help but notice how the animal seemed to just glide through the drifts and blowing snow as if it was all just air.

Barney stopped for a moment to catch his breath and listen for the sound of Bergen coming up behind him, but all he heard was the wind whistling through the branches of the trees. As he looked around, he could see what must have been trail markers along the way, but he couldn't read them because they were all covered in white. Of course, he didn't really care what they said; it had nothing to do with him. He was out here to bring down his target, not take a nature walk. He trudged right past them without even the slightest curiosity about what they might say. His eyes were locked on that flicker of red ahead of him.

He was becoming more irritated as the hours passed; he hadn't had one good shot yet.

"Come on, damn you. Stop for a moment, graze, take a bite of snow, take a crap, do anything that will slow you down or give me a shot," Barney muttered. "You can't keep hiding behind those trees forever—sometime you have to come out in the open, and then I'll have you."

As if it had heard and understood what Barney was saying—which, of course, was ridiculous—the animal paused to take a moment to rub its huge rack against a tree. It stood sideways to Barney, offering its side as a target.

"Now I've got you!" he said gleefully. He raised the rifle to his shoulder, sighted the animal in his scope, and squeezed the trigger. Nothing happened. He swore and opened the bolt to find it was a misfire. He yanked the errant shell from the rifle and slapped another one in as fast as he could and, raising the rifle to his shoulder, he looked through the scope to find his quarry gone.

"Where the hell did you go?" Barney screamed into the air. He headed for the last place he had seen it in the trees and trudged past another of the markers he had ignored.

If he had stopped to brush the snow off this one, he would have known he was only four hundred yards from the bottom of Hunter's Run. And nearby, but frozen over at this time of year, was Otter Creek.

Bern and Parker rode as quickly as they could without jarring Floyd anymore than was needed. The travois was attached to Bern's horse, as he was used to that sort of thing, while Parker rode behind, where he could keep an eye on Floyd in case there was a problem. Parker was the first one to see Floyd waking up.

"Bern, hold up. He's coming around," Parker called out. He had seen Floyd's eyes fluttering. "Hey there, Mr. Bergen. Can you hear me? Do you know where you are?" he asked.

"I … hear … you. Am … on … a … drag … sled … I … guess," Floyd painfully eked out.

"What happened to you, Mr. Bergen? Can you tell me how you came to be up here with a broken leg, Mr. Bergen?" Bern called back to him as he turned around in his saddle.

"Was … up … here … hunting," Bergen said through clenched teeth, pain visible on his face.

"Who was with you, Mr. Bergen?" Bern asked gently.

"Client … hired … me. Just … two … of us," he said just before he lost consciousness.

"He's out again, Bern," Parker observed. "He looks a little better, though. Seems to have a little more color in his face,"

"Yeah. But that color means he's likely to start bleeding again, and that don't say anything about what's wrong inside. I'm worried about him, Parker. We need to get him down to Dr. Fleming as soon as possible. I can't move very fast, Parker, but you can. You have to go find the others and bring them to me and him. You think you can do it, Parker?" he asked, worried.

"I can do it, Bern. Which way do you think they'll be headed? We've been riding all over the place, and I'm a little turned around up here. If you point me in the right direction, I'll get them and be back as quick as I can."

"Do you have a compass, Parker?" Bern asked him as he fished around in his vest pocket for his. Seeing Parker shake his head, he handed it to him. "I'm going to take a southeasterly course, heading to where we left the others. That means you need to ride northwest to find them. Once you locate them, bring Dr. Fleming and Gerry back here as fast as you can. Oh, and maybe you should bring the ranger back as well," he directed.

"I'll get them, Bern, don't you worry," Parker assured him as he headed out.

Bern watched him ride away, and then he got down and he saw Bergen twitching.

"Mr. Bergen, can you hear me?" he asked softly.

"Hear … you."

"Who is your client, Mr. Bergen?"

"You … know … who … client … is," came the reply.

"I think I know, Mr. Bergen, but I need to hear you say it," Bern said softly.

"Okay … Client … is … Warner … Barney," Floyd whispered before he passed out again.

"Warner Barney, you've got a lot to answer for," Bern said as he stood up, anger in his eyes. "I don't know how this happened, but you have a date with a judge if I have anything to say about it," he promised.

Getting back on his horse, he took one more look at the man on the travois and started moving out of the woods.

Three hours later, he heard Parker calling to him from off in the distance. He pulled his pistol and fired a shot in the air to get his attention. Twenty minutes later, he saw Parker, Dr. Fleming, and Oliver closing the gap between them very quickly, so he stopped and waited for them.

"Bern, it's good to see you again. This is a darn good compass you have," Parker said as he handed it back to him.

Oliver and Dr. Fleming jumped down from their horses and walked around to where Floyd was lying on the travois. Oliver stooped to kneel by his side while Dr. Fleming looked at his leg.

"Mr. Bergen, my name is—" Oliver started to say.

"Know … who … you … are … ranger," Floyd said weakly.

"How did this happen to you, Mr. Bergen?" Oliver asked him gently.

"Was … on … hunt … had … accident," he managed to say.

"Yes, I know, Mr. Bergen. But just how did that accident happen?" Oliver persisted.

"Shot … my … horse … by … accident," Floyd said hoarsely.

"You shot your own horse? By accident?" Oliver asked, clearly dubious about his story.

"Client … shot … my … horse … by … accident," Floyd clarified.

"Where were you standing that your client managed to shoot your horse, Mr. Bergen?" Oliver asked him. "And, for that matter, who is your client, Mr. Bergen?"

"Already ... told ... other ... man," Floyd said, his energy clearly failing fast.

"Well, I need to hear it from you myself, Mr. Bergen," Oliver said firmly.

"My ... client ... Warner ... Barney," Floyd said, and then he passed out.

"I hope you heard what you needed, Mr. Barry, I need him to be out while I work on his leg. I will need your help to set it properly. Bern, I suspect you know how to do this, so I want you, Mr. Woodson, and you, Mr. Barry, to hold him down while Bern pulls it out and I align the bones so it will heal properly. This is going to be painful, so he will probably pass out again even if he wakes up," Wanda explained.

She motioned everyone to their places and, with a nod to Bern, felt for the edges of the bones as he pulled the leg back. Once she felt them realign, she gave Bern the okay to release Bergen's leg. He never made a sound during the entire thirty seconds it took to reset it, but his face did get pale for a moment until Bern had released his hold. Once she was satisfied, she picked up the splints and reapplied them to his leg, tying them securely.

"Well, I've done the best I could. I don't have any painkillers with me, but I do have some antibiotics I can give him if we need to. I assume some of you might have some painkillers tucked into a saddlebag or something," she said as she looked around.

She didn't fail to notice that Parker looked over at Bern, who looked away, and so she just smiled.

"Do you think he'll come around again? I've got a lot of questions for him about Barney," Oliver said. "I want to know just what happened, and where he thinks Barney is now."

"I don't know, Mr. Barry. He's lost a lot of blood, he's in a lot of pain, and that's just the outside. I assume he was thrown from his horse, so there could be internal damages I can't tell about from an external examination. We need to get him back to town as soon as we can, so he can be seen by a real doctor," Wanda said, the urgency apparent in her voice.

"Maybe Charley can take him back. I'll speak to Gerry about it when he gets here. He should be right behind us. I have to go get

Barney. He's got to be stopped before he crosses into the ski areas. He's crazy as a loon, and he doesn't care who gets hurt if they're in his way," Oliver said.

He walked back to his horse and was getting ready to mount up when he heard the rest of the group closing in on them.

"How's he doing?" Gerry Junior demanded as he jumped down from his horse.

"Mr. Bergen's holding on, boss," Bern said. "Dr. Fleming, she set the break and gave him some antibiotics, but he's still in trouble. We got to get him back to a real doctor—no offense, meant, Dr. Fleming," Bern said as he looked over at her.

"None taken, Bern," she responded calmly.

"... real doctor soon as we can, boss."

"I'll get Charley and Axel to rig up something better than that travois you jury-rigged, Bern—although that was a right smart piece of work—and they'll get him back down the mountain in good shape and over to Dr. Hansen as soon as they hit town," he said gruffly.

"What's his financial situation, do you think, Gerry?" Oliver asked.

"Him? Piss poor, I'll warrant. Otherwise he'd never have taken Barney's money, although I'd bet the cost of this damn fool venture he'll never see a nickel of whatever it was Barney promised him," Gerry said with obvious disdain. "Why? You plan on paying his bills for him?"

"Tell Doc I'll cover the cost of his patch job," Oliver said to Axel, ignoring Gerry's sarcasm.

Wanda looked at him with respect and went to find Arnold.

Axel just touched his fingers to the brim of his hat and went looking for Charley. "That's a real generous offer, Mr. Barry. You're a good man," Axel said in a low voice as he walked by Oliver to get to his horse.

Oliver nodded that he heard, but his mind was elsewhere. Bern didn't say anything either, but he looked at Oliver and nodded slightly after Gerry turned away.

Oliver went over to him after Gerry was out of earshot, and told him what was on his mind. "Bern, I don't know if you're aware of exactly where we are, but the ski areas start about a mile from here, over Moosejaw Ridge. I've got to stop him before anyone else gets hurt.

This thing is getting way out of hand. I'm going to need some help to do it, and I'd like you to be the one to help me. I don't think I'll be able to get him with everyone traipsing through the woods, and that will just put everyone else at risk. I don't want to put the women in danger, and Arnold is too old for what we have to do. Ed isn't really an outdoors person, and Adam isn't an experienced rider, so I can't count on them. Axel and Charley are going to take Bergen back down the mountain, and that leaves me with you, Parker, and Gerry Junior," he said quietly.

Bern looked away for a second and then back at Oliver. "What you're doing for Mr. Bergen is something a real man would do, and more than most would even think about. But—" He held his hand up to shut off the words that he knew were coming, but he continued anyway. "But, no disrespect intended, Mr. Barry, but you're not an experienced rider either. This is likely to be beyond your skill level as well, you know. You could get just as hurt as any of them—or the rest of us."

"Hell, I know that, Bern. Boy, don't I know that. But—" He held his hand up to stop Bern from talking. "My turn. But I'm the one with the marshal's badge. I'm the only one who can arrest him, so I have to go. I have no choice," Oliver explained sadly.

Bern was silent for a moment. He then took off his glove and put out his hand. "You're a man to ride the river with, Mr. Barry. I'll go with you. On one condition," he said seriously.

"And that is …?"

"That you find me a job in case I lose this one," Bern said with a smile.

"That won't be hard to do, son. You can help me with my new spread I'm going to rebuild."

Neither man had heard or seen Arnold walk up behind them, so they were surprised when he spoke up. Both men turned around suddenly, and a guilty look covered both of their faces.

"Now the way I see it, boys, you two are cookin' somethin' up, and I'm willing to bet it involves Mr. Barney. And seein' the guilty look on your faces, I'm also thinkin' it means you two are trying to figure out how to leave the rest of us out of the play. Now I can't speak for Ed, or that reporter and her friend, but I can speak for Wanda, and we agreed there ain't no way in hell that you two are ridin' off and leavin' us behind. So. Now that we have that settled, what's the plan?" Arnold asked with a big smile.

"Arnold, this is going to be a very hard and dangerous chase, and—"

"Sounds good to me already."

"—and I don't want to put Dr. Fleming in any danger, anymore than I would my own assistant—" Oliver persisted as if he hadn't heard Arnold.

"Even if she wants to go along? Are you saying she can't make up her own mind?"

"Arnold, please stop fencing with me and twisting my meaning. I am responsible for stopping this situation before it gets any worse."

"Ranger, I don't think you understand what's going on here; let me explain it to you in a different way, and maybe you'll get the picture. You, this young man, and probably Gerry Junior over there—you three think you're going to slip away and find Barney and take him down while the rest of us slink on home like little children who have been sent to their room by daddy. You think, obviously, that because I'm older than you, I'm incapable of handling myself out here on a hard ride. Well, son, I've been doing that for longer than you've been up here. I will wear you out before I even yawn," he said.

Arnold was so clearly dead serious, Oliver just blinked. He heard Bern muffle a low snicker behind him, but Arnold was talking again, so he didn't turn around to give Bern a dirty look.

"Now, Charley and Axel are going to take that poor Mr. Bergen back to safety, but we are going with you, or we are going by ourselves—all of us—so you choose your poison, son," Arnold said with quiet emphasis.

Behind him, the others had gathered with their reins in hands, Eileen and Wanda in the front of the line.

Oliver looked at all of them, ready to ride—even Adam—and shook his head. "You people are all crazier than the man we're chasing," he said with a sigh, but there was no hiding the smile that crept across his mouth and into his eyes as he said these words.

Gerry Junior came back from giving Axel and Charley their instructions and looked around at the group in front of him.

"I don't like the look of this—you people are planning something really dumb, I can tell," he said sourly. "Where's my father? Is he involved in this nonsense too?" he asked, trying to find him in the crowd.

"Up to my neck and then some, son," came his father's voice from the back of the group.

"We came into this party as a unit, and that's the way it's going to be to the end," Gerry Senior said sternly. "*We* have a job to do, and *we* are going to do it. Everyone talked, and we all agreed—it is something that has to be done. We're counting on you and Bern to help us get it done right and without anyone getting hurt," Gerry Senior added.

"Of course, that don't include any mad animals we might come across," called Ed from the side, to the amusement of everyone.

"All right, if you people are determined to put yourselves at risk, I might as well stop trying to keep a child from putting a fork in the first electrical outlet he can find," Gerry Junior grumbled.

"I guess we might as well get started, so let's go get him. We're going to ride in a straight line; everyone will keep in sight of the person on their right and left. We are going to ride up the mountain, and we will find him or the elk, I don't care which. If we get to the top and we haven't seen him, we will come down the other side in the same manner, until we flush one of them out into the open. If you see him, don't call out," Gerry Junior instructed them.

"Then how are we going to let the others know we've seen him?" Oliver asked.

"I know. We can hold on to a rope and whoever sees him will pull on the rope so the others feel the pull!" said April excitedly.

"That's a real good idea, miss, but I have one question. How do we get the rope around or through the trees as we ride between them?" Ed asked sarcastically.

"Oh. I didn't think of that," she said, embarrassed.

"That's a good idea, miss, but just a little impractical. We need something else," Arnold said.

"Why do we have to be quiet, Mr. Bruce?" Wanda asked. "Aren't we trying to prevent him from shooting the elk? If he knows we are all out here, and all of us see him, won't that serve the purpose and perhaps save his life as well?"

"I'd rather just shoot the—" Ed muttered, but stopped when he saw Wanda looking at him.

"You know, you might be right at that, Dr. Fleming," Gerry said, after thinking about it for a few seconds. "Perhaps that is the best approach. Okay, new plan, everyone. If you see him, sing out, and we will swing the far end of the line around to circle him. But be careful—he's armed and dangerous," Gerry cautioned them.

"Yep. Armed and dangerous and as nutty as a fruitcake," Ed muttered to himself again.

"Adam, this is very exciting, don't you think?" April asked him, exhilaration lighting up her face. She was probably visualizing her story's scope expanding by leaps and bounds, and she liked what she was seeing. To her way of thinking, the potential risks were just part of the business.

"April," Adam responded, "sometimes I don't know who you are. You don't seem to understand what's going on here or what we're riding into. Someone's going to die out here because of this mess. I don't want it to be any of us—or that animal either," he said.

"No, it's you who doesn't understand," she said as she walked off to stand beside Ed Baxter.

"Where the hell are you? And just where am I?" Warner looked around as he followed his quarry across the mountain. He noticed the trees seemed to be thinning out slightly, and he could hear strange noises off in the distance that puzzled him—but not enough to investigate them to discover their source.

"I'm getting colder; this damn snow keeps coming down, and you keep just out of my reach! I want this to end today, damn it!" he swore to himself. "And where the hell is that idiot Bergen? Some tracker he is, he can't even follow my trail, and I'm not even trying to hide it. All that idiot has to do is just follow my … tracks …" His voice tailed off as he turned around to see the snow had filled in his footsteps. "Damn snow, it's wiping out my tracks. Okay, so he can't follow them. He can still hear me call, unless the snow filled in his ears too," Warner muttered.

He cupped his hands around his mouth and took a deep breath to call out to Bergen, but he hesitated … and let out his breath … without calling.

"Damn it, Bergen. If I call out to you, he'll hear me and run off. I can't do it now; I'll call for you when this is over. Right now, I need to get back to work. He's got to be here somewhere," Warner said to himself. His face was taut and anger-filled, and he was cold and damp. But he was determined to win this contest.

Standing thirty feet away from him and behind a massive oak, he was being silently observed by the animal he was chasing.

The elk was a magnificent example of its kind. It was strong and healthy. It had clean lines and well-defined musculature throughout its body. It had a very shiny coat, indicating its good health. It had an impressive rack of antlers, indicating its age and status in the herd. The many points at the ends were all sharp and dangerous. They were its weapons of defense. Its coat, a brilliant scarlet, was its signature and sign of its identity—as was its elusiveness.

The elk was accustomed to being hunted; it was just part of its life. It was used to it. The elk knew how to avoid being seen; it knew how to use the forest to hide and live in. This was his world, but another hunter was invading it. Again. This hunter, however … this hunter was different. This hunter liked to kill and he didn't care what he killed.

The elk sensed he was more dangerous than any other hunter, but it wasn't worried. After all, it knew this mountain much better than the hunter. It knew how to avoid being seen, unless it wanted to be. It turned away, the sunlight casting shadows across its face. As the sunlight passed across the dark stripes in its fur, it gave the appearance this beautiful red animal was wearing a mask—or maybe goggles.

Warner heard a sound and turned to see the animal looking at him—then it turned and walked into the trees again, apparently unconcerned about his presence.

"Gotcha!" he said excitedly as he raised the rifle to his shoulder and fired. He saw splinters fly from the tree behind the elk's shoulder. "Damn! How in the hell did I miss that shot? I had him cold, I couldn't have missed!"

Warner slogged his way over to the tree to see if he had possibly nicked him in the shoulder, but when he got to the tree, all he saw was a chip in the bark. It was clean—no trace of blood anywhere on the tree or in the snow. He walked around the tree and saw no signs of any injury to the animal.

"Damn snow!" he said, looking up into the sky. "That blurred my vision just enough to miss an easy shot. I have to take that into consideration, aim a little lower next time. Brr. It's getting colder here. I wonder what the friggin' temperature is, anyway."

He looked around and saw the flash of red in the distance, moving down the mountain. "There you are, boy. I see you, I'm coming for you. You can't get away from me now," Warner said lovingly.

"I heard a shot over that way, Gerry!" Oliver called out.

Everyone stopped in their tracks, and the tail end of the line of riders on Oliver's left began to swing around toward him. At the end of the line, April was talking to Ed, trying to get the information out of him about what he was planning on doing if he caught Barney.

"Mr. Baxter, why won't you talk to me about what you're going to do? I can write this to make you the hero of this soap opera, if you'll just give me something to work with," April said coyly. "You know you've got something planned, I heard you and the others talking about it."

"Miss Martens, I'm in a bad mood, and I don't feel so well. I'd rather not talk right now, if you don't mind. I've got a lot of thinking to do about what's coming up," Ed said in a surly tone.

Nothing on this outing had turned out as he had planned or expected. Ed was very much on edge, and the fact he hadn't had a drink in almost four days was making it even harder. Now he had this nosy reporter attached to him, and she was sure to ask questions about his background that would be hard to answer without tripping himself up … Unless he controlled the questions …

"Miss Martens, I'm sorry. I don't mean to give you a short reply. I'm just not feeling very well. What is it you want to know? Oh, yeah. When we catch up to him. Well, what we were talking about is that Mr. Barney is sure to hurt himself or someone else in this mad pursuit of his. He seems to be losing his objectivity and forgetting why he's here. Well, that's not exactly right. I guess it's more like he is developing a case of tunnel vision on getting his trophy. He's forgetting the ranger changed this to a capture hunt rather than just a kill hunt. I'm along to make the shot that brings him down so we can relocate him. I'm a member of the local NRA rifle team, and I've got the best record for long-distance accuracy, so they selected me for the job," he explained courteously. *Now comes the hard part,* Ed thought to himself.

"Mr. Barney's endangering everyone on the ride—and, for that matter, everyone on this mountain. Despite what I've said when I was joking, I don't want to hurt anyone," Ed said emphatically. "My nature is to grumble and complain, but I never mean it seriously. It's just how I relieve my stress," he said with a smile he didn't feel or mean.

"So all of those things you said back there, you didn't really mean any of them?" April asked skeptically. Her radar was telling her this was a line of bull, but she figured she'd let him run it out and catch him in a story later on.

"No, Miss Martens, I didn't mean them. What I'm hoping to do, however, is to get a line on him and sedate him so we can get him out of here safely. We don't want to hurt him, and we don't want anyone else getting hurt either. There's no real plot or conspiracy against Mr. Barney going on here, Miss Martens; we're just trying to do what we came here to do," Ed said earnestly.

"Mr. Baxter, is there something between you and Mr. Barney that you're not telling me?" she asked him, her reporter's instinct telling her there was more to this than met the eye.

"Miss Martens, why would you say such a thing? I never met the man before we started out on this thing, I assure you," Ed said indignantly, scowling as he spoke. "I admit he kinda riled me with his bragging and obnoxious ways, but that's no reason to want to harm someone."

"Well, Mr. Baxter, the thing is, I did some digging about the people going on this ride before we started out, and I heard from several people that you have a drinking problem," April said in a low voice as she leaned in toward him. "Now, I haven't seen anything to suggest that as long as we've been riding, but I've noticed that your hands have been shaking ever since you shot the bear. And I don't think I've ever properly thanked you for that," April said sincerely. "Lean over so I can," she said suggestively.

"You don't have to do that, miss," Ed said, embarrassed—but he leaned over anyway.

"Sure I do," April said with a smile, and she leaned over and kissed him on the cheek.

April wasn't done with him yet, however. Her instinct told her there was something between them, even if he wasn't going to talk about it. Maybe if she tried a little harder …

"So tell me a little about yourself, Mr. Baxter. Where do you come from, just what is it that you do, and how did you get into this line of work in the first place?" April asked, her tape recorder in her hand, and the *on* light bright red.

Here we go, got to watch what I let out, Ed thought to himself. He thought he kept his face impassive, but April was watching his expression closely and she caught the quick tightening of his eyes that told her he was nervous about one of the questions.

"Well, my life is pretty simple. I'm originally from Colorado—a little town called Centennial—and I've been up here for about twenty-five years. I started to work for the conservation group FARM—the Freed Animal Rights Movement—about fifteen years ago. I got into it because my parents were conservationists and really into the outdoors," he said with pride.

He was looking at a sight long gone, April could tell. She figured she would just let him talk; what she wanted to know would come out, she was sure.

"We used to go all over the United States to visit the national parks, and we'd go hiking in all of them. Our goal was to travel to all the national parks in the country before I left home. We had a lot of fun, and I saw some pretty interesting sights along the way," he said with a smile.

"So you and your parents visited every national park in the country? That's something to be proud of, I'm sure. How many parks are there, anyway?" she asked.

"There are fifty-eight, and no, we didn't get to see them all," Ed said brusquely, his mood instantly changed. His voice was no longer light; it was now hard and angry.

The pain in Ed's voice was very clear to April's ear. She was getting close to what she was looking for, she was sure, but she had to step carefully to avoid shutting him down.

She leaned over and put her hand on his arm as they rode. "Mr. Baxter, may I call you Ed?" she said softly. Not waiting for an answer, she eased into the heart of their conversation. "Ed, I couldn't help but hear the pain in your voice. Can I ask you what happened? Did one of your parents get sick?" she asked in a respectfully soft tone.

"No. They were killed in an accident while on the only vacation I didn't want to go on. I had a football game the weekend we would have gotten back, and I was playing offense. I didn't want to miss the game, so they didn't make me go along," Ed told her, the guilt all over his face.

"How old were you then, Ed?" April asked him gently.

"I was fifteen, and it was for the state title. I didn't want to miss the game—it was my first title game. You know the funny part? We lost the game when I dropped a pass in the final seconds," Ed said with an ironic and clearly bitter laugh.

"I'm sure they understood, Ed," April said consolingly, her hand still on his arm.

"So am I. They were always supportive of me, so they offered to stay home and miss their trip, but I knew how much they had been looking forward to it. Dad hadn't had any time off for the last two years, and this was to be sort of an anniversary vacation for them. I told them to go," he said sadly. His eyes were beginning to burn, but he didn't want to wipe them in front of her.

April saw the tears starting to well up, and she did something that was totally out of character for her, and she didn't know why—she took out a tissue from her pocket and wiped her eyes.

"Must be something in the air, Ed. I'm sorry, but my eyes are watering up on me. Is it bothering you too?" she asked innocently, giving him a way to not lose face in front of her.

"Yes, it's getting to me too, Miss Martens," Ed said gratefully, aware of what she was doing.

"Please tell me some more about your parents, Ed. They sound like they were very loving and gentle people," she encouraged him.

"They were, Miss Martens. They—" he started to say.

"Why don't you just call me April; it'll be easier to say," April said with a warm smile that she was surprised to discover she actually meant.

"Thank you, April. Anyway, as I was going to say, my mother took in every stray that came into our yard. It didn't matter to her what species it was—cat, dog, bird, turtle—she took them all in. She once took in a baby squirrel. He stayed with us for three years. She made my dad build a big enclosure for him in the backyard so he would have a tree to climb and grass to play in. It was so big, I'd go inside to play with the squirrel.

"He got so used to me, as soon as he saw me come into the enclosure,

he would come right up to me to see if I had any peanuts to give him."
Ed laughed as he remembered the sight of his friend. "I called him
Mr. May, because we found him in early May. He would ride in my
pocket sometimes, and he would always take peanuts from me as gentle
as can be. He was only about this big." Ed held his hands about six
inches apart. "But he had the thickest tail I ever saw on a squirrel," he
finished with a laugh, and April found herself joining in just from his
description of his little playmate.

April was very confused. She was getting the story she wanted, but
she was also finding herself actually caring about this gruff man. This
had never happened to her before. She missed the next thing he said
and had to ask him to repeat it.

"I'm sorry, Ed, I missed that. Would you mind repeating what you
said?" she asked him.

"I was just saying that my father was a hunter, but his goal was to
hunt for food, nothing else. He didn't hunt for trophies or just to put
heads up on a wall. My parents taught me to respect wildlife and not
to hunt for sport," Ed recalled fondly. "That's how I got started in this
kind of work. My parents taught me not to kill except for food or self-
defense. That's why I could shoot that bear—it was self-defense, and
I didn't need to kill her. I had the option to take her out of the way
just long enough for us to go past her. She was just doing what she was
trained to do by nature.

"And that's why I wouldn't hurt Barney; he's just doing what he was
trained to do by his nature. No matter how mad I might be at him, or
what grievance I might have against him—or anyone, I mean, I can't
take a life in anger or revenge," he said quickly.

"Do you have a grievance against Mr. Barney?" April asked, her
instinct at work once again.

"No grievance, April. I'm not jealous of him; he's got nothing I
want. He's never hurt me in any interaction I've ever had with him. In
fact, I'd never met him until this past week," Ed said truthfully. *That's
true as I said it, anyway,* he thought to himself. He looked April in the
eye as he spoke, and she was the one who broke the connection by
looking down at her recorder.

"One minute, Ed, I just need to turn the tape over," April said
apologetically. She quickly removed the cassette tape, turned it over,

and reinserted it into the recorder. She pressed the record button, but waited to speak until she saw the red light go on again.

"Okay, Ed. So what is it that you do for … what's the name of your organization again?" she asked him.

Okay, I got past that hurdle, Ed thought to himself. "The name of our group is FARM. That stands for Freed Animal Rights Movement. We are an organization that is dedicated to the care and preservation of wildlife in all areas of the United States. We are concerned with the quality of an animal's medical care and environment in any wildlife park, preserve, and even on the open range," he proudly explained to April. "Look!" he called out to her suddenly, pointing up to the sky.

"What is it, Ed?" April asked him excitedly, seeing what he was pointing at.

"That, April, is the majestic *haliaeetus leucocephalus*, also known as the American Bald Eagle," Ed said with evident reverence. He kept his eye on the bird soaring gracefully above them, and fell into his role as an educator, telling her all about it. "That's an adult—you can tell by the white head feathers. That means he, or she, is at least four or five years old. We'll say he, but I can't tell for sure … He's got a wingspan between seventy-two to ninety inches, and with those magnificent wings, he can fly as high as ten thousand feet and can reach a speed of thirty to thirty-five miles an hour."

"You're kidding! Really?" April discovered she was really interested in this information, to her own amazement. "What else do you know about him, Ed?" she asked.

"Well, he has about seven thousand feathers on the average, they can live up to thirty years, and they are known to be monogamous. The male will help with the incubation of their three eggs, unlike most animals, where the male leaves it all to the female," he told her with a smile.

"Unlike most males of any species, including humans, you mean," April said with a laugh.

"Yes, well, they can lift about four pounds, and they can swim, unless it is very cold water. Their hunting zone will cover between seventeen hundred to ten thousand acres per pair. He became our national emblem in 1782 when our Founding Fathers established the great seal of their new country." Ed was in his element, teaching someone about the wildlife of the country.

Suddenly, Ed began to smile and turned to look at April. "I'll bet you didn't know the eagle wasn't Ben Franklin's first choice for a national bird. I'll bet you a dinner out when we get back that you don't know what he wanted it to be. I get to buy the dinner and you get to choose the place if you don't know the answer," Ed challenged her.

April thought long and hard about this challenge. She knew the right answer—she just wasn't sure what she wanted to do. After a couple of minutes of soul searching, she made her choice.

"Was it a peacock? No! Wait, I've got it. It was a dove," April said with confidence.

"No! It was a turkey! Old Ben thought the eagle was a bird of prey and didn't think it was a fitting choice. He wanted the turkey, because it provided food to those who hunted it. You have to go out to dinner with me!" Ed said gleefully. "Unless you don't want to, that is," he added nervously.

He waited for her answer, which came quickly. "I'd love to have dinner with you, Ed. I have another question for you—if you don't mind, that is," April asked him. "What kind of vacation were your parents on when they died?"

"They were on a ski vacation. It was the first time they ever went skiing. It was someplace they had never been. They were killed right here in an avalanche thirty years ago," Ed told her.

CHAPTER 13

Warner passed by several unusual mounds of snow he assumed were signposts for something or other. Not caring what they might be indicating, he didn't bother to knock the snow off for a closer look. He was only interested in one thing, and that was chasing down his quarry. He only had eyes for the animal just out of reach. Although they were thinning out now, the animal seemed to be moving from tree to tree, slowly descending the mountain in a desperate attempt to evade his pursuit.

"That won't do you any good, my friend—I'm going to get you now. You made a mistake leaving the forest; now you're on my ground. I can move faster and keep up with you better, and there's less between us to deflect my shot," Warner gloated as he closed the gap between them. A break in the trees offered him a clear shot at the animal walking unconcernedly in the distance, but it unexpectedly stopped, and his shot went wild again. "Damn! You've got the best damn luck of any animal I've ever seen. No wonder you lasted so long," Warner admitted reluctantly.

"I heard it, Gerry," Oliver said.

"It sounded closer this time; I think we're gaining on him, Mr. Barry," Adam said excitedly.

"Mr. Barry, there's something I think you should know," Parker said at his shoulder. He was concerned about something, and was looking around the mountain slopes as he spoke.

"Parker, what seems to be the problem?" Oliver asked him absently. He was thinking about what he was going to do when he caught up with Barney.

"Mr. Barry, do you know where we are?" he asked quietly.

"If I am correct, we should be approaching the south end of Moosejaw Ridge," Oliver said after taking a quick look at his surroundings.

"Yes, we are. But there's more to it than that, Mr. Barry. We are approaching the place I was standing over thirty years ago when the avalanche occurred. I'm not sure of the exact point—the trees are a little different now—but it's right around here somewhere," Parker said confidently. "Max and the others were down there—" He pointed to a spot in front of them. "In a low place in the flat at the bottom of the slope over this rise, that's where the snow carried them away. I've got a bad feeling about being here, Mr. Barry, sort of like something bad's going to happen—or we're where we shouldn't be, I'm not sure. But I think we all need to be together, not spread out like this," he said anxiously.

Oliver turned in his saddle to look at Parker, and he could see in his eyes that he was serious in what he was saying. He thought about it for a moment and called out to the other riders.

"Everyone, hold up a minute. Parker has something he wants to say to all of you. I think you should listen to him," Oliver explained.

"Crap. What's the problem now?" Ed grumbled to no one in particular.

"I don't know, Ed, but I intend to find out," April said with intensity, her eyes narrowing.

"People, I want to tell you something that I think could be significant. All of you know what happened out here many years ago. What some of you may not be aware of is that we are approaching the very spot that it happened. I was standing up on the top of the ridge, looking down on the flats when I saw ... it happen," Parker said, his voice falling as he remembered that day.

"You mean we're at the very scene of that disaster?" April asked, her recorder running again.

"This is where my stepson died, Miss Martens; please be respectful of that," Arnold told her.

"But it looks so serene and beautiful out here," Adam said in disbelief.

"What does that have to do with anything, Adam? This is now, that was then. The *where* of a disaster is not the real issue; it is the *what* that shakes people and changes them," Wanda responded gently.

"Oliver, is there any danger of another avalanche here now?" Eileen asked as she looked out at the snow on the upper levels of the mountain and saw disaster everywhere.

"I don't think there's any real danger, miss, not so long as there's nothing to disturb the snow packs up there," Gerry Senior said when he saw the nervousness in her eyes.

"You mean, as long as no one shoots any guns up into the snow pack," Ed pointed out glumly.

Everyone just looked out into the fields ahead of them, knowing who was out there and what he was doing. And they were about to ride right into the snowfield behind him.

Warner kept his eyes open, looking for the elk. He hadn't seen it for several minutes, but he knew it was nearby.

"I've got a good view of the area, son, and you can't get away from me without my seeing you, so where the hell are you? You've got to be here somewhere, I know it. You can't have just vanished like a puff of smoke, damn it—you're flesh and blood, not a damn mirage! Where the hell are you?" he screamed in frustration.

As Gerry Junior and Bern reached the top of the ridge, they looked around them in all directions.

"It's a beautiful sight, Bern. Look out there, how quiet and peaceful it is. You'd never know the life-and-death battles that go on every day out there. Every day, something dies, and something is born—a tree sprouts, and a tree dies. We can't stop it, and anything we puny humans do, nature just brushes it aside and goes around us. Nature will always win out in the end. It always has and it always will, Bern," Gerry said calmly.

"Never knew you were a philosopher, boss," Bern said with surprise in his voice.

"Never knew I was, Bern, to be honest with you. It's just something that came over me at the moment. I guess I get it from Dad; he's the one who has the deep thoughts. Me, I'm the practical one. I'm the one who worries about the mortgages, the bills, the ranch, and even the payroll."

"Well, me and Axel are glad you do, boss," Bern said with a laugh. "You and your dad, you two are a real joy to work with. It's been a lot of fun these past years, boss," Bern said, a note of sadness in his voice.

"What do you mean, Bern? Are you two quitting me?" Gerry asked sharply, his face showing his confusion and annoyance.

"No, boss, not both of us. Just me. I'm going back to work for Arnold. He's going to rebuild his ranch, and he wants me to be the ranch manager. It's a big promotion, and one I can't pass up. I appreciate everything you've done for me, boss, but I need to move forward in my own career," Bern said apologetically. "I've talked to Axel, and he's ready to take my place here if you'll give him the opportunity. I think he'll do as good a job for you as I did—maybe even better."

Gerry didn't say anything for a few seconds while he looked out over the mountain, not really seeing it. Finally he let out a sigh and turned back to face Bern.

"Bern, it's been a pleasure to have you in the family, and to have you and Axel working for us these past few years. As far as I'm concerned, you are still part of the family, even if you're not working for us. I know Dad will say the same thing when you tell him, and yes, we'll give Axel the chance to fill your boots," he said sincerely as he shook Bern's hand warmly.

"I plan on telling Mr. Bruce as soon as we're done here, but you hired me, and I felt I owed it to you to tell you first, boss," Bern said appreciatively.

"Okay, Bern. You've always been your own man, and both Dad and I always knew this day would come up sooner or later—but we had always hoped it wouldn't." Stifling a sniffle, Gerry quickly changed the subject to something less painful. "Well, I don't see anything going on out there, so let's get everyone and ride down and see if we can find

Barney," Gerry said gruffly as he turned his horse's head around to look for a path down into the valley.

Bern had been watching the edge of the tree line for the last few seconds, as something hadn't looked right to him. And then, just as he started to follow Gerry, he caught a glimpse of movement at the edge of the trees. He studied it for a few seconds, until he was sure of what he was seeing.

"Hold it, boss!" Bern said suddenly. "Boss, get Parker and Adam up here right away! I think we'd better have them take a look at this," he cried, urgency palpable in his voice.

"Parker! Adam! Get up here right now! Hurry!" Gerry called, not knowing why, but trusting his man implicitly. He turned back to Bern to ask what he had seen, but then he saw it too, and he didn't need to ask anymore. He just stared down at the sight until Parker and Adam rode up a minute later, the rest of the group right behind them.

"Parker, look down there on the flat and tell me what you see!" Bern directed him. "And, Adam, you get your camera and put on one of those long-distance lenses and take a picture of what you see down there," Bern told him excitedly.

Parker looked down at the clearing from their place on the ridge, and it took him only a few seconds to see what Bern had called him up to see. He couldn't believe his eyes, but there it was, as plain as anything. Adam was just a few seconds behind him in locating the object. Within minutes the rest of the group was up on the ridge with them, and everyone was able to see for themselves what none of them had ever expected to find.

Warner saw the clearing in the distance, but didn't expect to find his quarry there, as that would afford it no cover or protection. No, he'd be hiding somewhere in all the damn trees.

"I'm getting hungry, I haven't eaten since breakfast, and I forgot to pack some energy bars in my pockets before I started chasing this damn critter. I just didn't expect it to take so long to run him down," Warner apologized to himself. He heard a noise behind him and froze. "You can't have gotten behind me again, damn it," he muttered to himself.

Slowly loading a round into the breech of his rifle, he quietly worked the action to seat it and turned around to fire it point blank in the direction of the noise. He discovered he had just killed … a fallen branch. His face very quickly becoming a mask of rage, he swore again at the elusive prey he was after.

"This is ridiculous! How the hell can one dumb animal continually outwit me? This can't be happening! I must have missed him. I know! I'll go back a bit into the trees and swing around to the edge, and I'll come up behind him for a change."

His confidence restored, he turned and slowly made his way back up the mountain, keeping his eyes open for his prey.

The entire group of riders was lined up on the ridge, looking down into the big clearing below. They were all staring at a solitary figure moving around down below them. They couldn't agree on who or what it was for sure, but there was one thing for certain all of them could agree on; that one incontestable fact being its color. It was bright scarlet, and it was big. They couldn't see it clearly, because it was far down, and the only field glasses they had were on their way back to camp with Axel.

"Adam, can you make out what it is down there?" Oliver asked excitedly.

"Not really, Mr. Barry. Every time I get a focus on it, it moves, and then I lose it and have to reacquire it in the viewfinder," Adam said patiently.

"Let me take a look, please?" Oliver asked him authoritatively.

Adam passed the camera over to him reluctantly, for it was a good camera. "This button is the focus control, Mr. Barry. You can extend the field of vision with this one, and the one on the right controls the degree of magnification you have. The red button on top is the shutter to take the picture. In order to—"

"Adam, enough instructions, if you please." Oliver finally expressed his frustration firmly but very politely. "Adam, I'm not taking a picture; I'm using the camera as a telescope."

"Yes, sir," Adam replied, properly subdued.

"Can you see anything, Oliver?" Parker asked him anxiously.

"Yes, but I think you ought to take a look yourself and tell us what you see," Oliver said as he relinquished the camera to Parker, and pointed to the object.

Parker looked at the object and then lowered the camera. He looked at Oliver, and then raised the camera again for another look. As he looked again, he spoke to Oliver in a very controlled tone. "Mr. Barry, just what did you see down there? Please tell me I'm not crazy," Parker pleaded.

"Parker, if you saw a figure in red skiing down there, then you're not crazy," Oliver told him.

"Mr. Barry, I think you should take another look. A little closer look, if you will," Parker responded after a few seconds.

He passed the camera back to Oliver, ignoring Adam's outstretched hand. While Oliver peered through the camera again, Parker turned to Gerry Junior and asked him a seemingly innocent question. "Mr. Bruce, you're quite familiar with this area, I believe. What's the elevation up here?"

"About eighty-seven hundred, I believe. Bern?"

"I believe that's correct, boss," Bern supported him.

"So what would you say the elevation is down there, Bern?" Parker asked, still looking at the scene below them.

"I'd have to guess it's about eighty-two, eighty-three hundred down there, Parker," Bern said.

"And, Mr. Barry, what would you say the angle is from the top end of that clearing to the bottom where our friend is moving around?" Parker asked casually.

"Well, if I recall correctly, that is a moderate slope, so I'd guess about twenty to thirty degrees of incline, most likely," Oliver said after a few seconds of thought, his eye still pressed to the viewfinder as he tracked the figure all over the flat.

"Well then, let me ask all of you this question. Are any of you competent skiers?" Parker queried in a very casual and amiable tone.

Everyone looked at the other, and no one raised their hand at first, then finally April spoke up. "I've been skiing for a few years, and while I'm probably not in your class, Mr. Woodson, I do believe I'm pretty good," she said modestly.

"Thank you for the compliment, Miss Martens. I think I'm pretty good myself. But I know this fact to be true—in any sport there's always someone who's better. Now the next question I have for you,

Miss Martens, or any of you, is just this: can you ski uphill? Can you ski up a hill with a twenty- to thirty-degree incline? Because if you can, then you're better than me, because I can't ski up a hill with a full twenty- to thirty-degree incline. I wouldn't even attempt to try it now, and I couldn't even do it back in my prime.

"To accomplish that trick requires a major violation of the very rigid laws of physics. But our friend down there—" He pointed down into the clearing. "He's doing it. He's been skiing *up* that hill just as easily as he's been skiing down the hill, and I don't know anyone living who can do that. Do any of you?" Parker emphatically asked them all, his face suddenly very ashen as he kept looking down into the clearing.

"Okay, enough of this. I'm going down there to see who this is and find out how he's doing that!" Gerry Junior said angrily as he searched for a path downward to the clearing.

Oliver nodded his head and handed the camera back to Adam. He started to follow Gerry, but both men stopped when they heard Adam call out. "Mr. Barry. He's stopped skiing, and now he turning to face us. What's he doing that for?" Adam said, puzzled by something. "He can't hear us up here, can he?" he asked, bewildered.

"Of course he can't, Adam. He probably can't even see us unless he has field glasses or a telescope," Gerry Senior said to relax Adam.

"Well, he sure seems to be hearing us. When you said you were going down there, he stopped skiing and turned in our direction. Now he's waving his arms kinda strangely," Adam said.

"Let me see that camera, Adam," Parker said suddenly. He grabbed it and looked at the figure down below them for several seconds. He slowly lowered it and turned to look at Oliver and Gerry Junior. His face, ashen before, was now getting even paler. "Mr. Barry, I think you and Mr. Bruce should stay up here. I think we should all stay up here, right where we are now. That figure, whoever or whatever it is, is sending us a message. He's waving his arms all right, but he's sending us a message. He's using an old signal system we had back in the days before we had radios," Parker explained, his voice starting to sound like he was having a hard time forming the words, much less saying them. "The message he's sending is an old signal for dangerous conditions on site.

"Adam, give me the camera and go up to the edge, but not too close. Do what I tell you to do, and maybe I can figure out what's going on. I want you to hold your arms over your head, hold one wrist with the other hand, and make a fist with the hand of the arm you're holding," he directed.

"Like this?" Adam asked, complying with Parker's request.

"Yes, that's perfect. Now, what's he doing?" Parker asked himself aloud as he watched the figure below move around some more. "Oh … my … God!" Parker said slowly.

"What is it?" escaped from everyone's lips almost at once.

"We are to stay here, out of danger; there's going to be another avalanche," Parker told them, never taking his eyes away from the camera. "What the hell does that mean?" he muttered. "Adam, raise both hands over your head and use your left hand … no! I mean your right hand, to grip your left arm at the elbow. Keep the angle square, if you can. Good," Parker said as he kept an eye on the figure below. "I told him we understood the first message, but that we needed him to clarify the second," Parker explained to the others.

"What was the second message? What did it say?" asked Oliver and Gerry together.

"He said something about us observing a righting. It doesn't make sense to me," Parker said.

"It makes sense to me, folks," Arnold said suddenly. When everyone turned to look at him, he shook his head in disbelief. "I can tell you what that means, but you'll think I've fallen out of my saddle once too often. It refers to something Max and I used to talk about all the time when he was upset about something he thought was unfair," he explained. "One time, when he was being teased about a fall he had taken, I told him the universe would always right every wrong somehow when the day was right.

"A little later, he made a jump they talked about for years, and he was the first to do it. He told me the universe righted his wrong, and we would laugh about it. Unless I am going dotty, I suspect that we are supposed to witness a wrong being righted, and I believe that the wrong was his death, and that we're going to see it corrected. Somehow," Arnold said, his voice quivering, and his eyes tearing up.

"Please, Arnold. Are you saying that mysterious figure is your stepson, Max, and he's going to come back to life?" Ed said sarcastically.

"No, Ed. That's not possible. What I am saying is that I believe he's sending us a message to stay up here, out of harm's way, while his death is corrected," Arnold said calmly.

"I could be wrong," Eileen suggested, "but it's my opinion the wrong that's being corrected is the fact his body was never recovered, and that's what is going to be righted."

"I thought the 'wrong' was that no one was ever held accountable for his death," Parker said.

After a moment of silence, while everyone tried to absorb everything that had just been said, Adam spoke up and expressed the thought in everyone's mind. "What if it's both things? What if both of you are right, and both events are going to happen?" he asked hesitantly.

"What's he doing now, Parker?"

"Nothing. He's not doing anything," Parker said slowly.

"He's not just skiing again?" Gerry Junior asked.

"He's not doing anything, because he's not there anymore. He's gone. And here's another little tidbit for you. There are no ski tracks in the snow down there either," Parker said evenly.

Everyone sat where they were for several minutes, until Oliver made the first move. He sat up and then dismounted. Everyone began dismounting until only Gerry Junior and Ed were still on their horses, but then Ed sighed and got down too. Gerry followed him a moment later.

"There you are! How did you get up here without me seeing you? Oh well, it doesn't really matter now; what counts is that I've got you. You can't get away from me now," Warner sneered at his foe. The elk was standing at the edge of the clearing, looking right at him, but not seeing him. Its head was up. It was sniffing the air for any sign of the hunter, Warner knew.

"You're not going to get wind of me, big boy. I'm staying downwind of you all the way. It'll be a little harder shot, but you stand out real good against that white snow backdrop. I'll be shooting uphill, but that's not a hard shot to make. You just hold still until I can get myself in a better position to take you down. I promise you, it will be quick. You've given me a good run, and I owe you that," he promised his foe.

Warner kept his eye on the elk, just in case it moved as he worked his way back down the hill, while staying in the trees until he was about fifty yards below the animal, who was just standing there as if it had given up the game and was too tired to run any further. Seeing the animal was just standing there, Warner eased himself to the edge of the clearing to get a better shot. The animal looked right at him, but apparently didn't see him, as it never moved a step and stood there like he was a statue.

"That's strange. I thought sure you saw me, but maybe not. Whatever. Just hold still and it will be over in a few seconds," Warner said to himself. He eased a cartridge from his pocket and noted that he only had two more rounds. As quietly as he could, he worked the bolt to open the breech and slid the shell in. He muffled the sound of the bolt closing as best he could and raised the rifle to his shoulder. He looked through the scope and turned the focus knob to get a clearer point. He raised the tip just a little and squeezed the trigger, feeling the familiar recoil in his shoulder as the bullet exited the barrel and went on its deadly way.

"The shot came from down there! There he is! There's Barney, I see him!" Adam exclaimed excitedly as he pointed to Warner standing at the edge of the tree line.

"Yes! I see him too, but what's he shooting at? Do you see the elk anywhere?" Parker asked him calmly, not even looking down into the clearing any longer.

He had walked back from the edge of the rim after finding Barney down below. Parker felt strangely calm now. He couldn't explain it, but he didn't feel guilty anymore either. He saw Arnold and Wanda sitting together by the horses, walked over to them, and sat down beside Arnold.

"You feel it too?" Parker asked him. "The sense of peace and being at ease, I mean, Mr. Wilcox?" He had seen the stress leave Arnold's face even before the shot had rung out.

"Yes, Mr. Woodson. I do feel it too. It's like a great and horrible weight has been lifted from my shoulders all at once—not all of it, mind you, but the bulk of it. I somehow feel very certain that the rest of it will soon be lifted as well, perhaps before we leave this place. I think

Max is going to be at peace at last, and his soul will be able to move on to whatever comes next for him," Arnold said with a smile. Wanda put her hand on his arm and her head on his shoulder.

"You know, Mr. Wilcox—"

"Arnold, if you please, Mr. Woodson."

"Then it's Parker, Arnold."

"Arnold, sometimes I think I held on to Max because I felt I failed him, and I wasn't good enough for him as a friend. I let him get killed by that … that …"

"Parker, that's not true. Max would talk about you from time to time, and he had nothing but respect for your abilities," Arnold said gently, placing a hand on his shoulder as he spoke. "You did all that you could do for him. You both had a job to do, and you did yours to the best of your ability, as did he. It was just his time, as it will be for all of us one day. He always wanted to go doing what he loved best, and that was helping people.

"I don't believe Max would want you to blame yourself or waste anymore of your precious time grieving for him. He'd want you to remember him as he was at his best, and to live for him doing your best." Arnold's voice was calm, but the tears were filling his eyes as he talked to Parker, who was crying silently.

Wanda got up to move over to Parker, sitting down next to him. She put her arm around his shoulder too and slowly stroked his hair.

April saw them sitting there, and she walked over with her recorder in her hand, but Ed reached out and took it away from her. She started to say something to him, but he just took her by the arm and steered her away from the three people sharing their grief.

Oliver began to head over to join them, but Eileen grabbed his arm and shook her head. He shrugged and turned back to observe what was going on down below. Eileen watched the three of them for a moment longer before rejoining Oliver.

Both of the Bruce men, Bern, and Adam were at the rim when Oliver rejoined them. They looked over at Arnold, Wanda, and Parker, and then at Oliver, who just shook his head and changed the subject by asking them about Warner Barney. "What do you suppose he's shooting at?" Oliver asked the other four men. "I don't see anything down there bigger than a stump or more alive than he is."

"I don't know what he's shooting at, but I can tell you what he's shooting into," said Bern as he pointed up the slope at the massive snow pack that was hanging out like an overextended lower lip. "I've been watching it, and he just fired into it and it started a little trickle of snow on the left end." He pointed it out. "See it? On the far left. I don't think it's going to take but one or two more shots to bring it all down," Bern said, concerned about the possible outcomes.

Both of the Bruces looked at the snowpack and then down at Warner Barney. Gerry Junior nodded and turned back to the snowpack. "Damn," was all he said.

"Yeah, that's a lot of snow," Oliver said, equally worried.

"No, that's not it. I'm just trying to remember if I cashed his check yet," he deadpanned.

Gerry Senior turned to look at his son, thinking he was joking, and realized he really was serious.

"Well, that should teach you, son. Always deposit the checks right away. It's easier to write a refund than cash a check from a closed account," Gerry Senior said with equal solemnity.

Warner was furious. His shot had missed its mark. Somehow he had missed the easiest shot he had ever had. It had to be the damn scope; it was set too low. He had to raise it a bit for his next shot. He pulled the rifle down and made the adjustment to accommodate the higher trajectory.

High above him, in the snowpack at the top of the mountain, the bullet had cracked some of the ice and crust that was holding everything together. The weight of all the fresh snow was creating additional pressure. It was slowly starting to give way, and it only needed a sudden shift of extra weight to cause it to collapse completely. If nothing else happened, it would likely repair itself and hold a little while longer.

Warner moved a little closer, as the elk wasn't showing any fear or concern for his presence.

"You keep on waiting for me, big boy. You're going home with me for sure. All those busybody do-gooders are going to be very disappointed when they find you back in my camp, hanging up to cool off before I dress you out," Warner assured the indifferent animal in front of him. He raised the rifle again, took aim once more—targeting the heart lying just behind the elk's shoulder—and slowly started to squeeze the trigger, stopping when the animal moved.

The elk raised its head, looked once more in his direction, and moved two feet to the right. It looked over his shoulder up the mountain, took two steps back, lowered its head, and went back to eating the snow, satisfied about whatever it had been concerned about.

Warner reseated the rifle against his shoulder and again looked through the scope at the target point. He slowly took up the slack in the trigger until it was taut, and then he squeezed it until it bucked once more.

High above him, on the rim of the ridge, the six people watched with great interest and curiosity. They could see him very clearly as he kneeled and aimed his rifle, and they could see the snowpack shifting more with the last shot he fired. What none of them could see was what he was shooting at in that direction. There was nothing living down there but him.

"What in God's name is that damn idiot shooting at?" Gerry Junior asked of no one in particular. "Can't he see there's nothing there? What is he, blind?" he complained to them all.

"I don't know what he sees, boss, but I know what I see, and I see that snow shelf starting to move," Bern shouted out as he pointed to the snowpack that was indeed starting to slide downward.

"Can't he hear it?" Adam asked Gerry Junior, worried about what was going to happen next.

"He probably can't hear it, or he is just ignoring it, would be my guess. Say, Adam," Gerry said, "you're missing out on some prize pictures here. Most folks never get to see an avalanche, so you might want to use that camera for what it used for, and maybe you'll get yourself some prize pictures," he suggested.

"Son of a ...! You're right! I forgot what I was doing up here. Thanks, Mr. Bruce," Adam said excitedly, and he began snapping the shutter as the snow began to slide down the upper levels of the mountain. "I'm getting some good shots, Mr. Barry!" Adam assured him as he worked.

"That's fine, Adam," Oliver said, clearly distracted by the disaster unfolding before his eyes.

"What in the hell is wrong with this friggin' scope?" Warner cursed to himself and adjusted it again. "This is my last damn shell. I've got to get him with this one, or all I'll be able to do is throw rocks at him! Maybe if I can move a little closer, I won't need the damn scope," Warner told himself. "Hmmm, sounds like water running somewhere. I must be near a stream. At least I can get some water when this is over,"

He moved a little closer and, again, the elk didn't seem to mind his presence. It looked up the mountain again and then at him. For a moment, Warner thought the damn thing was smiling, and then he told himself it was just chewing on a piece of grass or something.

"This hunt's getting to you, Warner; you know damn well that animal can't smile. Okay, steady now. Don't jerk the trigger. Hold your breath and then let it out slowly as you squeeze the trigger. You know how to do this—just stay calm. Quit shaking, you'll spoil your shot."

He squeezed the trigger and saw the bullet go right through the elk. He stood up slowly and replayed what he had just seen. "I saw the bullet go through the animal, and he's still standing. He looks strange though, kind of fuzzy somehow. And I'm still shaking."

Suddenly he realized that he wasn't shaking—it was the ground he was standing on that was shaking. The roar of water became the roar of the wall of snow heading right for him. He looked over at the elk, and his last conscious thought was the awareness that the elk had changed into the shape of a man wearing a red parka and goggles.

The man was on skis.

And then there was nothing else.

Eileen saw the wall of snow engulf Warner Barney, and she turned away from the rest of that scene. Adam took the last photo of the river of snow rushing madly down the little valley, and, as it rushed past the trees and bushes, it uncovered a small ravine that had been covered over by the avalanche of thirty years ago. He saw a flash of something red in the ravine and called out to Oliver—but by the time Oliver turned, the red had been replaced by white.

Parker and Arnold stood up, shook hands, headed to their horses, and mounted up for the ride down. Wanda walked between them, an arm around each of them. Not once had any of them ever come over to watch the avalanche.

Ed let go of April's arm and gave her back her recorder. As she stepped away from him, he called out to her, "April, are we still on for dinner when we get back?" Taking her lack of response as his answer, he smiled to himself and got up. He dusted off his jeans and went to his horse. Once there, he took a long case off the back of the saddle and began to break down the rifle. He had a feeling he wasn't going to need it anymore.

Eileen put a hand on Oliver's arm and looked at him, questioning.

He looked at her and shook his head. "Not a chance, Eileen. It's all over."

"Oliver, you want to come help me look for the remains?" Gerry Junior called out to him.

"Not really, but I suppose I have to as the authority here. Be right with you, Gerry,"

Adam walked over to Oliver, his camera still open.

"Mr. Barry. I have something here I think you need to see."

Oliver studied the picture and then called Gerry over. He examined it too, and then peeked over the rim at the valley below. Both men looked at each other and back down at the camera, ran to their horses and jumped into their saddles as fast as they could.

"Bern! Get everyone mounted—we've got a search-and-recovery job to take care of," Gerry called out.

Three hours later, everyone was on the valley floor. Adam had his camera out and was leading them to the ravine he had seen, checking for landmarks and comparing them to the picture. It only took thirty minutes before they found it. Everyone dismounted, stood on the edge, and looked in. What they saw there brought several of them to tears.

April told Adam to take a picture, but he refused until he was given permission by Arnold. Bern and Gerry Junior went back to their horses to get some blankets to cover up six of the skeletons that were lying at the bottom of the ravine.

They also found Warner Barney. He was apart from the remains of the others. He was tangled up with a seventh skeleton, one arm of it on top of him. The skeleton was wearing the remains of a once-scarlet parka. Max was coming home. The ghost skier and the Red Elk were never seen again.